THE MAN WHO WOULD BE KING

King Kelson and Dhugal were gone, betrayed by the sudden storm that had caught the expedition. Now, huddled under a borrowed cloak beside a small fire in the miserable campsite, Conall realized that they would never find Kelson—not alive, at any rate.

And that made Conall's father, Nigel, king—and Conall himself heir to the throne!

No need to suffer any pangs of guilt. He could forget that, but for the accident, Dhugal and Kelson might have drunk from the flask that Conall had drugged. That flask was gone forever into whatever watery grave had claimed Dhugal and the king.

Now Conall was only one small step from the throne—and from Rothana, Kelson's intended bride!

By Katherine Kurtz
Published by Ballantine Books:

THE LEGENDS OF CAMBER OF CULDI

CAMBER OF CULDI
SAINT CAMBER
CAMBER THE HERETIC

THE CHRONICLES OF THE DERYNI

DERYNI RISING
DERYNI CHECKMATE
HIGH DERYNI

THE HISTORIES OF KING KELSON

Volume I: THE BISHOP'S HEIR
Volume II: THE KING'S JUSTICE
Volume III: THE QUEST FOR SAINT CAMBER

THE DERYNI ARCHIVES

LAMMAS NIGHT

THE QUEST FOR SAINT CAMBER

VOLUME III OF
THE HISTORIES OF KING KELSON

KATHERINE KURTZ

A Del Rey Book

BALLANTINE BOOKS • **NEW YORK**

A Del Rey Book
Published by Ballantine Books

Library of Congress Catalog Card Number: 86-8249

ISBN 0-345-30099-8

Printed in Canada

First Hardcover Edition: September 1986
First Mass Market Edition: September 1987

Cover Art by Darrell K. Sweet
Map by Shelly Shapiro

For
Chevalier Scott Roderick MacMillan, GCJJ
"Steel True,
Blade Straight,
A Knight."

CONTENTS

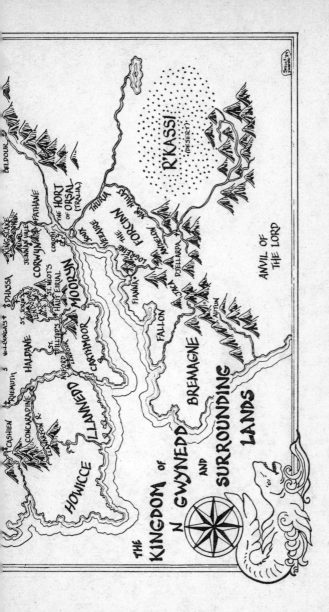

PROLOGUE

*Behold, thou hast instructed many, and thou hast
strengthened the weak hands.*

—Job 4:3

Thunder rumbled not far away, low and ominous, as
Prince Conall Haldane, first cousin to King Kelson of Gwynedd, pulled up with his squire in the meager shelter of a
winter-bare tree and huddled deeper into his oiled leather
cloak, squinting against the spatter of increasingly large rain-
drops.

"Damn! I thought we'd finished with storms for a while,"
he muttered, jerking up his fur-lined hood. "Maybe we can
wait it out."

Conall's comment was more a wishful aside than a statement of real belief, for March in Gwynedd was notorious for
its unpredictable weather. An hour before, when the two
young men rode out from Rhemuth's city gates, the sky had
been reasonably clear, but all too quickly fast-moving clouds
had closed the countryside in a flat, grey gloom more appropriate to dusk than noon, plummeting the temperature
accordingly. As thunder rolled closer and shower turned to
deluge, Conall could taste the acrid bite of lightning-charged
air moving just ahead of the storm. Had it continued only
to rain, Conall still might have borne the situation with reasonable good humor—for the day's outing was one of Conall's choosing, not someone else's notion of royal duty. But
his fragile forbearance quickly evaporated as the icy downpour turned to hailstones the size of a man's thumbnail, pelting prince, squire, and horses hard enough to sting.

"God's teeth! It's hailing plover's eggs!" he yelped.

"Shouldn't we make a dash for it, sir?" came the plaintive entreaty of the squire, Jowan, shivering on a drenched bay palfrey crowded next to Conall's grey. "I don't think it's going to let up very soon—and we can't get much wetter. Besides, your lady will have a warm fire on the hearth to dry us out. And the horses will be glad for her snug little barn."

Smiling a little, despite his increasing vexation with the weather, Conall nodded his agreement and set spurs to his mount, charging into the hailstorm with his squire right behind him.

His lady. Ah, yes. The lady to whom Jowan referred was not the principal reason Conall had decided to venture forth today, but she was pleasant enough, a side benefit. Nor was she a lady, in the genteel sense usually meant in court parlance. The pretty and pliant Vanissa was his leman, his doxy, his light o' love, or his mistress, depending on his mood, and he sometimes called her his "lady" in the throes of lovemaking; but even she knew she would never be his wife. That honor was reserved for a royal princess Conall had already picked out at court—though the object of his more honorable intentions had yet to be enlightened in that regard.

No, Vanissa would give him a child before summer's end, and Conall would see that mother and bairn were provided for, but visiting Vanissa was primarily a convenient cover for other activities that would raise far more questions than a royal mistress, were they to become known by the wrong people—and the wrong people, at least for now, included Cousin Kelson and all his closest confidants, especially those of the magically endowed race called the Deryni.

Conall often wished *he* were Deryni, despite the opprobrium and abuse heaped upon them by Church and State for most of the past two hundred years, for the Deryni possessed powers that gave them considerable advantages over ordinary humans, even if the Church officially condemned such powers as satanic and hell-spawned. By an odd quirk of history, Conall's own Haldane family had come to be possessed of the potential for powers not unlike those of the Deryni— but the gift was not for all Haldanes. Tradition insisted that only one Haldane at a time could actually wield the powers, and that was the man who wore the crown—in this generation, Conall's cousin, Kelson Haldane.

Conall had come to resent that restriction early on, having been born the eldest son of a Haldane king's second son. But his dissatisfaction came not so much of Kelson's having the crown and the Haldane power—for that was an accident of birth—but rather, that Kelson should have an exclusive claim on the latter, which seemed to Conall to have little to do with the kingship itself. That rationalization had led Conall to take certain steps during the past year to discover whether the wielding of the Haldane inheritance by more than one Haldane was a matter of *could* not or *should* not. And that was why, but a few days short of his eighteenth birthday and knighthood, Conall pressed on through such filthy weather—to meet his teacher. And if the outing also permitted him to indulge more physical appetites. . .

Anticipation of Vanissa's welcome lifted even Conall's flagging spirits as he continued through the storm, for he knew that the lass would provide her prince a far more warming fire than the one Jowan predicted burning on the hearth. The hail had slacked back to mere rain by the time the two pulled up before her secluded little cottage, but the puddles in the tiny yard were afloat with hailstones that crunched under Conall's boots as he lurched from the saddle and made a mad dash for the door, leaving Jowan to deal with the horses. The door flew back before he could even knock, an eager Vanissa bidding him welcome with a flustered curtsey, the curtain of her dark hair rippling like a rich mantle nearly to her knees.

"Ah, my good lord, I knew not whether still to expect you, with the storm an' all. Come take off those wet things an' warm yourself by the fire. You're shivering. You'll take your death of cold!"

He *was* shivering, but not only from the cold. Rain dripped from a small, silky mustache and from short-cropped black hair as he pushed back his hood and accepted a towel to dry himself, but her touch, as she reached to his throat to undo his cloak clasp, ignited a warming fire that sizzled through every limb and centered in his groin.

In heart-pounding silence, he watched her spread the dripping cloak over a stool near the hearth while he peeled off clammy gloves and sank down impatiently on another stool, inhaling the musty-sweet fragrance of the herb-strewn rushes underfoot and the sharper scent of mulling wine. He nodded his thanks as she handed him a cup of the steaming stuff and bent to pull off his muddy boots, his eyes gliding appreciatively along the sweet curve of her breasts as she struggled with the wet, slippery leather. Her exertions had them both panting by the time she finished.

"Shall my lord be warm enough with this?" she asked, bringing an armful of coarse wool blanket to lay around his shoulders.

Conall knew he really should not allow himself to be distracted until *after* he concluded business, but he had always found it difficult to moderate his pleasures. Vanissa was so eager to please him, so ripe for the taking, her body only just beginning to thicken from the child she carried. . . .

Almost overturning his wine in his haste to put it aside, he enfolded her with him in the blanket and bore her to the rushes before the cheery fire, losing himself in growing urgency and pleasure—until suddenly someone was grabbing a handful of his tunic and yanking him off of her and onto his back, slamming his shoulders to the rushes, a gloved hand pinning his sword arm while a wet knee jammed into his chest and the flat of a dagger pressed hard against his throat.

"Good God, boy, it doesn't even need a *Deryni* to take you by surprise when you're *that* stupid!" said a familiar voice, not Jowan's. "I could have been *anybody!*"

As the speaker's identity registered, Conall's reflex alarm and anger quickly shifted to indignation and then to grudging acknowledgement, though his hands still closed around the other's wrists to protect himself and move the blade aside, even as his mind tested at the other's decidedly Deryni shields.

"Here, now! Enough of that!" the newcomer said, abandoning his threat and pulling back. "You'll frighten the girl."

Conall subsided immediately, releasing his assailant and sitting up with a grunt of agreement. The stunned girl only cowered on the rushes and stared up at both of them in fear, skirts and bodice akimbo, cringing as the cloaked and hooded stranger sheathed his blade.

"Oh, for Christ's sake, Vanissa, no one's going to hurt you," Conall said, looking put upon as he reached across to touch her forehead with his fingertips. "Relax. Go to bed and forget what's just happened. I'll come to you later. And Tiercel, stop dripping on me!''

The offender drew back with a muttered oath, but he gave a hand up to the girl, who headed without comment toward the door to the next room, face devoid of emotion, mechanically smoothing her skirts as she went. When the door had closed behind her, Tiercel took off the offending cloak and laid it out next to Conall's. He was only a few years older than the prince.

"So. I was only half joking about just anybody walking right in, you know," said Tiercel de Claron, for more than a year now Conall's secret tutor in matters magical and Deryni—though without the knowledge or consent of the Camberian Council, who staunchly upheld the exclusive right of only one Haldane at a time to hold the Haldane legacy of magical power. Few outside the Council itself even knew of its existence—though Conall did, and the risk Tiercel took to teach him. "It mightn't have been so bad if Jowan had come in—"

"He's come in before and remembers nothing," Conall interjected, a surly note in his voice.

"That's undoubtedly true," Tiercel agreed. "At least *that* kind of control is better than I ever dared to hope you'd achieve. I wish I could say the same about your *self*-control. Couldn't you have waited?"

"I was going to, but I was cold," Conall said, as he lay back to do up his breeches before rolling to his knees and then getting to his feet. "I'm not anymore, though," he added, giving the Deryni lord a sly grin. "She's far better than a fire, Tiercel. Go ahead. Have her, if you want. I'll wait. She'll never know, if you tell her to forget."

Tiercel snorted disdainfully as he snatched up Conall's discarded towel to scrub at his own sopping hair. "Sometimes I wonder why I bother with you."

"What's the matter, Tiercel? Too fastidious to take a woman who's carrying another man's child?"

"What makes you so bloody certain it's *yours?*" Tiercel muttered, tossing the towel aside and unlooping the strap of a leather satchel from across his chest.

"How's that?"

"You heard me."

"As a matter of fact, I did. And I'm not at all certain I like your—"

"Just now, I don't much care *what* you like or don't like!" Tiercel said. He tossed the satchel on a well-scrubbed trestle table near the fireplace and hooked one of the stools closer with a booted toe, disturbing the rushes. "Sit down and act like a prince instead of a stablehand!"

Conall sat.

"Now. The point is, you were screwing around when you should have been paying attention to the business at hand," Tiercel said sternly. "*Anyone* could have walked through that door instead of me. *I* could have betrayed you. A prince must *never* neglect his defenses. And you had defenses available to you that ordinary men only dream of—but you didn't bother to use them."

"But—who was going to be out on a day like this? Besides, Jowan would have stopped them."

"Oh? He didn't stop *me*." Tiercel stalked to the outer door and wrenched it open, curtly beckoning a sleepy looking Jowan to enter. "Go lie down by the fire, Jowan," he said. "Take off your wet things and have a nap."

Conall's grey eyes narrowed as he watched the squire obey, but, by the time Jowan was snoring peacefully in the rushes, he had managed to push his anger down to a smoldering resentment.

"Very well, you've made your point," he finally said sulkily. "It won't happen again. I apologize. Am I forgiven?"

His bright smile was both compelling and infectious, and he knew it. Tiercel only sighed and nodded as he sat at the table opposite the prince.

"So long as you've learned from this little unpleasantness. Are you ready to work?"

"Of course. What are we going to do?"

"Something I've been meaning to do for several months now," Tiercel replied, feeling around inside his satchel. "I'm going to start you on proper warding. Wards are a type of magical protection or defense. Eventually, you'll learn to use them in conjunction with working other spells. It won't always be necessary to use a physical matrix to set the wards, but these will help, in the beginning."

As he extracted a well-worn brown leather pouch and

opened it, spilling a handful of thumbnail-sized black and white cubes into his cupped palm, Conall leaned closer.

"They look like dice."

"Aye. And so they might have been, a long time ago— or could have been disguised as dice, once it became dangerous to be Deryni. I've seen spotted ones, and they work just as well. Notice there are four each of the black and white. That has an esoteric significance, but we won't bother with that for now. Most Deryni children begin their formal training with cubes similar to these. Hold out your right hand."

Hesitantly Conall obeyed, flinching involuntarily as Tiercel tipped them from his own right hand into Conall's. The cubes felt cold and sleek, the white ones yellowed like old ivory but with little of ivory's warmth, the black ones more a charcoal grey than true ebon or obsidian.

"Now, close your eyes and tell me the first thing you sense about them," Tiercel said.

"They're colder than they look," Conall ventured, cautiously closing his hand to finger the cubes' corners and edges.

"Good. What else?"

Conall hefted the handful of cubes, considering, then opened his eyes and shifted the four black cubes to his left hand. He stared at them a moment, black cubes in his left hand, white in his right, then cocked his head at Tiercel.

"There's something different besides their color."

"Yes?"

"I—don't know what it is."

"Try changing them to opposite hands and tell me how that feels."

Dutifully Conall complied; but after a few seconds of concentration, he shook his head and switched them back.

"No, they definitely feel better this way."

"*Better?*"

"Well, more—*balanced*," Conall conceded. "Does that make any sense?"

Raising an appreciative eyebrow, Tiercel nodded. "It does, indeed. In fact, this may be easier than I dreamed. You've detected the polarities. Put the four white cubes on the table, forming a square, all of them touching. Then set the four black ones at the corners."

Conall obeyed, then looked up at Tiercel with a "what-next?" expression.

"Now, lower your shields and open your mind to me, to follow what I do," Tiercel said. "Setting wards doesn't require a great deal of power, but well-focused concentration is essential. That's what's hardest for children—and it's the reason I had you practice centering all winter. Pay attention now."

Setting his right forefinger on the first white cube, Tiercel breathed in deeply and spoke the cube's *nomen:* "*Prime*." Light flared in the cube as the energy was set and bound, then spread to the other three as Tiercel proceeded to name them as well:

"*Seconde.*

"*Tierce.*

"*Quarte.*"

Conall had grasped the procedure by the second repetition and glanced eagerly at Tiercel when the first four were complete.

"I can do that," he said confidently.

"Very well, then, *you* name the black ones," Tiercel said, sitting back with fists braced on hips in good-natured challenge. "Just keep to the same order, starting with *Quinte*."

"All right."

Narrowing all his concentration to the cube set diagonal to the white *Prime*, Conall touched it with a tentative fore-finger and spoke its name:

"*Quinte.*"

The light that flared in the cube was an inky green-black rather than white like the first four, but Conall hardly even blinked as he shifted his attention to the black cube next to *Seconde*.

"*Sixte.*"

The second black cube lit to match *Quinte*'s.

"*Septime . . . Octave,*" Conall continued, activating the remaining two black cubes in rapid succession. "Is that all there is to it?"

"Hardly," Tiercel replied, though he was grinning ear-to-ear and shaking his head slightly as if in disbelief. "They want balancing next. Watch how I combine the elements—first, *Prime* to *Quinte*, with the intent to bring the pairs of opposites into harmony."

He closed his eyes for just an instant, re-collecting his focus, then picked up the white *Prime* and brought it down on its black counterpart, speaking the word of power as the two touched with a faint flash and bonded.

"Primus!"

When he withdrew his hand, an oblong, silvery rectoid stood where two cubes had been. Conall gaped.

"No questions yet," Tiercel said, reaching for *Seconde*. "Just pay attention. Some magical systems equate the ward components with the Elemental Lords and their Watchtowers, or the Archangels of the Quarters. Some prefer the symbolism of the pillars. All are valid conventions. Watch again, now, while I do *Secundus,* and then I'll let you have a go at *Tertius* and *Quartus.*" He quirked a pleased grin at the prince. "God, I'm glad you're grown! Teaching this to children can sometimes be *so* tedious—but I think you're going to get it right the first time."

"Do you do that often?" Conall asked. "Teach children, I mean?"

"Often enough. Be still, now."

Tiercel brought *Seconde* just above *Sixte,* paused to draw a deep breath, then gently brought the white cube down on the black as he spoke its balance mnemonic.

"Secundus! Now you do the other two," he added, as he drew his hand away from a second silvery rectoid.

Conall complied without hesitation or difficulty, looking up expectantly as he drew his hand away from *Quartus.*

"Now what?"

"Now comes the tricky part, because there's some very specific visualization involved," Tiercel said. "May I borrow your signet for a moment?"

The ring, richly engraved gold on Conall's left little finger, bore the Haldane arms as differenced for a second son's eldest son: Nigel's bordured and crescent-charged Haldane lion overlaid with a label of three points. Conall removed it without discussion, setting it, at Tiercel's direction, in the central space Tiercel made by moving the four towers a handspan farther apart.

"Now, just watch, this first time," Tiercel said, poising a forefinger above the tower that was *Primus.* "I want you to observe the effect before you're involved with it."

As Conall sat back a little with a nod, Tiercel drew another deep breath, his tawny eyes going hooded, and pointed to the four towers in quick succession as he spoke their names.

"Primus, Secundus, Tertius, et Quartus—fiat lux!"

Conall gasped as misty light flared up in a shallow dome over the towers, enclosing the ring, but he immediately leaned closer for a better look.

"Is it solid?" he whispered.

"Touch it and find out," Tiercel replied. "Go ahead," he added, at Conall's hesitation. "It won't hurt you—not set this way, at any rate."

"I suppose that's meant to be reassuring," Conall muttered, prodding tentatively with a fingertip. It felt not quite solid, and made his finger tingle, as when an arm or leg went to sleep, but the sensation was not painful.

"Poke a little harder," Tiercel suggested, watching him closely.

Conall complied. His finger encountered more resistance, and a stronger tingling sensation, the farther he pushed it in, but even when he tried with all his strength, he could not quite manage to touch his ring.

"That's enough of that," Tiercel finally said, gesturing for him to pull back. "Now I'm going to make a subtle alteration." He held his hand over the domelet for a few seconds, not doing anything that Conall could detect, then blinked and glanced up at Conall again. "Now touch it."

Conall started to obey, but a blue-violet spark arced between the dome and his fingertip with painful consequences before he could even make contact. He gasped as he wrenched his hand away, looking up at Tiercel with only thinly veiled anger as he nursed his wounded finger in his mouth. It was all but blistered at the tip.

"What the devil did you do that for?" he demanded.

"So you would have some inkling of what this spell *could* do," Tiercel said mildly. "Now suppose it were covering an entire room rather than just your ring. Do you remember the protective dome that Kelson and Charissa raised, when they fought at Kelson's coronation?"

"Of course," Conall breathed. "But they didn't use ward cubes—did they?"

"No. But some of the principles are the same. Actually, the first version is the more useful for general purposes—

and there are variations between." Tiercel passed his hand over the dome again, then turned his palm briefly toward Conall. "Now try it again."

"Is it going to *kill* me this time, instead of just burning me?" Conall asked, still sucking resentfully at his wounded fingertip.

"Come, now. Would I kill you, after all the work I've put into you in the past year?"

Conall only snorted in answer; but after taking a deep breath, he did reach out gingerly to touch the dome again. This time, his finger passed through its misty outline with no more sensation than going through fog. With elation in his eyes, he speared the ring with his fingertip and pulled it out, looking up at Tiercel in triumph.

"*Got* it!"

"Of course. That time, the wards were attuned to you. Now, put it back, and I'll show you how we dismantle the wards. Then I'll let *you* practice."

Two hours later, Conall had formed and neutralized the wards several times under Tiercel's supervision—though only in the primary, non-lethal mode—and was confident he could now do so without assistance if the need arose.

"Hmmm, I daresay you probably could. But there's no need to rush things," Tiercel cautioned, when they had replaced the cubes in their pouch and Conall had made none too subtle inquiries about acquiring a set of his own. "Perhaps I'll have you a set by the time you return from the summer progress."

"So long?"

"Well, frankly, I didn't expect you to master them so quickly. Finding you the right set will take some time."

"Couldn't I borrow yours? That way, I could practice while I'm away."

"I—don't think that's a good idea," Tiercel replied. "For one thing, I may need them. For another, it wouldn't do for someone to find them and deduce what you've been doing with your spare time. Only a trained Deryni would have any business with a set. Besides, you're flexing abilities you've never used before. You have to build up your endurance. I'll bet you've got a headache just from this afternoon's work."

Conall nodded grudgingly, kneading the bridge of his nose

between thumb and forefinger and trying to will the dull throb to recede. He'd been trying to ignore it, but it was centered just behind his eyes.

"I have. It isn't too bad, though. Not as bad as some I've had."

"You're sure? I can give you something for it, if you like. You needn't play the martyr, you know."

"I know. But if I take one of your potions, I'll still be groggy at dinnertime. Someone might notice. I'll be all right."

"Very well. Suit yourself. I *am* pleased with your progress, however. Today's gains should make it *much* easier when we continue with your training. If only we'd had a few more weeks, I feel certain I could have taken you before the Council by Midsummer."

Conall grimaced, but not from his headache. "I know you won't want to believe this, coming from me, but under the circumstances, it's probably best we have to wait," he said. "The Council isn't going to like it when we prove that more than one Haldane can hold the Haldane power at a time. And when they tell Kelson, *he* isn't going to like it. If he knew, he'd never let me be knighted."

"What makes you so sure they'll tell Kelson?" Tiercel asked. "He isn't exactly their favorite Deryni right now, you know. If he were on the Council, it would be different, of course, but he isn't—the more fool, he."

"I still can't believe he turned down a Council seat," Conall muttered. "*I* wouldn't have—not that I'm ever likely to be asked."

Conall cocked his head thoughtfully at his prize pupil as he stashed the cube pouch in his satchel.

"That may not be as far-fetched as you think," he said quietly. "If you keep progressing, there's no predicting how far you might go."

"And wouldn't that be a feather in *your* cap?" Conall returned, not even blinking at the notion—which startled Tiercel. "You can't tell me you don't have ambitions, too, Tiercel de Claron."

Tiercel shrugged. "Oh, I do. But they had included your rather uncooperative cousin Kelson as well as yourself. And if declining the Council seat wasn't enough, he had to recommend Morgan or Duncan in his place—or Dhugal. . . ."

"Dhugal!" Conall snorted. "What does that upstart border bastard know about anything?"

Tiercel favored the sour-visaged prince with a wry little smile. "I must assume that you mean the term *bastard* in the purely pejorative sense rather than the literal one, since the holy fathers of the Church are even now about the business of legitimating young Dhugal."

"He's still a bastard."

"In that his parents were not wed according to the usual rites of Mother Church—perhaps. But a form of marriage *was* enacted, and both parents were free to marry at the time. That's enough for the king. And at his request, the bishops almost certainly will grant the necessary dispensation."

"A piece of parchment," Conall muttered. "It changes nothing."

"Why, one might almost think you were jealous," Tiercel said mildly.

"Jealous? Of Dhugal?"

"Well, he *is* of true Deryni lineage, after all, and the king's blood brother," Tiercel said pointedly. "That gives him a few perquisites that mere cousinship and usurped Haldane potentials don't confer, doesn't it? Don't worry, I won't betray your secret."

"I'd rather not talk about it," Conall said, turning his face away guiltily.

"No, I don't suppose you would." Tiercel stood. "Well, I must be away. You're sure you don't want something for your headache?"

"No. It's nearly gone already." Conall swallowed uneasily, fighting down a flush of embarrassment at his outburst. "Tiercel, I—"

The Deryni lord ducked under the shoulder strap of his satchel, then began drawing on his clammy cloak as he glanced back at Conall.

"Yes?"

"I—please don't mind me getting a little hot about Dhugal. I guess I *am* a bit jealous." He glanced down at his stockinged feet. "I suppose I'm a bit jealous of Kelson, too."

"I know," Tiercel said softly. He laid a comforting hand on Conall's shoulder until the younger man looked up and managed a shifty, half-hearted smile, then took his hand away.

"You have much to recommend you for yourself alone, Conall. Don't let jealousy make you lose sight of that."

"I'll try. Will—will we have time for any more sessions before I leave?"

"One more, perhaps," Tiercel said, "though not until after the knighting. You're going to be very busy between now and then. And I'd better come to you, rather than the reverse. You're going to be under increasing scrutiny—not because anyone suspects anything," he added, at Conall's flash of alarm, "but simply because, since the conferring of knighthood denotes a full coming of age in your rank as prince and knight, people are going to be interested in what you're doing and how you're taking the new responsibilities that come with the honor."

"I suppose that makes sense," Conall agreed. "Will you send word in the usual way, then?"

Tiercel nodded. "We'll plan tentatively for the night before you actually leave on the progress. Most everyone else will be otherwise occupied getting last-minute arrangements taken care of, so you're that much less likely to be missed."

"True enough." Conall stood as Tiercel gathered up cap and gloves.

"Good luck with your knighting, then," Tiercel said, clasping his hand to Conall's and brushing his mind briefly against the other's in leave-taking. "Mine was far less lavish than what they have planned for you, but I'll never forget it. Will you return to Rhemuth now, or are you staying a while with your lady?"

Conall smiled lazily as Tiercel withdrew from the hand-clasp and pulled on his cap, moving toward the door.

"I have some unfinished business here, I think," he said, hooking his thumbs in his belt as Tiercel paused with a hand on the latch. "And this time, I shall take suitable precautions to make certain I'm not interrupted."

Tiercel only flashed him a forbearing grin before dashing back into the rain.

CHAPTER ONE

I will make him my firstborn.

—Psalms 89:27

"Well, it's a relief finally to have official confirmation that my foster brother is not a bastard!" King Kelson of Gwynedd said.

He flung a playful arm around the neck of Dhugal MacArdry as the two of them followed Dhugal's father and Duke Alaric Morgan into Kelson's suite of rooms in Rhemuth Castle, Bishop Denis Arilan bringing up the rear. All of them were dripping rain. It was the Saturday before the beginning of Lent, the Vigil of Quinquagesima Sunday, the first day of March in the Year of Our Lord 1125, and Kelson Haldane had been King of Gwynedd for a little more than four years. He had turned eighteen the previous November.

"Not that I ever believed he was, of course," Kelson went on drolly, "or that it would have made any difference to me if he *had* been. I *am* glad that I won't have to defy the law to knight him on Tuesday, however."

The bluster evoked a chuckle from Morgan and a snort of disapproval from Arilan as everyone shed wet cloaks and gathered before the fire, for all were aware that the king might have done precisely that, if necessary, to see proper honor done to his beloved foster brother. Kelson had already waived the usual age requirement for the accolade—a royal prerogative whose exercise would raise no eyebrows, given Dhugal's outstanding service in the previous summer's cam-

1

paign, and Dhugal only just seventeen. Several others were also being knighted early, for the same reason.

But age was one thing—a somewhat arbitrary milestone that easily might be set aside for reasonable cause, even royal whim. The bar sinister was quite another. Even with royal patronage, illegitimacy was normally a serious, if not absolute, bar to knighthood.

Fortunately, Bishop Duncan McLain had proven today, to the satisfaction of an archbishop's tribunal, that long before entering holy orders, he and Dhugal's mother had exchanged vows that constituted a valid, if irregular, marriage. The proving had not been easy. The first sticking point had been that the vows were witnessed only by the two principals and the sacred Presence signified by the ever-burning lamp in the chapel of Duncan's father, at Culdi.

"Mind you, I don't dispute the precedent of *per verba de praesenti*," old Bishop Wolfram de Blanet had said, acting as devil's advocate as he and Arilan reviewed the case for Archbishop Cardiel in closed session. "Common law in the borders has long recognized the validity of a marriage declared before witnesses when no priest was available— though the Church has always urged a more solemn ratification at some future date."

Duncan, standing alone before the tribunal's long table, shook his head in objection, aware of the tension of his son and the others seated behind him. Other than one of Cardiel's clarks, taking down a careful transcript at the end of the table, only Dhugal, Morgan, the king, and Nigel had been permitted to attend.

"Your Excellency knows that was not possible," Duncan said. "I never saw her again. She died the following winter."

"Yes, so you have said. The salient point here, however, which must be addressed, has nothing to do with omission of a later regularization of the marriage, but whether a declaration before the Blessed Sacrament in fact fulfills the elements of *per verba de praesenti*."

Arilan, serving as Duncan's counsel, cleared his throat.

"Ah, there *is* a parallel precedent in ancient Talmudic law, Wolfram," he pointed out. "I doubt the comparison has often been invoked, but we have in the sacred tabernacle, before which the Presence lamp burns, a direct lineal descendant of the Jewish Ark of the Covenant. Interestingly enough, the Ark was permitted, in necessity, to substitute for one of the quorum of ten adult males required for many public rituals of Jewish worship.''

''Implying that the Ark functioned as a witness of sorts?'' Wolfram asked, frowning.

Arilan nodded. ''Beyond question. Surely at least equal in weight to the mere mortals making up the other nine— and in symbol, at least, the physical representative of the presence of the living God. If, as we believe, God is physically present in the Blessed Sacrament as the Body and Blood of Christ, then can the Holy Presence in the tabernacle before which Duncan and Maryse made their vows be any less valid a witness?''

Duncan scarcely dared to breathe as the import of the argument sank in; he sensed that the others, seated behind him, recognized it, too. Arilan had scored a point not easily refuted; for to deny the real Presence of God in the Sacrament housed in the tabernacle was clearly blasphemy.

Wolfram pursed his lips and looked to Cardiel for guidance, but the archbishop only raised an eyebrow, turning the initiative back to Wolfram. Cardiel was already far from neutral in this case, being Duncan's immediate superior. He did not *know*, in the way that many others in the room knew, that Duncan was telling the truth—but he sincerely believed he was. Unfortunately, neither believing nor knowing was sufficient in a court of ecclesiastical law, especially when the latter came of Deryni proving.

For Duncan McLain, besides being a bishop and the father of a son, was also Deryni—a member of that magical race whose powers had been feared and condemned by the Church for nearly two centuries. Duncan's identity as Deryni was not widely known outside the highest ecclesiastical circles, and even there was not officially acknowledged—for though the Church had long prohibited Deryni from entering the priesthood, Duncan McLain was an able, pious, and loyal churchman, Deryni or not—but speculation was rife. Thus far, Duncan had managed neither to confirm nor deny what he was.

There were other Deryni in the room as well, though only one besides the king was openly known to be so. Folk had always known who and what Alaric Morgan was. Protected by Kelson's Haldane grandfather and father through childhood and youth, he eventually had come to grudging acceptance at court because of his unswerving loyalty to the House of Haldane and because he had the good sense not to flaunt his abilities. Even the human Bishop Wolfram acknowledged guarded respect for the fair-haired man in black sitting at the king's elbow.

The fact that Morgan was Duncan's cousin must surely fuel old Wolfram's suspicions that Duncan was Deryni, too, though—and that Dhugal might also be, if Duncan was. What Wolfram did not suspect was that Bishop Denis Arilan also shared that distinction—though everyone else present except the clark knew it. And though any one of the Deryni could have verified the truth of Duncan's claim by using their magical powers—and some had—that evidence might not be presented, for the Church's official position regarding the Deryni race and their magical powers was still quite negative.

"You beg the question, Denis," Wolfram finally said. "Naturally, any declaration made before the Blessed Sacrament would have been witnessed in that sense." He jerked his chin vaguely over his shoulder toward the open doorway of the adjoining chapel. "The Light burns in there, too, and His Presence is among us in this room."

"Far be it from me to dispute that," Arilan replied, spreading his hands in a conciliatory gesture.

"It is usual, however," Wolfram added, "to be able to produce witnesses who can testify to what they've witnessed."

"Implying that God could not, if He wished?" Arilan asked.

"You know that isn't what I meant!"

"Of course not," Arilan agreed. "I would point out, however, that after eighteen years, even human witnesses are not always available."

"Aye, that's true enough." Wolfram scowled and turned his vexed attention back to Duncan, only partially mollified. "I don't suppose you confessed this alleged marriage before entering holy orders?" he ventured. "I needn't remind you, I hope, that marriage *is* an impediment to orders."

"Only if he had, indeed, been married and was still married at the time of entering orders," Arilan replied, before Duncan could answer. "But the lady, alas, had died. So you either ask a meaningless question, Wolfram, or else you intrude on the seal of privacy between a man and his confessor—who, I believe, is no longer with us, in any case. Am I correct, Duncan?"

Breathing a careful sigh, Duncan nodded once. "Aye, my lord. He was an old man even then. He lived only a few months past my ordination."

"Damned convenient," Wolfram muttered.

"Now, Wolfram, be reasonable," Cardiel chided gently. "The man would be past eighty, after all."

"It's still convenient, my lord."

"But not to the point, in any case," Duncan said softly. "Because even if he still lived, Excellency, and I gave him leave to speak of matters of the confessional, he could tell you little of Maryse. My sin was in failing to be more bold, in not trying harder to contact her in the months that followed, before she died. But she and I had committed no sin. We were married in God's eyes."

"Aye, so you say."

And that, indeed, was the ultimate question, for who would presume to claim he saw through God's eyes? A more practical question was to ask whether vows had, indeed, been exchanged, thereby contracting a valid marriage. If so, then Dhugal MacArdry was Duncan's true-born son, entitled to his name and all the other honors that went with that high lineage.

Or was Dhugal MacArdry only the result of innocent but unsanctioned fumbling between desperate young lovers who knew they would be parted on the morrow, and Duncan's present assertion but an attempt, after the fact, to legitimize the son he had never dreamed would come of that union?

Such an attempt certainly would be understandable. Indeed, it was to nearly everyone's benefit that Duncan should be able to prove his son's legitimacy. A direct legal heir would enable Duncan to resign his secular titles to his son during his lifetime, thus releasing his own energies for the high episcopal office he held. That would please the Church. Dhugal's accession to his father's estates would ensure loyal continuity for another generation in the ducal and county estates of Cassan and Kierney—which would please Kelson.

And of course, Dhugal himself would benefit. Through tanistry, from the man he now knew to be his maternal grandfather, Maryse's father, he was already Earl of Transha and Chief of Clan MacArdry. That would not change, regardless of the outcome here today. His Transha men adored him. But if, in time, he also succeeded to the vast estates of Duncan McLain, adjacent to his own Transha lands, he would be one of the most powerful magnates in all the Eleven Kingdoms.

In purely practical terms, Dhugal eventually would get his patrimony anyway, since, if Duncan died without legitimate heir, the last of the McLains, his lands would escheat to the Crown—and the king then could bestow those lands on whom he pleased. Or, for that matter, Duncan could resign his lands and titles to the king during his lifetime—and the king still could give them to Dhugal, bastard or not.

But grants of lands were far from the thoughts of most present here this morning. It was the honor of Dhugal's impending knighthood that stood to gain or lose, depending on the outcome of this hearing. If doubt remained that Duncan McLain had made his claim in utter honesty, it could color Dhugal's reception beyond even a king's ability to make it right. Thus had Wolfram de Blanet been appointed to argue against the case, in every way he could, so that no one might say, later on, that a biased court had found in Duncan's favor.

"We have only his word," Wolfram finally said, folding his hands on the table before him. "I see no other way around it."

Cardiel nodded unhappily, obviously feeling the weight of his official responsibility.

"I'm afraid I must agree. We appear to have reached an impasse, then. It all comes back to whether Duncan's oath can be deemed sufficient—whether he did, in fact, make vows with Maryse MacArdry before the Blessed Sacrament. As a private person, and Duncan's friend, I have no doubt that he is telling the truth. But as archbishop, I cannot accept his unsupported word simply because he is one of my bishops. I could not accept that from a layman, and I certainly cannot accept it from one of my spiritual sons."

"I agree," Arilan said, fiddling with the feathered end of a goose-quill pen as he glanced at the king and then at Morgan. "A pity we cannot accept evidence confirmed by Deryni powers. Duke Alaric's testimony would be prejudiced, in any case, since he is kin to Duncan, but you Deryni do have ways to verify whether a man is telling the truth, don't you?"

The question was for Wolfram's benefit, of course, for the Deryni Arilan knew full well what those of his race were capable of, but the scene he would now attempt to unfold had been carefully orchestrated by bishop, duke, and king the night before, to suggest a no less reliable verification of Duncan's oath that the Church *could* accept. For the Haldane line was also possessed of power—a power not unlike that wielded by the Deryni, though the Haldane power was held to be linked with that house's divine right to rule.

But much depended upon Wolfram's recognition of that fact, and his faith in it, and whether they had read their man correctly.

"Deryni are not the only ones to have this power, Bishop Arilan," Kelson said, staying Morgan with a hand on his sleeve as he himself rose to address the court. "Perhaps here is an answer to your dilemma. We Haldanes can tell when a man is lying. It is a power of our sacred kingship. If I were to question Bishop McLain and could ascertain beyond doubt that he is telling the truth about his marriage to Dhugal's mother, would that satisfy this tribunal?"

Arilan raised an eyebrow in guarded assent and looked to Cardiel, careful not to appear too eager, and breathed a cautious sigh of relief when his superior did not immediately veto the notion. Clearly, the human Cardiel understood what the king was proposing, but he still was archbishop, and forms must be observed.

And Wolfram, as devil's advocate, would be even more insistent that propriety be maintained. Wolfram de Blanet did not hate Deryni—which was one of the main reasons, besides being impeccably honest, that he had been appointed to this tribunal—but as an itinerant bishop, not often exposed to the few known Deryni at court, he knew little about them, other than through hearsay. Even the enlightened leadership of the past four years could not immediately overturn two centuries of suspicion and hatred. And some of the

Haldane abilities fell into a grey area about which Wolfram was quite unsure.

"What is it, Wolfram?" Cardiel asked quietly, noting the older man's expression of consternation. "I assure you, the king can do what he proposes. I have seen him question prisoners in the field. There is no evil in it. And his results were always verifiable by—those whose talents are less acceptable to this court."

"Meaning Duke Alaric?" Wolfram asked, flicking Morgan an uneasy glance.

"Yes."

Wolfram drew a deep, shuddery breath, visibly pushing aside his apprehensions to return to the task he had been assigned, and let out a heavy sigh.

"Very well. I would not presume to question His Majesty's ability to do what he says he can do—or the judgment of my Lord Archbishop that such an ability is benign." He paused to clear his throat. "Legally speaking, however, I wonder whether it is prudent to enlist his Majesty's assistance in this matter. Lord Dhugal is his foster brother, after all."

"Are you suggesting that I might distort the truth for the sake of the love I bear him?" Kelson asked.

Wolfram paled, but he did not flinch from the king's gaze.

"I suggest nothing of the sort, Sire. But others might."

"Aye, so they might."

Before Wolfram could do more than gasp, the king suddenly drew his sword and sank to one knee before the tribunal, reversing the weapon to grasp it beneath the quillons and extending the cross of the hilt at arm's length between them and himself.

"I swear on my father's sword, on my crown, and on my hopes for the salvation of my immortal soul that I have spoken and shall speak only the truth in the matter here before this court. In the name of the Father, and of the Son, and of the Holy Spirit, amen."

He kissed the sacred relic encased in the hilt, then let the tip of the blade rest on the floor before him, keeping his arm extended as he glanced toward Wolfram and the others.

"I am willing to repeat my oath, or any other you may prefer, in yonder chapel," he added, nodding toward the open doorway behind them. "And I assure you that I do not take such oaths lightly."

"No one questions that, Sire," Wolfram said, looking a little embarrassed. "But—" He sighed uncomfortably. "Sire, Duncan McLain is said by some to be Deryni."

"I don't believe that's at issue here," Kelson said mildly, getting to his feet. "The question is whether the man contracted a valid marriage with the mother of his son."

"But—if he *were* Deryni, Sire—could he not evade even your reading of the truth?"

With an exasperated sigh, Kelson turned toward Morgan, sitting at his right, and held out the hilt of the sword.

"Morgan, remembering the oaths of fealty and homage you have sworn to me and to my father before me, and further enjoined by your hand on this sacred sword, would you please tell Bishop Wolfram the limitations of Truth-Reading, *if* Duncan McLain were Deryni?"

Quietly Morgan stood, laying his bare right hand on the relic in the royal sword hilt. It was not often that Kelson invoked the name of his father, with all the very special associations that called up for Alaric Morgan.

"For simple Truth-Reading, whether or not the subject is Deryni has no bearing," Morgan said quietly. "His Majesty would have no difficulty distinguishing truth from a lie. The operative limitation to Truth-Reading is that the right questions must be asked. Nothing in Truth-Reading compels a man to tell the truth; it simply betrays him when he does not."

Wolfram swallowed uneasily, only partially reassured.

"Sire, is that true?"

"It is."

"You would know if Morgan lied?"

"If I wished it, yes," Kelson replied. "The process does require intent." He turned his Haldane eyes full on Morgan. "I cannot simply *know*, as I suspect the Deryni cannot, either. But if I will it, I can distinguish truth from falsehood. Morgan, before God and these witnesses, have you spoken the truth?"

"I have, Sire."

Kelson sheathed his sword as he returned his attention to Wolfram. "You have heard the truth, Excellency."

"I—see." Wolfram turned to confer with Cardiel, Arilan

nodding thoughtful agreement with whatever the archbishop said, then looked out boldly at Kelson again.

"Sire, I have only just confirmed something that I heard some months ago, but I am given to understand that—the Haldane talents are not limited to mere verification of truth. That more—compelling measures may be employed to elicit actual information from a subject. That—such measures were used routinely on campaign last summer to retrieve more complete reports from scouts in your service, not only by Duke Alaric, but by yourself."

Kelson allowed himself a tight, careful smile, wondering where Wolfram had gotten his information—though any of the scouts could have talked about it. No one had forbidden it. He wondered whether Duncan had used the method, too—though he would have been far less open about it, still feeling it needful to keep that aspect of his identity unconfirmed.

"My prince?" Morgan murmured.

"Tell him," Kelson said.

"We Deryni call it Mind-Seeing," Morgan said. "Do the Haldanes have another name for it, Sire?"

"No."

Inclining his head, Morgan continued. "We distinguish two levels of Mind-Seeing, depending upon whether the subject is cooperative or not. A consciously cooperating subject can recall events in great detail. And of course, there's no possibility of lying. An uncooperative subject *may* be able to block the efficiency of the process to the extent that he will not *volunteer* information. But his answers to specific questions will be truthful. Resistance produces varying degrees of discomfort for the subject, depending upon the level of resistance and the amount of energy being put into the demands for information. This holds true for Deryni as well as humans, though Deryni obviously will have the potential for greater resistance."

"I see," Wolfram said thoughtfully. "Then, if Bishop McLain *were* Deryni—"

"Even if he *were*," Kelson said pointedly, "—which I will not ask him, Bishop—any resistance to my questions regarding his marriage would be immediately evident, for I would put the full force of my power behind my questioning.

I will do that, if you wish—assuming, of course, that the findings thus obtained may be acceptable to this court."

The measure Kelson proposed was a uniquely Haldane solution to a situation they had all feared would have none, and the king had little concern that Wolfram would continue to object for long. Nor did he. When the peppery old bishop had conferred again with Cardiel and Arilan, finally giving reluctant assent by his expression, Kelson bade Morgan set two backless stools before the tribunal's table.

A glance in Duncan's direction brought him forward—an unassuming, black-clad supplicant today rather than duke and earl and warrior-bishop, blue eyes guileless and un-flinching, clean-shaven oval face framed by close-cropped brown hair, tonsured only in token, wearing no sign of his episcopal rank save the amethyst on his right hand. This he removed and laid on the table before Cardiel for safekeeping as he took a seat at Kelson's behest, scooting the stool closer to the table and laying his forearms on the table, palms upward, as Kelson directed.

"This questioning has nothing to do with my office as bishop," he explained to Wolfram, as the latter glanced in question at the ring. "I am here as a father who wishes to acknowledge his son."

"A Deryni father, acknowledging a Deryni son?"

Duncan managed a fleeting but stiff smile.

"I believe His Majesty said I was not to be asked that question."

"My Majesty did, indeed," Kelson said, setting a hand on Duncan's left shoulder. "Shame on you, Wolfram."

Wolfram shrugged. "I only ask what others are asking, Sire. I think he probably is—and I begin to wonder whether there is, indeed, harm in that, apart from the law—but, no matter, for now. I am not devil's advocate for *that* question, thank God." He glanced at the others, at the clerk, who had looked up furtively at this last exchange, and motioned the young man to continue taking his notes. "Shall we proceed?"

"With the understanding that *I* will ask the questions, yes," Kelson replied. He settled gracefully on the stool at Duncan's left, his hand sliding down Duncan's arm to grasp the wrist inside the loose-fitting black sleeve. In his peripheral vision, he could see Morgan sitting beside a stiff and anxious Dhugal, with Nigel leaning forward a little, the better to observe what was about to happen.

"For the benefit of Bishop Wolfram, who's never seen this done before, I'll explain what I'm doing," Kelson said, addressing the three bishops. "I've asked Duncan to lay his open hands on the table so that you will be able to observe any sign of tension as the questioning progresses—though I don't expect to see any. I have my hand on his wrist, partly for the same reason and partly because I've found that physical contact enhances control in this kind of procedure. Are you comfortable, Duncan?"

"Physically? Yes. Emotionally—" The Deryni duke-bishop shrugged and grinned, still playing innocent of direct Deryni knowledge. "I've watched this done before, Sire. I'm not sure I look forward to reliving the days of my brash youth. I was very ardent."

Kelson smiled fleetingly, feeling for Duncan, but there was no way around it. It had to be done.

"Nonetheless," the king said, as he turned his Truth-Reading talent on his friend. "Let's begin with a simple review of basics. Please state your full name for the noble lords of this tribunal, and all your offices."

"Duncan Howard McLain," Duncan said easily. "Priest and bishop. King's Confessor. Duke of Cassan and Earl of Kierney. Acting Viceroy of Meara. I also have some subsidiary titles and offices. Do you want those, too?"

"I don't think that's necessary. Did you contract a valid marriage with Dhugal MacArdry's mother?"

"I did."

"When was that?"

"It would have been early in April of 1107."

"And you were how old?"

Duncan smiled. "An intellectually precocious but very naïve fifteen, courting an older woman. Maryse was a year older."

"I see. But you were both of noble houses, you a duke's son and she the daughter of an earl. What made you decide to contract a secret marriage?"

Duncan shook his head wistfully, letting his gaze shift in the general direction of the ring before Cardiel, remembering.

"Youth. Impatience. Maryse and her mother and sisters

had come to stay at Culdi while our fathers took their levies into Meara on campaign. The two clans had been closely allied for several generations. The way I heard it told, one of my father's men killed one of her father's men in a drunken brawl. Unfortunately, her father's man was Ardry Mac-Ardry, her eldest brother—the heir.

"The culprit was tried and executed in the field, as was proper, but neither side was really satisfied. Our fathers feared a blood feud if contact continued between the clans. So old Caulay broke off his MacArdry levies and had them transferred to another command, separate from my father's, then rode back to Culdi with a small escort to get his wom-enfolk and hie them back to Transha."

"Maryse as well?" Kelson prompted.

Duncan blinked several times and nodded, his voice faltering just a little as he continued.

"I never planned to fall in love that spring. I had my studies and my vocation. I was to enter the seminary at Gre-cotha in the fall. I was old enough to go on campaign, but I'd stayed behind to host my father's guests while he and my brother went. Nothing like love was supposed to happen."

He shook his head, amazed anew at how events had upset all their plans.

"It did happen, though. Within a few weeks, we were all caught up in it. We kept it secret, because we knew my mother would be furious when I told her I would not be entering the priesthood, but we planned to ask our parents' permission to marry at the end of the summer, when our fathers came back from the war. Caulay's unexpected return changed all that—and the threat of a blood feud."

"What changed?" Kelson asked.

Duncan sighed. "We decided to marry anyway. We were thinking clearly enough not just to run away, but we knew none of the local priests would marry us without our parents' consent, especially at such short notice. So we agreed to meet in the chapel at midnight and make our vows before the only Witness we knew would not betray us."

"The Blessed Sacrament," Kelson supplied, glancing at the bishops and noting Wolfram's interest, in particular.

"Yes."

"And did you, in fact, meet? And did you, in fact, exchange marriage vows that you considered binding?"

"We did."

"Thank you." Kelson reached with his free hand to brush Duncan's brow, carefully avoiding eye contact with Wolfram.

"Close your eyes now, Duncan. Close your eyes and slip deeper into memory of that night. In a moment, I'm going to ask you to recall exactly what you and Maryse said to each other. Are you willing?"

As Duncan complied, nodding dreamily, Kelson pressed his fingertips lightly on the closed lids, extending control without encountering resistance, then slid his hand down to rest on Duncan's sleeve, his other hand still circling the relaxed wrist. Only then did he look at the bishops again.

Arilan, who knew exactly what Kelson was doing, and how truly Deryni it was, had raised one hand casually to shield a faint smile from Wolfram. Cardiel looked alert and fascinated, as he usually did when watching the king work. Wolfram himself appeared a little apprehensive, but that was only to be expected. He started a little as Kelson nodded in his direction and glanced deliberately at Duncan's passive, upturned hands.

"He's been telling the truth exactly as he remembers it, my lords," the king said softly. "There's been no flicker of resistance, no hint of deception. I have no doubt that they did exchange marriage vows. Is it necessary for me to go on?"

"It—won't hurt him, will it?" Wolfram asked.

"Not at all—though, as he said, the intensity of some of those memories may be a bit uncomfortable. In a sense, he'll actually be reliving the incident."

Wolfram swallowed. "I—don't wish to cause him distress, Sire, but I would like to hear the words. The words can confirm much of his intent."

"Very well." Kelson sighed and turned his attention back to Duncan, waiting docile and ready beneath his hands. "Duncan, I'd like you to go back to that night when you and Maryse exchanged vows. Think back to the chapel at Culdi. You're fifteen years old, and it's midnight. Did Maryse come to you?"

"Yes," Duncan breathed.

"And what, if anything, did you say to each other?"

"We knelt before the Blessed Sacrament," Duncan whispered. "I took her hand in mine and made my vow.

"'Before Thee as the Supreme Witness, my Lord and my God, I make this solemn vow: that I take this woman, Maryse, as my lawful wedded wife, forsaking all others until death do us part.'" His free hand lifted vaguely to his left shoulder, then subsided as he went on.

"'I give thee this token of my love and take thee for my wife, and hereto I plight thee my troth.'"

"And what did you give her?" Kelson prompted softly.

"A silver cloak clasp, shaped in the likeness of a sleeping lion's head."

"I see. And what were the words she spoke to you?"

Kelson could feel Duncan trembling beneath his touch, but it was the trembling of emotion, not resistance to the probe.

"'I take thee as my wedded husband. I give thee this token as a sign of my love, and hereto I plight thee my troth.'"

"And she gave you—"

"A *shiral* crystal, smooth from the river bottom and drilled to receive a slender leather thong," Duncan replied, swallowing with difficulty. "It was—still warm from her body as she placed it around my neck. Her perfume clung to it."

"Be easy," Kelson murmured, soothing the poignancy of the memory and shaking his head a little. "I know this is uncomfortable for you."

But he had caught a glimpse of something else, something he knew Duncan had never even told his old confessor. It was intensely personal for Duncan, but not particularly notable of itself. Still, it certainly would seal the validity of his intent.

"Tell me what happened next, Duncan," he whispered. "Before you left the chapel, you did something else. What was it?"

Duncan drew a deep breath and let it out audibly, making a conscious effort to relax.

"We knew that marriage was a sacrament that two people give to one another. We also knew that our own administering of that sacrament was irregular. But we wanted to make it as special and holy as we could, without a priest. So I—went up to the altar and—took a ciborium from the tabernacle."

"Wasn't it locked?" Wolfram muttered.

But Cardiel only hushed him as Kelson shook his head and urged Duncan to go on.

"You took out a ciborium," Kelson repeated, glossing over the opening of the tabernacle and the memory of Deryni powers brought into play to drop the tumblers of the door's tiny lock into place. "Then what did you do?"

"I—brought it down to the altar step and knelt beside Maryse. Then we—gave one another Holy Communion. We—knew it wasn't normally allowed, but I was accustomed to handling the altar vessels when I served Mass. And we couldn't have a nuptial Mass. . . ."

"I take it," Arilan interjected softly, "that everything was done with due reverence for the Blessed Sacrament?"

"Yes," Duncan breathed.

"I think there can be no doubt that the intent was there to solemnize a valid and sacramental marriage," Cardiel said quietly. "Arilan? Wolfram?"

As both nodded, Cardiel went on.

"But one final question must be asked, then. Where and when was the marriage consummated? You need not give any further details beyond that."

Duncan smiled dreamily, grateful for the kindness.

"After we had finished in the chapel, we stole away to the stable loft, snug and hidden in the sweet-smelling hay. Innocent that I was, it never even occurred to me to wonder whether our one painfully brief union might have borne fruit. And communication, once she would have known, was impossible, given the bad blood between our two clans. Perhaps she tried to write to me and tell me, but no messenger ever reached me. It was only a full year later that I learned she had died the previous winter, ostensibly of a fever. The first inkling I had otherwise was when, a year ago, I saw Dhugal wearing the cloak clasp I had given Maryse."

When Duncan had finished, it remained only for Dhugal himself, the offspring of that union, to come forward and offer as final evidence the tokens his parents had exchanged that long ago night in the chapel of Culdi: the cloak clasp bearing the sleeping lion's head, its concealed compartment still containing the ring woven of Duncan's and Maryse's hairs intertwined, and the honey-colored lump of *shiral* that Dhugal had worn since that day, now a year long past, when he and his father had finally discovered their true relationship.

"Keep it," Duncan had said, "in memory of your mother."

"But, that leaves you with nothing of hers," Dhugal had protested.

"It leaves me with everything," Duncan had replied. "I have her son."

Now father and son stood a little shyly in a windowed alcove opening off the king's dayroom, still savoring the heady triumph of the archbishop's tribunal and the more creaturely satisfaction of the hot meal Kelson had ordered sent in upon their return. The king, Morgan, Nigel, and Arilan continued to converse over the remnants of that meal, but Dhugal had felt the need for more private counsel with his father. As he and Duncan moved a little farther into the alcove, out of sight and earshot of the others, the coppery streak of his border braid made bold contrast against the unadorned black that he, like his father, had donned for the morning's solemn proceedings.

"I know you told me before, but I'd forgotten that you and Maryse gave one another communion after you made your vows," Dhugal said in a low voice, looking out at the rain while he fingered the *shiral* crystal that had been his mother's. "Of course, you would have. In fact, you were a priest even then, weren't you?—even though you'd not been ordained or even started in holy orders. Yet you were willing to give it all up for her."

Duncan sighed and set both hands on one of the horizontal bands of iron supporting the mullioned window panes, leaning his forehead against the cool glass as he stared, unseeing, at the rain beyond. At midafternoon, it was nearly dark already, but not nearly so dark as that dark night of the soul through which he had gone that long-ago summer.

"I thought I was willing," he said, after a moment. "I fully intended to give it up, at the time. And yet, I suppose I *was* already a priest. I guess I've always known that, but I—put it aside when I met your mother. I used to wonder if that was why God took her from me—because I was His priest."

"Why did He let you fall in love, then?" Dhugal demanded. "Was He only testing you? And then, when you failed the test, did He kill her, so you couldn't have her?"

Duncan looked up sharply at the bitterness in Dhugal's voice, hearing an echo of his own rebellious anger when he learned that Maryse had died.

"Dhugal, no!" he whispered. "It's true that she died, son, but He didn't kill her. If I've learned anything in thirty-odd years of living, it's that He's a loving God. He doesn't slay His children—though, for His own reasons, He sometimes lets them suffer adversities that we don't understand. She might have died bearing anyone's child. I don't think she was singled out because she dared to love a man God intended as His own."

As he looked out at the rain again, remembering what it had cost him to truly believe what he had just said, Dhugal snorted and turned away, shoulders rigid with rebellion.

"I understand what you're feeling," Duncan said, after a few seconds. "In some ways, you may be right. It may well be that God *was* testing me—and that I did, indeed, fail. For a while, after I heard she'd died, I used to think so. But now I wonder if there wasn't another reason He brought me and Maryse together. He still wanted me for His own, but— maybe that's the only way *you* could be born."

"Me?"

As Dhugal turned to stare at him aghast, Duncan smiled gently.

"You're so like Alaric sometimes. He's another who doesn't like to think he's been the subject of Heaven's special attention. Ask him sometime, if you don't believe me."

"Well, it does take some getting used to."

"Why? Don't you think God has a plan for each of us?"

"Well, of course," Dhugal said uncomfortably. "But only in a general sort of way. We have free will."

"To an extent," Duncan agreed. "But what was *my* will, set against the will of God, Dhugal? He wanted me to be His priest. I'm not sure I ever had a choice in the matter—not really. Not that I mind," he added. "Not now, at any rate, and not for many years—though I certainly minded after your mother's death.

"But there's a certain heady comfort in knowing one has been chosen, warts and all. I don't know why He wanted me so badly, but other than that one brief flare-up of rebellion—which may have been all in His plan anyway—I've been content in His service. No, more than content. He's brought me joy. And one of my greatest joys, though I didn't know it for a long, long time, is that He let me sire you—and all without compromising His honor."

Dhugal, much moved, turned awkwardly to gaze out the window again, all but blinking back tears.

"What about His laws?" he asked after a moment. "The ones that forbid Deryni to seek the priesthood."

"Laws are written by men, Dhugal, even if God inspires them. Sometimes men misunderstand."

Dhugal glanced sidelong at his father.

"What if Maryse *hadn't* died, though? Would you still have become a priest? For that matter, did she know what you were?"

"That I was Deryni? Of course. I told her that afternoon, before we were wed."

"And she didn't mind?"

"Did she mind? Of course not. To her, it was the same kind of odd but useful talent as the second sight some of your borderers have—just a bit more diverse. I'm not sure she ever quite understood what all the fuss was about, though she knew it could mean my death if I were discovered. The border folk have always been a mystical people. Perhaps the terrible persecution of Deryni in the lowlands never quite reached the same proportions in the borders and highlands."

"Aye, that's true enough," Dhugal agreed. "But you haven't answered my other question. What would you have done, if she hadn't died?"

Curiosity about what might have been, loyalty to the mother Dhugal had never really known—Duncan could hardly fault his son for any of that, but neither could he really give an answer. How was he to explain, without shattering whatever idealism might remain to this keen-eyed young man who had already lived so much and in such adversity?

"I honestly don't know, Dhugal—and believe me, I asked myself the same question many times in those early years." He twisted the bishop's ring on his hand as he went on. "The reality is that it would have been several years, at least, before the bitterness between our two clans had died down enough that we could acknowledge our marriage openly. Maryse's pregnancy would have been seen as a dishonor to her clan, even if she'd told her mother we were really married—which she may have done, since it was your grandmother who saw that you eventually got the cloak clasp I'd given Maryse as a bridal token. And there's no telling how long it might have been before she could get word to me. As it was, she never did."

He sighed. "In any case, because of the circumstances, you probably would have been brought up as a son of her mother, regardless—the easiest immediate way to cover up a daughter's increasingly apparent indiscretion and save the honor of the clan. You *were* old Caulay's grandson, after all, even if you weren't his son. And he'd just lost a son. In time, when anger eventually cooled between the two clans, there would have been no problem acknowledging the marriage and you."

"And would you have?" Dhugal persisted.

Duncan shrugged. "We'll never know, will we? I entered the university at Grecotha in the fall, as planned. Not to have done so would have aroused suspicion—and besides, I loved the academic life. But I delayed taking my vows, waiting for the bad blood between the clans to dissipate.

"Then, when I heard the news the next summer—that she'd died of a fever—there was no reason not to go ahead and make my profession, no reason to suspect you even existed. I grieved and I raged at heaven over the injustice of it, but life went on. I was tonsured at Michaelmas, and soon the memory of my brief flirtation with a secular life had taken on the aspect of a pleasant but fleeting dream." He looked directly at Dhugal, catching the amber eyes with his blue ones. "Does it bother you that I can't say, 'Yes, Dhugal, I definitely would have acknowledged the marriage and the son I didn't know I had'?"

"I—suppose not," Dhugal said in a small voice. "As you said before, we'll never know." He swallowed noisily and raised his chin higher, but he could not sustain eye contact.

"There's something else I have to ask, though," he said. "And in light of how things have turned out, perhaps it's even more important."

"I'll answer if I can, son."

"You went ahead and made your vows. You became a priest. But you knew you were Deryni."

"Well, of course, but—"

"Why do you continue to deny what you did, then, and what you are?" Dhugal blurted, turning to gaze at his father with the uncompromising eyes of youth. "You're Deryni and you're a priest. And you're a *good* priest! You've proven by many years of faithful and righteous service that the two are *not* incompatible. There were Deryni priests before the Restoration, for God's sake, and they were good ones, too!"

"That's true," Duncan whispered.

"Then, why don't you admit it? Why keep playing these games of not answering either way? What can they do to you?"

Duncan could feel his heart pounding like a battering ram at the walls of his chest and he prayed Dhugal would drop the line of questioning.

"There are a great many things they could do, son."

"But they *won't*. They *didn't*. Some of the bishops know, and all of them surely suspect. You heard Wolfram today! And they knew it *before* they elected you a bishop."

"Yes, and Edmund Loris knew, too," Duncan retorted, fists clenching involuntarily as the memory of the renegade archbishop's tortures loomed unbeckoned in his mind's eye. The nails had grown back on his fingers and toes, and his other wounds had healed, but the nightmare of being chained to the stake, with the flames leaping up around him, beginning to lick at his flesh, would be with Duncan McLain until the day he died.

But the invoking of Loris' name had brought Dhugal back to the reality of what *could* happen, for it was he who had fought his way through the fire and Loris' men to save his father. Dhugal gasped as he realized what memories he had stirred and he shifted his gaze out to the rain again.

"I'm sorry," he said quietly. "I have no right to ask that

of you. I'm new to knowing what I am. You've had to live with it all your life. It has to be *your* decision. It's just that Morgan and Kelson are able to be so open—''

"And you'd like to be, too, wouldn't you?" Duncan replied softly. "I know, son. Believe me, I've thought about it often, but—''

He broke off as Morgan stepped into the opening of the alcove, clearing his throat to announce his presence.

"Sorry to interrupt," Morgan said. "Duncan, had you forgotten we have some important further business with Bishop Arilan?''

Duncan blinked and shook his head. He had not forgotten, but he was not looking forward to it. Dhugal and Kelson did not know it yet, but tonight was the night that Morgan and Duncan had agreed Arilan should expose the two young men to *merasha* for the first time. The very notion made Duncan's stomach queasy, for Loris had given *him* the drug when he fell captive of the renegade archbishop the summer before. It acted only as a sedative in humans, but even a minute amount could render a Deryni totally incapable of using his powers. Morgan, too, had cause to know *merasha*'s dangers from bitter firsthand experience, but it was important that both Dhugal and the king experience its disruptive effects in a safe, controlled setting before they chanced encountering it in less favorable circumstances. There was no antidote, but sometimes the effects could be minimized or made to work somewhat positively, if the subject was familiar with them.

Back in the supper room, Kelson was already seated at the now-cleared table before the fireplace, Nigel across from him—for they had agreed that the king's uncle should be present, as regent, since the king would be incapacitated for the rest of the night. Dhugal glanced questioningly at Kelson as he sat down at Kelson's left and his father sat beside him, but the king only shrugged as Morgan took a place on Kelson's right. Arilan came back to the table with a tooled leather flask in his hands and an odd, tight expression on his face.

"I apologize if this may seem a bit abrupt," the Deryni bishop said, sitting opposite the two younger men and ignoring their expressions of apprehension as he set the flask on the table between them. "However, I have my reasons. Sire, I doubt you saw this flask on the day your father died— or that you remember it, if you did. You should, though. This is what killed your father."

CHAPTER TWO

Open thy mouth, and drink what I give thee to drink.

—II Esdras 14:38

"This is what killed your father."

Arilan's words pierced like steel in the hearts of the four present who had known Brion Haldane intimately. Kelson's face drained of color, grey eyes like dead coals in a death-white mask. Nigel gasped soundlessly, stricken, in that instant looking uncannily like the beloved elder brother who had died in his arms. Duncan crossed himself in horrified disbelief. Only Morgan responded with action, half coming to his feet to lunge between Kelson and the bishop, an open hand stretching toward Arilan's throat.

"Don't touch me, or you'll regret it!" Arilan snapped, not even flinching as Morgan's hand pulled up in a fist a hair's breadth from his face. "Sit down. You'd think *I* killed Brion. Actually, neither did this—though it's what enabled him to be killed in the way he was. Surely you guessed it was *merasha* that made him vulnerable—or *do* you think I somehow had something to do with it?"

As Morgan drew back and sat down, not trusting himself to speak, Duncan slowly exhaled and glanced at Arilan, a hand staying Nigel, whose mouth was working, but without words coming out.

"No one is making any accusations," Duncan said carefully, at the same time bidding the others, with his mind, to keep silent while he sought an explanation. "Though I think it occurs to all of us, now, that you could have done. I assume

24

that's the flask that Colin of Fianna shared with the king that day. We never learned how *merasha* got into it, however.''

Arilan sat back with a snort of derision, crossing his arms on his chest. His lean, handsome face, blue-jowled this late in the day, looked a little satanic as the shadows came and went in the flickering firelight, and his deep blue-violet eyes were nearly the color of his cassock in the dimness.

"Don't be absurd. If you'll recall, Nigel, it was I who first told you that Colin said he'd gotten it from a mysterious lady."

"Then, where did *you* get the flask?" Nigel countered. "We searched high and low for it, but we never found a trace. Colin said he guessed he'd lost it on the ride back from the hunt."

Arilan nodded. "And so he did. Only, I was the one who 'lost' it for him. I knew, the moment I reached Brion's side and saw that he was dying, that he'd gotten *merasha* in him from somewhere—and I'd seen him drinking with Colin only minutes before.

"So I waylaid Colin in the courtyard after we got back, while everyone was milling around and seeing Brion's body brought into the great hall, and I relieved him of the flask—which was, indeed, the source of the *merasha*. He never remembered that part of our conversation, of course. I left it to the rest of you to draw the correct conclusion that Charissa had been the giver of the deadly gift—something I couldn't tell you then, or even about the *merasha*, without betraying that I was Deryni."

"I—assume there was nothing you could do to save my father, either," Kelson finally said, speaking for the first time. "I don't want to believe that you could have done something and didn't, just to protect your precious identity."

Arilan glanced down at his clasped hands. "Kelson, I will not deny that I have been guilty of that accusation on more than one occasion. The nightmares I suffer because of it are worse than you can possibly imagine and only a foretaste of the answering I shall have to make one day before a higher Judge. But your father's blood is not on my hands. The damage already was done by the time I got to him. I doubt that even a Healer could have saved him—if we still had qualified Healers."

"Is that the truth, or are you just saying it to placate me?" Kelson replied, daring to turn his Truth-Reading ability on the Deryni bishop for the first time.

Smiling gently, quite aware of the feather-light probe, Arilan shook his head and opened his hands in a gesture of submission.

"I have told you only the truth, Kelson," he breathed. "There was nothing I could have done for your father save to prolong his agony a few more minutes. He would not have chosen that, I think. You were there. You know how he suffered."

"Aye." Kelson swallowed down the lump rising in his throat and looked away for a few seconds, shutting himself off from the mental query of Morgan and even Dhugal's timid attempt to comfort. He tried not to look at the flask still on the table before him.

"So," he finally said, risking a glance at Arilan again. "You've had the flask all this time. Why bring it out now?"

"I think you know."

Very deliberately, Arilan reached into his cassock and pulled out a small, stoppered glass vial, which he set deliberately beside the flask.

"It's time you faced the thing that can set all your powers at naught, Sire," he said. "You've never experienced *merasha* disruption directly. Nor has Dhugal. For Deryni fortunate enough to receive formal training, it's an important part of that training, because even though *merasha* is probably the single most devastating substance that can be employed against our powers, an informed subject can sometimes minimize the effects and even use some of them to his advantage. Duncan can attest to that, I'm sure."

Tight-lipped, Duncan nodded, covering one of Dhugal's hands with his own, and Kelson shifted an accusing glance to Morgan.

"Alaric, did you know about this?" he demanded.

Morgan drew a deep breath and let it out audibly.

"Not about the flask, no. Duncan and I had discussed with Arilan the need to expose you to *merasha* before you left on your summer progress. We had agreed that tonight was the logical time to do it. I didn't tell you, because I didn't want you to be apprehensive about that when you needed all your concentration for the hearing this morning. As you may have gathered, however, I was not expecting him to produce the very *merasha* that Brion was given. That was a foul blow, Arilan.''

Arilan spread both hands in a gesture of conciliation. ''For that, I apologize. I had not realized the wounds were still so raw. But it seemed a vivid way of underlining why it's important they face *merasha*. In that, at least, I believe I have made my point.''

''Amply,'' Kelson muttered. He picked up the stoppered vial and held it to the light, conjuring handfire with his empty hand to see it better. Through the greenish glass, he could just make out the shadow of a clear liquid filling it halfway. He shivered as he put it back down and quenched the handfire with an impatient closing of his fist.

''So, that's *merasha*.''

He glanced uneasily at Dhugal, who looked even more apprehensive than he himself felt, then made his gaze continue on around the table to Duncan, solemn and sympathetic, no doubt remembering his own most recent brush with the drug, to Nigel, who was trying hard not to transmit his dry-throated fear to the rest of them, full of dread even though he was not being asked to endure the testing, past the inscrutable-looking Arilan, and on, at last, to Morgan.

''I think I would have preferred some time to get used to the idea, Alaric,'' he said softly, managing to keep most of the reproach out of his voice. ''You could have told me.''

''Forgive me,'' Morgan murmured. ''I misjudged. We did talk about the advisability of doing this—one night late in the fall, as I recall. Dhugal, you were there. But I suppose you put it out of mind when I was unable to procure any *merasha* on my own. The need is no less important for having been postponed, however. It's vital that you know what you could come up against and how to deal with it.''

''What's the urgency?''

''Because you aren't a child any more, my prince,'' Morgan said a little sharply. ''Because in three days' time, you'll be knighted. For those who will never wear a crown, that's the official seal of manhood. It makes you fair game for those who might have spared you before, because of your youth—especially as your talents become more widely known. When you go on progress, and especially when you meet the Torenthi legates in Cardosa, you'll be particularly at risk.''

"Implying that I haven't been for the past four years?"

"You've been lucky. You can't be sure your luck will hold. If Brion had known what you'll know, he might not have died. That's *my* fault. I knew what *merasha* could do, at least in theory. I should have made certain he did, too."

"Don't flatter yourself, Alaric," Arilan said. "It would have done no good in Brion's case. Brion was never really comfortable with what he was and he never learned to utilize his powers the way he might have done. That isn't your fault; you were only half-trained yourself. No, there was something in Brion's own makeup that held him back, that made him just a little too reluctant to use what powers he had. I think I know, but I mayn't speak of it. Remember that I was his confessor for the last six years of his life."

"He spoke of these things to you?" Kelson asked.

"Only peripherally and very rarely, at that. But why do you think he never taught you anything about the Haldane potential? Think back. Alaric and Duncan were the only ones who even tried to expose you to magic and esoteric philosophy."

Kelson swallowed uncomfortably and reached out to touch a hesitant fingertip to the side of the leather flask.

"If—if my father *had* known how to minimize the effects of the *merasha*, would that have saved him?"

As all eyes turned to Arilan in question, the Deryni bishop slowly shook his head.

"I can't answer that, Kelson. It might have done so. If he'd known—if he'd been fighting it when I realized what was happening—it's possible. But *not* knowing, he definitely didn't have a chance. That I can say without reservation."

"I see."

Kelson picked up the flask and tipped it from side to side, with an answering gurgle of liquid still inside.

"Very well. Is there enough in here to do the job, or has it gone bad in four years?"

Nigel paled, and Morgan and Duncan exchanged startled glances, but Arilan only smiled slightly.

"I fear the wine has gone a little sour, and the *merasha* has lost its potency after so long, but I think I understand what you're really asking. I'd intended to start with new wine, but we can use what's in there, if you wish."

"Is that safe?" Morgan asked, before Kelson could reply.

Arilan nodded. "As safe as *merasha* ever is. What's in there is nearly spent—exactly how much, is difficult to determine—so I'll still have to add some from what I've brought." He gestured toward the green vial. "But I wanted a higher dosage anyway. Even new, the original was too subtle for our purposes. I believe, however, that His Majesty means this trial partially as a remembrance of his father. For that purpose, I'm willing to sacrifice strict accuracy of dose in favor of spiritual resolution. And I've brought a sedative, for afterward, to take the edge off."

He handed a small parchment packet to the reluctant Duncan, who went immediately to fetch a cup of water. Meanwhile, as the others watched in taut fascination, Arilan matter-of-factly unstoppered the leather flask and sniffed at the contents, wrinkling his nose at the smell. A distracted snap of his fingers brought two empty goblets floating over from the dishes cleared away after supper, one of which he filled from the flask. After adding most of the contents of the glass vial, he poured the mixture back and forth several times between the first and second goblets, ending with half the mixture in each. These he set on the table before the king and Dhugal without ceremony. Beside him, Duncan had returned and was stirring a cup of water with a little horn spoon.

"That's the sedative?" Morgan asked.

Duncan nodded. "Aye, nothing unexpected. A good, stiff dose, but they'll need that. Dhugal, I think you're familiar with this one."

Dhugal, trained as a battle-surgeon, sniffed at the cup Duncan held out to him, frowned, then gingerly touched a fingertip to the liquid and then to his tongue, grimacing at the taste.

"Aye, I know it. We won't wake before morning, and that's for sure. Next to a Deryni, it's the best thing I know to knock out a patient so you can work on him. They don't feel much."

"And neither will you," Arilan said, taking the cup from Duncan and setting it back in the center of the table. "Nor will you want to."

He glanced at Kelson, then at Morgan and Duncan, finally sparing a look and a smile for Nigel, who bit back a grimace of apprehension and clasped his arms across his chest, one nervous hand massaging the opposite bicep.

"Whenever you're ready, then, gentlemen," Arilan said quietly. "Actually, why don't you go first, Kelson, so we don't have to watch both of you at once? I know you don't much trust me right now, so Alaric can monitor. I'd recommend you have a very modest taste first, so you can experience the subtler effects, and then toss it off as neatly as you can. In this concentration, it has a particularly nasty aftertaste, as I'm sure Duncan can attest. I suspect this is similar to the strength Loris and Gorony used on him."

If Arilan had intended his words to be reassuring, he failed utterly, for Kelson had seen the end result of Duncan's ordeal—and of his father's. Picking up the *merasha*-drugged goblet of his own volition was one of the most difficult things he had ever done.

This is what killed your father! his fear screeched at him, even though he knew it was not true. *You will taste his death again!*

His hand trembled as he brought the cup to his lips, and he had to steady it with his other hand. Try as he might to prevent it, images of his father's death began crowding into memory—the well-loved face contorted with pain and bewilderment, the chest heaving for breath—and sometimes the face was his own. Sternly he told himself that he was *not* his father, but dread continued to scurry just at the edges of awareness, constantly dipping deeper into that well of vague and even more soul-chilling fears that every man has, that would always resist reason.

But to counter it, he could feel support all around him: magical bolstering, the likes of which his father had never known—the quick, timid caress of Dhugal's mind, backed by Duncan's, and then the more powerful surge of Morgan's exhortation for courage, as the Deryni duke laid his hand on the back of Kelson's neck. He could sense Arilan's mind only sketchily, though what did come through was benign, but even Nigel, all potential and no power as yet, displayed a fierce glow of fortitude that was another source of comfort.

Heartened, Kelson tipped the cup to taste of the temporary death of mind, barely testing with the tip of his tongue. Unlike his father, he would not *really* die. Surely he could endure this tempering ordeal, so that his father's death might not have been in vain.

The wine was pungent and tart. Arilan had been right

about it going sour. It was not yet vinegary, but almost—probably not a Fianna varietal, but it would have been a good vintage red, four years before. He knew his father had approved. He wondered why it had not lasted better.

Perhaps it was the *merasha*, he decided, as he ran his tongue across his lips. Perhaps the old *merasha* had changed it, as it lost its potency. Odd, but the tip of his tongue suddenly felt a little numb. And as he swallowed, the sharp tang of the turning wine left a bitter aftertaste at the back of his tongue—not unexpected, in light of what Arilan had said. He swallowed again and became aware of a faint buzzing that started in his throat and quickly spread to the back of his head.

"Drink it down now," Morgan murmured, suddenly at his right ear, standing now to rest both hands on his shoulders. "You might as well avoid the worst of the transition. Fast is better, believe me."

Kelson might have argued with Arilan, if only because he resented the Deryni bishop's highhandedness in this entire matter, but not with Morgan. He could feel an unpleasant tingling already extending into his lips and down his arms. He raised the cup again in hands that were fast losing sensation.

"All of it, in one big gulp," Morgan urged, as Kelson set it to his lips.

Kelson managed it in two, almost immediately fighting nausea as the sour wine hit his stomach. But it was not the wine that made him want to retch. He knew that with a cold, gut-cramping fear, triggered by yet another image of his father dying, that would not respond to the rational awareness that he was safe here, among friends. Morgan took the empty goblet before he could drop it, but then all his senses began shutting down and he was alone—more alone than he had ever been, even before he came into his powers.

His vision began to blur, tunneling down something like the way it did when he was going into trance for a very deep working. Only, instead of letting him focus inward, the tunnel kept closing in, constricting, shutting him off from both outward and inward sensation until he was blind.

And blind with his powers as well as his eyes. He tried to open his mouth to ask if anyone was still there, but the movement made his stomach churn—though not enough, unfortunately, to heave up what was lying there like a belly full of coals, sending jerky streamers of fire into all his limbs.

"Kelson, can you hear me?" a voice said, close in his ear, its sound like the rasp of rusty metal against his raw nerves.

He managed to nod, but he had to close his eyes to do it—which didn't matter, since he couldn't see anyway. A vague, faraway part of him knew his hands were gripping the edge of the table for dear life, his only anchor in the world now inaccessible to him, but what touched his face, clamping his head between, might have been tongs of fire, had he not somehow sensed they were Morgan's hands.

"Keep your eyes closed, take a deep breath and let it out, and try to concentrate only on my voice," Morgan commanded. "Your shields are nearly gone. Try not to resist what I'm about to do. This isn't going to be pleasant for either of us, but I'll show you what's happening and how to make the best of it."

Kelson could not have disobeyed, had his soul's salvation depended on it. The touch of Morgan's mind was far worse than the touch of his hands. All he remembered of the next hour or two was screaming—though they told him, later, that he had uttered not a sound.

He supposed they had finally given him Arilan's sedative, at the end, because when he finally woke, it was the next morning, and Jatham, his senior squire, was rousing him for Sunday Mass, and his head hurt worse than any hangover he could ever remember having or even hearing about.

"God, how did Duncan function at all?" Kelson whispered, hardly even able to lift his head as he waited for Jatham to fetch Morgan. "The *merasha* disruption, on top of everything else they did to him!" He shifted one arm over his aching eyes to shut out the light. "And my *father!* I doubt he even knew what was happening to him."

Dhugal, stirring from the cot where he had slept at the foot of the king's great bed, groaned as he managed to raise himself far enough to clamp both arms around one of the bedposts and look muzzily in Kelson's general direction.

"You mustn't let yourself dwell on it," he said, "just as I mustn't let myself think about what my father suffered. It does no good. What's important is that we've learned what can be done if *we* ever have to face *merasha* again—God forbid!''

But though it was their resolve not to dwell on such troubles, both of them did—until Morgan's arrival shifted their attention to more practical concerns.

"We *have* to go to Mass this morning, Alaric," Kelson replied, when Morgan suggested that a day in bed would do both young men far more good than attendance at any ritual. "Cardiel will be reading the tribunal's dispensation from the pulpit. Dhugal should be there."

Morgan could not fault that reasoning, though he warned both of them that any immediate relief he might bring them was but a temporary measure, cautioning that only another good night's sleep would really complete their cure. After applying what healing measures he might, he underlined his advice by going to bed himself.

At least Cardiel's announcement proved popular. After Mass, dozens of well-wishers flocked around Dhugal and the king to offer their congratulations, for the young border lord had made himself well-liked at court in the past year and more—and doubly so, now that the social onus of bastardy had been laid to rest. A contingent of Dhugal's borderers, come to Rhemuth to attend his knighting two days hence, cheered him as he and the king left the cathedral, though Ciard O Ruane, Dhugal's aged gillie, was quick to observe—and to point gleefully out to his clansmen—that both their young chief and the king apparently had over-celebrated the night before, judging by their bleary eyes and aversion to light and loud noises.

Neither Dhugal nor Kelson disabused them of that notion, of course. Even were it not expected that all those to receive the accolade should retire early that evening, before plunging into the two-day round of ceremonies and festivities officially marking the event, a hangover gave both of them added excuse to seek seclusion. By the time they had crossed the castle yard and mounted the steps to the great hall doors, only Jatham was still with them, for the clansmen and young warriors who had buzzed around them after Mass or accompanied them back to the keep had drifted on about their business. Besides, Jatham, too, was a candidate for knighthood two days hence, and had his instructions from Morgan, though he did not know the true reason for them.

No ceremony attended the entry of king or border lord into the great hall, though individuals noted the king's passage with informal salute when he passed nearby. Jatham led them briskly down the left side of the hall, intending to take them via a back stair and avoid the more direct and populous route that skirted the gardens—for the previous day's storm had brought a glorious, sunny day, unusual for March, and half the court had repaired to the garden to enjoy the unseasonable warmth.

The sunshine had also brought Nigel's duchess, Meraude, down from the ladies' solar for the afternoon, to stitch and read with two companions in the good north light. Meraude's baby daughter Eirian dozed placidly in a basket at her mother's side. The Princess Janniver tended the baby from time to time, sad-eyed and wistful beneath her mane of yellow curls—Janniver, whom Kelson and his men had been too late to save from dishonor at the hands of Mearan rebels the summer before, now rejected by father and betrothed and left no refuge save the court of Gwynedd. But the other young woman—

Kelson made himself draw a deep breath and tell himself again that the other one was no more for him than Janniver was. At just seventeen, Rothana of Nur Hallaj was beautiful in a dusky, eastern way that made Kelson's knees weak if he thought about it too long. Her breeding was impeccable, for she was a princess of the Forcinn and Richenda's kin by marriage, but she was also *Sister* Rothana, a novice nun of the Order of Saint Brigid, even if her vows were not yet final.

She was also Deryni, perhaps as powerful and certainly as self-willed as Morgan's Richenda, if less thoroughly trained—which made her doubly fascinating to a Deryni king now more than a year a widower from a marriage never consummated and being pressed increasingly by family and royal counselors to take another bride.

At least Kelson had managed to postpone *that* inevitability for the moment, ostensibly out of respect for his slain first bride. But to avow that he still mourned his lost Sidana carried less and less weight as the months passed. He continued to wear the ring he had given her—a narrow gold band with a ruby-eyed Haldane lion carved on a facet pared from the top—but it bespoke habit rather than conviction, more than a year after Sidana's death. Nor had he worn black for her since returning from his Mearan campaign the previous summer, other than to observe the anniversary of her death, in January.

He had met Rothana on that campaign, while he scoured the Mearan borderlands for traces of his dead bride's rebellious elder brother. He had first seen her in the desecrated ruins of her abbey as she tried to comfort the weeping Janniver—pale blue habit smudged with soot and her heavy, blue-black hair escaping from a braid as thick as a man's wrist. Though Rothana herself had been untouched by the raiders, at least in body, her Deryni senses had amplified the terror and humiliation of those around her and left a uniquely Deryni anger.

But the psychic cost to Rothana had not occurred to Kelson, most interested just then in finding out who had been responsible for the attack. That night, after setting his guards and returning to the abbey church where the remaining sisters had set up a hospice to care for the injured, he had wanted to use his powers to read Janniver's memory of the attack and perhaps identify her assailant. But Rothana had held that to be too intimate a contact with the already violated princess and had forbidden it—though she did agree to read the memory herself and transmit to Kelson the information he required.

Only, when she did, she had also given him a taste of the rape from *Janniver's* point of view, with all its hurt and humiliation and anguish. It had *not* been pleasant. Kelson himself was yet a virgin, for a variety of tiresome but practical reasons that seemed valid to him, as king, but occasionally he had wondered, since that night, whether the intense psychic experience of reliving Janniver's ordeal would unman him when the time came for his own sexual initiation. He had been taught to believe that rape and the act of love were as different as night and day, but until he knew for certain, from his own experience, his imagination sometimes inspired far more apprehension than confidence.

That Rothana had been the one to trigger that apprehension made Kelson even more wary where she was concerned—especially since it was her shadow-face and form that occasionally intruded, all unbidden, on the increasingly erotic fantasies that he, like most eighteen-year-old males, experienced in his dreams. There were other faces, to be sure, but none whom he could identify as living, breathing women.

That only made the apprehension even more concrete, for Rothana *was* a living, breathing woman—and vowed to God. Despite that avowal, something more frighteningly personal and intense than the violence of Janniver's rape had also surged across their brief psychic link. Both of them had been denying it all winter, with only indifferent success, neither willing to admit or accept that the attraction was mutual.

"Good afternoon, Kelson," Meraude said, she and both girls rising to make him dutiful curtsies as Kelson and his companions approached—though Rothana kept her dark eyes primly averted to the scroll she had been reading, as was seemly for a female religious in the presence of three virile young men just coming into their prime. Janniver dared a glance at them, but she blushed prettily and retreated all in a fluster when Jatham eased a little closer to his master's side—and to her—and tried, unsuccessfully, to keep from smiling.

"Why, Aunt Meraude, what a pleasant surprise," Kelson said, suddenly aware of the chemistry between his soon-to-be ex-squire and the princess and making an effort to be courtly, despite the ache behind his eyes. "Pray, ladies, be seated. I see that the spring sunshine has brought out the flowers."

His frankly appreciative survey of the three of them left no doubt that he was *not* talking about flowers that grew in the castle gardens beyond.

"Why, here's a fair rose of Rhenndall," he went on, with a bow flourished in Meraude's direction, "and Mary bells, to honor our Blessed Lady." He gave restrained and proper salute to Rothana's pale blue habit. "And surely here is a golden jonquil, Princess, unless I disremember all my lessons in botany. Dhugal, have you ever seen fairer blossoms? Or you, Jatham?"

As a blushing Janniver ducked her head and fumbled for a hank of yarn in her embroidery basket, Jatham knelt to retrieve one that tumbled from her lap.

"Never, Sire," he breathed. "'Tis the loveliest bouquet that *I* have ever seen."

"Why, my lords, you shall turn our heads with such flattery," Meraude scolded, though she could not keep the mirth from her eyes. "Besides, 'tis far too early for most flowers."

"But not too early," Rothana said, lifting her eyes boldly to Kelson's, "to ask His Majesty about the greenery for the basilica tomorrow. May I speak with you for a moment in private, Sire?" she continued, touching his sleeve as she brushed past to lead him away from the others. "Please to come into the next window with me and look into the garden, where I may point out what might be useful. At this time of year, the possibilities are somewhat limited, but there are a few that might suit. After all, it is not fitting that young men should keep their knight's vigil before an unadorned altar."

She had said all in a low voice, so that only he and their immediate company could hear; but, by the time they were well into the next window bay, Kelson was certain that every eye in the hall must have turned to observe their withdrawal. Nor were they safe from curious eyes in the garden itself.

"Come and pretend you are looking at the garden, my lord," Rothana murmured, setting a finger against the glass and only watching him sidelong. "I have something I must ask you that could not be said before the others—though, with your head still smarting from the test of *merasha*, perhaps we should delay until another time."

Kelson swallowed nervously and moved closer, though he was careful not to touch her, dutifully pretending to follow the discourse she was *not* giving about flowers and such.

"Did Meraude tell you that," he asked, "or is it that apparent?"

"Why, both, my lord. I should be dull-witted, indeed, if I should fail to recognize such aftereffects in one of our race."

"I see." He made himself draw a deep breath to steady out both the noted aftereffects and the effect *she* was having on him.

"If you are too ill, we *can* delay, my lord," she said quietly. "I would not increase your discomfort."

"If you know what I went through last night, then you know what it's costing me to function today—but, no, there's no need for delay." He drew another deep breath. "What did you wish to ask me?"

"Very well, my lord. It concerns your squire. What can you tell me of him?"

"Jatham?"

He knew immediately that her interest was in Janniver's behalf, for he had seen the Connaiti princess' reaction when his squire came into her presence; but even so, he felt a quick pang of alarm clench at his throat as he feared, just for an instant, that Rothana asked for her own sake. Something of that fear must have slipped past his still unsteady shields, for suddenly she blinked and seemed to bite back a distressed smile, though she covered most of the reaction by turning deliberately to look out at the garden again.

"Nay, do not look in his direction, my lord. We are here to inspect the garden. And pray, keep your voice down. But you saw how he and Janniver looked at one another. I can tell you that she is quite taken with him—and it seems there is a certain attraction on his part as well, though I suspect he believes himself too far beneath her ever to have his suit encouraged. What is his lineage, if I may ask?"

The question annoyed Kelson, perhaps because he had heard it asked all too often about potential royal brides.

"Oh, come, my lord, he cannot be baseborn, or he could not be a royal squire," Rothana murmured, her soft voice tinged with impatience. "Therefore, he must be of gentle, if not noble birth—and he will be *Sir* Jatham, come Tuesday, will he not? And the accolade well deserved, from everything I hear."

Kelson snorted. "If you have heard all that, my lady, I wonder that you need to ask *my* counsel."

"Oh, fie, that is but common gossip around court, Sire! I had hoped you might tell me more of the *man*. I would see my little princess honorably wed—" Her face fell. "Or, is Jatham one of those men who would not deign to offer marriage to a ruined girl?"

"Ruined?" Kelson found himself saying, not a little defensively. "Isn't that a trifle harsh, my lady, and you her friend?"

Rothana looked out at the garden again, dark eyes shuttered.

"Pray, remember that there are others nearby, my lord. The world is sometimes harsh. And the harsh truth of this matter is that most men prefer their brides unsullied. Kings and princes insist upon it."

"*This* king would not!"

"No?" she returned. "Would *you* marry her, then, my lord? I think not. Nor would your lords of state permit it, even if you so desired. Besides, could you truly take her to your sacred marriage bed, knowing that Ithel of Meara had had his pleasure of—"

"Pleasure?" Kelson remembered only just in time that he must keep his voice down and managed not to shout. "Madame, there was precious little of pleasure in *that* act, for *either* of them!—as you, yourself, should know!"

Rothana recoiled a step at that, herself obviously reminded of the intimacy of that moment when she had forced the memory of Janniver's rape upon him in the ruins at Saint Brigid's—and what else had passed between them.

"Forgive me, Sire. I should never have done that to you," she whispered. "I am occasionally far too willful for a nun. It was an unconscionable liberty on my part."

Breathing out audibly, Kelson managed a taut, careful nod.

"Aye, it was," he conceded, at least partially mollified. "But probably a valuable piece of education for a king. And you're right that I wouldn't marry Janniver—though not because of anything that happened to her at Saint Brigid's. I suppose I still dare allow myself to hope that love will have a part in the selection of my next wife."

"I hope that it may, my lord," Rothana murmured.

"And I. Still, I won't have you speaking that way of Janniver. The poor girl didn't ask to be raped, after all—though one might think she had, judging from the correspondence I've had in the last six months from her father and her former husband-to-be." He sighed. "I'm afraid they're two princes of the kind you were talking about."

"Alas, I must agree, Sire," Rothana replied quietly. "But your Jatham, I pray, is not a prince, or even such a man."

"No."

"Then, would he have her to wife, do you think?"

Kelson managed a wry smile. "I think he might, given the slightest encouragement."

"*Royal* encouragement, Sire?" she asked, looking at him sidelong.

"Well, I can't *command* the man to fall in love."

"Oh, no one said anything about commanding, Sire. You

need not even *persuade* him, as only one of our blood could do.''

She turned her gaze to the forgotten garden once more.

"Well, then, that's settled," she murmured. "Just say that you will do your best to encourage him—and then we can get on with this dreary business of picking out the greenery."

"Dreary—greenery?"

"Well, that *is* why we're standing here, looking out at the garden, is it not?"

"Why, *Sister* Rothana, you *love* this, don't you?" Kelson blurted, in that instant, amazed beyond thinking of his own romantic interests. "Can it be that the little nun is actually called to be a matchmaker?"

He regretted that, the instant he had said it, for it was all too near his own wishes in the matter. He was horrified to realize that he was blushing, but mercifully she had kept her gaze riveted to the garden, pretending that she had not heard.

"Now, then," she breathed, after he had had time to recover. "We were selecting greenery—and we really should go back to the others. Yes, ivy, I think, for the knighting of a winter king and his compan—"

"Kelson, should you not be in seclusion, preparing for your impending knighthood?" a cool female voice asked, unexpectedly close behind them in the opening of the window embrasure as they turned to go. "And Sister, I cannot imagine that your lady abbess would approve of private speech with a young gentleman."

The speaker was Jehana, Kelson's mother, and where she had come from, Kelson had no idea, for she had not been in the hall when he entered. He wished she were not now, for he had no energy to spare for dealing with her, especially after the exchange he had just had with Rothana.

Jehana had returned to court the previous spring, immediately stating her intention to have a hand in the choosing of Kelson's next wife, for she believed that the right woman could make him renounce his powers as she had done with Kelson's father, thereby mitigating the evil of his Deryni blood. She had brought her chaplain and a sister called Cecile and continued to wear the stark white habit of a novice of Saint Giles' Abbey, but she had not yet managed to reconcile the vast potential of her own Deryni blood. Nor had the renunciation of her own powers been nearly as successful as she might have wished. More than once, since her return, she had been driven to use those powers, always at great cost to her notions of morality about such use.

She still paid lip service to her intention not to use them again, however, and heartily resented any Deryni who did use the powers she believed Satan had given. Rothana's abbess and the rest of the sisters of her order continued to reside within the castle precincts, awaiting the milder days of summer before journeying back to abandoned Saint Brigid's, so Jehana had taken to attending their Masses and other offices, though she habitually shunned Rothana. She deemed it an abomination that the Deryni girl should have presumed to take religious vows—a thing she longed to do, but dared not.

"*Sister,* I am speaking to you," Jehana continued pointedly, when the two merely turned to gape at her. "Should you not be about your devotions? I would have speech with my son. Please be so good as to leave us."

Rothana lowered her eyes and made the queen a dutiful curtsey, ready to obey, but Kelson stayed her with an arm out-stretched to bar her way.

"Sister Rothana and I have not yet finished our conversation, Mother," he said crisply. "And for your information, I *was* preparing for my impending knighthood. We were discussing the altar decorations for the vigil tomorrow night. Is it to be ivy, then, Sister?"

He could sense the smile Rothana dared not show as she made him a slight bow, hands tucked demurely in her sleeve openings and eyes still downcast.

"I think so, my lord. And holly, if there's any left this late. That will lend some color. I would suggest mistletoe as well—that's apt, for virgin knights—but the archbishop would probably forbid it as a pagan practice. If you will excuse me, Sire, I'll see to it." She made him a curtsey that included Jehana, though with just a hint of defiance. "Good day, Your Majesty."

Jehana was speechless until Rothana had entirely quit the hall.

"The insolence! The *cheek!*" she murmured. "I'll speak to her superior."

"You'll do no such thing," Kelson replied, firmly taking

her arm to lead her deeper into the window bay. "You were very rude. That's graceless in any woman and inexcusable in a queen."

"How dare you speak to me that way?"

"If you wish to continue welcome at this court, you'll curb your tongue, madame!" He had not raised his voice, but there was no mistaking his anger. "You were rude because she is Deryni. I won't tolerate that."

"But she's a *nun*, Kelson. As Deryni, her soul was already in jeopardy, but to take vows—"

"I believe the lady's soul is her own business, Mother—and that of her confessor."

"Who is, himself, Deryni, and he a bishop!" Jehana challenged. "Or didn't you know she'd begun going to your precious Bishop Duncan?"

"Careful, Mother. He's my confessor, too."

"And damned, for having defied the Church to be ordained, knowing what he was!"

Kelson turned away to look out into the hall and caught several people staring—though they immediately pretended not to be.

"It's pointless to continue this discussion," he murmured. "You're making a scene. And you're absolutely correct that I should be in seclusion, preparing for my knighthood. I'll do that now, if you don't mind. Dhugal, Jatham, attend me, please."

He had raised his voice to call them from the next bay, and they appeared almost at once, both looking frankly embarrassed, for they could not have failed to overhear much of the exchange.

"Gentlemen, my lady mother has correctly reminded me that we should all be making preparations for tomorrow," he said, stepping past Jehana to join them. "We shall keep a nightlong vigil on the morrow, so tonight should see us early to bed. Jatham, this means you as well. You're hereby relieved of all further squiring duties. Dolfin will serve tonight, and you'll dine with Dhugal and me in my quarters. There's something I wish to discuss with you," he added, glancing at the door whereby Rothana had exited. "Mother, I and my companions bid you a respectful good night."

His brisk bow before turning on his heel to leave was echoed a trifle more respectfully by the two who followed him wide-eyed from the hall. Blessedly, no one apprehended them again on their way to his chambers. He and Dhugal even had time for a nap before Dolfin brought a hearty supper—a meal that quickly took on festive overtones when Kelson broached the subject of the Princess Janniver to Jatham.

Afterward, Duncan came to them briefly, to ensure that all three slept soundly in preparation for the ceremonies of the next two days. They rose at noon, sober but refreshed, to pass the remaining hours until sunset in quiet reflection, as was seemly for young warriors about to undergo their knightly initiation.

The formal observances began at Monday Vespers, with the assembly of all the candidates and their sponsoring knights at Saint Hilary's Basilica. Prince Nigel stood for Kelson and Conall, and Morgan for Dhugal, and there were more than twenty candidates, each with his sponsor armed and formal at his side. Monks from the cathedral chapter came up from Saint George's to sing the Office, and their voices floated celestially pure among the roof beams of the ancient church.

Archbishop Cardiel preached the sermon that night, instructing all present on the duties and obligations of the estate about to be entered. As a part of the service, all the sponsoring knights renewed their knightly vows as a group, that they might better assist their charges. Afterward, assisted by Bishops Arilan and McLain, the archbishop presented each novice knight with the traditional garments of knightly profession: the long, loose-fitting white tunic, symbolizing purity; the shorter overtunic of black, with hose and boots the same, reminder of death and the earth to which all must eventually return; and the crimson mantle, betokening nobility, but also the blood that a true knight must be prepared to shed in defense of his lord and in the service of his vows.

These the candidates donned after undergoing the prescribed ritual bath, each assisted by his sponsor. They returned at midnight, in solemn, candlelit procession, there to make their own vows before the high altar, witnessed by their sponsors and the bishops. After that, following special prayers and blessings, the candidates were left alone to keep watch over their arms through the rest of the night.

Kelson knelt on the lowest altar step, hands resting on the quillons of the Haldane sword, sometimes resting his forehead against the pommel when he bowed his head in prayer. Conall knelt slightly behind and to his right side, Dhugal to his left. It was not until nearly dawn, when the altar candles had nearly guttered out and Kelson's attention was drifting, that he realized there were tiny cuts of mistletoe mixed in with the holly and ivy on the altar.

CHAPTER THREE

Many seek the ruler's favor.

—Proverbs 29:26

As steel descended toward his unarmored shoulder, King Kelson of Gwynedd suddenly found himself helpless to move or even to blink. Eyes as grey as his own, Haldane keen and as little to be swayed, held him frozen as the blade flashed inexorably downward. Kelson had the chilling impression that he could not have broken that immobility even if his life depended on it—which, thank God, it did not.

For it was his Uncle Nigel's hand on the hilt of the weapon—the royal sword that had knighted Nigel and nearly every other seasoned warrior present in the great hall of Rhemuth Castle—and the loyal Dukes Alaric and Ewan MacEwan stood solemn witness to either side of Nigel, sanctioning the deed. What held Kelson was not fear, but awe at joining the ranks of knights such as these, as the flat of the blade pressed briefly to his right shoulder, left shoulder, then to the top of his uncrowned head.

"In the name of the Father, and of the Son, and of the Holy Spirit, be thou a good and faithful knight," Nigel said, lifting the blade to kiss the sacred relic in its hilt before handing it off to Morgan, who sheathed it with characteristic economy of motion. "Arise, Sir Kelson Cinhil Rhys Anthony Haldane, and receive the other symbols of thy new estate."

Released at last from his immobility, Kelson grinned and obeyed, letting Nigel and old Ewan assist him to his feet.

45

The golden spurs of knighthood were already on his heels, set there by Morgan and Ewan before he knelt to receive the accolade. The spurs, like the sword, had been his father's.

Two other items of this morning's attire also had been his father's, though they had to do with kingship rather than the accolade he had just received. One was the great ruby in his right earlobe, worn by every Haldane sovereign since the great Cinhil of the Haldane Restoration. The other was the fist-sized disk of red enamel clasping his crimson mantle, bearing the golden lion *rampant guardant* of the House of Haldane.

Only noble significance—not royal—attached to the rest of the king's garb this morning, however. For beneath the crimson mantle, he still wore the traditional garb of any novice knight, received from the archbishop the night before. He held his arms a little away from his body as his mother, Queen Jehana, buckled the white belt of knighthood around his waist. Like the white undertunic, it signified purity, but in the sense of chastity, or faithfulness to one's chosen state—a fitting virtue for any upright man.

That symbolism was behind Jehana's now customary white novice's habit and wimple, too, though Kelson thought she might have worn more queenly attire today, of all days. It was one thing for professed nuns like the Sisters of Saint Brigid to wear religious garb to such an important court function; it was embarrassing when one's mother, who had taken no vows as yet, retained her austere adopted garb as a personal statement of protest against her son's way of life. The queen's sole concession to rank this morning was a cross-embellished circlet holding her veil in place, which paled almost to insignificance beside the jewels and Haldane crimson worn by Meraude, the only other woman seated on the dais. Even the men outshone her—Nigel, resplendent in a heraldic surcoat richly appliquéd with his arms in silk and gold bullion, a voluminous mantle of Haldane crimson falling from his shoulders, collared with black fox; old Ewan in his fur-lined robes of fine wool and highland tartans; and Morgan—

Of course, if Morgan had wanted to, he could have overshadowed every other person in the hall by his mere presence. He could wear sack cloth and ashes and still be more a prince than most men born to the purple and dressed in the richest raiment and most costly jewels. Clad in forest green velvet as he was today, ducally crowned with gold and with Kelson's sword in his hands, he looked like some elemental godling—sunlight on forest leaves and pine boughs, puissant and vital, but focused only on his king and liege.

It was Morgan who approached Kelson now, to bow his golden head and lay the sheathed sword of state across his king's outstretched hands—the royal sword, King Brion's sword, a potent symbol handed down through the Haldane line for generations—and sometimes, in the duly consecrated hands of an anointed Haldane king, a magical implement. King Brion was more than four years dead now, but his legacy both of crown and of magic seemed secure at last in this slender eighteen-year-old who had just been dubbed knight. Kelson wondered, as he brought the hilt of the sword to his own lips in salute, whether Brion would have approved of what his son had done with the kingdom left him so untimely; he wished his father could have lived to see this day.

At least Morgan had lived to see it—Alaric Morgan, the Deryni Duke of Corwyn, who had been closer to Brion Haldane than probably any other man. It was Morgan to whom Kelson owed much of what he had gained in the four years of his kingship, even unto survival itself; for Morgan, like a handful of others present in the hall today, was of the seemingly slim minority of his Deryni race who had always turned their awesome powers to the service of the Light—despite the Church's longtime suspicion of such powers.

Such service was Morgan's lot today, if of a less than magical sort, as he lent the weight of his own achievements as a knight to assist in the knighting of his king. Morgan's swift, boldly defiant thought of Deryni congratulation slipped into Kelson's mind with an impression of delighted laughter as the king solemnly crossed the dais to kneel briefly before Bishops Cardiel, Arilan, and Wolfram for their blessing. The golden spurs of Kelson's new-made knighthood chimed on the Kheldish carpet as he returned to take his seat on the throne of Gwynedd and laid his father's sword across his knees. As soon as his mother and Nigel had also sat, the king took his state crown from the cushion that his cousin Rory offered on bended knee.

Prince Rory Haldane, Nigel's second son. As Kelson put

on his crown and nodded Rory his thanks, waiting for the participants in his own knighting to rearrange themselves for the next set of ceremonies, he found himself almost wishing that it was Rory being knighted today, instead of Rory's older brother. Rory had always been such a merry child—in sharp contrast to the sulky and sometimes petty Conall. And his skill with weapons, though yet untried in battle, was everything one might hope from one of Nigel's sons, even at fourteen.

But Rory's knighting would not even be an issue for another four years. Only rarely was the accolade given before a candidate turned eighteen, and hardly ever to royal princes, who must set the example. After all, most young men were *not* ready for knighthood before the age of eighteen, and many were still immature at twenty or more. Kelson feared that such might be the eventual case with Conall.

Still, if one dared not knight a royal prince early, so could one hardly *decline* to knight him, once he came of age for the honor—not if one hoped to keep his ambitions in check and retain his loyalty in the future. Conall no doubt found life difficult enough, forever being pushed into second place by the accident of birth that made Kelson king and Conall only the eldest son of a second son, though the blood of Haldane kings flowed in the veins of both. By giving Conall precedence over all candidates but the king himself on this important day—for that was his rightful place, as heir of a royal duke—perhaps some of Conall's increasing restlessness could be mollified. Kelson had also given him an official seat on the privy council to mark his coming of age. Surely more experience would temper him into a proper knight and prince.

But Conall's loyalty was not in question today. Nor was he at all *un*worthy of the honor soon to be bestowed upon him. Like all of the young men being dubbed today, Conall had more or less proven himself during the Mearan campaign the previous summer. If he had not precisely distinguished himself, at least he had not disgraced himself or his family. Following in the footsteps of a father like Nigel was asking a great deal of any novice knight.

The king scanned the hall again, impatient to continue, as old Duke Ewan bowed himself from the dais and went to escort the troop of young boys who would be sworn to pages' and squires' service next. The break also would set off Conall's knighting further from the shadow of following Kelson's, by making him first of the remaining knightings. Only now, with the first, personal intensity of the day safely past, did Kelson truly have time to notice that the great hall was filled almost to capacity by those who had come to see their king and his companions knighted. Even the side galleries were thronged with ladies and pages—and watchful Haldane archers, gently dressed and with bows well concealed behind arras and railings, but ready to deal with anything untoward that might transpire later on—for there were political ramifications to the taking of one of the squires a little later in the ceremony.

The youngest boys came first, ages six to ten, to kneel and pipe their carefully rehearsed oaths in chorus at the foot of the dais steps before Nigel and Ewan invested each with the crimson tabard of Haldane pages' livery. After that, the new crop of junior squires approached, a dozen or so, most of them twelve to fourteen years of age and already seasoned by several years' duty as pages.

These swore their oaths individually, each one being assigned to a particular knight who would act as his sponsor until he achieved full knighthood. Kelson took two into his direct service, one to replace the junior squire moving into the place vacated by Jatham's forthcoming knighting and another simply to assist with the increasing work as Kelson became busier and in need of more assistance.

Nigel also took a new squire—the ten-year-old King Liam of Torenth, a vassal of Kelson since the death of his elder brother two summers before, whom Kelson had taken hostage the previous summer to ensure Torenthi neutrality while he fought his Mearan campaign. It was this squiring that was likely to cause an uproar when Kelson revealed it to the Torenthi ambassador waiting for audience just outside the keep, for Liam's regents expected both Liam and his mother, the Lady Morag, to be released by summer's end. Negotiations to that end were to be held in Cardosa, at the conclusion of Kelson's summer progress, but the Torenthi were not yet aware that only Morag's release would be discussed—and that was contingent upon the king's satisfying himself that Morag and her children's uncle, Duke Mahael of Arjenol, were not plotting treachery against him, with

Morag's sons the first victims. The youngest, Prince Ronal, was in Mahael's hands already, but the Torenthi duke would not get his hands on Liam as well.

As for Liam himself, Kelson had plans that he hoped would make the young king an ally rather than an adversary by the time he came of age. The boy was Deryni, like his mother, but he was ill-trained in the use of his powers and tamed by a year's exposure to the more normal pursuits expected of a noble-born boy of his age. Kelson expected no trouble from Liam, now receiving his blued-steel squire's spurs from Nigel; and the Lady Morag was not even at court anymore, having been secretly moved to Coroth during the winter. Richenda was Morag's gaoler now, ably guarding her Deryni hostage while she awaited the birth of her and Morgan's second child.

No, trouble today, if it came, would come from the Torenthi ambassador, even if it only evidenced as a verbal altercation. As Liam and the last of the new-sworn squires filed back to their places at one side, Ewan remaining among them to curb any youthful restlessness during the lengthy ceremonies to follow, Kelson smiled and put the whole thing out of mind for the moment. Gradually the hall quieted as the rest of his attendants took up their places to continue. Vestigial murmurings hushed to utter silence as Nigel came from among the squires and moved before his nephew's throne to bend his knee and speak the ritual phrase.

"Sire, I would ask a boon of you."

"Name it, Uncle. And if it be within my power to grant it, saving my honor and the honor of the realm, I shall gladly do it."

"Then I may ask with joy, Sire, for I would request that you grant the accolade of knighthood to my eldest son Conall, who today has attained his eighteenth year."

"Right gladly shall I grant it, Uncle. Please to bring the candidate before us."

With a slight nod to acknowledge the command, Nigel rose and moved down the steps, sweeping back through the hall to where Conall and the other candidates waited.

There was no mistaking the Haldane lineage of sire or son as Conall came slowly down the hall at his father's side—half a handspan taller than Nigel, if more slightly built; lightly mustached since the previous winter, with night-black hair barbered in the close-shorn style favored by most of the older fighting men, including Nigel, though the king and many of the younger men, including Conall's two brothers, had adopted Dhugal's border braid. The brooch securing his crimson mantle was larger and more ornate than that of anyone save the king; but beyond that concession to pride, he wore the same traditional raiment of any novice knight, for all that he was a prince.

"My Liege," Nigel said with a formal bow, as Conall slowly knelt on the bottom step of the dais and bowed his head, his father's hand on his shoulder. "I have the honor and privilege to present my eldest son, Prince Conall Blaine Cluim Uthyr, as a candidate for knighthood."

Kelson returned the bow with a nod. "Let Prince Conall be vested with the spurs."

Instantly, Conall's youngest brother, Payne, came proudly forward with the spurs on their damask cushion. Nigel knelt long enough to affix them, then stood and moved to Conall's left, making Kelson another bow, deeper than the previous ones, before he dropped to one knee.

"The candidate has been vested with the spurs, Sire."

Kelson stood, the sheathed royal sword still held across both hands, and leaned forward to speak quietly to Conall.

"I mean you no slight, cousin, but may I offer your father the privilege of giving you the accolade? I think it would please him greatly—and he is a far greater knight than I, who have myself been dubbed but a short while ago, and by his hand."

Kelson could read the leap of relieved assent in Conall's eyes without recourse to any of his magic and knew he had found the perfect sop to Conall's tender ego, to be spared receiving the accolade from one only months his senior. He noted pleased approval on Nigel's face as well as he turned his attention there.

"I think there can be no question of your son's desires, Uncle," he murmured, "and rightly so, for you are one of the most honorable knights I know. May I deputize you to perform this happy duty for your son?"

Nigel all but grinned as he gave the king a nod and got smoothly to his feet.

"It will be my privilege and honor, Sire."

"It is a father's right, if he be a knight himself," Kelson

replied. "Come and stand beside me, Conall, with what sword would you be knighted?"

Conall's grey eyes darted to the sword in Kelson's hands and then to his father's face.

"With all due respect, Sire, I would be knighted with my father's sword."

"So be it."

A murmur of approval whispered through the hall as it gradually became apparent what was about to happen. Conall's face seemed almost to glow as he raised his eyes to Nigel's and watched his sire draw a sword nearly as distinguished by its battle honors as Kelson's was hallowed by Haldane magic. Both Jehana and Meraude, Conall's mother, were blinking back tears as Nigel reverently kissed the blade and then raised it above his son's head.

"In the name of the Father, and of the Son, and of the Holy Spirit, be thou a good and faithful knight," Nigel said, dubbing Conall firmly on both shoulders and the crown of the head. "Arise, Sir Conall Haldane."

Kelson smiled and made appropriate murmurs of congratulation as Conall was girded with his new white belt by his mother, and presented by his father with a goodly sword that his brother Rory brought forward, but his thoughts were already flying to the next candidate, with whom he shared far more by spiritual kinship than he ever would share by blood with his eldest cousin. Dhugal had appeared at the far end of the hall now, waiting with the other candidates to be called forward next; and Kelson sent him a tight-focused greeting, mind to mind, before returning his attention to Conall. He slipped his sheathed sword into the hangers at his belt as the newly dubbed Conall knelt once more and placed his hands between the king's to swear him fealty.

"I, Conall, Prince of Gwynedd, do become your liege man of life and limb and earthly worship; and faith and truth will I bear unto you, to live and to die, against all manner of folk, so help me God."

No trace of Conall's usual resentment marred the moment as Kelson returned the oath, pledging his justice and protection for Conall's loyalty, and then raised Conall up with words of honest congratulation. He gave Conall his full moment of unshared glory while his parents and brothers embraced and welcomed him to his newly adult status. Only when Conall had put on the coronet of his rank and taken a seat on a stool to his right, just to the other side of Nigel's chair, did Kelson turn to glance at Morgan, still waiting behind and to Kelson's immediate right. Morgan stepped forward at Kelson's slight nod.

"Duke Alaric, I believe it is your intention to sponsor the next candidate. Please bring him forward."

Whispered asides rippled all through the hall as Morgan made his way down the aisle to where Dhugal waited, many a curious glance looking for Duncan, now legally and openly recognized as Dhugal's father, but apparently to have no part in the knighting of his son. By most folk's reckoning, that was only as it should be—for, notwithstanding the decree of the archbishop's tribunal, the oddness of a bishop with a legitimate son still had many people off balance. An act of legitimation might have removed the last legal and religious impediment to Dhugal's reception of the accolade or succession to his father's titles, but there would always be those who continued to call him bastard, especially as his Deryni heritage became more widely known. Fortunately, most folk had not yet made that connection, just as most preferred not to believe that Duncan really was Deryni, no public evidence having been presented to the contrary.

Today, therefore, Duncan was present, to be sure, but he had attempted to appear no kind of a bishop, lest his episcopal presence further confuse the court's reception of his son. Rather than standing on the dais with the king, as was his due as bishop or duke, he waited anonymously in the ranks of other, lesser nobles come to witness the day's ceremonies, but with no part to play. He also had eschewed his customary purple cassock in favor of a dove grey tunic and breeches of very conservative cut, with a plaid of McLain tartan brooched to his left shoulder and across his chest, green and black and white. A soft grey cap of maintenance covered most of his tonsured brown hair, fur turned up around the edge almost to obscure the simple, cross-embellished coronet of silver circling the crown—the only hint of either ducal or episcopal rank.

Rather than a sword, he wore a border dirk at his hip, its pommel and scabbard set with cairngorms—for among the highland and border clans, he was chief of his name in addition to his other titles. A captain-general's chain lay around his shoulders, and the bishop's amethyst on his right hand, if one did not look too closely, could have been simply the ornament of any secular lord.

With those around him, Duncan craned his neck to see, ignoring the faces that turned to watch his reaction as much as Dhugal's, as Morgan escorted Dhugal down the length of the hall—for in that moment, Duncan saw only his son.

Dhugal MacArdry McLain. He was no longer the rustic border lordling of his upbringing, first fostered from the borders to King Brion's court, where he and Kelson had bound their friendship, then tempered to a true borderman as he rode patrol duty for the man he had thought his sire up until last year. Today, rather than the distinctive border attire that had become his personal trademark, he sported the traditional garb of the other knightly candidates, though he still wore his coppery hair pulled back cleanly in a border braid. The mustache that had been a smudge of reddish down a year before had reached bushy proportions over the past winter, bristling across his upper lip and drooping at the corners of his mouth, but revealing large white teeth when he smiled, which was often, though not now. He was taller by a handspan, too—nearly Morgan's height as the two of them mounted the dais steps, just before he dropped to his knees.

"My Liege," Morgan said, from the step behind Dhugal, "I am honored to present Lord Dhugal Ardry MacArdry McLain as a candidate for knighthood."

"We are most honored to receive him, Your Grace," Kelson replied, looking inordinately pleased with himself as he hooked his thumbs in his new white belt and glanced out at the thronged hall, apparently looking for something. "But before we proceed with this well-deserved honor, we command that Duncan, Duke of Cassan, come before us."

The command startled Duncan, and he considered briefly and futilely trying to melt back into the crowd; but eyes were already turning toward him, and he knew there was no escape. Setting his left hand on the pommel of his dirk, he worked his way reluctantly among those standing between him and the dais, murmuring apologies to those he had to jostle, and made the king a puzzled but respectful bow as he came to a halt beside Morgan and a little behind his son.

"Sire?"

"Thank you, Your Grace," Kelson said. "We require your assistance. Attend us please—here on the dais."

As Duncan uneasily mounted the steps, suddenly wondering whether the king planned what Duncan feared he might, Kelson drew his sword, smoothly reversing it to offer Duncan the hilt across his forearm.

"I see you're not wearing a sword today—and a man should never be knighted with a dirk—so you can use mine."

"Sire, I—"

"Come, now. We've already established that a son should be knighted by his father," Kelson said. "Please do the honors."

"But—"

Joy mingled with chagrin and showed on Duncan's face, but before he could even begin trying to explain why he could not oblige, Morgan was at his side, leaning forward to whisper in Kelson's ear.

"But, that's impossible!" Kelson blurted, drawing back to stare at Morgan in astonishment. "What do you mean, he was never knighted?"

"'Tis true, Sire," Duncan murmured, wishing he could sink through the floor and disappear, for it was this that had made him choose not to sponsor Dhugal, as much as any fear of notoriety from his episcopal office. "I was in holy orders by the time I was of age for the accolade. It was my brother Kevin who was to have carried forward the family honor and name. After I inherited, it—never occurred to me that I should seek to rectify the matter."

"Well, I'll jolly well rectify it today," Kelson muttered, so low that only Duncan, Morgan, and Dhugal could hear, though Conall strained to catch what they were saying. "If I'd known, it could have been done in the field a dozen times over. Why, good *God,* man, *any* knight would have been proud to acknowledge you!"

He reversed his sword, which had been resting with its point against the carpet at his feet while they disputed, then glanced sharply at Morgan as he let the blade lie back across his right shoulder.

"Don't even think about lecturing me," he said. "Either of you. I know what I'm doing—and *hang* those who still think there's anything untoward about a bishop having a legitimate son or being a knight. Alaric, I'll thank you to loan

Duncan your spurs for the occasion. This won't be as formal as I would have liked, knowing Duncan's penchant for ceremony, but I think he's waited long enough for the honor. Duncan, will you *please* kneel! I can't knight you if you insist on standing up."

Misgivings still loomed in Duncan's mind, for fear Kelson might one day rue this act of friendship untempered by more considered reason, but Morgan's resigned grin, as he knelt on the steps and began unbuckling one of his gilded spurs, told Duncan it was no use appealing to *him*. He fell to his knees, removing his cap and coronet as he did so, and the delighted Dhugal stood and backed off a pace to watch.

"My lords and ladies," Kelson said, lifting his head to address the mystified court—most of whom had no idea what was going on. "It seems that we have committed a grave injustice against our most loyal Duke of Cassan." He controlled a grin as Morgan eased closer on his knees to slip the first spur onto Duncan's right heel. "In asking said duke to knight his son, as is often done, we find that we have inadvertently asked the impossible of him—for only a knight may make a knight, and we find that Duncan McLain has never himself received the accolade.

"That certainly is not for want of merit," he added, holding up his empty hand to still a murmur of surprise, "for on the basis of last summer's campaign alone, he could have been knighted many times over. Nor is there any doubt that he has served our crown most loyally, in any number of different areas, since our accession."

Morgan had by now finished with the second spur and bit back a pleased grin as he rose and slipped his sheathed sword from its holders to hand it to Dhugal before stripping off his white belt.

"It is therefore my honor and privilege to confer upon you, Duncan Howard McLain, the ancient and honorable estate of knighthood." Kelson raised the Haldane sword and brought the flat of the blade down smartly on Duncan's right shoulder. "In the name of the Father, and of the Son—" The blade shifted to the left shoulder, "—and of the Holy Spirit—" The blade came to rest upon his head. "—be thou a good and faithful knight, as thou hast been hitherto."

He raised the blade and again rested it across his right shoulder. "Rise, Sir Duncan, and be vested with the white belt of thy rank.'' He glanced at Duchess Meraude rather than his mother. "Aunt, would you perform this service?"

Meraude came forward willingly as Duncan rose, receiving the worn leather from Morgan with a grave nod and taking her time as she slid it around Duncan's waist to fasten it.

"I imagine you know that the white belt is a symbol of chastity," she whispered, as she worked the knot. "Which is not necessarily the same as celibacy, as I'm sure you also know, though it can mean that as well, for you—now. Your son is very lucky to have such a father. This is a well-deserved honor."

"Why, thank you, my lady," Duncan murmured, surprised, for he had not realized Meraude regarded him so highly.

"There," Meraude said aloud, backing off to make him a little curtsey. "Be thou steadfast and true, Sir Knight."

"My lady, with all my heart I shall endeavor to do so."

"Good. That's done," Kelson said, rising up and down on the balls of his feet in a posture very reminiscent of his father. "You've already given me your fealty as a duke and your homage as a bishop, so I think we can dispense with any further oaths. I believe we were about to knight your son."

He snapped his fingers for Brendan, Morgan's seven-year-old stepson, to bring Dhugal's spurs forward, and Dhugal gave the lad Morgan's sword before dropping to his knees again, grinning from ear to ear.

"Let the candidate be vested with the spurs."

Doing his best not to chuckle at the coup the king had just accomplished against both the court and Duncan, Morgan took the spurs and bent to do the honors, leaving Duncan to exchange uneasy glances with the king as he put on his cap and coronet again. Morgan knew what argument Duncan was about to offer, and about how much good it would do.

"Kelson, I'm flattered beyond reckoning, but are you sure you want me to do this?" Duncan murmured, as Morgan finished with the spurs. "I think I understand what you're trying to achieve, but Dhugal is your blood brother. That's important, too. Don't you think it's more appropriate that he have the link of chivalry with *you*?"

"He'll *have* that, by my having knighted you," Kelson

said, setting the hilt of his father's sword in Duncan's hand
with an expression that brooked no further argument. "He'll
also have it through my sword."

Read him, if you don't believe me, Kelson continued,
mind to mind. *Do you think he could lie, in a situation like
this, given what we are?*

Swallowing, Duncan glanced at his son and read the awe
and adoration there, catching a little of Dhugal's wonder at
the glitter of the Haldane blade heavy in his hand. Its weight
brought to mind another matter weighing heavily upon Duncan for the past three days; and all at once he knew how
that quandary, as well, must be resolved. He had no doubt
that Dhugal would approve; nor would Morgan have any
objections. And his meek, tentative query to the king returned royal approval and even glee, almost before he could
frame the silent question with his mind.

"So be it, then," he murmured aloud, squaring his shoulders resolutely as he let a tendril of his coiled, tight-leashed
power probe into the royal blade.

It held the magic of a long line of Haldanes—no doubt of
that. With his Deryni senses, Duncan could feel it pulsing
in his fist. Trembling, he steadied it with his other hand on
the pommel so that he could bring it slowly to his lips to kiss
the sacred relic encased in its hilt and, in doing so, loosed
his own Deryni essence to show as silver light along the
blade—a light that flowed bright as water down the steel and
welled as quickly up his hands and arms to settle like a cloak
of light around his head and shoulders, openly and unmis-
takably Deryni at last. The awed gasp of those watching was
immediately caught in rapt silence as Duncan dipped the
glowing blade, two-handed, toward Dhugal's right shoulder.

"In the name of the Father." The blade touched. "And
of the Son." The blade shifted to the left shoulder. "And of
the Holy Spirit. Amen."

But as the sword touched the crown of Dhugal's head,
and Duncan sighted down the blade to his son's eyes, Dhugal's own Deryni aura flared like a halo around his coppery
hair, sunburst golden, his eyes blazing an exultation so fierce
that the rest of the formula nearly went out of Duncan's
head.

"Be thou a good and faithful knight, my son," Duncan
managed to say, himself surprised at the steadiness of his

voice and the pristine silence into which his words fell. "Be faithful and true, and may God prosper thee in thy great love for Him and for our Lord the King."

"Amen to that!" Kelson said heartily, daring anyone to gainsay it as Duncan lifted the blade to kiss the hilt again, and first his and then Dhugal's auras died away. "Rise, Sir Dhugal, and receive the other tokens of thy new-made knighthood."

As Dhugal rose, proud tears shimmering in his eyes, Duncan whispered, "Thank you, Sire," and reversed the blade again, offering it back to Kelson across his forearm as he bent his knee once more.

And though you did not ask it, Duncan continued, mind to mind, *I do reaffirm my fealty, unconditionally, in all things saving my holy office—as Deryni, now openly so to serve you, if you will have it.*

The sword trembled with the emotion between them, with Kelson's hand on the hilt and the blade still resting on Duncan's sleeve. With a little flick of his wrist, the king shifted the weapon to lie across his outstretched palms, silently inviting Duncan's response.

No word passed aloud between them, and few in the audience caught the significance of the action that followed, being now released to startled speculation, albeit whispered, as the significance of what they *had* seen registered—that both Duncan and Dhugal were Deryni. But as if the two had rehearsed it, Duncan briefly laid his hands atop Kelson's and bent to brush the blade between with his lips, silently affirming a most holy oath.

Then he was bounding to his feet, and Kelson was sheathing the sword, beckoning Dhugal forward to be girded with the white belt that Meraude slipped around his waist, Jehana already having retired from the dais and, indeed, from the hall when Duncan's intentions became clear.

"I, Dhugal, do become your liege man of life and limb and earthly worship," Dhugal proclaimed, kneeling once more to set his hands between those of the king.

And when he had finished his oath, the hall erupted to the raucous whoops of his MacArdry borderers, noisily proclaiming their approval of all that had been done and daring anyone to speak against their young lord or his father. After all, Dhugal was their chief, chosen by their chief, the grandson of their chief, regardless of who his father was.

Even a piper added his salute, on pipes smuggled into the hall past the watchful eyes of the chamberlain Rhodri and his assistants, who were always trepidacious where border custom was concerned. The cheering and the piping ceased only when Kelson himself raised open hands to beg their forbearance, grinning and shaking his head as the MacArdrys hefted both Deryni father and Deryni son onto broad shoulders and paraded them to the side of the hall to savor the moment.

Even then, it was some little while before sufficient decorum had been restored that the rest of the knightings could continue—somewhat anticlimactic, after the spectacle of the MacArdry acclaim, but satisfying, nonetheless, for the young men who received the accolade.

When Kelson had done, twenty-two new, crimson-mantled knights were ranged near the king's throne, eleven on either side, with Conall still seated beside his father's chair, as was the prerogative of a royal prince, and Dhugal now posted directly to the king's left, where Morgan had been. The new knights' sponsors occupied the front ranks of those standing in the main part of the hall, assembled there as each finished the duties attendant on knighting his candidate—for what came next would require a show of strength, a display of the finest of Gwynedd's chivalry, old and new.

As Saer de Traherne came into the hall to inform the king that all was in readiness to admit the Torenthi ambassador and his party to the keep, Duke Ewan drew his flock of young charges farther to one side, close by Cardiel and his bishops. Morgan and Duncan moved quietly among the squires to flank young Liam.

"Well, we can bring them in whenever you're ready, Sire," Saer muttered under his breath, kneeling at the king's knee. "Just wait until you see them, though."

Kelson smiled as he caught a flash of what Saer had seen—it *was* an exotic contingent, by Gwynedd standards—but he only pulled his sheathed sword from its belt hangers and laid it across his knees again.

"Very well, then. Let's see them," he said.

As Saer rose and turned to signal to one of his men in the rear gallery, Kelson caught the eye of the elderly Lord

Rhodri, who had been waiting for his cue at the far end of the hall. Lifting his head proudly, the old man strode halfway up the hall, clearing an aisle, and rapped weightily with his chamberlain's staff.

"Your Majesty, an emissary of the Court of Torenth seeks audience."

At Kelson's nod, the doors at the end of the hall swung back.

"They may approach."

Kettle drums, struck with the hand rather than with sticks, heralded the entrance of the visitors. The black-clad drummers were Moors of some sort, as were the twenty white-robed warriors who followed them as an honor escort to the ambassador himself, who had not yet come into view. Scale armor glinted beneath flowing desert robes as the men impassively swept a clear path down the widening center aisle. They bore spears and small metal-studded targes as ceremonial adjuncts to the curved blades thrust through wide sashes of a pale yellow silk, and their carefully wrapped turbans only partially concealed pointed steel caps.

The Moors gave brisk salute to Kelson with spears against their shields as, by pairs, they split to either side to line the end of the aisle. And then, as the unexpected clatter of hooves on the stairs outside the hall heralded the approach of the ambassador himself, the Moors turned inward as one man and lowered their spears to the man they escorted.

By his dress, the Torenthi ambassador, too, was a Moor, though darker complected than any Moor Kelson had ever seen. He rode a tawny-colored desert barb, taller by several hands than the usual of the breed, and his flowing desert robes were of the same amber hue as the animal's shiny coat, though his turban was snowy white, a fold of it covering the lower part of his face. Most impressive of all was the vast cloak of spotted catskin curved around the man's shoulders, dappled and sun-tawny, the great fore paws clasped on his breast and the ponderous head resting on his left shoulder, all gleaming in the sunlight as he paused briefly in the doorway to take stock of the situation he was about to enter.

He bore himself like a prince as he minced his barb delicately down the center of the stone-flagged hall. He appeared to be unarmed—but any number and manner of weapons might be secreted beneath the cloak of spotted fur.

Or perhaps he had no need for weapons, since cautious psychic probes from Kelson and several of the Deryni around him encountered closely guarded shields.

Deryni himself, then—or at least well protected by someone who was. His black eyes flashed, vibrant and aware, as he drew rein in the center of the hall.

Only, as he dropped the barb's reins and flung one leg over the pommel of his saddle, preparatory to dismounting, the golden eyes of the great cat's head on his shoulder blinked, the mighty head lifting as the jaws parted in a mighty yawn.

Chapter Four

It is good to keep close the secret of a king.
                                                   —Tobit 12:7

Kelson's gasp was echoed by nearly every throat in the hall as the great cat carefully disengaged its paws from around the Moor's neck and sprang lightly to the floor. The movement, plus the soft plop its landing made—punctuated by something that sounded like a muted growl, cut off in mid-rumble—released the assembled court of Gwynedd to surge back from the center aisle like the sea parting before Moses. What had begun as a breathless murmur of speculation and grudging respect at the man's first appearance became a wave of exclamations trailing into hushed silence as the cat's master dropped nimbly to the floor beside the beast.

The Moor walked the cat to the very foot of the dais steps. One of his men led the barb back to the door of the hall and waited there. The cat sat at once as its master halted, looking up attentively as the Moor slowly tugged loose the cloth veiling his lower face and allowed the faint glow of a Deryni aura to flare visibly around his head for a few seconds—which elicited yet another murmur of foreboding from the courtiers still edging away from the pair. The man's nose was thin and aquiline, with a slight hook to it, made more prominent by a close-clipped beard and mustache.

"May Allah the Compassionate, the Merciful, grant peace and health to all within this house," the man said, touching a graceful hand to breast, lips, and forehead in sa-

63

lute as he made his bow. His voice was deep and melodious, with only a hint of accent even in the speaking of the ritual phrase.

"I am Al Rasoul ibn Tarik, emissary of my Lord Mahael II of Arjenol, guardian of my Lord Prince Ronal of Torenth and regent for my Lord King Liam in the absence of his royal mother, the Lady Morag. My Lord Mahael sends his personal felicitations on this, the day of your Christian knighting, my Lord Kelson, and prays you will accept this small token of his esteem, one knight to another, as a remembrance of this happy occasion. My Lord Mahael had it especially blessed by the Patriarch of Beldour."

While he spoke, he had drawn a small, silk-wrapped object from his sash and extended it on one outstretched palm.

"Please accept, as well, my personal congratulations," Rasoul went on, as Dhugal, at Kelson's signal, came close enough to retrieve the gift—though both young men kept a wary eye on the cat. "We have not the equivalent of your knighthood among the faithful, but we recognize the honor it betokens among your people. My respect to these other young men as well."

The gift was a heavily enameled cross done in the eastern manner, but Kelson gave it only a cursory glance when Dhugal had brought it back—enough to reassure himself that it carried no malignant glamour. The greater part of his attention was still diverted by the cat.

"Please convey my thanks to your master, my Lord Rasoul," Kelson said carefully, still wondering what he was going to do if the animal sprang. It had sunk into a crouch as Rasoul began speaking, lithe tail slowly lashing, but its golden eyes watched every movement on the dais with great interest. One giant paw had already crept onto the bottom step, claws flexing lightly against the priceless Kheldish carpet. Nor would archers be much help, if the cat did decide to attack, though they had come to half draw at the animal's first movement.

I don't think she likes the cold floor, came Dhugal's surprising comment in Kelson's mind, not at all concerned. *Most cats don't. Isn't she beautiful, though?*

The notion so startled Kelson, in the process of handing the cross to Rory for safekeeping, that he glanced quickly at Dhugal before continuing what he had been about to say to Rasoul. He had forgotten about Dhugal's uncanny knack with animals.

"Say also, my Lord Rasoul, that I pray peace and health for all in his house, and that our two kingdoms may abide in peace and health."

"I shall do so, my lord."

Rasoul sketched another brief, distracted bow, right hand to his breast, but he was already sweeping his gaze pointedly along the upper galleries as he straightened—looking for Morag, no doubt, since he had already seen Liam, still standing quietly among the squires between Duncan and Morgan, the latter with a proprietary hand on the boy's shoulder. He plainly did not care for the archers, either.

Neither he nor Kelson said anything, but Kelson slowly raised one hand in sign for the archers to stand at ease. He could afford that concession. If the cat *did* attack—and Dhugal seemed not at all concerned that she would—then mere arrows would not be swift enough to stop her.

"Thank you, my lord," Rasoul murmured, with another inclination of his turbaned head. "My next message is for my Lord King Liam and his mother—though I do not see the Lady Morag present in the hall today. I trust she is in good health."

"Her health is excellent, my lord," Kelson replied coolly. "Had her courtesy been as notable, I am sure her sojourn at my court would have been far more agreeable for everyone concerned."

Rasoul snorted and gave an impertinent jerk of his chin, causing the great cat to lift its head and look at him, the rumbling purr faltering.

"I will concede that the Lady Morag's *patience* may occasionally have been lacking, my lord," the Moor allowed, "as might be that of any noble lady held hostage against her will for close on a year, though her release was promised six months ago."

So. Rasoul was pulling no punches, going immediately to the heart of the matter. Fine. It eliminated the need for playing diplomatic games. As Kelson framed his reply, he carefully extended his Truth-Reading talent to gauge the Moor's responses—difficult at this distance and to read another Deryni, but Rasoul would find the reverse no easier.

"That promise, my lord, was made before Torenthi

agents attempted to assassinate my uncle last summer in my absence," the king said. "According to the letter of the law, either I or my regent would have been wholly within our rights to execute both hostages, were it not for certain indications that Liam's own death was also intended by the assassins."

"Sir, your insinuation is not only insulting, it is preposterous!" Rasoul retorted. "If, indeed, these were agents of Torenth who acted in such a manner—for which I have only your word, my lord—" The Moor made a curt, insolent bow, "—why should they wish their king dead?"

The man was good, never making any statement that was not the literal truth, but Kelson knew how many lies could be hidden in what Rasoul did *not* say. Besides, both he and Morgan had questioned the prisoners still languishing in the dungeons below the keep. *Someone* had wanted Liam dead.

"That, I do not know, my lord," Kelson said. "Perhaps their master wished him dead. I make no particular inference that their master is indeed your master, but one must wonder who stands most to gain, should our young royal guest perish before he comes fully into his inheritance. I assure you, it is not I—if only because your master has the governance of King Liam's heir."

The Moor bristled at that, prudently silent, but the great cat's rumbling purr rose in volume, verging on a growl, its tail lashing vexedly in response to its master's obvious agitation. Both front paws were now on the lowest step, up to the elbows.

"I decline to answer an allegation so patently absurd," Rasoul said at last. "If carried to its logical conclusion, it implies that the Lady Morag countenanced her own son's murder." He glanced at Liam and made him a bow. "Do not listen to their lies, my prince. All is being done that may, to secure your release."

"Which will occur in due time, my lord," Kelson replied, before the boy could speak, "but not today and not in the very near future. For the present, it is my intention that Liam of Torenth shall remain the guest of Gwynedd until he attains his fourteenth year—to which end, I have this day squired him to Prince Nigel Haldane, Duke of Carthmoor—"

"*Squired* him—"

"Hear me, my lord! Your king is yet of tender years. Nor

was it anticipated that he would one day rule Torenth. It was not *I* who encompassed his elder brother's death," he added, letting Rasoul read the truth of *that*. "But it is my responsibility to see that he is properly trained to rule his land when he comes into his legal majority."

"And whence derives this alleged responsibility, my lord?" Rasoul challenged.

"Because last year, King Liam did me homage for his kingdom," Kelson replied, "as was agreed between myself and his uncle, the late King Wencit. That places him under my protection."

"Say, rather, your servitude," Rasoul muttered.

Kelson sighed. "Hardly servitude, my lord, saving such servitude as any child owes his elders while he learns the lessons of maturity. That is a servitude which I myself have borne, and gladly, and under direction of the same goodly knight. Your king must learn his statecraft somewhere, after all."

"Then let him learn it at his uncle's knee!" Rasoul responded. "Your ways are not our ways. To keep him hostage, apart from kin and countrymen—"

"—is no different from the fosterage that most highborn youths endure, sir," Kelson replied. "He studies with my own royal cousins," he swept an arm in the direction of Payne and Rory, "and he spars with the flower of Gwynedd's chivalry—which is precisely how he would spend his next four years, were he nobly born in Gwynedd and not in Torenth. Surely you cannot think that ill."

Rasoul let out a perplexed sigh. "It is not I whose approval you must gain, my lord. My Lord Mahael will not like this."

"I do not require that he like it," Kelson said. "I do require that he accept it, as regent of my vassal, the King of Torenth. Missives have been prepared by my chancery, detailing my intentions in this matter, and you will deliver these to your Lord Mahael upon your return to his court. I shall expect his presence in Cardosa in June."

Rasoul's dark face went very still.

"You *expect*—"

Kelson leaned back a little in his chair, never taking his eyes from Rasoul's. He could feel the tension rising among the Moors, but their master suddenly had become a tightly shielded blank.

"If you prefer, I shall *command* it, my lord," he said carefully. "And once I have met your master face-to-face and assured myself of his peaceful intentions—and Prince Ronal's well-being—I have no doubt that terms for the lady's release can be arranged."

"Ah." The one word seemed to dissipate all the pent-up tension that had been building in both Rasoul and his men, further reinforcing Kelson's belief that he was wise to tread softly, that something was afoot in Torenth. "Then, you do intend to set the Lady Morag free."

With but the faintest flare of his own shields, apparent only to another Deryni, Kelson smiled conspiratorially and gave the Deryni lord a shrug.

"Our kind are few at the Court of Gwynedd, my lord. She will be far less trouble to Duke Mahael than she has been to me. Do you take my meaning?"

The observation contained just enough wry irony to restore the Moor's good humor. Chuckling aloud—to the mystification of most of the court—Rasoul nodded, giving Kelson another bow.

"I do, indeed, my lord. I—don't suppose I might have brief audience with Her Highness?"

"Alas, no, my lord," Kelson replied. "I trust you will understand why."

Of course, he did not volunteer the more practical reason for his refusal—that Morag was no longer in Rhemuth—and Rasoul had no reason to suspect it. As the Moor shrugged and bowed again, Kelson stood, cradling his sword in the crook of his arm.

"Good, then. I believe we understand one another. May I invite you and your men to join the feast that will shortly be served in honor of today's knightings? Or, if you prefer, may I offer you less formal refreshment while the missives for your lord are brought? Archbishop Cardiel, would you see to that immediately, please?"

Rasoul, gracious once more, inclined his head, and the great cat stirred at his feet, stretching languidly.

"I thank you, my lord, but our ship waits at Desse, and we must be on our way as soon as possible, if we wish to catch the tide. Might I present my compliments to my Lord Liam, however, since I am not to see his mother?''

"In our company and here before the court, you may speak with him, yes," Kelson said.

With silent signal for Dhugal to accompany him, the king came slowly down several steps, keeping a wary eye on the great cat, but Dhugal went ahead of him, several steps closer, and crouched to hold out his hand to the beast—to Rasoul's obvious surprise.

"Young lord—"

"It's all right," Dhugal murmured.

Kelson cleared his throat nervously and glanced at Rasoul, himself a little taken aback at Dhugal's boldness.

"Permit me to make known to you my foster brother, the Earl of Transha, my lord," Kelson said. "I confess, sir, he is more daring than I, to offer his hand to your most magnificent companion, not knowing whether she would prefer to make a meal of him."

Rasoul chuckled, but honest amazement showed in his face as the cat stretched its head closer to sniff at Dhugal's hand, then wrapped an enormous tongue around his fingers, and Dhugal only laughed.

"Ah, I thought as much," Dhugal murmured. "You're a great, huge, hearthside cat, aren't you, girl?" As he shifted his hand to scratch behind one tawny ear, the animal crawled up a few more steps and butted its head against him, sinking down on the Kheldish carpet with a contented sigh.

"Ah, I was right about that, too, wasn't I?" Dhugal crooned. "You didn't like the cold floor, did you, my pretty? May I ask how she is called, my lord?"

Rasoul raised one eyebrow as the great cat's purr rumbled and it closed its eyes, rubbing its head harder against Dhugal's knee.

"If you mean her name, young sir, she is called Kisah, which means Light," the Moor said. "If you refer to her breed, she is a cheetah. They alone of all the great cats can be tamed with any reliability. My people use them for hunting as well as for bodyguards. But—you are not afraid of her?''

Dhugal shrugged, grinning as the cheetah butted him hard enough to knock him back on his haunches and continued to purr as Dhugal's hand kept up its caress.

"She knows I will not harm her, my lord," he said. "We border folk seem to have a way with animals—don't we, Kisah?"

The cheetah only closed its eyes and leaned more heavily against Dhugal's hand, purring even louder. After a few more seconds of this display, Rasoul shook his head and glanced up at Kelson, a smile twitching at his beard.

"It seems there are wonders at the court of Gwynedd that I had not anticipated, my Lord King," he said respectfully. "But I truly have not the time to tarry. Perhaps the young tamer of cheetahs will conduct me to my Lord Liam . . . ?"

The cheetah lurched alertly to its feet as Dhugal stood and made Rasoul a bow, then padded calmly between him and Rasoul as Kelson led the strange trio across the front of the hall to where Liam waited with the other squires. Boys and courtiers retreated at their approach, but Liam stood his ground, still flanked by Morgan and Duncan. At Morgan's nod, the boy went forward to fling his arms around Kisah's neck, giggling and laughing as the great cat wrapped its paws around his waist and licked his face. When Liam at last made the cat stand down and raised his head to greet his ambassador, one arm still around the cat's neck, Rasoul made him formal obeisance, fingertips to breast, lips, and forehead.

"May Allah give you long to reign, my prince."

"My Lord Rasoul, I am glad to see you."

"And I you, my prince, though it seems I might have sent only Kisah, and you would have been content. Are you treated well, my lord?"

"Aye, of course." Liam glanced sidelong at Morgan and Duncan while he continued fondling the cat. "Many things are different here, but I am learning so much! And now, to be squired to Prince Nigel—it is a great honor. When I am grown and I return to Torenth, I hope to be as great a warrior as he!"

Rasoul laughed dutifully as Liam buried his face in Kisah's neck to hug her playfully, dark head against spotted, tawny fur, but the Moor's eyes were mirthless as he crouched down opposite the boy, the cat between.

"Why, that is well to hear, my prince, and you have surely grown taller since last I saw you. But do you not miss your brother? He is page to your Uncle Mahael now—who would be honored to squire you as well. Do you not think that a king should learn the ways of his own people before studying the ways of other lands?"

Liam looked stricken, and his lower lip started to quiver, but Morgan moved closer to set his hand on the boy's shoulder and meet Rasoul's eyes in veiled challenge.

"It is a king's duty to learn the ways of many peoples, my lord," he said quietly. "And those who love their king ought not to play upon his childish fears to turn him from that duty. If you persist in this, you do him no service."

Kelson felt the brush of Rasoul's shields as the Moor scanned all of those close around the young king and found only other Deryni. Smiling, Rasoul rose and bowed, right hand to heart.

"I see that you are well served, my Lord King of Gwynedd," he murmured, "so I shall not press the matter. And that being the case, I shall take my leave as soon as I have received the documents you have commanded me to carry—for I would not have it said that Al Rasoul ibn Tarik did aught to bring unhappiness to his king. But here comes your esteemed archbishop now, I believe."

Arilan was at Cardiel's side as the archbishop approached with a leather courier pouch in hand, and Rasoul favored both prelates with a respectful bow before turning back to the wide-eyed Liam. Kelson, as the bishops came nearer, became suddenly aware that neither man looked happy and wondered whether Arilan had come along to shield the human Cardiel from possible probing by Rasoul. But he had no time to consider that question further, because Rasoul was bowing to Liam again, and reaching out one hand as if to try to touch him.

"My prince, I shall convey your dutiful greetings to your uncle and hope that circumstances soon will permit you to convey those greetings in person. In the meantime, I would kiss your hand in leave-taking—" He pulled up short as an attempt to do just that was thwarted by Duncan's outstretched arm. "But I see that it is not to be permitted, so I shall merely take my leave with a most loving farewell. *Salaam aleikum*, my prince. May Allah hold you safe in the hollow of His hand."

"No doubt He shall, my lord," Kelson remarked dryly. "My Lord Archbishop, are all the documents complete?"

Cardiel gave the king a cool inclination of his head and handed over the pouch.

"They are, Sire. And might I recommend that Your Majesty assign an honor escort to see the Lord Rasoul and his company at least partway to their ship at Desse?" He flicked his gaze pointedly at Duncan. "Perhaps one of your senior dukes would be good enough to go, since I should hate to deprive any of your new young knights of these festivities in their honor. Perhaps His Grace of Cassan."

"I concur, Sire," Arilan agreed. "Duke Duncan is an excellent choice."

The ducal form of address from both men, coupled with their unexpected desire to see Duncan gone from court, suddenly jarred Kelson to wonder whether Cardiel and Arilan were angry with their fellow bishop. Of course! Duncan had not consulted them before confirming, before the entire court, that he was Deryni!

But before Kelson could do more than glance in Duncan's direction, Morgan moved a step closer and laid a warning hand on his sleeve.

"By your leave, Sire," he said softly, "I shall accompany Lord Rasoul as well. Even two dukes are scarcely fitting escort for a man of his caliber—and this evening's festivities, as His Excellency has said, are intended for the new young knights."

The celebration for the new young knights began almost as soon as Morgan and Duncan had escorted their exotic visitors from the hall, though it was close on an hour before Kelson was able to relax enough to begin enjoying it. Cardiel and Arilan vanished before he could get a private word with either of them. Nor was Wolfram anywhere to be found, once the feasting started. It boded ill, but there was nothing he could do about it without creating an uproar; and they had had uproar enough for one day.

"Do you think they're angry that my father revealed himself as Deryni?" Dhugal asked Kelson, while the two of them dismembered a fat game hen stuffed with dates and licked greasy fingers, pretending to watch a troupe of acrobats.

The musicians were playing far too loudly in the rear gallery, but if Kelson could only barely hear Dhugal, sitting right beside him, he knew there was no danger of anyone else overhearing.

"Probably," he replied. "They were unhappy about *something*, but there were too many Deryni around for me to figure out what. And you and that damned cat didn't help matters any."

Dhugal grinned, but let the point pass.

"It may have been a good thing, though, to get Duncan out of here for the rest of the evening," Kelson went on. "You're not that different from Alaric, as far as being Deryni is concerned, so no one's going to bother you, now that they know—not sitting here beside me, at any rate. But Duncan's already stepped on a lot of toes—being a bishop, having you, and now confirming that he's Deryni, too. It'll die down in a while, I'm sure, but there's no sense asking for trouble. Besides, it was a very good idea to send a couple of Deryni along to make sure that the Moors left. A Deryni as powerful as Rasoul could make a lot of trouble, if he put his mind to it."

"Hmmm, you're probably right," Dhugal agreed, chewing thoughtfully at a bite of bread as his eyes roamed the hall. "I don't suppose it does any good to spoil our evening worrying about it, in any case. Incidentally, did you notice who's sitting with your Aunt Meraude, down there near Saer and Duke Ewan?"

Taking a deep pull at his wine, Kelson glanced in the direction of Dhugal's vague gesture, flicking his attention past a pair of indifferent jugglers. The Princess Janniver was sitting on Meraude's left, nearest Kelson, shyly sharing a trencher with his ex-squire, Sir Jatham—well, that was nice! But Kelson had to look twice before he recognized the young woman seated on Meraude's other side—and nearly choked on his wine when he did.

It was Rothana. Had she been wearing the expected pale blue of her novice's habit, he would have noticed her immediately, but he had never seen her in secular attire before. Her gown reminded him of the color of the wine he was drinking, lavished around its high neck and flowing sleeve hems with silver tracery. Her hair was covered by a gauzy pinkish veil draped in eastern fashion and held in place by a silver circlet set with purple stones the size of grapes, framing sultry brown eyes a man might drown in.

"Good God almighty!" Kelson whispered, when he could breathe again.

Dhugal only chuckled and shook his head. "Good God, the man says. One would think you'd never seen a pretty girl before, Kel. And she *is* a nun, after all."

"Then where's her habit?"

"I dunno. Shall I ask her?"

"You do, and I'll have to kill you," Kelson muttered, clutching at Dhugal's sleeve and only half joking, when Dhugal shifted in his seat as if he might do exactly as he threatened.

Dhugal only smiled and sipped at his wine, letting his eyes rove over other parts of the hall.

"Don't worry. I have better things to do this evening than play matchmaker for a man who doesn't want to be matched. I wonder if the Earl of Carthane's daughter will give me a dance or two? And then, there's the Lady Agnes de Barra— if one can work one's way past her ever-watchful brother. *You* might be able to get past. Shall I introduce you?"

"I don't know how you do it," Kelson said, shaking his head. "Go on, then. I don't think I'm drunk enough for that yet."

By the time the feasting was over and the center of the hall had been cleared for dancing and entertainment, Dhugal was already making good his boasts, flirting boldly with nearly every lady present—as were most of the other young men. Kelson dutifully led off a *pavanetta* with his Aunt Meraude, since his mother had declined to attend the feast, and watched both Dhugal and Conall claim a dance from Rothana as the afternoon wore into evening—but at length he found himself sitting quietly next to Nigel during a lull in the entertainment, drinking more than he should and worrying about bishops and Torenthi ambassadors and hostage Torenthi princesses.

He tried not even to think about the bishops. He was sure that matter could be resolved without too much difficulty. It wasn't as if Cardiel and Arilan hadn't known what Duncan was, after all, though he supposed some of the other bishops might not be too happy, once the word spread.

The Torenthi matter was far more vexing just now, however. Rasoul had raised many doubts in Kelson's mind—as he was sure the Moor had intended.

Could he have misjudged the danger? Was the promise to consider releasing Morag a mistake, even if he took Prince Ronal hostage in exchange? Liam, and Ronal after him, were the rightful heirs to Torenth, as blood nephews of Wencit, and Kelson had no designs on their crown; he had enough to manage, keeping his own kingdom at peace. But their mother's children by a second marriage might be said to have equal claim to Wencit of Torenth's bloodline, even if not the senior claim, and might be better supported by the nobility of Torenth than two princes in fosterage to the king of a neighboring land—especially if the father of the junior claimants were one of them and as strong a leader as Mahael of Arjenol appeared to be.

Kelson did his best to appear attentive as Lord Rhodri announced a troupe of players and the servants lit more torches to dispel the growing twilight; but in the face of his own concerns tonight, he was little interested in the exploits of the semi-legendary Sir Armand, flattered though he was to be compared to that goodly knight. By the time the play had ended, Kelson knew that he needed more perspective than his own analysis could give him. Nor was such input likely to be forthcoming tonight.

Dhugal was no help. He had retreated to the other end of the hall to flirt shamelessly with the Earl of Carthane's daughter. His bishops were even less use—taking off in a snit, just because Duncan finally had come clean about being Deryni.

Nigel was telling jokes with Rhodri and Ewan at the other end of the table, Meraude had returned to her chaperone duties with Janniver and Jatham, Rothana was dancing a spirited *gavotte* with Rory, and his mother was off being penitent.

He had no idea where Morgan and Duncan were.

CHAPTER FIVE

A feast is made for laughter, and wine maketh merry.

—Ecclesiastes 10:19

By twilight, as the court of Gwynedd relived the legend of the saintly and chivalrous Sir Armand and Kelson mulled the problems of Torenth and bishops with increasing uneasiness, Morgan and Duncan were within an hour's ride of Desse and the ship that would convey the Torenthi ambassador back to his lord. Riding to either side of the Deryni Rasoul, it had been necessary to forbear exchanging speculations about Cardiel and Arilan, though both men longed to do so. Verbal discussion might have revealed far more than a Torenthi ambassador ought to know about the inner affairs of Kelson's court. And while, in theory, a mind-to-mind exchange could have been effected without Rasoul's knowledge, that was not possible in fact—not while carrying on a conversation with their guest.

For the colorful and clever Al Rasoul ibn Tarik had proven loquacious as well as articulate as they waited for the escort of Haldane lancers to form up and then made their way from the keep to the city's outer gates, first complimenting the vaulting of the hall they had just left in some detail and then firing a seemingly endless string of knowledgeable questions about architectural features of the city proper. Rhemuth the Beautiful was justly famed even outside the Eleven Kingdoms, after all; and it seemed the Moor had pretensions as a master builder himself, with several castles and fortified towns to his credit in Torenth and in the northern Forcinn.

Which made for novel diversion until they had passed through the city gates—especially whenever one of the Haldane horses went into a bucking fit for fear of Kisah, riding like a queen on her pillion pad behind Rasoul. Whatever Deryni powers Morgan and Duncan employed during that first part of the ride were confined to controlling their mounts, not surreptitious mental converse. The lancers stayed well back with Rasoul's Moors, to avoid similar difficulties.

The scenario changed, once they passed the city gates and picked up speed for the long dash down the river road to Desse. Not even verbal conversation was possible then. The cat loped along a few lengths ahead of Rasoul's barb at that speed, to the relative relief of Morgan's and Duncan's mounts; and Rasoul's two dozen Moors followed by twos, with pairs of Nigel's Haldane lancers interspersed. They had just passed the last barge landing before Desse, less than an hour away from their goal, when Rasoul suddenly raised his arm in signal and pulled his barb to a walk, then to a halt; Morgan and Duncan reined in as well. Behind them, Rasoul's men and the lancer escort also drew up, and the great cat circled back at a lope, head raised attentively.

"What's wrong?" Morgan asked, instantly suspicious, for this particular stretch of road was set somewhat apart from the neighboring villages.

Holding a finger to his lips, Rasoul shook his head slightly.

"Nothing, my lords. I merely wish a word with you in private. May we draw ahead of the others for a moment?"

Questions flashed between Morgan and Duncan, but Duncan had detected no danger either. Curious now, though he kept a wary eye on the approaching cheetah, Morgan glanced back over his shoulder.

"Saer, take charge until we come back."

"Aye, Your Grace."

"Thank you, my lord," Rasoul murmured, calling the cat to heel with a silent gesture. "Kisah, stay."

The great cat sank to its haunches, then onto its belly, head resting on its front paws, as the three Deryni drew ahead of their respective troops, perhaps twenty yards.

"Very well," Morgan said, turning his horse to sit knee to knee with the Moor, with Duncan on Rasoul's other side. "What did you wish to say to us?"

Rasoul smiled. "To your most noble companion, actually, my lord. That archbishop—Cardiel, was it? He is not Deryni, is he?"

Duncan went instantly on guard. "Why do you ask?"

"Because, my dear Duke Duncan of Cassan, he was very vexed with you and wanted you away from there—you, who are so obviously well loved by your noble young king. Can you tell me why? I ask only from personal curiosity, one Deryni to another, and because you seem a man of honor."

Morgan exchanged a startled look with Duncan, but Duncan only smiled.

"Yes, I can tell you exactly why, my lord," he said. "You were not present at the earlier part of the king's court. My son was knighted today. He's the one who charmed your Kisah. Very few people knew until today that he and I are Deryni, but they did know that I'm a bishop."

Rasoul's face fell. "A bishop. And he, a bishop's son. Ah, I *am* sorry. Then, the boy is—"

Chuckling, Duncan shook his head. "No, he's true-born, my lord. I married his mother before he was conceived, but she died soon after he was born. *Then* I became a priest. People will get used to that, in time. Many already have.

"No, it's being *Deryni* and a bishop that has my archbishop angry with me. Actually, that's not strictly true, because he's known for some time what I am and chosen to overlook it. It's that I ought to have told him beforehand that I was going to make the Deryni part public. I'm afraid it never occurred to me, at the time."

Rasoul nodded gravely. "I see. Or rather, I do not see, entirely, though I have heard how your Church harbors a great intolerance for our race. You Christians are a strange lot, my Lord Bishop-Duke—seeing evil in what is different, simply because it is not understood. It is not thus among my master's people, who are also mostly Christians. We Deryni of Torenth, whether we follow the Prophet or your Christ, have never warred over *that*."

"Perhaps we should learn from you, then," Duncan replied. "At least I don't need to live a lie anymore. And as my son pointed out only a few days ago, what can they do to me? Alaric has been public all his life, after all."

"And Alaric," said Morgan, "has had his share of problems—but never mind." He glanced back at the men, Christians and Moors, who were beginning to look restless. "Was that all you wanted to say, my lord? I don't wish to sound rude, but I would not wish you to miss your tide."

Rasoul sketched an amused bow. "I do sympathize, my lord. Of course, you wish to return to your king and see what has transpired in your absence. You need not tarry on our account, however. We shall make our tide easily, being this close to Desse." He raised a hand and shook his head as both Morgan and Duncan started to object. "Nay, my lords, you need have no fear of treachery. We came in peace and we shall depart the same way. Our countries are not at war, after all. Not yet, at any rate. I give you my word, neither I nor my men shall stray from this road, or delay our passage, or do mischief to any in Gwynedd."

"Do you give it as one Deryni to another?" Morgan asked, eyeing the Moor carefully, for he *was* anxious to start back for Rhemuth.

"Of course."

"Will you swear it with your hand in mine, open to my reading of the truth?"

Rasoul smiled and held out his hand, and Morgan reached across to grasp it, stretching all his ability to detect any sign of deceit and urging Duncan to do the same.

"I give you my parole that I and my men shall ride directly to Desse and take ship for our own land on the next tide," Rasoul said softly. "We shall do no harm to any man, nor conspire to do any harm, so long as we remain on Gwynedd's soil. And may Allah strike me dead if I speak not the truth or contrive to deviate one jot from what I have sworn, after we have parted. *Amin.* So be it."

Morgan retained the Moor's hand for a heartbeat more, still unable to detect any trace of guile in the mind behind the black eyes, then released it, at Duncan's confirming nod, with a nod of his own. If Rasoul was lying, he was more skilled and powerful than Morgan could cope with—in which case, he and Duncan were probably best off to let the Moors go anyway.

"Very well," Morgan murmured. "You and your men are free to go, my lord. I wish you a safe journey."

Rasoul bowed again. "Thank you, my Lord Duke. And my Lord Duke-Bishop. *Insh'allah*. As God wills it."

Even leaving Rasoul and his men short of the port of Desse, the night was well advanced by the time Morgan and Duncan clattered back into the yard of Rhemuth keep. The sounds of revelry floated out on the frosty night air as Saer de Traherne led the lancers around to the parade court to dismiss, nearer the stables, but Morgan and Duncan dismounted in the forecourt before the main doors.

Leaving their exhausted mounts with a groom, they started slowly up the stone stairway, wearily pulling gloves from cramped fingers and stripping off fur-lined caps. They had refrained from conversation during the hard ride back to the city. A few revelers had strayed out on the landing for a breath of air, so Morgan paused midway up the steps.

"I'm getting too old for this, Duncan. But before we go in, why do *you* think Cardiel wanted you out of here? How angry will he be?"

"I don't suppose I'll find out until morning," Duncan replied. "He has the first Mass tomorrow, so I doubt he's still about. He needs his sleep."

Morgan snorted. "He's not the only one, but I don't think we dare go to bed yet. I'll bet Arilan isn't sleeping either. He's probably off telling the Council all about what you've done. Why *did* you do it, by the way? I'm glad you did—I think—but why today?"

Duncan shrugged, flicking his bunched gloves uneasily against his thigh. "It seemed like the logical thing to do, at the time. And Dhugal wanted it."

"Well, I suppose that's as good a reason as any. It certainly makes things easier for *me*." Morgan buffeted his cousin on the shoulder as they started up the stairs again. "First, then, why don't you see how Dhugal is holding up, and I'll find Kelson and let him know we're back. There's no sense worrying. It's done; and in the long run, it's going to be for the best. We'll weather whatever temporary difficulties it's generated."

Inside the hall, the night's festivities were still in progress but all the signs indicated that things were beginning to wind to a halt. Tonight's principal honorees had slept not at all the night before, after all—unless they snatched a few minutes on their knees during their vigil—and wine had been flowing freely for hours. Dancing had further depleted the waning energies of the young and not so young.

By silent agreement, the two dukes separated as they entered, Duncan watching until Dhugal should finish the rowdy circle bransle winding its way back and forth across the floor and Morgan heading for Nigel to check in, since he did not immediately see Kelson.

Kelson saw Morgan, however. He would have gone to him immediately, but he had only just gotten up the courage to approach Rothana, on the pretext of requesting her presence at a privy council meeting he had set for the following noon to discuss the Torenthi situation.

That mission accomplished, he now suddenly wished himself almost anywhere else. The deep magenta of Rothana's new gown set a disturbing flush on her dusky features, little diminished by the wisp of veil she had drawn across her lower face after dining. Her long, dark hair hung over one shoulder in a heavy braid, blue-black and shiny as a raven's wing in the torchlight. The effect was not lost on the king.

Nor was it likely that Morgan would come soon to rescue him. He and Rothana were standing in one of the northern window bays, in plain enough view for the sake of propriety; but with so many knights wearing crimson mantles tonight, it might take a while for Morgan to spot him.

"Ah, I see that Duke Alaric has returned," Rothana said, following the direction of Kelson's attention as he glanced distractedly in Morgan's direction again. "Which brings me to a somewhat delicate question, while we have a few moments in private. Did you know, beforehand, that Bishop Duncan would finally make public confirmation of his lineage?"

Kelson glanced at the wine remaining in his goblet, then took a careful sip before looking back at her.

"No, I didn't know," he said quietly, "though he asked, before he did it, whether I approved. Of course I did."

From their vantage point, a step above the level of the floor, he saw Duncan working his way toward the dais, watching Dhugal dancing, but Morgan had disappeared from sight.

"It's certainly what Dhugal wanted, though," he went on, turning back to her uneasily. "Apparently the two of them even quarreled about it, a few days ago. I'm not certain what finally made Duncan decide to do it, but I'm glad he did—and he did it so well! Now Dhugal can be open about it, too. After all, we can't hope for acceptance of Deryni if we don't set the example."

"Aye, Bishop Duncan will be a good example, all around," she agreed. "Few have not heard of what he suffered for you in Meara—though, to look at him, one would never know. No scars show on the outside. I wonder if he has nightmares."

"Sometimes," Kelson said distractedly. "But less and less often, he says. I think seeing Loris and Gorony hang helped a lot. Whatever else may have happened, he knows they can never touch him again."

"Wicked, spiteful men!" Rothana murmured. She moved farther into the window bay to lay one hand flat on the glass and stare unseeing at the moonlit garden beyond. "I don't understand how it could have come to that in Gwynedd, Kelson. We Deryni have never had to tread so softly in the Forcinn."

Kelson glanced into his cup again and shrugged.

"You didn't have a Deryni conqueror murder your royal house and impose despotic rule for four generations," he countered. "When my ancestors were restored to their rightful throne, two hundred years ago, they'd had a bellyful of Deryni. I suppose a backlash was almost inevitable. If Saint Camber had lived longer, perhaps things might have been different."

"Perhaps. Tell me, do you really expect to find Saint Camber's relics this summer?"

"I hope to. It's important to me." He gulped another swallow of his wine. "Does that interest you—the prospect of restoring his cult in Gwynedd?"

"As a Deryni? Of course it does. We haven't many Deryni saints—even discredited ones. His cult was never really strong in Nur Hallaj, but it never quite died out, either—perhaps because so many Michaelines fled through the Forcinn, after they were expelled from Gwynedd."

Kelson swallowed, suddenly awkward as he saw the opportunity to ask the question he had been wanting to ask all evening.

"How about as a religious?" he murmured. "Does your order support what I want to do?"

"My order is not Deryni, Sire," she said demurely, from under lowered lashes. "Nor have I made a point of telling them what you want to do."

"Did you—ah—receive some special dispensation to wear—er, not to wear your habit today?" Kelson dared to ask.

She looked him full in the eyes for just a second, far more boldly than he had dreamed she would dare, then quickly glanced at her feet, slippered in purple velvet.

"I—did not think it needful to ask, Sire. I am a princess of royal blood, privileged to reside in the household of a most noble king. On the day that king was to receive his knighthood, it seemed fitting that I dress in a way appropriate to my station, to do him honor."

Kelson swallowed, still not satisfied with her answer.

"I appreciate the honor you have done me, Princess, but I would not have you compromise the honor you owe to God. I am a man. I am not made of iron."

"I know that," she said, a blush staining her cheeks, even beneath her veil.

"And?" he persisted.

"And I—have found, in these past few months, that I am no longer certain I mean to take my final vows," she managed to whisper. "I—have never questioned my vocation before now."

When she did not go on and would not look up at him, Kelson slowly nodded, cautious relief flooding into his breast. Thank God Morgan had *not* come to rescue him when Kelson first had wished it.

"You need say no more, my lady," he murmured. "In a few days, I shall be leaving again for several months. Perhaps—both of us might spend some of that time apart in careful consideration of what your words might mean. I pray that you—and God—will forgive me if I dare to hope you do *not* take final vows."

"There is nothing to forgive, Sire—or, if there is, I forgive you freely, as I know Our Lord will also do. This decision is mine to make. It is I who must resolve the questions rising in my own heart. You are not the cause of those questions; you are only a catalyst. It might well be that I would have reached this point even if we had never met."

"Perhaps."

Kelson tossed off the rest of his wine, then glanced out uneasily into the hall again. *Now* was the time for Morgan to show up. He had learned what he set out to learn and was well content with what he had found out—at least for now—but he did not wish to risk destroying it by dwelling on the point, or by encouraging court gossip that might also put pressure on this fragile victory. Fortunately, rescue was ready at hand, for Morgan was, indeed, approaching.

"Ah, Morgan," he hailed him. "I see that you've returned. Do you have a report for me?"

"Most assuredly, Sire," Morgan said, bowing and then handing Rothana down the step from the window bay. "My lady, I apologize if I've interrupted your conversation."

"Nay, Your Grace, methinks I should see how the Princess Janniver fares. If you will excuse me, Sire."

When she had made her curtsey and retired, Morgan turned back to Kelson.

"All's well?" the king asked.

"Aye. Rasoul and his men should be underway by now. We left them just short of Desse. Rasoul gave me his solemn oath that he wouldn't go anywhere but there. If he was lying, *I* couldn't tell. What's happened while we were gone?"

Kelson shrugged and came down out of the window bay, and the two of them headed slowly toward the dais where a rowdy handful of Dhugal's bordermen had surrounded him and Duncan and were singing them a bawdy song.

"Nothing much," the king said. "I was a little uneasy about our Torenthi plans, after some of the things Rasoul said, so I've called a meeting of the privy council for noon tomorrow. I'd rather have done it tonight, but this was hardly the time or place. It occurred to me that Rothana might have some additional insight on Rasoul's thinking, since he used to frequent her father's court when she was a girl, so I've asked her to join us."

Morgan nodded. "What about Cardiel and Arilan? Are they coming?"

"I suppose. After you and Duncan left, they disappeared." Kelson hunched down in his crimson mantle and studied his spur straps as they continued to walk. "I suppose they retired early; it *was* a long day. Anyway, I sent pages to both their apartments with written notice."

Morgan nodded grimly. "I—think they were not pleased with Duncan's revelation. It remains to be seen what they'll do about it—though it shouldn't affect tomorrow's meeting. Even Rasoul recognized that there was *something* wrong, however. And I think Duncan may be having second thoughts now."

They had nearly reached the dais, and Dhugal's jubilant bordermen turned to greet them with a ragged chorus of border cheers and upraised goblets, most of them empty. The newly knighted Jass MacArdry had removed his crimson mantle and draped it ceremoniously around Duncan's shoulders, and one of the MacArdry drummers was beating a slurred tattoo with his sticks on the edge of a stool, his drum having been temporarily "lost" through the good graces of the efficient deputy of Lord Rhodri.

"*Urram do'n Righ!*" said Ciard O Ruane, sloshing wine into Kelson's cup and thrusting another into Morgan's hand as a pair of pages saw to the others. "Homage to our king! Th' MacArdry's men salute ye, *Ceannard Mhor,* fer rightin' the wrong tha' was done t' this fine son of th' McLains! 'Twas well done, t'knight Sir Duncan. *Slainte!*"

"*Air do slainte,* gentlemen," Kelson responded with a grin, lifting his cup in salute. "To your very good health! And I'm glad you approve."

"*Slainte, Ard Righ . . . slainte!*" the bordermen responded, draining their cups to the dregs and sweeping great bows to the high king.

"I thank you for your vote of confidence, gentlemen. That's heartening, after the words of the Torenthi ambassador. Dolfin—"

He snapped his fingers to catch the attention of his new senior squire, waiting attendance at the back of the dais.

"Aye, my lord?"

"Dolfin, please tell Lord Rhodri that I said to break out a beaker of our best Fianna wine for the enjoyment of these leal MacArdry men."

"Yes, my lord."

"And have I anyone on duty in my apartments tonight, or are they all here reveling?"

"No, my lord. Ivo Hepburn awaits your pleasure."

"Ah, good. You can retire, then, after you've run that errand to Rhodri. I shan't need both of you tonight."

"Yes, my lord."

When the lad had hurried off to do Kelson's bidding, with the MacArdry men trailing after to claim their promised reward, Kelson sighed and glanced around the quieting hall. The musicians had finished their last piece and were packing up instruments in the rear gallery, and inebriated revelers who had no other quarters in the castle were beginning to bed down on pallets along the edges of the hall. The ladies largely had withdrawn.

"God, I'm tired," Kelson breathed.

"*You're* tired," Dhugal said with a snort. "*I'm* the one who's been doing all the dancing."

"And your father and I," said Morgan, "are the ones who rode nearly to Desse and back while you and our gracious king feasted and drank yourselves nearly to happy oblivion. And *that* being the case, I, for one, am about ready for some serious drinking before I go up to bed." He loosened the throat of his tunic and glanced wistfully at the other three. "Anyone care to join me? Ewan brought Nigel a fine old flask of Vezaire port to celebrate Conall's knighting, and the good dukes have invited Saer and me to sample it. We might even talk about bishops. There's room for a few more, if anyone wants."

Duncan shook his head wearily. "Not I, I'm afraid. Vezaire port may be smooth going down, but in the morning you'll wish it had done no such thing. And *tomorrow* morning, I have to be a bishop again." A worried look flitted across his face for an instant and was as quickly replaced by a roguish grin. "In case any of you have forgotten, tomorrow is Ash Wednesday. I expect to see all three of you at the cathedral for my first Mass and ashes. No pious knight would miss it."

"I hate it when he puts things that way," Morgan muttered, with a pained grimace. "I suppose that means he isn't coming. Either of you care to join me? If you shiny new knights don't mind drinking with tired old generals, that is."

"I think Dhugal and I will pass as well," Kelson replied

with a grin, "though not because of the company. It *has* been a long day, and this shiny new knight who's king has something he'd like to discuss with another of his shiny new knights, before either of them passes out from exhaustion. Do you mind, Dhugal?"

"Me? Not at all, Sire."

"We'll walk out with you, though," Kelson said.

They parted just outside the hall, Morgan and Duncan quickly disappearing in separate directions, and Kelson and Dhugal making their way briskly to Kelson's tower apartments. Squire Ivo, a perky twelve-year-old with a thicket of dark, curly hair, had Kelson's slippers laid out and a fire already lit on the hearth, anxious to please, but he obviously was put off balance when Kelson requested water for himself and his guest instead of the wine the boy had ready.

"Just—water, my lord?"

"That's right. Just water. God knows *I've* had enough wine. Or would *you* prefer wine, Dhugal?"

"Water is fine for *me*, Sire," Dhugal replied, carefully formal in front of the new squire, as the two of them sat before the fireplace.

"Water it is, then, Ivo."

Ivo brought the water dutifully enough and set pitcher and cups on the hearth as directed before crouching to remove his new master's spurs and boots, but Kelson could see at once that the boy was all set to be *too* attentive, once his duties were completed. Nor would he be dismissed as easily as the more experienced Dolfin, who had already been in Kelson's service as junior squire for a year or more and knew his master's preferences.

I suppose I'd better get this over with, once and for all, the king whispered in Dhugal's mind, flicking him a resigned glance when Ivo had ducked his head to wrestle with a balky buckle on the right spur. *Pay attention. You may need to do something like this for yourself some day.*

And as he casually dropped his right hand to the boy's bent head, he reached out with his mind for control.

"Relax, Ivo," he commanded, intensifying his mental touch as the young mind unexpectedly sensed the intrusion and the body started to tense. "No, close your eyes and don't fight me. I promise I won't hurt you—on the oaths we exchanged."

Kelson sensed that the boy had been half-expecting something of this sort—one could hardly spend much time around court and not have heard at least rumors of what the king could do with his mysterious powers—but he was pleased when the resistance immediately ceased and the young mind tried to still, though he could feel a faint trembling beneath his hand.

Continuing to croon words of encouragement and reassurance, the king drew the boy's dark head gently against his knee and deepened control, then sat forward slightly so he could ease both hands to either side, thumbs resting against the boy's temples and fingers sliding among the crisp curls for closer contact yet. Immediately the trembling stopped. He let his gaze shift to focus through the fire as he set his instructions.

"That's much better. No need to be frightened. Listen carefully now. When you've finished with the boots, you're to lie down on your pallet and go to sleep. You'll not stir unless someone from the outside should knock. If you should overhear anything spoken between myself and Earl Dhugal tonight, you'll forget it. In fact, if at any time in the future you should overhear conversation between myself and any other person, you're to forget it unless I, personally, ask you to remember. This is something I require of all my squires and pages, do you understand?"

"Yes, my lord," the boy whispered.

"Good." Kelson sat back quietly, keeping contact only with a light touch of one hand on the side of the boy's neck. "You can stop being anxious, then. I doubt we'll ever need to have this conversation again. In fact, this is the most I'll ever do to you without your consent, unless it's a life and death situation. If you pay attention to your duties, you'll find I'm extremely easy to work for. All right? You can look at me now, if you want—really."

The boy lifted his head and blinked a little tentatively, just slightly glassy-eyed, but the former tension was gone.

"I'll do my best, my lord."

"Fine. That's all I'll ever ask of any man: his best. Now, you'll follow the instructions I've just given you, but you'll forget I gave them." He clasped his hand once on the boy's shoulder with a smile and released control. "You can finish with the boots now."

As he sat back with a deliberately vocal yawn, stretching his arms to either side, the boy returned immediately to the recalcitrant spur strap, leaving Dhugal the opportunity to cast an impressed glance at his blood brother as he poured himself another cup of water, yawning.

"I must learn how you do that," Dhugal said, saluting Kelson with the cup.

"What, yawn? You're doing very well without instruction, I should think. And we've certainly earned the right." As Ivo pulled off the offending spur, followed quickly by its boot, and scrambled to his feet, boots and spurs in his arms, Kelson yawned again and gave the boy a reassuring wink.

"Well done, Ivo. You see, the king's feet stink just like anyone else's, after two nights and a day inside boots. I put those on before the vigil last night and haven't had them off since."

He grinned as the boy tried to stifle a surprised gasp, and deliberately shifted his gaze as he gestured toward the spur strap dangling from the boy's hand.

"Incidentally, I think Duke Alaric must have gotten that strap one hole too tight, when he was putting it on me this morning. That's why it gave you trouble. Perhaps you can work on it in the morning."

"I'll—be happy to, Sire," the boy managed to reply, eyes shining as he clutched the boots and spurs to his breast. "Will there be anything else tonight, sir?"

"No, Ivo. Nothing else. You may go to bed. Incidentally, you'd best wake me in time for Mass at Terce. If I don't show up, Bishop Duncan will have me saying *Pater Nosters* until I'm fifty. It's Ash Wednesday, you know."

"Aye, my lord," the boy agreed. "Ah—how long will you need?"

Kelson smiled. "You'd better allow an hour. With as much wine as I drank tonight, I may find it a little difficult to get going. Oh, and Ivo—"

"Yes, my lord?"

"It's a prerogative of royal squires to attend Mass with the king, if they like. You're most welcome to come along."

"Oh, yes, my lord!" the boy breathed, his face wreathed in smiles as he gave the king a parting bow.

When he had left the room and closed the door, Kelson sighed and stretched his legs closer to the fire, luxuriating in the warmth and the feel of the bearskin rug against his stockinged feet.

"Ah, that Ivo's going to be a good one, Dhugal," he murmured.

"You're not so bad yourself," Dhugal said admiringly. "God, how I love to watch you work with your men. I hope I'm half as good someday."

Kelson snorted and picked up his cup of water. "I wish I could work as well with women. That's what I wanted to talk to you about."

"Women? Or one woman in particular?" Dhugal asked, raising an eyebrow in speculation.

"Does it show?"

"Well, since the only woman you spent any time with at all this evening was Rothana—assuming we can discount your Aunt Meraude—I gather that you must mean her. But no, it doesn't show. Besides, she's a nun, isn't she—or going to be?"

"That was the assumption, up until tonight. I didn't expect you to have noticed, though. You were too busy trying to figure out how to get the Earl of Carthane's daughter off in a dark corner. You're no help at all."

"I *did* get Carthane's daughter off in a corner—and got a kiss for my trouble, too!" Dhugal said with a wicked grin. "But, what do you mean, 'that was the assumption'? *Isn't* Rothana going to be a nun?" He cocked his head. "Good God, come to think of it, she *wasn't* wearing her religious habit, was she? Something sort of—purplish, and foreign looking."

"She *said* it was because of the formality of the court, to do honor to the knightings, as a prince's daughter." He sipped at his cup. "Two breaths later, though, she said that she—was no longer certain she intended to take her final vows."

"Sweet *Jesu*," Dhugal breathed.

Tentatively, he reached out his mind to Kelson's, not surprised or offended when the other's thoughts remained shielded from him.

"Are you in love with her?" he asked.

Slowly Kelson shook his head, not looking at his friend, holding the cool side of his cup against his forehead.

"I don't know."

"Well, she *is* Deryni, and royal," Dhugal ventured. "And she's certainly beautiful. Those are all excellent recommendations. Is it because she was supposed to become a nun that you're unsure?"

Smiling, Kelson shook his head again, gazing unseeing into the fire as his thumb played at the ring on the little finger of his left hand. Dhugal saw the gesture and guessed another possible reason for Kelson's uncertainty, for the slender band had been Kelson's bridal token to his dead first wife Sidana, the Mearan princess whose name meant *silk*—second cousin to Dhugal himself, and slain by her own brother before her marriage vows with Kelson were even minutes old. Dhugal had never been able to decide for certain whether Kelson had actually loved Sidana. He knew that Kelson had tried to convince himself that he loved her, especially after the fact; but perhaps guilt over her death was as much a motivation as love.

The king had kept official mourning for a full year following her death, even though it would not have been required or expected, since the marriage was never consummated. He had said, in the beginning, that he only wore the black to remind him of his vow to bring the Mearan rebels to justice. He had said he wore the ring for the same reason, since court protocol required that he sometimes put aside his mourning attire.

But though the last Mearan rebel had been brought to bay by the previous fall, it was only two months ago, on the actual anniversary of her death, that he had finally ceased wearing black. And he still wore the ring.

"Did you love Sidana?" Dhugal asked softly, as he had asked a dozen times before.

Kelson shrugged, as he always had, and put down his cup, but his actual answer, this time, was slightly different.

"What does it matter? She's dead. Even if I did, it doesn't mean I can never love again."

Amazed, Dhugal raised one eyebrow, nodding carefully.

"I see. Then, you *are* falling in love with Rothana."

All Kelson could manage was a silly grin.

"Maybe."

"Well, I'll be. . . ."

"Neither of us is going to make any binding decisions

before I leave for Torenth. We both need the time apart to think things out.''

"Sweet *Jesu*, do you really think you'll marry her?" Dhugal breathed.

"It—ah—wouldn't be a placid marriage," Kelson hedged. "You remember how I told you what she did to me, the *first* time we disagreed."

"Well, she *is* Deryni, after all."

"And I'm a king, Dhugal. A lot of things would have to be worked out. And chiefest among them, for starters, is whether she's even inclined to marry someone besides the Church. I hate to think of competing with God."

Dhugal grinned wickedly. "Oh, I don't think you need worry too much about that. Sometimes I think you'd give even Him a run for His money."

"Dhugal, that's *blasphemy!*" Kelson gasped. "Take it back right now!"

"Well, you *might*," Dhugal insisted. "Hey, easy!" he yelped, as Kelson launched himself at Dhugal and both their chairs went over with a crash.

"Take it back!"

"No, it's true!"

Dhugal ended up half on his stomach and half on his side with Kelson straddling him, one arm pinned beneath his own body and the other fruitlessly trying to fend off the choke-hold the king had just about succeeded in locking across his throat from behind. He could not help laughing, despite the fact that he was losing. Their wrestling upset the pitcher of water on the hearth, soaking the bearskin rug and making the fire hiss and steam. It also brought Dolfin and Ivo charging into the room with drawn daggers, to see what the commotion was.

"Go back to bed!" the king ordered, taking advantage of the diversion to make his choke-hold secure and beginning to see the humor of the situation. "My brother and I are having a difference of opinion. I don't need any help. Dhugal, if you don't take it back right now, I'm going to put you out! And with as much as you've had to drink tonight, you'll probably puke when you come to!"

The squires disappeared immediately, Dolfin dragging the wide-eyed Ivo by a sleeve—he had seen the pair's high jinks before—and Dhugal went limp, no longer putting up a fight.

The pressure across his throat was already beginning to make things go black around the edges, and he could feel a wave of nausea threatening as well.

"Take it back, or I'll still do it!" Kelson demanded.

"All right, all right! I take it back," Dhugal gasped. "Hey, let me up! I'm breathing soggy bear hair!"

He wormed onto his back and managed a game grin as Kelson released him, even though the other still was half sitting on his protesting stomach, and he lay there for a few seconds to catch his breath as Kelson got to his feet.

"Are you all right?" Kelson asked.

Dhugal sat up with a nod and took the hand Kelson offered to help him up.

"If I don't throw up in the next thirty seconds, I will be. But, *Jesu*, I must have hit a nerve! I mean, what flesh and blood woman in her right mind would want to marry the Church when she could have the King of Gwynedd for a husband?"

"Watch it," Kelson warned.

Wagging a finger at Dhugal, still breathing a little hard, the king righted the overturned chairs and helped the queasy Dhugal sit in one and put his head briefly between his knees. He was not really angry, but Dhugal had touched a spot Kelson had not realized was so sensitive. One did not joke about God that way. Not when the stakes were this high.

"I'm sorry," Kelson murmured, when Dhugal had straightened and gingerly laid his head against the chair back. "I guess I overreacted." He picked up the overturned pitcher and began mopping the worst of the spill with a towel. "Some day, though, you need to sit down with your father and have him explain about religious vocations. I confess, I don't really understand them either, but I respect them. And however much I might find myself attracted to Rothana, and however good a wife you think she'd make for me, I wouldn't marry her if I thought I'd made her give up the Church."

"Well, she wouldn't really have to give up the *Church*, after all. She just wouldn't be a nun," Dhugal said, rubbing at one wrist where Kelson had pinned him.

"You know what I mean," Kelson said. "Anyway, this is all premature. I'm not even going to think about it any more tonight."

But he *did* think about it, of course. After Dhugal had gone and he had reassured his squires that nothing was amiss, he lay awake for nearly an hour and was the worse for the lack of sleep when Ivo came to wake him again at eight.

CHAPTER SIX

*For he offereth the bread of thy God; he shall be
holy unto thee.*

—Leviticus 21:8

"*Memento, homo, quia pulvis es, et in pulverem reverteris . . . . Memento, homo . . .*"

Kneeling at the altar rail in Rhemuth Cathedral, huddled
deep in the collar of his sable-lined cloak, Morgan waited
blearily to receive the ashes that marked the beginning of
Lent.

"*Memento, homo, quia pulvis es. . . .*" Remember, man,
that thou art dust, and unto dust thou shalt return. . . .

His head felt as if it were filled with dust this morning,
and his mouth tasted of it. Worse, Duncan would not even
lecture him, later on, about the folly of overindulgence. But
it *had* been a fine Vezaire port. . . .

"*Memento, homo, quia pulvis es. . . .*"

Morgan had missed Mass, too, though perhaps Duncan
had not noticed. The Deryni bishop was far toward the left-
hand end of the line of penitents kneeling at the altar rail,
solemnly bending to smudge a young page's forehead with
ashes. Both he and Father Shandon, the young priest assisting him this morning, wore the somber violet vestments
appropriate to the beginning of the Lenten season, but suddenly it occurred to Morgan that far more people were waiting on Shandon's side of the sanctuary than on Duncan's,
despite the fact that people usually preferred to receive anything from a bishop rather than an ordinary priest.

Ah, but that assumed that the bishop was also ordinary,

95

Morgan suddenly realized—and a Deryni bishop was far from that. Given the official position of the Church regarding Deryni, was it any wonder that, as news spread of Duncan's display of the day before, many folk would have qualms about having an admitted Deryni touch them? No matter that the archbishop and two other bishops had witnessed the incident and had done nothing. Who wanted to be among the first to test whether harm might, indeed, come from a Deryni priest's touch?

Clearly, not everyone felt that way. Thank God for that. The men kneeling to either side of Morgan—a young MacEwan man-at-arms and an even younger sergeant of lancers that Morgan *knew* had been present in the hall the day before—could hardly fail to know who and what both he and Duncan were; but they seemed to have no hesitation either about kneeling next to Morgan or receiving ashes from Duncan, who was proceeding back along the altar rail toward them, now tracing a sooty cross on a Haldane archer's brow.

"*Memento, homo, quia pulvis es, et in pulverem reverteris. . . .*"

In fact, Morgan suddenly noticed, the common factor among most of those apparently willing to have Duncan minister to them was that they were young, most of them younger than Morgan and Duncan themselves—which at least bespoke hope for the future, if Duncan could ride out the immediate outcry.

"*Memento, homo, quia pulvis es. . . .*"

Intrigued by that observation, Morgan scanned the altar rail again. There *was* a correlation by age, though it was not iron-clad. In fact, as Father Shandon reached the center of the altar rail and crossed back, to resume at the far end of the rail again, Morgan saw several older men, just past where Shandon had left off, rise and edge surreptitiously into the queue of men and women waiting to kneel on Shandon's side. It was quietly done, but it was done, nonetheless. He supposed it was too late for some men to change.

"*Memento, homo, quia pulvis es. . . .*"

Duncan was giving ashes to the lancer sergeant now, and Morgan raised his head to meet his cousin's eyes as the Deryni bishop finished and came before him.

"*Memento, homo, quia pulvis es, et in pulverem reverteris,*" Duncan murmured, tracing the cross on Morgan's brow with special attention. *So glad you could finally make it this morning,* he added mentally. *Meet me in the sacristy, after.*

Morgan had to duck his head to keep from smiling, waiting until Duncan had finished with the MacEwan man-at-arms and moved on before crossing himself deliberately and easing to his feet. He withdrew into the relative shelter of one of the pillars of the clerestory aisle, shadowed and anonymous, to continue watching until the last penitents had received ashes. No one actually got up and left when Duncan began helping Shandon finish with those kneeling on Shandon's side or refused to receive ashes from Duncan, but Morgan could feel the apprehension and tension radiating as the people left the rail, their duty done at last. He even saw one man scrub surreptitiously at his forehead to remove the ashes Duncan had placed there, as soon as he thought no one would notice.

Morgan knew that it would take a few minutes for Father Shandon to unvest and leave, so he waited quietly for a few more minutes before heading for the sacristy. But by the time he got there himself, he could hear angry voices within, neither of them Shandon. Deryni shields, not Duncan's alone, tingled against Morgan's own as he pushed the door open in alarm and entered.

"I really don't want to talk about it, Denis," Duncan was saying, though neither he nor Arilan even glanced aside as Morgan drew the door closed and leaned against it, watching and listening warily. Over on a stool beside a vestment press, Father Shandon slumped asleep or unconscious, still fully vested in surplice and stole, obviously taken unawares by one of the two Deryni when the argument began to get too specific for outsiders to witness.

"Well, you'd better think again about talking about it," Arilan said. "Don't you realize that you may have put the entire Church at jeopardy? You saw what happened out there. It was one thing when they only thought you *might* be Deryni. God, Duncan, couldn't you have waited?"

"And just how long was I supposed to have waited?" Duncan countered. "Twenty-odd years, like you? Is that how long you've been a priest? And you *still* haven't owned up to what you are! *Someone's* got to be the first, if there's ever going to be a change."

Too angry to reply, Arilan spun away to glare unseeing at the tiny window above the vesting altar. It was filled with colored glass in a random pattern suggestive of ocean waves, and the sunlight cast sickly greenish blotches on Arilan's face and hands and on the plain black working cassock he wore. Morgan glanced at Duncan, not daring to intervene beyond his mere presence, but Duncan was focused only on his fellow bishop.

"I *was* the first, once," Arilan finally said, very softly. "Or, no, I wasn't the first—Jorian came before me—but I was the first one to make it through successfully that I know of." He leaned the heels of both hands against the edge of the altar and stared down at the white-worked linen covering it, then glanced back over his shoulder.

"That's not such a poor distinction, is it, Duncan? To be the first Deryni successfully ordained as a priest in nearly two hundred years? And *you* were ordained. And after you, in the past two or three years, there have been a few others, too. I'll bet you didn't know about those. But if I'd tried to do it all when I was the first, I'd be as dead as Jorian and all the rest that they killed before him! So, damn it, don't you *dare* talk to me about *someone has to be first!*"

As he turned to confront Duncan again, Morgan felt himself sag against the door, closing his eyes against his own memories.

Jorian. God, he remembered Jorian! Morgan had been just barely thirteen, a squire at Brion's court, when one of the royal chaplains had insisted that the king's pet Deryni be taken to witness the execution of the Deryni ex-priest Jorian de Courcy, whose defiance of the law had been betrayed by the very hand of God at his ordination. Morgan was sure his own almost paralyzing fear of death by fire must spring from that terrible day, from being forced to watch the flames engulf de Courcy's helpless, writhing body. Nor was it the last time he had witnessed such horror.

He found himself sweating inside his heavy cloak as he opened his eyes, all but shaking physically in reaction, but his reaction was nothing compared to Duncan's. The younger bishop had blanched nearly as white as the alb half-unlaced at his throat, and his shields were absolutely impenetrable, even to Morgan.

"What do you mean, there have been a few others?"

Duncan whispered. "Are you saying there are more of us now? Other Deryni priests?"

"Not enough—but some," Arilan said stonily, half turning back toward the ocean window.

"And—you were the one to arrange it?"

"At some cost, yes. Being a secret Deryni in the ranks helped enormously. And being a Deryni bishop who isn't known to be Deryni helped even more.

"But now everyone knows, or soon will know, that there's at least one of us who's infiltrated even to the episcopate; and where there's one, there could be more. That may not bother the sane, honest churchmen like Wolfram, once they've had a chance to get used to the idea, but suppose there are a few more bishops or would-be bishops out there who are more like Edmund Loris than Thomas Cardiel? Do you want to unleash *that* on the innocent again?"

Duncan recoiled almost as if struck a physical blow. Arilan was sparing him not a whit.

"It's exactly to stop that from being unleashed again that I did it," Duncan murmured, sinking down on a bench behind him. "We have to show the world that we *aren't* evil, by the example of our lives. I did it so that my son will have the chance to be a part of that example."

"And *that's* truly the crux of it, isn't it?" Arilan said quietly. "Dhugal, your son." He sighed and crossed his arms on his chest, glancing down at his feet. "Perhaps that's why we don't permit our clergy to marry, Duncan. We grow too fond of the flesh of our flesh; and when the time comes that we have to make a choice, it's awfully difficult to choose for God rather than one's child. Few men can do it. Nor should they be asked to do it."

Drawing breath audibly, Duncan looked up. "I'll stand by my decision, Denis. I'm a father *and* a priest, and I intend to continue being both. In fact, that's part of what finally led me to do what I did: the sheer wonder that God worked His magic the way He did, to lead me to His service but also to let me sire that young man."

Arilan snorted. "How poetic. Is that supposed to move me not to be angry anymore? And you're absolutely right that you'll stand by your decision. You haven't really got much choice."

"It was a decision made in good conscience," Duncan said defensively, a brittle edge to his voice.

"Oh, I'm sure it was. I just don't know whether you considered that this act of conscience of yours might cost you your mitre—and maybe even your office as a priest."

As Morgan held his breath, Duncan slowly straightened and stood, as grey as the smudge of ash on his forehead.

"What do you mean?"

Arilan tried to maintain eye contact, but failed.

"You're aware that the general synod meets next week in Valoret. There's been some talk this morning of suspending you, at least until the synod has had a chance to consider what to do," he said, nervously clasping and unclasping his hands. "Cardiel doesn't really want to, but Wolfram isn't sure. And it could go further than suspension."

"How much further?" Duncan whispered. "The mitre doesn't really matter. I never particularly wanted to be a bishop in the first place. And I've been suspended before—even excommunicated. It was unpleasant, but it passed. It didn't change what was in my heart. But *what else might they do to me, Denis?*"

"Just be glad that the Church doesn't burn Deryni anymore," Arilan said gruffly. "Not officially, at any rate. We won't count renegades like Loris, or what still goes on occasionally in the outlands. And even if enough bishops wanted to try, the king would never permit it. Which could precipitate another, entirely different kind of crisis—the king attempting to interfere in episcopal matters—but we needn't worry about *that* for the present. Neither Cardiel nor Bradene would ever let it get that far."

"So they won't burn me," Duncan said impatiently. "That's been tried and failed. What about my priesthood?"

"Don't get cocky!" Arilan snapped. "You might not be so lucky, next time around. Or your luck might not hold for Dhugal."

Duncan shuddered and bowed his head. "Forgive me. I suppose I shouldn't have said that. But what about my priesthood?"

Arilan shrugged and sighed. "Well, they can't take it away entirely, as you know. *Tu es sacerdos in aeternum.* Thou art a priest forever. That's why the original Ramos conventions specified the death penalty for Deryni who actually managed to get ordained—one can't unmake a priest. They *could* degrade you from the priesthood, however. I don't think I need to remind you what that means. You may know about suspension and excommunication from firsthand experience, but you've never had to deal with *that*.''

Morgan shared Duncan's sick dread at that prospect. Though the imprint of priestly ordination was indelible, lasting for all eternity, degradation stripped a priest of all authority to exercise the sacred office so imparted. It did not cut him off from reception of the other, usual sacraments at another priest's hands, as excommunication would; but if he defied the restrictions of degradation, excommunication was but one of the further penalties the Church might impose in an attempt to bring a wayward son to heel.

Morgan knew how Duncan had suffered from mere suspension when his Deryni blood first began to be suspected; and the later excommunication the two of them had shared, though imposed unjustly, had taken a similarly heavy toll on Duncan's spiritual health, which was already scarred by the necessity to balance his priestly call against the Church's stand regarding ordination of Deryni. Degradation from the priesthood that Duncan loved so well and to which he was so obviously called would be the greatest injustice of all.

"I hope it won't come to that," Arilan went on, obviously aware of Duncan's distress. "And since you're directly under Cardiel's jurisdiction, I doubt he'll do more than just suspend you from *public* function until this all blows over. That's assuming he doesn't receive too much pressure from the other bishops, of course."

"You mentioned that Wolfram's unsure," Duncan whispered. "What will the others say?"

"I wish I knew," Arilan replied. "Bradene's the real key, if it goes beyond local jurisdiction—which it's almost bound to do, with the synod meeting next week. Just thank God that up until yesterday, your record was excellent, even if speculation was rampant. In fact, before you were elected to the episcopate, probably half our fellow bishops had pretty much decided that you *were* Deryni, but that it probably didn't matter. Of course, that was before you decided to confirm the rumors and flaunt what you are in front of the entire court. It could be worse, I suppose. You could have done it at the altar, in full pontificals. Now, wouldn't *that* have been a coup?"

"But, I never would have—"

"I don't know *what* you never would have done!" Arilan snapped. "Not anymore. All I know is that you've made a great deal of trouble for a great many people. I hope you're quite satisfied."

Duncan breathed out audibly, not quite a snort, and clasped his hands in a careful gesture of control, fingers intertwined, gazing at his bishop's ring. Would Arilan never let him be? Morgan wondered how much more of this he could take.

"I—suppose I—should have thought through the possible consequences more carefully before I acted," Duncan said after a few seconds, in a conciliatory tone. "I'm sorry if I've made your position more difficult." He looked up at Arilan tentatively. "Any advice, now that it's done?"

With a wry, grudging nod, Arilan turned to face Duncan squarely, still totally unyielding in posture and expression.

"So," he said softly, "have I finally made you realize the seriousness of the situation?"

Miserably, Duncan nodded.

"Good, then. Maybe now we can do something constructive." Arilan paced back to the little altar, thinking, then came back to look down at Duncan again.

"Very well. You're probably safe enough for now, and so am I. So are those other Deryni priests you had no idea existed. You're still also a bishop as well as a priest—for now—but if I were you, I'd keep a very low profile."

"No more ashes today?" Duncan said, with a strained attempt at a smile.

Arilan nodded. "*Especially*, no more ashes. In fact, it might be wise if you became seriously indisposed, indefinitely. Perhaps you shouldn't even go to the synod. And if you do intend to continue public celebration of Mass, at least for the time being, I suggest you let it be known that you intend to take the earliest one, since it's already sparsely attended. That way, people can make their own decision about whether they want a Deryni priest to minister to them."

He picked up a black cloak with capelets and slung it around his shoulders.

"You're just damned lucky no one bolted this morning, when you were distributing ashes. I hope you realize that. You and I both know that if you'd wanted to, even that brief contact—long enough to trace a cross on a man's brow—would have been long enough to take over just about any mind that approached that altar rail. Fortunately, they don't know that. And Ash Wednesday only happens once a year."

Duncan sighed, shoulders slumped dejectedly, and Morgan started to move quickly out of Arilan's way as the Deryni bishop glanced at the door, but Arilan stepped on the squared cross of the Transfer Portal in the center of the room instead.

"Very well, then," Arilan said. "I'll leave you now. I may or may not be back in time for the privy council meeting. If I'm not, please give Kelson my regrets. Now that I've gotten *your* explanation of why you did what you did, I have to try to explain it to some other people who already look on the two of you with a somewhat jaundiced eye."

"The Camberian Council," Duncan breathed. "Well, I don't suppose it can make matters any worse."

"Not for you," Arilan replied, without a trace of humor in his voice. "And as for you," he went on, for the first time even acknowledging Morgan's presence, "I'd better not *ever* find out it was you who put him up to this."

Morgan only shook his head, truly afraid of Arilan in that instant for the first time in his life. But Arilan only gave him a final, stern look, then bowed his head and closed his eyes to make the Portal connection—and disappeared. Only when several seconds had passed did Duncan heave a great, shuddering sigh and sign for Morgan to lock the door.

"I'm sorry you had to witness that," Duncan said, rising woodenly to begin unknotting the girdle of violet silk binding his waist. "He was waiting for me when we came back from Mass. Poor Shandon never knew what hit him."

Across the room, the younger priest still slumped against the vestment press, oblivious to what had gone on. Morgan went to him, checking for a pulse and extending his own controls to override what Arilan had set, then glanced at Duncan.

"No harm done, though it was damned inconsiderate of Arilan to leave us his dirty work to finish up. Shall I put him through the motions while you finish changing?"

Duncan's muffled assent came from inside the alb he was

pulling off over his head. Smiling mirthlessly, Morgan returned his attention to the unconscious Shandon, shifting one hand to the man's brow.

"All right, Father, you've napped long enough. You're not to remember anything that's happened since you came back from Mass. Not Bishop Arilan's presence, or what he did to you, or any of the conversation that took place—or even these instructions. When I tell you to, you're just going to open your eyes and finish unvesting. I came in while your back was turned. Be aware of your heartbeat now and, when you've counted ten, wake up and follow the instructions I've just given you."

He released the man then and went to help Duncan do up the buttons of the plain black cassock he had exchanged for his more formal purple one.

Part of your new, low profile? Morgan sent silently, as Shandon stirred and began taking off his own vestments, as if there had been no interruption whatsoever.

"I suppose I should be glad you got here at all," Duncan replied verbally, one eyebrow raised in wry disapproval as he wrapped the cassock's plain, black silk cincture around his waist and let Morgan help fasten it. "Assisting the priest to dress is no substitute for hearing Mass, though. What *am* I going to do with you?"

It was an old game they played, though Morgan could sense the edge of leftover turmoil beneath the familiar banter. But they must keep it up for Shandon's sake.

"Why, continue to pray for me, I should imagine. I—ah—didn't get as much sleep as I should have liked. You were right about the Vezaire port."

"Hmmm, I dare say."

Duncan thrust his arms distractedly through the sleeve openings of a black, fur-lined mantle that Morgan held for him. Then, almost as an afterthought, he picked up his jewelled pectoral cross, kissed it, and looped its chain over his head, though he tucked the cross itself inside his cassock so only the chain showed. He was cool and distant now that Arilan was gone, his mind close-shuttered, almost as if he were angry with Morgan.

"Is the king waiting for us?" Morgan asked, to get conversation rolling again.

"Yes. He and Dhugal are poring over maps in the library.

He was disappointed you didn't join them for Mass. Father Shandon, we'll be in the library for the rest of the morning. After that, we'll be at a privy council meeting. Alaric, are you coming?"

Not until they were outside the sacristy and moving along the ambulatory aisle that ran behind the high altar did Morgan dare to speak again.

"You're shutting me out, Duncan," he murmured. "Don't do that to yourself. It's Arilan who put you out of sorts, not I. Do you want to talk about it?"

"No. I think Dhugal and Kelson should know what's happened, first. Then all four of us can talk about it. Arilan is right in one respect, though. I *didn't* think out all the consequences of what I did, before I decided to do it. And maybe I did let my love for Dhugal cloud my duty to my church. God, what if it eventually puts one of those other priests at greater risk?"

He stopped short in the shadow of a doorway leading to a side chapel and simply started to shake, eyes tightly closed and clasped hands jammed hard against his teeth.

"God, what have I done, Alaric?" he managed to whisper, for an instant transported back in memory to the hot flames leaping up around him. "I may have put them nearer the fire!"

Himself deeply shaken, Morgan laid both arms around his cousin's shoulders and simply held him close for several seconds, trying to ease comfort past Duncan's static, brittle shields.

"You don't know that, Duncan," he murmured. "At this point, you don't even know who they are. And there isn't going to be another fire."

"What if there is?"

"We have enough to worry about, without taking on all the 'what ifs' as well. Let's go on to the library, shall we? This isn't the best place for a discussion."

"You still haven't explained *why* he did it," someone said an hour later, not for the first time, when all seven of the presently filled seats on the Camberian Council were occupied and Arilan had made his report. His fellow councilors were *not* happy with his news.

"I've told you, I don't know," Arilan replied. "I'm not certain *he* knows, though I'm sure that Dhugal was a strong motivating factor. As a Deryni, I must point out that there *are* pluses to this entire matter, of course. Having two more Deryni openly at court and as strongly under the king's protection as they are can only help our overall cause. As a bishop, however, I'm appalled. And I can tell you that Cardiel is not exactly overjoyed, either."

Barrett de Laney, senior to any other member of the Council, touched bony but agile fingers lightly to the co-adjutor's wand lying on the ivory tabletop before him. The spring sunshine washing the faceted dome of the Council chamber flooded the chamber with purplish light and danced rainbow flashes off the head-sized crystal suspended from the center of the arched ceiling, but Barrett could not see it—though he could feel its warmth. The emerald eyes had been blind for more years than most of his fellow councilors had been alive. He cocked his head in Arilan's direction, however, seeing with Deryni senses far more clearly than mortal eyes had ever seen.

"What will Cardiel do, Denis?" Barrett asked. "Will he try to take Duncan's mitre?"

"I don't think *he* will." Arilan glanced at the table, running a fingertip along one of the bands of gold set into the ivory surface. "Unfortunately, it isn't entirely up to him. Bradene is senior archbishop."

"Bradene is in Valoret, preparing to convene the synod," said a voice at Arilan's left elbow—Kyri, the youngest of the three women at the table. "He has been occupied with cleaning up after Loris and running the affairs of the Church in the northern half of the kingdom. He has two vacant bishoprics, with no one to see to the care of the souls resident in them, and several bishops under disciplinary consideration. To me, that suggests that Bradene will follow Cardiel's recommendations for matters in the south. So, what will Cardiel recommend?"

Arilan shook his head. "I can't answer that. He wouldn't *initiate* a move to take Duncan's mitre, but he might allow himself to be pressured into such an action if enough of his bishops were adamant enough. He's come to love Duncan almost like a son, even knowing he's Deryni—in fact, he's fascinated by our powers. But he's an archbishop, first and foremost. He'll do what he feels is best for the Church. A lot will depend on how the other bishops take the news."

"That's all at least a week away, then," said Laran ap Pardyce, from the other side of Kyri. "What about immediate repercussions? Will Cardiel suspend him?"

Arilan shrugged. "He did mention the possibility—though that was last night, in his first anger at what Duncan had done. I think he was as much hurt as angry that Duncan didn't consult him first. Early this morning, though, when he'd cooled down a bit, he said he'd wait and see how public reaction went, that perhaps just a voluntary suspension of public function would be sufficient, at least for now. I think he means to talk to him this afternoon. Kelson called a privy council meeting for noon."

Tiercel de Claron, seated across from Arilan and Laran, tilted his high-backed chair slightly onto its back legs, looking thoughtful.

"What about your Deryni priests in human clothing, Denis?" he asked. "Are they safe?"

Arilan nodded. "For the present. They're all very young, though. Not one is over twenty-five. I'd planned to ordain two more at Easter. *Damn*, why couldn't Duncan have waited!" he exploded, slamming a fist on one arm of his chair. "In another few years, he could have had a see of his own, and then *both* of us could have been ordaining Deryni priests. Even if he keeps his mitre now, they'll probably never let him ordain—for fear of just that result."

"Perhaps, then," said a slender, ageless-looking woman seated two chairs right of Arilan, "you had best turn your energies to making sure the law changes to allow Deryni to be ordained, rather than continuing to work around the law."

Arilan glanced at the woman almost guiltily. He might have known that Sofiana would come up with that argument.

"If I knew how to do that, don't you think I *would?*" he said. "Do you think I *like* having to live the way I've lived for the past twenty years, knowing how much more I *might* have done, but not daring, for fear of losing all? And we've gotten the death penalty removed, for God's sake! I'd hardly call that 'working around the law.'"

"Perhaps what Sofiana is saying," said Vivienne, farther to Arilan's left, "is that now you have an admitted Deryni within the episcopate—as well as yourself, who are unknown to all but him and Cardiel. And I gather that this Bishop Wolfram was not wholly antagonistic to the notion that Duncan might be Deryni, when he sat on the tribunal last week. That's possibly four, then, counting Duncan himself, who could probably be counted upon to support a change in the law.''

"I've already suggested that Duncan not go to Valoret,'' Arilan replied. "At least not in the beginning, until I can ascertain which way the wind is blowing. We have some bishops to replace, however, and some of those remaining were all too eager to support Edmund Loris, not a twelve-month ago. Still, I suppose it's a start.''

"Of course it's a start,'' Vivienne muttered, pausing to cough into a wadded square of embroidered linen. "Miserable catarrh! You start working on that, Denis, and keep us advised on further developments. Now I want to know about this other Deryni who spoke for the Duke Mahael yesterday. Al Rasoul, was it?''

Wearily Arilan nodded. He supposed that in the larger scale of things, a Deryni priest-*cum*-bishop *was* no more important than the latest posturings of a Torenthi ambassador, even if that ambassador *was* Deryni.

"He defies mere verbal description,'' he said, leaning his head against the back of his chair and reaching to either side for his neighbors' hands. "It's easiest if I show you. You really had to be there to appreciate it, but I'll recreate it as best I can.''

As he sank into easy trance, focusing on the crystal above their heads, he felt the calm of the familiar link envelop him like a cloud, warm and comforting, and he closed his eyes to let the images flow.

CHAPTER SEVEN

Ye have set at naught all my counsel.
—Proverbs 1:25

Arilan returned to Rhemuth Castle in time for only the tail-end of the privy council meeting, but he was just in time to follow Cardiel and a very subdued Duncan into a private withdrawing room afterward, where Cardiel gave the younger bishop a royal dressing down in Arilan's presence.

"It isn't that I didn't know what you were, Duncan. I've known for some time what Denis was, too. I suppose I thought you realized that my overlooking of that fact was a personal act of conscience, and that I could only continue to overlook it as long as you played your part. When you chose to make it public, it became a concern of my office, not just my conscience."

When Duncan only continued staring at his folded hands, Cardiel went on.

"Well, fortunately or unfortunately, the law is not clear at this moment just what I should do with you next. We've been successful in rescinding the death penalty for doing what you did in letting yourself be ordained, but the Statutes of Ramos still say it's illegal for a Deryni to be a priest."

"At one time," Duncan said quietly, "it was illegal for a Deryni to own land or hold any kind of office or noble title, too. But Alaric's been a duke for years, and Queen Jehana still holds her rank and dower lands."

Cardiel exhaled with great forbearance. "Those are exceptions, and you know it. And maybe, just *maybe*, you'll prove to be an exception, too. But it won't be by throwing legalistic quibbles in your archbishop's face. Now, are you going to argue, or are you going to listen to what I have to say?''

"Listen," Duncan whispered.

"All right, then. Officially, I'm going to ignore this entire matter for as long as I can. Thanks to your impetuosity, however, the synod in Valoret will have to deal with the Deryni question far sooner than I might have wished. You can be certain you will be the subject of many heated discussions when they meet next week.

"But you will not go to Valoret. So far as the Church is concerned, you are to become invisible. Denis has suggested—and I concur—that you develop a convenient illness making it unwise for you to travel. I must also ask that you not undertake any public function as a priest or a bishop.''

"Am I suspended?"

"No, much as you sorely tempt me. You may continue to celebrate Mass privately, but I do mean privately—for yourself, for the king, for Alaric, for Dhugal. Period. You may also hear confessions, but from them only, unless it's a matter of life and death. If you attend privy council meetings or any court functions, you're to do it as a duke. I'm not going to forbid you to wear canonicals, but you'd better be discreet. I'd be happier if you stuck to secular attire whenever possible.''

"For how long?" Duncan asked.

"Until I can get the bloody law changed, goddammit, man!" Cardiel retorted. "Duncan, I can't overstress the importance of this. If you keep out of sight and don't make any more damned-fool demonstrations of what you are, this may blow over. The *only* thing that's enabling me to give you as much slack as I am is that you weren't functioning as a bishop when you blew your cover—and you didn't actually *say* anything. And you'd better *not* say anything—you *or* Dhugal. Do I make myself clear?''

It was all *too* clear, though not as bad as it might have been. Duncan obeyed Cardiel's strictures, counterfeiting a cough and fever that kept him to his rooms in the episcopal palace, and counted himself very fortunate when no further repercussions descended during the days that followed. The isolation also gave him a welcome excuse to spend more time with Dhugal, before his son left on the summer progress with the king. Morgan and Kelson came to dine with them almost every night, usually staying to talk, long into the early morning hours. The last night that the king and Dhugal would spend in Rhemuth, Duncan came to the castle to dine.

That night, since the royal progress would also incorporate a quest for relics of Saint Camber, Morgan presented the two new knights with Saint Camber medals, cast from the one he himself had inherited from his Deryni mother. After Duncan had blessed the medals, however, Kelson excused himself to seek out another blessing. Sending Dolfin as his emissary, he requested Rothana to meet him by the fountain in the center of the garden.

Propriety required that she be attended, of course. One of the older nuns accompanied her as companion and chaperone, both of them cloaked and hooded against the chill night air; but the woman succumbed without resistance to Kelson's suggestion that she walk abroad in the gardens with Dolfin, who likewise would remember nothing of what he might see or hear. The king led Rothana into the relative shelter of a nearby arbor.

"I wanted to show you this before we left in the morning," Kelson said, pulling the silver disc of his Saint Camber medal out of his tunic by the chain. "It takes a Deryni really to appreciate it. Duncan's blessed it already, but I wondered if you might also give it a blessing."

"I, my lord?" She glanced at the medal with interest, obviously recognizing what it was, but made no attempt to touch it. "Such blessing is reserved for priests."

"Nonetheless, I would value *your* blessing," Kelson said. "Surely that can do no harm, since it already has a priest's saining."

"That's true."

Smiling cautiously, she came close enough to take the medal in her left hand and inspect it, then signed a cross above it with her other and bent to touch it with her lips.

"Thank you," Kelson murmured, taking it in his own hand and kissing it, too, as she straightened and released it. "I shall treasure it the more for it having felt your kiss."

She blushed and ducked her head.

"Please, my lord, you must not say such things."

"Must I not? Rothana, it's been nearly a week. I'd like to know what you've been thinking. Not about the things we discuss in the privy council. Not about the Torenthi situation, or the bishops, or even Saint Camber. About us."

She glanced at him surreptitiously, then returned her gaze to her hands folded in her sleeves. The movement made her hood fall back on her shoulders. Underneath the dark blue mantle she had donned for the venture out of doors, she still wore the sky-blue habit of her order, but she had changed her customary linen coif for filmier stuff that surrounded her face like a madonna's veil. The thick mass of her hair was not braided tonight, but coiled beneath the veiling in a heavy, shining mass at the back of her head, apparently held only by a pair of silver pins.

"What about us, my lord?" she replied. "I thought we had agreed we would spend the time apart in contemplation."

It was all Kelson could do to make himself clasp his hands behind his back. "We had. But I, ah, hoped that this—departure from strict conformance with your habit," he nodded toward her veil, "might mean that—"

As he groped for words, she snared him with her eyes.

"Might mean what, my lord?" she whispered. "That my vocation as a religious is wavering? Well, it is. And I lied to you before, my lord. You *are* the cause of it."

He could feel his pulsebeat soar as the blood pounded in his ears, and he was not sure the words would come out as he gazed down into her eyes.

"Sweet, dear lady, don't toy with me," he breathed. "If I thought you were lying to me right now, I might not recover. And I won't chance finding out, either. Sometimes our powers tell us far *too* much."

"Do they tell you that I think I love you, Kelson Haldane?" she said softly. "Do they tell you that when I was arranging the greenery for your knight's vigil, I pretended it was for our nuptial celebrations?"

Slowly he brought his hands from behind him and raised them toward her face, daring to ease back the veil.

"There can be a *true* celebration of our nuptial vows at

the end of the summer, when I return," he whispered. "Is that what you want?"

"I—think so, my lord," she breathed. She raised one hand to brush her fingertips across his lips. "But we should not speak of it now. We—"

To keep any further protest from lessening that incredible admission, Kelson crushed his mouth to hers, her face between his hands. He could feel the sweet, aching rush of fire stirring in his loins as her lips parted under his, hesitant at first, then more bold, and he thrust his fingers deeper into her hair to draw her closer, both of them trembling. The motion dislodged the hairpins, and masses of blue-black hair tumbled down his hands, each strand an electric tingle across his skin.

"My lord, we mustn't," she managed to whisper, drawing back with a doe's frightened eyes, though her arms had slipped around his waist as they kissed and held him still.

Smiling, he pulled two great handfuls of her hair over her shoulders and buried his face in them briefly, inhaling of her perfume.

"What mustn't we do, my princess, my queen?" he murmured, raising his eyes to hers again and trailing a strand of her hair against her cheek. "Did you not just say that you think you love me? And most assuredly, I do love you."

"It's too soon," she whispered. "I must have more time to think. I never meant that we should make any promises until the end of summer, after we'd had the chance to consider—ah, my lord!"

While she made her protests, Kelson had allowed one hand to fiddle with the ties at the neck of her gown, at the same time nuzzling tiny kisses along her temples and eyelids. An opening parted in the fine blue wool, and he slipped his hand gently within to cup the curve of a breast.

"I told you before, I was not made of iron," he murmured.

"Nor am I," she said, withdrawing his hand but then kissing the back of it, still trembling. "But we must not do what both our hearts urge. Not now. Not here."

"Then, where, my heart, and when?" he insisted, breathing a kiss across her palm and brushing it with his tongue.

"I pledge you a king's love, Rothana. I would make you queen of my land as well as my heart."

Shaking her head, Rothana drew herself straighter with a sob and turned her hand so that it only clasped his, safe from his lips.

"My lord, I pray you, do not do this to me. You are a king, and may take what you please, where and when you will, but I am still under vows. I pray you to respect my habit."

Kelson smiled wistfully and brushed the back of his free hand against her veil, then against her cheek.

"Does one under vows take such a veil, my lady, or wear her hair so fetchingly tumbled?"

She swallowed and averted her eyes. "I should not have worn this veil, my lord. It was a vanity that I shall probably regret. I must repent me of it, when next I confess."

"Best not confess it to Father Duncan, then," Kelson murmured, smiling still, "for he has been my confessor for many years. If I tell him I wish to take you as my bride, he will give you a strict penance for enticing me thus."

She extricated her hand from his and pulled off her veil the rest of the way, giving it to him to hold while she half turned away to retie the neck of her habit.

"Father Duncan is no longer my confessor, my lord. Haven't you heard? The archbishop has forbidden him to confess anyone but you, Dhugal, and Morgan."

The revelation was like a dash of cold water in Kelson's face. He had wondered at Duncan's reticence to talk about his conversation with Cardiel after the privy council meeting. He could feel the ardor drain out of his body as if someone had pulled a plug as he straightened from picking up Rothana's fallen hairpins.

"What do you mean, he's forbidden it? Duncan isn't suspended."

"No, but he's been ordered to cease voluntarily all public function as a priest. Haven't you noticed that he's not celebrated Mass at the cathedral since Wednesday?"

Kelson watched numbly, almost hypnotized, as her fingers began plaiting the thick strands of hair that, not minutes before, had set every nerve atingle.

"But that's because he's supposed to be sick, so he won't

have to go to the synod," Kelson managed to say. "He said Mass this morning."

"Yes, for you, Dhugal, and Morgan, very early, in the Chapel Royal. Duchess Meraude told me. Didn't you wonder why no one else was there? It's Sunday, after all."

"Well, I—"

She coiled her braid neatly at the back of her head and secured it with the pins she took from Kelson.

"Of course you didn't. You're all excited about riding off on your quest for Saint Camber—and that's as it should be. He wouldn't want to spoil it for you. You've already agreed to address the synod, after all. What more could one ask?"

"I thought there wouldn't be any further repercussions yet," Kelson murmured. "No one has said anything all week."

"No, but you can be sure they're thinking it. Fortunately, Duncan is well liked and respected. And Dhugal may turn out to be an unexpected asset. A priest with a legitimate son is unusual enough that one who's also Deryni may not make that much difference to the average person. The bishops will have to grind through the process of officially changing the law, but that may not be before the end of Lent. They've got bishops to discipline and new ones to elect, after all."

As she put on her veil again, though she left her face uncovered, Kelson considered all that she had said.

"You're right," he murmured. "Now is not the time or place for us." He glanced at his feet, then looked up at her again.

"But when *will* be our time and place, Rothana? Did you mean what passed between us earlier, or were you only telling me what you thought I wanted to hear, to save your honor?"

She lowered her eyes and swallowed noisily. "What passed between us earlier was very real, my lord," she answered. "As for our time and place, I can only say that I— have already mentioned to my abbess that I begin to doubt my vocation. I'm sure she thinks it has to do with the attack on the abbey last summer. I have not told her the true reason or mentioned your name, of course."

Kelson allowed himself a smile, more relieved than he could say, and took both her hands in his, though he only held them close between them at chest level.

"The old harridan. When she finds out what or *who's* behind it, she'll probably think I've tried to compromise your virtue. Which I have—*tried*, at least—but what happens next? I'll tell her you wouldn't be swayed, if that will help."

A smile escaped Rothana's lips, but she would not look up at him, and he suddenly realized how difficult this must be for her.

"The next step is to ask for a dispensation from my vows," she said steadily. "I made them to the Bishop of Meara, who is dead and has no present successor, so my request can go directly to the archbishop. I am certain it will be granted without difficulty, especially when I tell him the true reason for my request."

Kelson allowed himself a wry chuckle. "Are you joking? There'll be dancing in the streets. They've been after me to marry again almost since they closed Sidana's tomb."

His face clouded as he saw Sidana's ring on his hand, and he wondered suddenly whether he dared to offer it to Rothana—as a pledge only, for he knew it would not do to seal even a promise of a second marriage with the symbol of old blood.

"What is it, my lord?" Rothana whispered.

"This ring you've always seen me wear," he murmured, rubbing his thumb over it, though he did not release her hands. "I—don't suppose you ever knew that it was Sidana's ring. I wore it initially to remind me of the vow I made to bring her murderers to justice. I've worn it since then to remind me that I wanted never again to have to wed for reasons of state. I wouldn't want you to wear it—and it's tainted with her blood—but if you're willing, I'd like you to keep it while I'm gone, as a sign that she and all of that are behind me."

"I am deeply moved, my lord," she said, searching his eyes with hers. "Are you sure you want to do this?"

"As sure as I am that I want you to be my wife when I return," he said, slipping the ring off his finger and holding it out to her. "Because of your vows, this isn't a betrothal or even a promise of betrothal, but it's my personal commitment to readdress the subject when we're both free to do so. And if, while I'm away, you should decide that you've changed your mind, that this was all just a pleasant flight of fancy wound up in the romance of knighthood and court intrigues, you have only to return the ring. No explanations will be necessary.''

He quirked her a wry smile to dispel her solemn expression as she took the ring and closed it in her fist.

"I have to qualify it that way, Rothana," he added, pausing to brush her closed hand with his lips. "I've done all of this without reckoning on God. Technically, you still belong to Him. And I won't compete with Him, despite the fact that I've already driven my own blood brother to blasphemy on the subject."

"Dhugal? Does he know?"

"More than I knew, until tonight," Kelson said. "No one else does, though."

"Well, they'll know if I don't soon rescue Sister Marian and go on to bed," Rothana whispered. "Not *yours,* my lord, though you sorely tempt me, despite my vows. And I mustn't miss the night Offices, or we shall have more than Dhugal suspicious."

"I could just *tell* Duncan and Alaric," Kelson ventured, folding her in his arms again and nuzzling at her throat. "They're going to know anyway, eventually."

"Eventually, but not tonight," she said, drawing back to look him in the eyes. "And not before you leave. I doubt not that they would keep their peace, my lord, but if it were to become known while I am still under vows, it could compromise my honor. Your bride must be virginal above reproach when she gives herself to you before God's altar."

Kelson sighed. Her logic was inescapable.

"Very well, then. Shall I see you tomorrow, before we leave?"

"Why, of course, my lord," she said gaily, giving him a chaste kiss on the cheek and drawing back farther, only her hands in his. "I shall be waving a kerchief with all the other ladies of the court, to wish the brave young knights Godspeed on their quest. And I shall pray for your safe and speedy return."

He stood there gazing at her for several heartbeats, then slowly nodded.

"I shall treasure the sight, my heart," he whispered. "But may I not hope for a more lingering kiss to last the summer long?"

Shyly she stepped toward him, their joined hands lifting

to either side but not separating, only their lips meeting between. It was a chaste kiss on the mouth, sweet and lingering after they had drawn apart, but no more. And Kelson was content as he watched her go. He stayed a few more minutes to breathe in the sharp chill of the night air to clear his senses, then himself headed off in the opposite direction, to rejoin Dhugal, Duncan, and Morgan.

And from a tiny window overlooking the garden, Conall sipped at a goblet of rich, red wine and observed all with more than passing interest—and had seen almost the entire exchange, though even near-Deryni senses could not discern what was said.

The actions had been clear enough, however—clear enough for Conall to decide that *he* would not have drawn back when Kelson had, sparing Rothana her virtue. Were it he instead of Kelson in the garden darkness with Rothana, he would even now be enjoying her lithe, sweet body, making it tremble beneath his, taking her as his own in a way that even her vows could not set aside, if he then demanded that she accept his suit of marriage or else face having her dishonor made public.

For it was Rothana on whom Conall had set his sights, since escorting her and her sister nuns back from Cùilteine the previous summer; and it was Rothana whom he meant to wed, however he could, regardless of what dear Cousin Kelson might desire.

As he tossed off the rest of his wine and prepared to go to his own assignation, he wondered whether Tiercel had some means of encouraging a lady's affections—though Conall knew that influencing a Deryni woman would involve far more risk than bending any mere human quarry to his will. He had done *that* before, starting with Vanissa and not ending with several serving maids and ladies of the court.

But Rothana—here was a bride fit for a prince, and especially for a prince now nearly Deryni. And if Conall could, he meant to win her openly, perhaps right from under the nose of Kelson. Neither he nor the king would be able to pursue the matter for the next few months, but when they returned . . .

He heard the bells in the basilica ringing Compline and he pulled a dark cloak over his indoor attire. It was time to meet his mentor. Tiercel had promised an extraordinary lesson for tonight, surpassing anything Conall had experienced before.

And after that, Conall would see about Tiercel procuring him a bride.

CHAPTER EIGHT

Teach me, and I will hold my tongue.

—Job 6:24

Conall tried to put out of mind what he had seen as he made his way toward the library, where he was to meet Tiercel. Fantasies of bedding the fair Rothana were not conducive to the kind of concentration his mentor usually demanded of him, and he had no idea what to expect from tonight's session. Tiercel's message had said only to be in the library an hour after Compline. It was not one of their usual meeting places, but Conall had come to expect the unusual when dealing with Deryni.

The library was still and quiet as Conall entered—but he knew he was a little early. Shielding his rushlight with a cupped hand, he paused a moment with his back to the closed door to look around. He did not come here often. Reading held little interest for Conall unless it concerned military strategy and tactics. His Uncle Brion had amassed a fair collection of scrolls and bound books on such subjects, several of which Conall had nearly memorized by now, but Kelson's tastes ran more to histories and, increasingly, to obscure esoteric subjects—though, in light of what Conall had been learning recently, perhaps some of them were not as obscure as Conall first had thought.

Kelson had even expanded the library since Brion's time, cutting a connecting doorway through to an adjacent room to house his growing collection. Conall remembered the up-roar, two winters ago, when Kelson had had the work done, breaking through the thick interior wall and then sealing off the new room's former door from the outside corridor, so that access could only be had through the library. It seemed a great deal of trouble, when the library simply could have been moved to larger quarters, but perhaps Kelson wanted to retain the link with his father. Conall could understand that.

What he did not understand was why Tiercel had instructed him to come here rather than one of their usual rendezvous points. So far as he knew, Tiercel had never ventured into the keep before; it was far too risky, even for a skilled Deryni who could make guards forget he had passed.

Still puzzled, but impatient now, Conall moved on between the rows of shelves, heading for the second chamber. That was probably a better place to wait, just in case anyone came looking for some late-night reading. The temperature seemed to drop as he drew aside the heavy curtain across the connecting doorway and ducked to go through, but the feeling passed as he straightened on the other side. Shelves had been added across the opposite wall since he last had been here, but the room was still barer than he had expected. He also thought he was alone until a silvery glow suddenly flared in the deep window embrasure and Tiercel stepped out, only his face visible against the dark stuff of his hooded cloak, lit by the sphere of handfire in his gloved left hand.

"Oh, so you *are* here," Conall murmured, turning to face him squarely.

"Yes, but not for long—either of us. Someone might come. Besides, I have important things to show you tonight."

"All right. Where do you want to go? Dhugal's room has that secret passage that can let you out in the castle yard or even outside the keep, if it comes to that. He'll never know. He and Duncan are dining with Morgan in Kelson's apartments. When I get back from the progress, I mean to speak to Kelson about that room. *I* should have had it, not Dhugal."

Tiercel's grin flashed in the shadow of his hood.

"Ah, Duncan's dining with the king, is he? Good. That

eliminates one potential problem. Blow out your rushlight and put it over in that niche. You won't need it where we're going."

The instruction gave Conall a twinge of apprehension, but he did as Tiercel ordered. When he turned back, the Deryni lord had pulled off one glove with his teeth and was hunkered down in the middle of the floor, brushing his bare hand over one of the stone flags. His handfire still hovered at head level above him.

"What are you doing?" Conall murmured, coming closer to crouch beside Tiercel.

"Do you see the edges of this flagstone?" Tiercel said, with an amused glance up at Conall. "Notice that it's the only completely square one here in the center of the room."

"Yes. Why?"

"Lay your hands flat inside the square and tell me what you feel."

Without answering, Conall obeyed.

"It tingles," he murmured, quickly shifting one hand outside the square to compare the difference, then putting it back beside the other. "There's magic here, isn't there? What does it do?"

"That, my friend, is a Transfer Portal," Tiercel said, standing and dusting his hand against his leather-clad thigh as Conall did the same. "It's a Deryni way of getting somewhere in a hurry. More specifically, that's *the* Transfer Portal that Charissa used to gain access to the library the night before your cousin Kelson's coronation. Morgan and Duncan found it a couple of years ago. That's why all this was done." He gestured around him to indicate the room.

"In any case, I felt you ought to know about such things, so I've decided to give you your first taste of Portal travel tonight—and as sort of a reward for your hard work all winter. It isn't something I ordinarily recommend just for recreational purposes, since it does use energy, especially if one has to go very far, but there are three I'd like to show you here in Rhemuth, all quite close. This is the first."

Conall glanced at the innocuous-looking flagstone again. He had heard his father and Morgan speak of Portals before and had a vague notion what they did, but he had never seen one and certainly had never suspected there was one right here in the library.

"Whenever I've heard of Portals, I've always pictured a door," he murmured. "There's nothing here but a square on the floor."

Tiercel smiled. "Oh, there's far more than that, my practical young friend. Stand here in front of me, inside the boundary of the square, and close your eyes. There isn't going to be anything to see, anyway."

He quenched the handfire as he guided Conall into place and set his hands on the younger man's shoulders from behind, standing close and shifting one hand farther around Conall's neck to span lightly across the carotid pulse points with the vee of his thumb and first two fingers.

"Go ahead. Close your eyes. And let down your shields. This first time, all I want you to do is relax as much as you can and let your mind be as still as possible. I'll do the rest. The first time, the sensation of the actual jump is a little startling, but you mustn't fight it or me. If you do, I'll have to help you along. Relax now."

Though Conall did as he was directed, stilling his mind easily under his mentor's guidance, he still could feel his heartbeat pulsating under the increasing pressure of Tiercel's fingers. But then, in a sudden, sickening swoop of vertigo that made him clutch instinctively at Tiercel's arm to keep from falling, the pressure was released and he was staggering against Tiercel's body, trying to catch his balance, and they were closely surrounded by walls, about where the outline of the Portal square would have been if they were still on it—but they were not.

"Easy," Tiercel murmured, close beside his left ear. "You're fine. We're now in a Portal that opens into Father Duncan's old study, adjoining the basilica."

He conjured handfire practically in front of Conall's nose, causing the startled prince to recoil harder against him for just a second, then reached out to finger a barely noticeable stud projecting from one of the corner stones lining the chamber. Instantly, the wall to their left withdrew with a soft sigh, revealing a heavy tapestry curtain which Tiercel pushed aside with his forearm as he stepped through and gestured for Conall to follow. The silvery glow of Tiercel's handfire lit the room eerily, but Conall recognized it as soon as he had crossed the threshold.

"I know this room," he murmured. "When Kelson and I were children, Father Duncan used to hear our confessions in here sometimes. I haven't been here in years."

"It's a very old part of the basilica building," Tiercel replied. "If you've ever wondered why Duncan never moved his study to some more convenient location, as he rose in rank, now you know. There's something else you should see, since we're here."

Crossing softly to the prie-dieu set facing the corner to their right, Tiercel dropped to one knee and ran his hand tentatively under the arm rest. His touch caused something to move behind the tapestry covering the Portal entrance.

"Go ahead and have a look," he said, at Conall's questioning expression. "Other than ourselves and the Council, I doubt more than half a dozen people even know it's there. This is where they brought your father to set his potential, and presumably where they'd bring you, if it ever came to that."

It was a tiny, ancient chapel, only half the size of the study. The warm red gleam of a Presence lamp hanging to the left of a narrow altar gave only a vague suggestion of the dark crucifix suspended above, though it reflected more brightly from tiny giltwork stars studding the blue-painted wall behind the altar. And as Tiercel pressed past him and moved farther into the chapel with his handfire, to bend his knee briefly in prayer, Conall could see that the walls were decorated with frescoes depicting the lives of saints. Though Conall himself rarely felt the need for any outward religious observance, he, too, knelt and bowed his head, waiting until Tiercel had crossed himself and stood before doing the same.

"I hope you made a petition to Saint Camber," Tiercel said, turning to face him, "because this chapel was once sacred to him." He nudged the handfire higher and stood with his hands on his hips as he looked around again. "I suppose that's why Duncan and his friends are so fond of it. I confess, I rather like it myself. I hope your quest is successful. I'd like to see the day when Camber can claim his proper veneration in the open again."

"Why, because he was Deryni?" Conall asked, a little uneasy at this talk of saints.

"Partly that. I think he would have been a great man even

if he hadn't been Deryni, though. And maybe he'd have kept his sainthood longer, too.''

He grinned and called his handfire to hand with a snap of his fingers as he indicated it was time to leave.

"In any case, you have that adventure ahead of you, and we should be about showing you more of Portals. I'll take you through under my control again," he said, closing the chapel door behind them before guiding Conall back into the Portal chamber with one hand on his shoulder, "but I'll let you experience the jump in its full glory this time, now that you know what to expect.

"Before we go, though, I want you to close your eyes and probe this Portal. Be aware of what it feels like. Every one of them is slightly different, or we wouldn't know where we were going. And one almost has to have been to a particular Portal in order to go to it unassisted—either that, or else get a *very* specific image from someone else who's been there. Notice everything you can about this one and commit it to memory. I'll verify, when you're done."

Obediently, Conall closed his eyes and cast out with his mind to the Portal beneath his feet. Now that he knew what to look for, he could feel its tingle even through his boots, and it *did* feel different from the one in the library.

He let his heightened senses mull the feeling for several seconds, classifying everything he could about what made it feel different, then opened his eyes and glanced over his shoulder at Tiercel, still holding the images for his mentor's inspection.

"Good," Tiercel breathed. "You shouldn't have any trouble getting back here if you needed to." He quenched the handfire with a thought, but his mind was still wrapped around Conall's.

"Now we'll go to the next one. It's in the sacristy at the cathedral—which we'll hope is unoccupied at this hour; but if it isn't, I'll bounce us right back here before you or whoever's there even realizes something's happened. That's another good reason for me to keep control, even if you knew where we were going."

Tiercel's control this time was more a melding of their perceptions than an actual taking over, so Conall was able to follow the process with far more understanding as Tiercel seized and balanced the energies, then bent them just—so. And apparently there was no one in the sacristy, for Tiercel conjured handfire again, as soon as he had assured himself of Conall's well-being and released his mind.

"Have you been *here* before?" Tiercel whispered, glancing casually around the little room as Conall did the same.

"I don't think so."

"Well, it doesn't matter. Have a look at what you're standing on. This one is marked out in the floor mosaic. Do you see the squared cross motif?"

As Tiercel backed off a few steps and nudged the handfire closer to the floor, Conall crouched to look. By appearance, the square was but one of many, all very similar, but his heightened senses told another story altogether as he ran his fingertips along the design's perimeter.

"That's right. You've found the physical marker for this one," Tiercel murmured. "Now take a few minutes to file away this location, the way you did the other. You're really taking to this far more easily than I had feared. I keep underestimating your talents."

"I have a good teacher," Conall said with a grin, in rare compliment.

"Hmmm, we'll see how good he is when you try the jump yourself for the first time. Do you think you've got this one?"

Opening his shields to the other, Conall said, "See for yourself."

"Very good. How about seeing if you can get back to the one in the study now. You haven't quite got the library squared away, since you didn't know what you were looking for when we started out, so there's nowhere you can end up except here or in the study. Are you game to try it?"

"By myself?" Conall squeaked.

Tiercel grinned. "Well, it's safer than having you try to take me through, too. Only one person can control the operation—and if it's you, I'd only be a hindrance anyway. I'll follow right behind, as soon as you've gone. Just don't move physically at the other end, until I get there."

Conall drew a deep breath. "You're sure I'm ready?"

"Have I asked you yet to do something you weren't ready to do?"

"No."

"Then I suppose you must be ready."

Conall exhaled slowly and stood, aware of Tiercel watching intently. He did not need to look down at his feet to know he was standing squarely on the Portal. He could feel it tingling beneath his feet, vibrant and alive. He summoned up the memory of the other Portal's location, brought it into balance with the one he was standing on, then glanced at Tiercel uncertainly. The Deryni did not appear to have done anything to prepare.

"Just—go?" Conall asked.

"Did you want a royal fanfare?" Tiercel countered, with a wry grin.

Conall did not answer that. Instead, he closed his eyes and drew another deep breath, linking in with the energies beneath his feet the way Tiercel had done and then bending them to where he wanted to go. And then he was staggering in darkness again, and a split second later, Tiercel's arms were bracing him around his shoulders, the warmth of his congratulation wrapping him like a mantle as he realized they were back in the study Portal again.

"Well done!" Tiercel whispered in his ear. "Oh, well done! How do you feel?"

"A little—giddy," Conall said. He could feel himself grinning ear to ear like an idiot. "I *did* do it, didn't I?"

"Does this look like the cathedral sacristy?" Tiercel countered, making his handfire flare brightly around them to reveal familiar stone walls.

"Let's do it again," Conall said happily. "That was so quick, I hardly got to realize what had happened."

"No, we'll not risk going back to the sacristy," Tiercel said. "Besides, I told you that this uses energy. We'll go back to the library, so you can memorize that location, and then, *maybe*, I'll let you bounce us both back here one more time. I'll need to get home when we're done, after all. And you'll need a good night's sleep to be able to ride out in the morning. I suppose you'll have a lot to think about, at any rate."

"That's for certain," Conall agreed.

He let Tiercel take control again for the jump back to the

library Portal. He was less disoriented this time and was able to kneel immediately to finish assimilating the characteristics of this location. And when he had done it to Tiercel's satisfaction, he asked whether *he* might control the return.

"I can do it, I *know* I can," he pleaded.

"I don't know," said Tiercel. "It's much harder, taking through someone else's mass besides your own. I don't want you to exhaust yourself."

"So you can use that fatigue-banishing spell on me if you have to, or give me something from your trusty drug satchel. I can do it, Tiercel, I know I can. Please let me try. If I have any trouble at all, I'll let you take over."

Tiercel sighed. "Oh, very well. I can leave from there as well as here, after we've gathered up the loose ends. I want you to promise to return through the secret passageway, though, after I've left, rather than coming through the Portal again on your own. I'm serious about the energy drain."

"I promise."

It felt odd to be taking the active part. As Conall moved closer to Tiercel and set his hand on the other's wrist, making the physical contact necessary to ease the control, he sent his mind cautiously against Tiercel's shields, starting a little when the primaries dropped immediately and exposed the control levels necessary.

"Ease up a little," Tiercel said, closing his eyes and drawing a deep breath to make it easier for Conall. "With someone who knows what to expect, you don't need as tight a control."

Conall obeyed, taking a few seconds to shift everything into balance with the energies pulsing beneath their feet, then paused.

"Do it," Tiercel whispered. "Don't leave us hanging here all night."

Conall did, and they were back in the niche in the study. He felt a slight flicker of impatience when he was a little slow releasing Tiercel, but he did not try to hold the control. Tiercel sighed as he conjured handfire again and opened the door so they could go into the room.

"You certainly did it," he said. "Conall, I'm proud of you. Have a seat." He waved his hand in front of the door leading from the study—setting wards, Conall knew, to warn against potential discovery—and pulled a chair from under the table set before the dark fireplace. He passed a hand over a candlestick there as he sat, and the candle flared to life immediately. Tiercel quenched his handfire as soon as the wick had caught.

"I hope that wasn't too rough," Conall said, sitting opposite. "I didn't mean to make you uncomfortable."

"No matter. You were trying to juggle a lot of things at once. One expects a few training scars for the trainer as well as the trainee."

Conall nodded. "I suppose so."

"Anyway, that's about all the work I'd planned for tonight—and you did far better than I'd expected. You *will* need a good night's sleep, though. I wasn't joking about the energy drain. One doesn't normally jump more than two or three times in a twenty-four hour period, and we've done—what?—four, five? And I came to you from—well, farther away than any of these—and will need to get home. Fortunately, all of *our* jumps were close together."

"And where *is* home, Tiercel?" Conall replied, asking a question he had been wanting to ask for months. "Where do you go, after we've met?"

Grinning, Tiercel shifted his satchel into his lap, easing the strap across his shoulder. "Lately, at least off and on, home has been a set of lodgings in the city. But there's no Portal there. I'm sorry, but I can't tell you where my real home is."

Conall shrugged. "Well, I didn't think you would, but I had to ask. Are there many Portals?"

"Not a great many, no. I'm aware of a few dozen—but they're not all accessible to me. For security reasons, some are attuned to the use of only selected individuals, or they have special warding at the other end to keep a user from leaving the immediate vicinity of the Portal until the owner authorizes it. And then there are Trap Portals that will prevent an intruder from jumping back out of an unauthorized Portal until the owner releases him. That may not sound particularly dangerous, but suppose the one in this room were trapped, and we'd come into it while Duncan was on campaign last summer? A person could starve."

"Good Lord, can you tell, before you jump, whether a Portal is trapped?" Conall asked, aghast.

"Sometimes. Sometimes not. It depends on the skill of the trapper and the trappee—which I hope will give you pause before trying any of this on your own, if you should find any Portals on your journey. As I said earlier, I don't recommend Transfer Portals for recreational purposes."

Conall swallowed and nodded.

"That Portal in the library, then—it can't be a Trap, because we wouldn't have been able to use it, but—is it warded to keep someone from leaving the vicinity? Is that why you haven't used it to come to me before?"

"*Very* good," Tiercel said, nodding approval, "though you haven't got it exactly right. There's warding involved, but it's on the passageway connecting the Portal room with the old library. I'm surprised you didn't sense it when you came through."

Conall thought back, remembering the slight change in temperature he had felt.

"Was that a ward? But I walked right through."

"Yes, because you're a Haldane. Kelson and his friends set up that very specific ward to permit my fellow Councilors to use the library resources, but to keep us out of the rest of the castle unannounced. After Charissa, one can certainly understand his reasoning. In any case, the only way I could have left that room was the way we did or else for you to take me through under your shields. It isn't a foolproof situation, but it serves the purpose."

"And that's all been done *since* Charissa," Conall added.

"Correct."

Conall mulled that for a moment, but Charissa made him think of Rothana. He wondered whether he dared ask Tiercel about another kind of magic—far more ancient, he suspected, than even the Portal knowledge.

"Tiercel, can I ask you something, one man to another?"

"Certainly."

"Tiercel, do you—have any love potions in that satchel of yours? Or do you know any love spells?"

"Love spells?"

"Don't you dare laugh!" Conall muttered, his tone so deadly serious that the smile beginning on Tiercel's face immediately disappeared.

"Why, what do you want with love spells?" Tiercel asked, after a few seconds. "Your lady loves you already. She's carrying your child, she—"

"She is *not* my lady," Conall said coldly. "She's my mistress. The fact that she carries my child is incidental. I could never marry Vanissa."

"Ah, then you mean to *marry* the object of your affections—except that I gather she does not return your advances."

"Don't use that tone with me," Conall snapped. "She would if it weren't for—no matter about *that*. But, she's my perfect match, Tiercel," he went on plaintively. "I danced with her after my knighting. She was like a feather in my arms. Her touch made the blood pound in my head—"

"It made all your brains fall into your crotch!" Tiercel muttered. "Conall, do you take me for a fool? Even if I had a love spell or some magical potion that I could give you, don't you realize how unethical that is?"

"I want her love, Tiercel! I'm a prince. I don't care what it takes—"

"It can't be bought, Conall. Don't you understand? It's worthless unless it comes of free will. A man named Rimmell found that out the hard way, and two other innocent people paid for his folly with their lives. Morgan's sister, and Kevin McLain," he added, at Conall's belligerent look of question. "And it was a 'love spell,' as you so quaintly put it—actually, a 'love charm.' God, I would have thought you'd grown beyond such peasant nonsense!"

"Don't you dare patronize me!"

"My, we *are* agitated about this, aren't we?" Tiercel murmured, shooting out a hand to block Conall as the prince lurched angrily to his feet and took a swing at him.

Conall's continued hostility made Tiercel come half to his feet himself as he caught the prince's wrist and gave it a deft twist, forcing the younger man back into his chair with a *whoof* of pain. Raging at his physical helplessness, Conall even made a tentative mental foray against Tiercel's shields. The shields held, but not without far more effort on Tiercel's part than he had expected, and he wrapped a blanketing lock around Conall's shields in return, hardly able to believe the other's strength and determination.

"Let it go, Conall," he ordered, not letting up on his wrist lock as the prince continued to fight him, both with body and with mind. "Give it up! I don't want to hurt you. This is a stupid argument. I couldn't give you a love spell if I wanted to. I don't know any. *Will* you stop it?"

The fight seemed to go out of Conall all in an instant. With a little groan, he collapsed across the table and buried his face in his free arm, all resistance gone, so that Tiercel nearly staggered physically from the sudden yielding before his pressure.

"Easy," Tiercel whispered, as he edged around to Conall's side of the table, keeping contact with mind and one hand, until he could help the trembling Conall to sit up.

The prince's primary shields had collapsed at his surrender, under the pressure of Tiercel's blanketing lock, but the secondaries held as Tiercel tried a stronger probe, shielding what lay in the deeper levels of consciousness that Tiercel himself had sequestered off, months ago, to protect the knowledge of what he and Conall did from detection by Morgan or Duncan or any of the other Deryni at court. Now Tiercel wondered what was going on in there and what *had* been going on in there, since last he'd had free access to Conall's mind. He did not like the flash of willfulness he had just seen; and Conall's unexpected strength could be cause for even greater concern.

"Do you mind telling me what that was all about?" he said softly, avoiding Conall's eyes as he continued to probe what he could.

"I'm sorry," Conall whispered. "I don't know what came over me. I guess I lost my temper."

"I guess you did," Tiercel replied. "Do you think it's going to happen again?"

Conall managed a careful smile and shook his head, drawing back from Tiercel's touch, and the Deryni lord withdrew.

"All right. I'll accept your apology—but on one condition."

"What's that?"

"I think I ought to do a very deep probe on you tonight. I want to find out what made you react the way you did. We'll go back to your own rooms, so I can give you a sedative and not have to worry about how you're going to get back. You'll sleep the better for it anyway, after all that's happened."

Conall swallowed visibly. "I said I was sorry."

"So you did," Tiercel said, setting a hand under Conall's elbow to assist him to his feet. "And so am I—because it's partially my fault for letting you overextend—too much Portal travel, all at once. For that reason, we'll go back through the secret passageway rather than risking another Portal jump."

He was glad Conall did not ask what would happen if Tiercel did not like the result of the deep probe, for Tiercel did not know himself. Neither of them said anything else as they set the room in order and Tiercel released the guard ward on the door so they could leave, but the incident continued to trouble Tiercel as he and Conall slipped out of the study, locking the door behind them and making their way out of the basilica. Conall's insistence on arcane assistance to win the lady of his desire touched on something Tiercel could not quite isolate; something said in Council, perhaps; something very important.

They were deep in the heart of the keep, climbing a narrow stair by the light of Tiercel's handfire, Conall leading, when the answer finally came to Tiercel.

"Rothana," he murmured, stopping dead in his tracks to stare at Conall in disbelief as the prince whirled on him with stark panic in his grey Haldane eyes. "Arilan talked about her only days ago. It's Rothana you've taken a fancy to—*and you know that Kelson wants her*. It's your goddamn jealousy again!"

But he got no further with his accusation, because suddenly Conall, in a blind rage, was shoving him backwards down the narrow stair.

Too startled even to cry out, Tiercel tried to break his fall, to catch himself against the narrow walls with outstretched arms. But his cloak tangled between his legs and tripped him worse as Conall, instantly sobered, tried to catch him. The Deryni lord went over backwards, his handsome face contorting as the back of his head smacked against a stair tread. His open mouth, gaping in a soundless cry of agony, was the last thing Conall saw of him as he tumbled into the curve of the stairwell to disappear in the darkness.

After a few seconds, the frantic sound of scrabbling, of flesh and bone thudding dully against stone, was punctuated by a hollow, sickening snap and then replaced by an all too total silence. And then, where Tiercel had been standing when it all began, the handfire left hanging there flickered, then faded and was no more, leaving Conall standing terrified in the darkness, alone.

CHAPTER NINE

*An inheritance may be gotten hastily at the
beginning; but the end thereof shall not be blessed.*
—Proverbs 20:21

"Tiercel?" Conall squeaked, not daring to move as utter
darkness pressed in on him from every side. "Tiercel, are
you all right?"

No answer—and the heavy silence, underlined by darkness, made Conall's already racing heart pound even faster.

"Tiercel?" he repeated, more softly this time.

When still no answer came, Conall made himself take
several deep, ragged breaths and cupped his hands to conjure
handfire. The light grew slowly in his trembling hands, ruddy
and uncertain until he forced more control on his growing
panic. He tried not to think about what he might find at the
bottom of the stairs.

He kept his handfire cupped in one hand as he began his
tentative descent, fearing with each step to see what lay
around the curve of the stairwell, until at last, just before
the landing of the next level down, he saw a boot, a leg, and
a tangle of russet cloak. Somehow he managed to scramble
over the motionless form without repeating Tiercel's mishap,
but he knew, even before he crouched by Tiercel's lolling
head, that the man was dead.

Conall choked back a whimper as he gently lifted Tiercel's
head to see if there could be some mistake, but the slack
movement only confirmed his worst fear. Tiercel's neck was
broken. The supple mind that had roused him to undreamed
of potentials was stilled forever, the almond-colored eyes

135

already filming over, sightless, the formerly impenetrable shields already half-gone as the physical processes of death continued.

Dear God, what had he done? And worse, what was he going to do? He dared not go for help—not that anyone could help Tiercel de Claron now. Tiercel's death had been an accident, but who would believe it? Conall *had* pushed him, and they *had* quarreled. If that came to light—and it would, under close interrogation by any Deryni, along with the reason for the quarrel—not only would Conall lose all chance of eventually winning out over Kelson for Rothana's hand, but his magical connections with Tiercel over the past year would be discovered, the latter with potentially far worse consequence than merely being bested at the chancy game of love.

He dared not confess, then. If, on the other hand, he simply left the body where it was—or, better yet, dragged it the rest of the way down to the next landing and left it in the shadows to one side—days or even weeks might pass before anyone discovered it. Maybe even months.

And when the body eventually *was* found, why should anyone suspect Conall? He didn't think anyone was aware that he even knew about the secret passageway. And it connected with Dhugal's rooms, after all. Let someone else figure out what the Deryni Tiercel had been doing here.

The plan was not the best of all possible solutions, perhaps, but it seemed workable. When Conall had dragged the body the short distance to the next landing, he took great care to arrange things so that it looked as if the dead man could have tumbled into that position by falling all the way down the stairs. Tiercel's russet cloak blended well with the shadows, so that any passerby not actually looking for something unusual probably would never notice him. Not until the body began to decompose, of course—but Conall would be well gone on the royal progress before that happened.

One thing he did do, before setting the final touches to the scenario, and that was to remove the leather satchel that the Deryni lord had always brought to their sessions. A quick search confirmed that the coveted ward cubes were there in their pouch, and some of the drugs might come in very handy. Perhaps a little *merasha* in someone's wine. . .

He shook off such thoughts as he knelt a moment longer beside the dead man, searching again for any visual clues that might betray him and reviewing whether he had left anything undone.

"I'm sorry, Tiercel," he murmured under his breath, preparing to retreat into the darkness. "I'm sorry you had to die unshriven, too. That would have mattered to you, wouldn't it? I wonder, did you make your last prayer to your precious Saint Camber, there in the chapel?"

But as he bent closer self-consciously to trace a cross on the dead man's brow, mildly regretting the uncharitable thought about Camber, his mind brushed the surface of Tiercel's disintegrating shields, the memory dissolving beyond, and a daring idea came to him.

He had Tiercel's legacy of the ward cubes and the Deryni drugs, some of which he knew how to use to continue his psychic growth on his own. And he had his training. But what if he could learn even more by trying to read what was left in Tiercel's mind? He had seen Kelson try it on a dying man, and extend the reading beyond death—with very useful results. The man had not been Deryni, but with Tiercel's shields gone, did that matter? And to gain the secrets of a full Deryni lord, and a member of the Camberian Council, at that—

He did not pause to consider further. How much might already have slipped away, gone beyond all possible hope of retrieval, while Conall attended to the mundane details of making good his escape? Calling on all the skills he possessed, he wrapped his shields tightly around the fading, shifting knot of energy that was Tiercel's essence and probed deep, bypassing the trivial memories of Tiercel's day-to-day living and seizing only on those things that had to do with being Deryni—ritual procedures, outright spells, mental exercises, methods of arcane combat, snatches of Tiercel's interaction with the Camberian Council, with which, apparently he often had been at odds. . . .

There was too much to assimilate with any real understanding, and few items were really complete—*damn*, why had Conall not thought of this sooner?—but any additional knowledge was better than none at all. He could sort it all out later, when he had some leisure. He read all he could, until his knees ached and the body was cold beneath his hands and he could take no more of contact with the increasingly fragmented impressions that were all that remained. He avoided, once he had touched them, those final and most recent memories—the horrified disbelief as Tiercel fell, the pain, and then the final darkness putting an end to all future. He was sweating as he withdrew from Tiercel's mind for the last time, his whole body shaking with fatigue and sheer after-reaction, but he managed to pull himself together as he stood.

Well, Tiercel, I fear you've taught me far more than you ever intended, he thought, throwing his cloak back on his shoulders to cool off a little as he prepared to go on up the stairs. *But I'll try to put the knowledge to good use. Fare thee well in the next life, at least—if there is a next life.*

By the time Conall reached the hidden entrance to Dhugal's apartments, voices were conversing on the other side—servants packing Dhugal's things for tomorrow, Conall gathered—so Conall retraced his steps to let himself out into the castle yard near the basilica. As he passed the landing where Tiercel's body lay, he was pleased to note that even he had to look closely to see anything amiss—and he knew what to look for.

The yard before the basilica was dark and deserted as he left the secret passageway and secured the entrance behind him. En route, he had considered trying to use the Portal in Duncan's study to get back to the library, but only briefly. Conall was certain he could do it again, properly rested; but aside from the risk that someone else might be in the library, even at this late hour, Tiercel already had been concerned about Conall overextending—and Conall had pushed himself far beyond that to read Tiercel's memories, not to mention the sheer emotional and physical expense of the entire incident. Best not to risk losing all, when he had gained so much.

No, best simply to walk around through the parade ground and stable yard and let himself into the apartment wing through a side door—or go through the great hall, if too many nosy guards were about. If stopped, he could always come up with an appropriate excuse—he had gone out for a stroll or to check the horses for the journey tomorrow. The guard had not seen him leave? Why, he must have passed before the guard changed.

It would work. He was confident it would. Shifting Tiercel's satchel around behind him, so that only the strap could be seen across his chest, Conall made his way back to his rooms as planned, whistling snatches of an old R'Kassan love song under his breath.

"Dhugal, I feel the complete fool," Kelson said the next morning, as his foster brother helped him finish dressing for their departure. "I was holding a beautiful woman in my arms last night and all I did was kiss her. If I'd pressed the matter, who knows where it might have ended, but she stopped me—and I let her."

Dhugal, brightly decked out in MacArdry tartan and border leathers, perched himself casually on one of the trunks in Kelson's dressing room, uncoiling the belt wrapped around Kelson's sword while the king buckled a white belt over crimson riding leathers.

"Goodness, such self control," he teased, noticing but not mentioning that Kelson no longer wore Sidana's ring. "Do I know the lady in question?"

"What do *you* think?"

Snatching his sword and belt from Dhugal and buckling them on over the white belt, Kelson let Dhugal lay a hooded, fur-lined riding cloak over his shoulders, thrusting his arms through the front slits and turning so Dhugal could snap the clasp at his throat.

"I think," said Dhugal, after reflection, "that my brother the king is in love—and that the lady will never be a nun. And seeing that you have given her a ring—"

"I didn't exactly give her a ring," Kelson said.

"No? Your finger says otherwise."

Kelson glanced at his bare finger, at the white stripe left untanned, and immediately began rummaging in a jewel cask.

"Well, it wasn't what it might appear," he murmured. "I didn't give it to her in that sense. We've made no promises. She's—keeping the ring for me, as a token that I've put Sidana behind me. She isn't going to wear it."

"No?"

"No."

Fishing a small, emerald-set band out of the jewel box, Kelson jammed it onto the finger in question, then snatched up a pair of black leather gloves and a fur-lined riding cap. The cap had a circlet worked around the crown in metallic stitchery, gold against crimson kidskin, far more comfortable for denoting his rank than a coronet would be. When he had put on the cap, he stood glaring at Dhugal for several seconds, snapping his bunched gloves against his thigh in annoyance. Then he grinned, shook his head, and began laughing helplessly.

"Why, was it something I said?" Dhugal asked, all the wide-eyed innocent.

Still laughing, Kelson shook his head.

"This is stupid. Virgin knights are supposed to have an advantage on quests. Especially holy quests. So why am I so upset that I *am* one?"

Sheepishly, Dhugal ducked his head to glance at his boots, then back at Kelson. "If you are, then that makes two of us," he said quietly.

"*You*?" Kelson gasped. "But, I thought—"

"Oh, I talk a good line," Dhugal admitted. "And for a while, I thought that the Earl of Carthane's daughter and I, the other night—"

His sly wink and the eloquence in his shrug spoke far more revealingly than words ever could have, and for several seconds both he and Kelson laughed uproariously.

"Good God, *two* virgin knights," Kelson gasped, when either of them could speak again. "I thought I surely must be the last. And old Carthane's daughter. Lord in heaven, you're playing with fire, man! He'd kill you if he ever found out! The way he guards that girl—"

"Well, he wasn't guarding her well enough to keep me from claiming a kiss," Dhugal replied, wiping tears of mirth from his eyes. "I think Conall managed to steal one, too. He may have managed even more."

Kelson's grin turned to a chortle as he pulled on his gloves. "Conall. Now there's one I'm afraid is fated to fail this quest miserably, if virginity really *is* a prerequisite. Tell me, has anyone ever actually seen this leman of his? Is she pretty?"

"I dunno. One presumes his squire has seen her. What's his name? Jowan? Unfortunately the lad's deadly dull and discreet." A wicked grin came across Dhugal's face. "We could ask him, though—I mean, really *ask* him. . . ."

"And if I didn't trounce you for that kind of foolishness, your father would—or should," Kelson retorted, with a wry look of disapproval that quickly changed back to mirthful speculation. "Seriously, though, we could ask Jowan in more usual ways. He's got to know something. And maybe we could Truth-Read him, just a little . . . Conall certainly comes back tired often enough."

They were still snickering about it as they went out to meet the rather boisterous party forming up in the yard. They raised gloved hands in greeting to Morgan and Duncan, who were watching indulgently from the great hall steps with Nigel, Meraude, and other senior members of the court; but they had said their good-byes to family the night before, and Duncan had celebrated a special Mass, just for the four of them, right at dawn. Jehana and her chaplain, Father Ambros, stood apart from the others, and Kelson and Dhugal both paused to make the queen a dutiful salute, but their attention was soon caught by Conall, as they continued on toward their horses.

Kelson elbowed Dhugal in the side and tried to keep from laughing again, for a grouchy and bleary-eyed Conall was railing at his squire for some unknown offense. Prince Rory, who would captain a band of younger squires and pages as an escort for the first few miles, sharing the excitement, looked totally disenchanted with his elder brother, and young Prince Payne appeared to be on the verge of tears.

"My, my, touchy this morning, isn't he?" Kelson whispered. "What did I tell you? Look at the circles under his eyes."

"Aye, no virgin knight, *he*," Dhugal murmured in return, as they mounted up. "That's lack of sleep, an' for sure. He probably sneaked out last night for one last assignation with his lady-love."

"I don't doubt that you're right," Kelson replied, as he gathered up his red leather reins. "While I check on our baggage train and see what mischief the squires have managed to work, do you want to see if you can cheer up poor Payne and Rory? Other than my grumpy cousin, this is beginning to take on the appearance of a circus, rather than the dignified departure of a holy quest."

Dhugal laughed aloud at that, and Kelson was still chuckling as he moved off to exchange morning greetings with Ciard O Ruane, who was supervising the servants and squires making last-minute adjustments to the loads on the sumpter animals. Most of the servants were of mature years, but the young squires were laughing and joking among themselves as they worked and barely subsided at the king's approach.

"Morning, Ciard," Kelson said indulgently. "Are these lads going to prove too unruly a lot for you to handle?"

The squires quickly bent to their work again as the old gillie grinned and touched two fingers to his border bonnet in salutation.

"Nae problem a'tall, Sair," he said in his broad border accent. "'Tis only th' excitement o' leaving on th' journey. An' if their high spirits dinnae settle doon by th' time we ride out," he warned, eyeing the squires sternly, "I've nae doubt that extra work can be found tae occupy idle fingers when we stop each night."

The mild threat had the desired effect, quickly subduing youthful exuberance to an acceptable level in the squires' ranks. Other than the dour and irritable Conall, however, those riding out with the king and his foster brother that morning were still in high spirits: six of the other young men knighted the previous week, including Sir Jatham and Dhugal's Sir Jass MacArdry; Saer de Traherne and Roger, Earl of Jenas, to provide a balance of greater experience and maturity for the fledgling knights, should it be required; and Archbishop Cardiel's battle-surgeon, Father Lael, to see to the party's spiritual needs as well as any physical mishap along the way, though Dhugal was almost equally qualified to deal with the latter. Eight Haldane lancers and three more MacArdry men also accompanied them, with a modest baggage train and sufficient squires and other servants to care for the lot—nearly thirty in all.

Duncan gave them his blessing as they passed in exuberant if ragged review, and many of the servants and attending nobles, both men and women, hurried up to the battlement walks to continue watching and waving farewell when the company had clattered out through the gatehouse arch to make their way northward through the city and on to the river road toward Valoret. Meraude and Janniver went, Meraude with a nurse carrying the infant Eirian and Janniver waving excitedly to Sir Jatham, accompanied by young Brendan and an excited Squire Liam. The Sisters of Saint Brigid were also there to see them off, singing a short hymn of thanksgiving as the royal party rode off.

As the few other observers still milling on the steps began to disperse, Nigel let out a heavy sigh and turned to glance at Morgan and Duncan.

"God, I feel old," Nigel murmured. "All our fledglings are flying the nest. It's going to be awfully quiet around here."

Morgan grinned and clapped the prince regent on the shoulder. "You'll get used to it," he murmured. "They say that fathers find it easier to let go than mothers do."

"Not being a mother, I suppose I'll never know," Duncan quipped. "It isn't easy for a father, though."

Morgan only nodded. "I'll let you know when Brendan's a little older. At least they aren't riding off to war, this time."

"No, but the Torenthi negotiations could get tricky later in the year—especially when they find out Morag isn't even in Rhemuth any more," Nigel replied. "But I suppose that's another matter entirely. Besides, what can happen on a quest?"

"With luck—nothing," Morgan said. "Right now, I'm far more concerned about the bishops. Kelson seems to have his arguments well in hand, however."

Nigel snorted. "Yes. Well, let's just hope everything goes as planned. Incidentally, Alaric, when do you have to leave?"

"Oh, midafternoon or so. *Rhafallia* is tied up at Desse, so I thought Brendan and I would sleep aboard tonight and catch the morning tide. As long as the weather holds, we'll get home much faster that way than overland. It will still be very wet in the Lendours."

"Hmm, just hope that young Brendan is a good sailor, then," Nigel said. "In any case, you've time for a meal and a last cup before you head out. Meraude will make certain Brendan eats. Duncan, why don't you join us as well—if this morning's public exertions haven't overtaxed your strength, that is? How long must you keep up this charade of illness, now that the other bishops are safely on their way to Valoret?"

Duncan managed a wry smile as they went inside.

"I don't know that I'd call anything about them 'safe,'" he quipped. "But now that Kelson's gone and the rest of court focus will be shifting from Rhemuth to Valoret, I think I'm feeling stronger by the minute. With any luck, Cardiel will summon me within a week or two, and my recovery can be complete."

"Just pray that he summons you for the right reasons," Morgan murmured.

"Oh, I do—several times a day."

Not quite a week later, in Valoret, Kelson reiterated a version of that same prayer as he prepared to address the bishops gathered there. It was a bleak, dreary Sunday morning, the Second of Lent. The day was wet and cold, and Kelson was nearly certain he was coming down with a cold.

The rain had begun the second day out of Rhemuth and had hardly let up since. They had tried holing up en route with one of the local lords to wait it out, but they dared not delay too long, else Kelson would miss the opening of the synod and the opportunity to address the bishops before they began their deliberations.

He and his party had arrived early the previous evening, several days later than expected and drenched to the bone, tired and irritable from having to cope with the torrential rains, some of their number already falling victim to colds and coughs—conditions only partially improved by dry clothes, roaring fires, and the hot, hearty meal the archbishop's servants quickly served up in the refectory. Rain had continued to pelt down through the night and was still falling heavily the next morning when it was time to go to the cathedral for the solemn High Mass that would open the synod. Neither Kelson nor Dhugal slept well.

It was cold in the cathedral, despite heavy clothing—

damp and dreary and *dark*, despite the blaze of candles burning on the altar and the torches lighting the aisles. Kelson had begun to wonder if he would ever see the sun again. He huddled down in his cloak and tried to get warm as he knelt beside Dhugal in the choir and heard Mass, but he was miserable. And most of his carefully rehearsed speech was going out of his head as his sinuses filled up—and more being lost, every time he sneezed.

By the time Mass was over and everyone began moving on to the chapter house, Kelson hardly cared that this was the place where a similar gathering of prelates and other clergy had declared Camber MacRorie a saint, two hundred years before—or even that, for a time, one of the cathedral's side chapels had been consecrated to the Deryni saint. He sneezed repeatedly in the relatively short length of time it took him to go from the choir, through the south transept, and out through the processional door to the cloister walk. The state of his humor and his already damp handkerchief were not improved by having to dab continually at his reddened nose.

Nor did it count for much that the cloister walk was covered, for Archbishop Bradene's secretary bade Kelson and his party wait outside the chapter house entrance while the milling prelates and other clerics found their places and an episcopal chamberlain tried to bring the gathering to order. The entryway was cold and windy, even standing in the lee of Dhugal's cloaked and hooded form, with rain blowing through the arched and pillared colonnades of the cloister's inside perimeter and puddling on the paving stones. Kelson was surprised the puddles were not icing over and said as much to Dhugal. He only barely resisted a show of royal temper when the rest of his party were invited to go in and find seats on the top tier of benches, leaving him and Dhugal to freeze.

The filthy weather had not even permitted the king to wear the court garb customary for such an important occasion. He had been reduced to wearing his thickest wool breeches and not one but two heavy wool tunics, with heavy, thick-soled riding boots that came to mid-thigh—not that anyone was likely to notice, under the bulky, fur-lined cloak. Nor had he bothered with the heavy state crown, in this weather. The bishops would just have to settle for the plain band of hammered gold that was constricting his forehead inside his fur-lined hood.

At least the hall looked reasonably dry inside, though several puddles growing near the open doorway might bespeak roof problems rather than just blowing rain. And it was hardly more light inside than out, despite the torches set in cressets around the walls for general illumination and the rushlights on the table where the clarks would take down the proceedings—though it *had* to be warmer inside. Half a dozen firepots had been positioned around the perimeter of the room at floor level, with a seventh smoldering cheerily between the archbishops' thrones on the dais—probably vain attempts to take the edge off the damp and chill, but Kelson resolved to end up near one of them, no matter what else happened.

As he slipped his sheathed sword from its hangers and gave it to Dhugal to hold, crowding a little closer to move out of the puddle growing at his feet, he had about reached the point that he was ready to go inside anyway, regardless of what the archbishop's secretary wanted—though it really had not been that long, he knew.

Then he sneezed again, several times in rapid succession; and when he could see properly, after blowing his nose, the chamberlain was nearly at his side already, with a look of extreme solicitude for the king and a reproving glance for the archbishop's secretary.

"Father, you should have let His Majesty wait inside the doors, out of the wind," said the chamberlain, a portly priest of middle years named Father Elroy. "Sire, I'm dreadfully sorry. The weather has everything askew. Please come in. Would you prefer to sit or stand for your address?"

"I'd prefer to lie down," Kelson said sourly, "though, since that doesn't seem to be one of the available options, I suppose I'll sit. I don't know that I could speak from a supine position anyway—I'm sorry, Father," he amended, cutting himself off at Father Elroy's recoil to his sharp answer. "It isn't your fault I've got this beastly cold or that the weather's rotten. Do you suppose we'll have forty days and forty nights of rain, for our sins?"

Father Elroy managed a prim smile, uncertain whether to be mollified by the king's apology, annoyed at the slightly irreverent reference to Scripture, or still affronted.

"Your Majesty surely recalls that the Lord vowed never to mete that punishment again and gave us the rainbow as sign of His promise." The priest's reply had started out stuffy, but then his strait-laced expression softened to one of very human commiseration. "On the other hand, Sire, thirty-nine days and nights would not surprise me, judging by what we've seen so far."

And at his wink, Kelson chuckled despite his misery and clapped Father Elroy on the shoulder in appreciation as he moved on into the hall, wiping his nose again and then pushing back his hood. Perhaps he could get through this after all. It did seem a little warmer, now that he was out of the wind and damp.

"My Lord Archbishops, Your Excellencies, Reverend Lords," said the chamberlain, rapping his iron-shod staff to call them all to order, "His Majesty the King."

All those not already standing rose as Kelson strode across the tiled floor to approach the dais where the archbishops were enthroned. Dhugal did not accompany him, but slipped into a place at the rear of the hall near Saer de Traherne and Jass, his back against the doors the archbishop's secretary closed and barred.

The prelates and other clerics bowed as Kelson passed, some of them with familiar faces, many not. All of the bishops had chairs on the ground level of the circular chamber, each with a chaplain attending at his side; the rest stood in two rows along the tiered stone benches ringing the hall, some of them crowded very close. Five of the chairs were empty: Duncan's, beside Cardiel; that of the vacant See of Meara, whose incumbent had been so brutally murdered more than a year before—and whose sainthood would be under consideration during the days and probably weeks to come; and those of the three titled bishops currently under suspension for their parts in or acquiescence to that murder, at least one of them almost certain to lose his office, if not his life, in addition to the freedom that he, like the other suspendees, had already lost.

No chairs had been set out at all for the five itinerant bishops also under suspension for the Mearan misadventure, though doubtless at least a few vacancies would be created and filled by the time the prelates finished disciplining their wayward brethren. Father Lael had shown Kelson a list of the seven itinerant bishops who were *not* under suspension, assuring him that every one of them would make a point to be present, and Kelson believed it. He and the little priest had linked up all seven names with faces while they waited for Mass to begin, between Kelson's sneezes. Lael had never used precisely the imagery of vultures gathering to dine off the carcasses of their fallen fellows, but that was the impression with which Kelson was left.

And if some of the itinerant bishops expected to become titled, then *their* offices would fall vacant—to be filled, perhaps, from the ranks of the many abbots and priors and other high-ranking churchmen who had also made a point to be present for consideration. It was far worse than the jockeying and maneuvering that had gone on to choose the *last* Bishop of Meara. This synod must replace that office again and also choose several more prelates. Kelson wondered if there had been so profound a shakeup of the episcopate since the first massive reorganizations following the Restoration.

"Welcome to Valoret, Sire," Archbishop Bradene said, bowing over Kelson's hand when the king had ascended the steps of the dais and bent his knee to kiss the primate's ring. "I am most sorry that our prayers were not more efficacious in bringing finer weather for your journey. Perhaps you would have been better served had you ridden directly here with Archbishop Cardiel and Bishops Arilan and Wolfram after your knighting—on the occasion of which, incidentally, all of our colleagues here present who were not able to witness that most momentous event offer their most sincere congratulations, along with their prayers that Your Majesty may ever find the fulfillment of your knightly vows a joy, rather than a burden."

"Thank you, my Lord Archbishop," Kelson murmured, waving off a monk who was trying to approach surreptitiously with the chair the chamberlain had ordered. "Thank you, Father, I'll stand, after all. It will encourage me to be brief. Pardon me, my lords."

He stepped up between the two archbishops, gathering up the edges of his cloak to hop over the firepot, then turned and pushed it nearer the edge of the dais with his boot, so he could stand behind it and still be even with the archbishops. The warmth was blessed respite from the cold and damp he had just left outside, and he shook the front edges of his cloak a little to either side to trap and hold the heat. The fur-lined wool was a deep, subdued crimson, so dark as to be almost black in the dim light, and parted to show only the white gleam of his knight's belt against unadorned grey as he held his gloved hands over the firepot to warm them. The hilt of a dagger protruded from one boot top, but that was his only visible weapon. He wore no apparent jewelry save his golden circlet and the Eye of Rom that had been his father's.

"Pray, be seated, my lords. The rain has me a trifle indisposed, so I hope you will forgive me if what I say seems more blunt than my usual wont."

As the assembly obeyed, settling with an expectant murmur, Kelson rubbed his gloved hands together a few times, surveying his audience, then gave his nose what he hoped would be the last wipe for a while and tucked his handkerchief into one sleeve.

"I bid you good afternoon, Reverend Lords," he said, warming his hands again as he inclined his head in respect. "I thank you for your felicitations and for the opportunity to address you before you begin your deliberations. Many of you I have met before, but I have yet to make some of your acquaintances. If I do not succumb to this chill I seem to have taken from the rain that Father Elroy assures me will not last forty days and nights—though it could last for thirty and nine, he tells me—I shall look forward to meeting all of you this evening at dinner."

His quip brought a modest ripple of amusement, but Kelson feared it might be the last such as he hooked his thumbs in his belt and prepared to make the transition to the real meat of what he had to say.

"Now, as I have assured many of you in the past, I value your advice and counsel greatly, in temporal as well as spiritual matters. I hope, therefore, that you will not think it too presumptuous if I offer my advice and counsel on a few of the spiritual matters which you will be considering during this synod."

A few murmurs whispered through their ranks at that, but he had not expected otherwise. At least they were not hostile. And he was feeling better, now that he was speaking to them, having to think on his feet. He simply must be careful that he was not too candid and risk turning them against him.

"First of all, I do not envy you your task of disciplining those among your number, none present here today—" He quirked them a grateful smile. "—who broke faith with you and with me during the unfortunate business of last summer. As you no doubt have already been informed, I rendered justice then—with the advice and consent of Archbishop Cardiel and Bishop McLain—to three clerics whose treason against me and against your chosen hierarchy was so great that, in conscience, I should have felt compelled to intervene if the Church had not herself voluntarily surrendered them to temporal justice.

"Fortunately, the crimes of all three individuals were such that there was no disagreement among their superiors and myself regarding disposition. Former Archbishop Edmund Loris, Monsignor Lawrence Gorony, and Prince-Bishop Judhael of Meara were executed by my command in July of last year—the latter primarily for reasons of state, which I regret, though his canonical betrayals and disobediences were such that his superiors did not dispute the political necessity, under the circumstances. And it is my understanding that the other two would have been hanged by an ecclesiastical court, had I not been there to do it.

"With those three executions, and several more purely secular ones necessitated by trial of certain individuals for particular crimes against chivalry and the conventions of wartime, the letter of the king's justice has been satisfied. I seek no additional deaths, for far too many have died already as a result of last summer's treachery and its terrible aftermath. However, I wish it noted that, should you see fit to impose the death penalty on additional parties involved in the Mearan unpleasantness, I will support your decision. I believe there are eight men in question, all of them bishops, all of them now in custody of the Archbishop of Valoret."

He let them ruminate that for a moment while he paused to cough and blow his nose. That part had not been too difficult. He had simply been reiterating what most of them already knew. Nor was the next topic apt to draw much controversy.

"The second item I wish to address is connected with the first, for it concerns the election of a successor to the See of Meara, presently vacant, and of successors to those vacancies likely to be created by your actions in the first item—

for even if the lives of some or all of those offenders be spared, I suspect that you will find at least a few of those men no longer fit to hold high episcopal office.

"Regarding those elections, I will say only that I am aware of the qualifications of some of the candidates considered during your deliberations two years ago and believe that some of those men are probably even more qualified now than they were then. I am sure you will give them all due consideration, as well as new candidates who have come to notice since. Several weeks ago, after consultation with several of my temporal advisors, I gave Archbishop Cardiel a letter outlining some of my own observations and recommendations regarding candidates known to me. He will share that information with you at the appropriate time. I trust I need not remind you, however, that you and those you elect wield and shall wield extensive temporal power as well as spiritual and that your choices must, therefore, be considered in a temporal light as well. The events of the past few years and of last summer, in particular, have shown us amply that it is no longer sufficient for a bishop merely to be a pious churchman and shepherd of his flock. He also must be an administrator and sometimes a politician—though I should point out that he ought never to allow his spiritual obligations to be overshadowed by the latter occupation. In the matter of elections, then, I shall simply wish you clear minds, honest hearts, and souls that listen to the direction of the Holy Spirit, as you deliberate to choose new Shepherds of the Flock."

A mild stirring whispered through the chapter house at that, as Kelson paused to dab again at his miserable nose—which was beginning to tickle, in the warmth from the firepot—but he knew he could quell that with his next statement.

"The third point I wish to address concerns one of your number no longer with us—Bishop Henry Istelyn, of blessed and much missed memory, who, I believe, is to be considered for canonization."

The murmuring instantly ceased. He knew he had their complete and undivided attention.

"I can only say that my own dealings with His Excellency were always of the most satisfactory nature and that his loyalty to crown and cross was unshaken to the end. If martyrs have merit, if only in providing examples to all of us, then surely Henry Istelyn was one such shining example and ought surely to be recognized for the courageous and godly life he lived, as I am sure Our Lord already has recognized him in heaven. It is my fervent wish that at some time not very far in the future, we shall be able to make official petitions to *Saint* Henry Istelyn, Bishop and Martyr.''

A sigh of agreement whispered through the hall at that, and Kelson knew he had set the stage properly for the last and most difficult thing he had to say to them this afternoon. This was the one that was most important, in the long view, and would require the most delicate balance. He wished he could think more clearly.

''Finally,'' he said—and here several of his listeners shifted uneasily in their seats. ''Finally, I would commend to your careful consideration the continued modification of the Ramos Conventions, which have governed the interpretation of our law, both civil and canon, for nearly two hundred years. I will not attempt to tell you that all the statutes of Ramos should be struck down, for they should not. Nor will I deny that some of the statutes are worthy and honorable laws.

''But for those laws dealing specifically with members of any particular—let us be candid, gentlemen. For those laws dealing specifically with those known as Deryni, I would ask your careful and prayerful consideration.

''Civil law regarding Deryni has been gradually changing in the past few decades, as individual Deryni have begun guardedly to prove their worth and loyalty to the crown—as was surely true in many instances even during the worst of the Interregnum times. My own father, may he rest in peace, dared to rescind or amend several of the most troublesome civil statutes, such as those forbidding even Deryni of proven loyalty to hold office or noble titles or even to own land, like any yeoman farmer.

''But canon law has not been as forgiving of what, I begin to believe, was more often political avarice, such as I warned you of earlier, than any moral or spiritual deficiency inherent in Deryni as a people. You, yourselves, in the past year, finally have agreed that the death penalty ought not to be imposed on a Deryni who simply seeks, in the passion of a true vocation, to be ordained a priest—though, thank God, no test of this deviation from the still-extant section of the Ramos statutes has been called for. I wonder if most of you even know how, over the last two centuries, the discovery of would-be Deryni priests has been ensured.''

"Do *you* know, Sire?" called a voice from the right side of the hall.

"Who asked that?" he countered, searching the upturned faces. "Speak up. You won't be punished for your honest question—I swear it.''

Slowly a man in the black habit and blue girdle of the *Ordo Vox Dei* stood. Kelson noted him well for further investigation, then nodded for him to be seated.

"Yes, I know," he said quietly. "Not all the details of implementation, but I am aware of the method itself. Steps are being taken to deal with it, for it is the hand of man, not God, which singles out so and which has sent so many to the flames.''

"Has Bishop McLain told you this, Sire?" asked another man, from the left, though Kelson saw him before he finished speaking and fixed him with his gaze.

"Bishop McLain knows about it now, but he was not the one who told me. Nor was he the instrument of his own salvation when he was ordained, more than twenty years ago.''

There. Let them sweat *that* little piece of information, to prepare them for the likelihood that others besides Duncan might have gotten past their precious system. He dared not look at Arilan, who must be even more on edge than he was.

"I put it to you that an entire rethinking of the Deryni question is in order, gentlemen. Man's ways *are* fallible, as God's are not. God calls men to be His priests when and where and how He wills, whether they be human or Deryni or some mixture of the two. It is time to remove all human penalties whatsoever from this crime that is not and has never been a crime, and to judge a man's worthiness for the priesthood by the kind of life he leads—not by the gifts he may or may not have been born with. If you insist upon maintaining this cold and illogical stance regarding Deryni, then you do me no honor either—though all of you have sworn to defend and uphold me, as I have sworn to defend and uphold you. For my mother, however vehemently she may try to deny it, has given me a legacy of Deryni blood that I value no less highly than the Haldane blood that runs in my veins. I pray you, keep that in mind as you deliberate in these next weeks."

CHAPTER TEN

A day of darkness and of gloominess, a day of
clouds and of thick darkness.

—Joel 2:2

Rain was still bucketing down by late afternoon, when Kelson had finished his speech, both archbishops had addressed the assembly, and the synod had adjourned to the archbishop's palace for supper. Kelson's cold had not improved, so he retired soon after eating and let Father Lael give him a physick in a shot of hot and potent Rhenndish brandywine. He doubted it would do much to cure the cold, but it made Father Lael feel better—and it did feel good going down, balm to his scratchy throat. After he had dutifully tossed it off, he bade Dhugal help him into deep, controlled trance-sleep—which, if it did not cure him, would at least release him from conscious misery through the night. The last thing he heard, before he slipped beyond caring, was the soft drone of Dhugal's voice, coaxing him deeper into trance, and the steady patter of rain on the leaded roof.

And it was raining in Rhemuth, later that night, when Duncan, working late in his study, laid aside his quill and knuckled at bleary eyes. During his "indisposition" of the past week, he had begun to take on occasional secretarial duties for Nigel—a sometimes mindless and often boring pastime, but it kept his mind off what might be happening in Valoret and it helped Nigel. The transcription he had been working on for the last two days was of the latter sort, even more boring than most, but at least it was finally finished and could be taken to the prince. The hour was late, but not so late that Nigel would be already abed—though, judging from the sound of the rain pelting down outside, that was probably the best place to be on a night like this.

Indulging in a leisurely yawn, Duncan drew back one of the heavy velvet drapes covering the window and shaded his eyes against the leaded glass to peer outside, trying to gauge how hard it was actually coming down. The amber panes distorted, but not enough to change his original estimation that the weather was abysmal; and he could hear it battering the leaded roof as well.

Making a face at the rain, Duncan let the curtain fall and rolled up his transcription in a leather scroll tube, rising to slip it under his cincture before putting on a fur-lined cap and gloves and throwing a heavy black cloak around his shoulders.

At least he did not have to go all the way back to the archbishop's palace in the rain—though getting to Nigel's quarters even somewhat dry would be difficult enough. Since Dhugal's departure with the king the previous week, and in light of his own supposed indisposition, Duncan had all but moved into Dhugal's apartments in the castle. It was only natural that, during his "convalescence," he might be expected to derive comfort from being near his son's things; and, as he gradually resumed sedentary duties, it was far more convenient to sleep in the castle than to trek back and forth between there and his old quarters, especially on a night like tonight, or when he worked late in his study, or he and Nigel talked too late—an increasing occurrence, for he had taken to spending many of his evenings in the prince's company, often dining with him and Meraude. All of them missed their sons—and with the mass exodus of nearly every Deryni from Rhemuth the week before, Nigel was the only one who could even begin to give Duncan the companionship he needed.

Being Deryni offered no particular advantages tonight, however. As Duncan straightened a few last things on his desk and put out the candles, he briefly considered using the study Portal to go to the library Portal and thence to Nigel—but only briefly. One never knew who might be in the library to witness his arrival—and how could one explain being dry on a night like this?

No, blatantly Deryni frivolity of that sort was unthinkable

just now, when his position was so precarious vis-à-vis his future with the Church. However, he *could* use the secret passageway that connected Dhugal's apartments to the basilica yard, rather than slogging through the muddy parade ground and stable yard to enter through the great hall. He generally avoided taking the secret route, because the stairs were steep and he disliked closed-in places, but it was better than getting soaked or sleeping in his chair in the study.

He got wet enough, even in the short dash across the churchyard to the alcove where the entrance to the passageway was hidden. En route, he slipped and nearly took a nasty fall. And then, rain running down his face and inside his hood, he had to stand in a puddle until he could find the stud that opened the entryway.

It was dry inside, though—and dark. From habit, and because the use of handfire could have been potentially fatal to a Deryni priest until very recently, Duncan struck flint to tinder to light a rushlight in a niche beside the closed door. The flame gave little actual warmth, but its fitful yellowish light was cheering in the damp and gloom and made him feel warmer.

There were fifty-five steps to the first, straight flight of stairs, steep and irregular, and Duncan paused to catch his breath on the landing, just slightly winded, before starting doggedly up the winding treads of the next set. He was preoccupied, thinking about what he wanted to say to Nigel regarding the document he carried. But he had not gone more than two or three steps on the stairs before he became aware of a faint, sweetish odor tickiing at his nostrils.

He stopped and sniffed the air, instantly alert and casting out with his Deryni senses. Something was dead down here—something larger than the odd rat or other rodent one might expect in such a place.

He turned and took another whiff, holding his rushlight higher as he concentrated on the smell, then briskly retraced his steps to the landing and looked around. The odor was stronger here. He wondered how he had missed it before. Something was definitely dead. He had smelled that smell before, more times than he cared to remember, in the aftermath of far too many battles. There was no mistaking it.

He conjured handfire to augment his rushlight, flooding the landing with silvery light and then he saw the russet shadow crumpled against the far wall, a leather boot protruding at one end and an outstretched arm visible at the other.

"I have no idea how long he's been there," Duncan said to Nigel, as he led the prince down the steep stair from Dhugal's apartments, half an hour later. "Long enough to begin decomposition, though—probably a week or two, in this weather. It looks as if he fell coming down the stairs and broke his neck. What I can't figure out is what a member of the Camberian Council was doing in this passageway. I thought they couldn't get into the keep from the library Portal."

Nigel only shook his head as they reached the landing and he bent to look as Duncan pointed things out.

"I didn't think they could," he said. "That's what Kelson told *me*. You say his name's Tiercel de Claron?"

Duncan nodded. "I've only seen him twice, and beginning stages of decomposition could have me fooled, but it sure looks like him. Arilan is the only one I can think of who would know for sure."

"And Arilan's in Valoret, where you should be," Nigel replied, straightening to stroke his mustache with a worried hand. "Sweet *Jesu*, if this *is* a member of the Council, they're going to be livid."

"Well, not with us," Duncan muttered, crouching down beside the body again. "*We* didn't do it. Do you want to help me turn him over, so I can see whether it looks like anyone else did? I didn't want to move anything too much before you saw him. I just turned his head enough to see his face—and to realize his neck was broken—and scanned to see if I could pick up any residual information from his mind. Of course I couldn't, after this long. His brain is probably like pudding."

Making a face, Nigel swept the skirts of his night robe back, out of the way, and knelt down.

"I'll never make a surgeon," he said, as the two of them gently turned the body on its back. "I've brought enough men to this state in my time, but I usually don't have to deal with them after they've been dead this long. You have a stronger stomach than I do," he concluded, rising to back off a few steps as Duncan bent to the grisly task of further examination. "Any wounds?"

Duncan shook his head. Rats had been at the body, but there were no signs of any other trauma besides the broken neck and associated bruising one might expect if Tiercel truly had fallen down the steps to his death.

"None that I can see offhand, though I'd like a closer look when the body's stripped for burial. How do you want to handle that?"

As Duncan stood, Nigel shook his head.

"I don't know. It isn't really our place to bury him. He must have family—or perhaps the Council itself will wish to handle the arrangements. But our only link with the Council is through Arilan. So if you're sure he's theirs, I suppose you'd better have an official relapse, so you can go to Valoret and tell Arilan. I don't suppose there's a Portal there, to make things easier?"

"I've heard vague rumor about one, but I don't know where it is. And even if I did, it wouldn't do me much good if I've never been there." Duncan sighed. "I'll plan to leave at dawn. You probably should draft a letter to Kelson as well, which I can forward from Valoret. He'll probably have gone on to Caerrorie by the time I get there, but he ought to know."

Nigel's sigh echoed Duncan's.

"Very well. There's some additional correspondence that I can send as well. I would have sent a courier in a few days, in any case. In the meantime, I suppose the body ought to be coffined. It isn't going to get any prettier, lying here in the damp. How are we going to get him out of here?"

"We can rig a sling with his cloak and carry him down to the yard," Duncan replied, suiting action to words as Nigel bent gingerly to assist. "We'll put him on the basilica porch while I get some monks to take charge of him. Then no one else need know about this passageway."

"No one except whomever de Claron may have told," Nigel muttered. "Can you trust these monks of yours?"

"For what they have to do, yes. I'll put my chaplain over them while I'm gone—Father Shandon. He's discreet and loyal—and I can make sure he doesn't remember anything he oughtn't. I don't like to do that, but sometimes there's no choice. Shall I send for him?"

"Not until we've gotten our friend safely to the bottom," Nigel said. He grunted as they picked up the cloak-sling between them. "I'll wait with him on the basilica porch until you've done that and gotten the monks. Between us, we ought to be able to dissemble well enough to divert any untoward curiosity. We'll say we found him in one of the cellars."

By dawn, Tiercel was decently coffined and lying in state in Duncan's study, with Father Shandon set on watch there to pray by the body and ensure against intrusion. And Duncan was galloping through steady rain, already near to wearing out the first of several dozen horses that he would ride in relays to reach Valoret as quickly as possible.

Dawn brought a break in the rain in Valoret, however, and Kelson's cold was much improved as well—so much that by early afternoon, after a brief inspection of the chapel where Saint Camber once had been venerated and where his body had lain before being transported to the ancestral home in Caerrorie for burial, the king had decided to press on toward Dolban, much to the dismay of some of his entourage, for many of them had looked forward to dining again in the archbishop's refectory. Sparse though the Lenten fare was by the standards of the court at Rhemuth, it still was far more than they were likely to be served in the more austere surrounds of Dolban—or at Saint Mark's Abbey, en route to Dolban, where they must surely spend the night in pilgrim's lodgings, because of leaving so late from Valoret, and sup on pilgrim's fare.

But Kelson was adamant that they must be on their way. Having delivered his speech to the bishops, he felt it best to let them conduct their business in peace, without the specter of the king's presence hanging over them and possibly making them balky, where they might otherwise move ahead. Besides that, the weather was clearing to the north and east. If they could make it to Dolban before another storm hit, they could rest there for a few days while he and Dhugal queried the monks about the former patron of their house. For Dolban, though currently the home of an order dedicated to teaching, once had housed the first Camberian religious community, the Servants of Saint Camber. And though the shrine to the former Deryni saint had been destroyed at about the time of the Council of Ramos, Kelson hoped to find some further hints there that would help him understand Camber better.

Consequently, Kelson was long gone from Valoret by the time Duncan arrived there, three days later. With Nigel's concurrence, Duncan had decided to travel anonymously as an ordinary royal courier, using the badge of his office to procure the fresh horses he needed at relay stations along the way. Two of Nigel's Haldane archers rode with him as escort, but even they were unaware who he really was.

Thus it was that Duncan drew rein before All Saints' Cathedral of a Wednesday morning, just after Terce, exhausted and mud-stained, to leave his spent mount in the charge of his escort while he dashed up the steps, praying that the bishops were not already in conclave for the morning. Fortunately, Mass was still in progress, and his royal courier's badge admitted him without question to work his way quietly down a side aisle, there to wait until Mass should end and he could approach Arilan. A bishop named de Torigny was the celebrant.

He longed to go forward for Communion, for it had been several days, but it was clear that this Mass was for the bishops and their attendant clergy only, and he dared not risk being recognized, anonymous though he was in black riding leathers and dark, hooded cloak. He kept all trace of his Deryniness tightly shielded, lest Arilan somehow detect his presence while transported in that peculiar psychic ecstasy and extension of senses that he was sure Arilan, like himself and every other religious Deryni he had met, often experienced at the peak of the Mass. But when Mass had ended, he was waiting with his courier's badge by the south processional door to accost Arilan before he could file past with the other bishops.

"In the King's service, Excellency," he murmured, thrusting the badge in Arilan's face but letting his shields slip to identify himself, though he kept his face averted from the others. "I have urgent dispatches. May I deliver them in private?"

Duncan! What—

Arilan's surprise and consternation reverberated in Duncan's mind, but the other bishop did not betray even a hint of his reaction outwardly as he shut down again and nodded, leading Duncan wordlessly into the shadow of the night stairs so the other clerics could pass into the sunlit cloister yard beyond.

"So, what 'dispatches,' courier?" he said coolly, as he turned to face Duncan again. "Am I to take it that a certain bishop has suffered a relapse?"

"He has, so far as anyone in Rhemuth knows," Duncan said softly. "And I *do* have dispatches to be forwarded to the king. But what I had to tell you in person is that Tiercel de Claron is dead."

He winced at the intensity of Arilan's recoil.

"That's impossible. Who told you that?"

"I saw the body, Denis," Duncan whispered. "At least I'm fairly certain it's Tiercel, but you're the only one I know who could verify that. I hope you're not angry that I left Rhemuth without permission, but there was no one else to send, under the circumstances."

"No, you did right to come," Arilan breathed. "*Jesu-Maria,* so *that's* why he didn't show at the last Council meeting. How did it happen?"

"An accident, we think."

"Who is *we?*"

"Nigel and I," Duncan replied. "I had to tell someone. I found the body in the hidden passageway that connects Dhugal's apartments with the basilica yard. It looks as if he fell down the stairs and broke his neck. He'd been there for a while."

"How long, do you know?"

Duncan shook his head. "It's hard to say. A week? Two weeks? More?"

"Not as long as that. I saw him the morning after Kelson's knighting. That was Ash Wednesday—what, two weeks ago? And you found the body when?"

"Sunday."

"But what was Tiercel doing in that passageway?" Arilan went on. "I didn't think he knew about it."

"Did he know about the Portal in my study?" Duncan asked, looking the other bishop in the eyes.

Arilan went close-shuttered, as if he were considering whether or not to answer, and Duncan wished he dared try to Truth-Read whatever response the bishop made. But he knew Arilan would resist him, and there were still other clerics milling outside the processional door, some of them growing curious about the prolonged exchange between the Bishop of Dhassa and a royal courier. Duncan dared not put them both at risk, just to satisfy his own pique.

"Yes, he knew," Arilan said carefully. "I informed the Council of its location last spring, after you showed me where it was. I felt they ought to know, in case it was ever necessary for one of our number to reach one of you in an emergency. It would have been far more convenient than the ones in the cathedral sacristy or the library."

Duncan sighed. He supposed Arilan was telling the truth, but it made little difference just now. Somehow, Tiercel had learned of the passageway and met his death there. Odds were that he had come through the study Portal and entered the secret passage from the basilica yard, bound for some unknown destination in the castle, but equally possible—and a concern that had been bothering Duncan through most of the ride from Rhemuth—was that Tiercel had entered through Dhugal's apartments, after somehow getting past the wards on the library Portal. Duncan was sure his son could have had nothing to do with Tiercel's death, but that possibility would occur to someone else, eventually.

"I'll want to see the body immediately, of course," Arilan suddenly said, breaking into Duncan's flight of speculation. "And then I'll need to summon the Council. As you may have surmised, there's a Portal here in Valoret. We'll use it. Are you alone?"

"I have two men waiting in the yard," Duncan murmured, "but they only know me as a courier named John. Shall I dismiss them?"

"No, I'll see to that. Wait in there." With a nod of his head, Arilan indicated a chapel opening off the south transept. "You shouldn't be disturbed. And if you can think of any good prayers appropriate to the situation, this is the time to say them. I have to manufacture a good excuse to explain my absence for the next few hours."

Duncan obeyed without demur, kneeling unobtrusively at the altar rail in a far corner of the little chapel and keeping his face well in the shadow of his hood, but his mind was racing too busily for him to pray. A fatigue-banishing spell was in order, too—for the third time in as many days, though he could not keep this up indefinitely. But the jump back to the Portal in his study was a long one. He had gone farther before, but never as physically exhausted as he was now. He wondered where the Portal was at this end.

And poor Father Shandon, Duncan thought, when he had run through the spell twice to reinforce it, and recentered his remaining energy as best he could. Without doubt, the loyal priest would be dutifully reciting prayers for the dead man in his care; but Duncan's precipitous arrival with Arilan would necessitate yet another tampering with the poor fellow's memory.

Duncan dozed a little in the more than half hour it took Arilan to return, though he came to attention immediately when the elder bishop beckoned from the chapel doorway. Arilan had exchanged his episcopal purple for the caped black cloak Duncan had last seen him wear in Rhemuth, and he wore a plain black cassock underneath. They were twin black shadows as they silently moved back through the south transept and right, toward the sacristy. The door was standing open, the room empty, and Arilan closed the door softly behind them, after glancing back the way they had come. No one appeared to have noticed their entry.

"This is a little risky, using this Portal in the daytime," Arilan said, "but we daren't wait until tonight. I want a look at that body, before all trace of residual memory is gone—if it isn't already."

"It is," Duncan said, "unless you're that much better at reading than I am. I did my best to leave a stasis on the body to retard further decay, but I don't know how well it will have held, without tending. The coffin's warded, too, for whatever good that may have done."

Arilan grimaced. "I suppose that means you've moved the body."

"Well, we could hardly leave him down there in the damp, for the rats."

"No, no, I'm not criticizing. You did everything else properly. Of course I'll want to read *you*, after I've had a look at him, to pick up everything I can about the actual death site and the situation of the body, but that can wait a while. Who's apt to be waiting at the other end, now?"

"Only Father Shandon," Duncan replied, as Arilan indicated a circular design set into the floor tiles.

He did not relish the thought of having to open his mind to Arilan's probe, but he could hardly refuse. At least he did not have to do it now. Palming across his eyes to reinforce the spell he had already worked, he drew a deep breath to collect himself, trying not to let it turn into a yawn.

"Give me a moment before you come through," Duncan added, "and I'll put him to sleep."

"It looks like *you* could use the sleep. Are you sure you're up to this? I can take us both through, you know."

"And Shandon will see you," Duncan replied. "Besides, it's possible he isn't alone. Don't worry, I'll sleep after you've gone to deal with your precious Council. See you in Rhemuth."

He flashed Arilan a game smile as he stepped onto the circle, but he did not wait for any further objection. Closing his eyes, he reached his mind into the tangle of power he could already feel throbbing under his feet. The Portal was a potent one and required far less effort than he had anticipated to lock into its pattern. As he reached for the link in the study Portal, he wondered briefly whether active use reinforced Portals.

Then he drew the link closed with his mind and felt the pit of his stomach give a little wrench, and he was in close darkness, in the familiar confines of the Portal in his study.

He drew a deep breath to steady his balance and felt for the stud that would open the door. He thrust beyond the door with his mind, but only Shandon's presence radiated, prayerfully immersed in supplications for the dead, as Duncan had expected. The priest was kneeling beside the pall-covered coffin, his back to Duncan. Even as the opening door stirred the tapestry covering it and Shandon turned in alarm, Duncan was slipping from behind to slide one arm around the man's shoulders, his other forefinger going to his lips in a sign for silence as his mind seized Shandon's.

"Relax, Father," he whispered, just before shifting his further commands to a non-verbal level. "And when you've carried out my instructions, you'll remember none of this."

By the time Arilan came through, a few minutes later, Shandon had left on his errand and Duncan was folding back the pall to expose Tiercel's shrouded body to the waist. He had already dispersed the wards. He backed off and sat down near the fire as Arilan approached, letting himself doze again while the other bishop spent long moments with his hands on the forehead of the corpse.

"Nothing," Arilan finally said.

The word brought Duncan back to consciousness with a start.

"I told you there wouldn't be."

"Yes, so you did. Where is Shandon? Wasn't he here?"

Duncan leaned his head wearily against the high back of his chair and smiled, knowing Arilan would see the intended second meaning behind what he was about to say.

"I sent him to fetch Nigel. It seemed like a good idea for someone to know we're both here, especially since he thinks we're still in Valoret. He *is* the regent in Kelson's absence, after all."

Chuckling, Arilan came to sit on the edge of the table next to Duncan. "You don't quite trust me, do you?"

"Should I?"

"Well, if I *were* trying to deceive you, I should say yes, whether it were true or not, so what good is that question? But I give you my word, as a Deryni and as a priest, that our present dealings have nothing to do with our past differences regarding the Council or your status as a cleric. Read the truth of what I say. Go ahead. You've gone to a great deal of trouble to do me a personal favor, and I shan't take advantage of the situation. I *would* like to see how you found Tiercel's body, however."

"Make your probe, then," Duncan said, smiling again as he closed his eyes. "I'll help you all I can. I'm so tired, I don't know whether I could resist if I had to, so I'm glad you promised not to make me fight you."

As he slipped into trance, Arilan's mind edging close behind him, he sensed the impression of gentle, even affectionate laughter, quickly overshadowed by a warm, comfortable greyness, reinforced by Arilan's hand across his eyes, which carried him swiftly to depths so far from consciousness that he was only barely aware of his memory being sifted, carefully restrained to only the subject of Tiercel.

The next thing he knew, someone was knocking on the door, and he was bobbing back up to consciousness, curiously refreshed for the short time he knew he had been under, and Arilan's hand was leaving him. He opened his eyes to see Nigel standing over him, Arilan to one side. Beyond them, Father Shandon was closing the door.

"Are you all right?" Nigel asked.

"I'm fine. Just tired. What time is it now?"

"Just past noon. How long have you been here?"

Duncan smiled. "Only long enough for Father Shandon to go and get you. But not quite three hours ago, I was just riding into Valoret. At least I know where another Portal is."

Nigel nodded grimly. "Should Shandon be hearing all this?"

Shaking his head, Arilan took the priest's arm and directed him, glassy-eyed, toward the prie-dieu in the far corner of the room, facing away from them.

"Go and pray awhile, Father," he murmured, "and remember nothing of what you've heard and seen." As the priest obeyed, Arilan turned back to Duncan and Nigel.

"You've been a great help. Now I'd like to take Tiercel to his brethren. Will you help me get him to the Portal? I can manage from there alone. Duncan, I don't expect to need your direct testimony, but I'd appreciate it if you could stand by, just in case. Get some sleep, by all means, but do it here, if you don't mind."

When Arilan had gone with his grisly burden, Duncan did just that, curling up on the carpet and a pile of cloaks before the fire, with Nigel to watch and Shandon praying in the corner.

CHAPTER ELEVEN

We will return and build the desolate places.
                                        —Malachi 1:4

Arilan, when he returned some hours later, was able to inform Duncan that he would not need to testify to the Camberian Council regarding his finding of Tiercel's body, but the Council *was* interested in having Arilan query Dhugal as to how and why Tiercel might have happened to be in the passageway connecting with Dhugal's quarters.

"Surely they don't think Dhugal had anything to do with Tiercel's death," Duncan said, rubbing sleep from his eyes as Arilan crouched by the hearth to warm his hands.

Arilan shook his head. "Of course not. Everything points to an accident. It's possible that Dhugal heard or saw something, however, if he was in his quarters when it happened—which is by no means certain, though we did narrow down the time of death somewhat."

"Really? You can do that?"

"Oh, yes. We estimate a week to ten days ago, based on the absence of any psychic traces. That would place it right around the time Kelson and the others left, perhaps a little before."

As Duncan propped himself up on his elbows, Nigel edged forward in the chair where he had been napping while he waited with Duncan, awake now. They had moved Father Shandon to the hidden chapel, deep in forced sleep.

"Hmmm, I suppose Tiercel might have cried out when he fell," Duncan agreed. "Most men would. What I can't understand is what he was doing in there at all. And which end did he enter from? To come in from the yard is one thing, but—dear God, you don't suppose he was going to do something to Dhugal, do you? Or that he *did* something?"

"Did something?" Arilan cocked his head. "I'm not sure what you mean."

"Well, Dhugal is an unknown quantity to your Council folk. No one besides yourself has had any kind of look at his mind, and even you haven't tried to read him since you've known he's my son. You don't suppose Tiercel would have taken that upon himself, do you?"

"You mean, to come into Dhugal's room while he slept and try to do a probe without him being aware?"

"Well, yes."

Arilan sat back on the edge of the hearth and considered, his amethyst glittering in the firelight as he pleated an edge of his cloak between restless fingers.

"No, I shouldn't think so. Nigel, I could possibly see him being interested in you, because of his preoccupation with the notion that the Haldane potential is not limited to the sovereign and his principal heir. For that matter, he might even have had an interest in Conall—though Conall's such an arrogant little son of a bitch, I shouldn't think Tiercel would bother. Sorry, Nigel, but your eldest son can be very tedious."

Nigel sighed. "I know. I keep hoping maturity will temper him."

"Hmmm, no doubt it will," Arilan replied. "As for Dhugal, however—and no slight intended to *your* son, Duncan—he really isn't anything that would particularly interest Tiercel: only part Deryni, and hardly trained at all. Given Tiercel's snobbery about such things, it simply doesn't make sense."

But neither did any of the other half-dozen explanations they tried on one another in the next little while, before Arilan reluctantly prepared to make the jump back to Valoret.

"There *is* something else that may or may not mean anything," Arilan said. "If Tiercel *was* intending any mischief with someone here in the castle complex—Dhugal or anyone else—he probably would have been carrying a set of ward cubes. There were none on him, and so far we've found none in any of the several houses we know he kept. Or he might have had them in a pouch or satchel, along with Deryni-specific drugs. He used to do a fair amount of training for us. But you didn't find anything like that, did you, Duncan?"

Duncan had not found anything, but that proved nothing, either. So Nigel wrote the appropriate letters informing Kelson of Tiercel's death and querying Dhugal further. These Arilan agreed to forward to the king's party the next morning, along with the other, routine correspondence that Duncan already had taken as far as Valoret. When the bishop had gone, Father Shandon was roused and sent off to bed with suitable instructions to forget what he had seen and heard, and both Duncan and Nigel retired for much needed sleep, only mildly concerned for Dhugal. The next morning, life in Rhemuth resumed its usual routine when the king and court were not present.

And Arilan's activities in Valoret settled back into routine as well, once he had written his own letters and sent an episcopal courier off to find Kelson. He had missed little the previous afternoon that could not be filled in by a quick perusal of the day's transcripts and counted himself fortunate that he could fill in what gaps remained by means of a few minutes casual reading of a willing Cardiel, who knew what had happened back in Rhemuth and had covered Arilan's absence quite handily. The synod was proceeding apace with the business of chastising and replacing many of its number.

The first major item on the bishops' agenda had already been accomplished before Arilan was called back to Rhemuth—the election of a new incumbent to the vacant See of Meara, whose filling the previous year had so convoluted the Mearan political situation. The choice this time was one John FitzPadraic, an itinerant bishop considered somewhat prematurely before Henry Istelyn's election, but whose levelheaded conduct in the Mearan outlands during the Mearan cirisis—always on the move to avoid contact with the Mearan rebels—had only enhanced his reputation as an even-tempered, moderate churchman of proven loyalty to his legitimate superiors as well as the crown, well suited to take command of the still volatile see that was junior only to Valoret and Rhemuth.

Bishop FitzPadraic's election had raised the number of titled bishops not under suspension to nine—Valoret, Rhemuth, Meara, Grecotha, Dhassa, Coroth, Cardosa, Stavenham, Marbury—giving the synod the three-fourths quorum desirable for trying the remaining three. The trials of those three had proceeded *pro forma*, with unanimity uncertain only over the question of whether Creoda, the suspended Bishop of Culdi, should also be turned over to secular justice for trial on the charge of treason—and an almost certain capital sentence—in addition to being deprived of his office and imprisoned for the rest of his life, as was the decision regarding Belden of Erne and Lachlan de Quarles, the suspended bishops of Cashien and Ballymar, respectively.

In the end, Creoda was spared secular trial, but only by the narrowest of margins. And disposition on the three being agreed, the nine wasted no time filling the newly vacant sees with three of the most promising from among the itinerant bishops: the loyal Hugh de Berry for Ballymar, in Kierney, as further reward for his continued service to the crown after leaving Loris' employ four years before; for Culdi, one Bevan de Torigny, a former abbot of the respected *Ordo Vox Dei* in Grecotha and a master lecturer at the university there, young and flexible regarding the Deryni question, who had long ago stated his support of the move to restore Culdi's most notorious son to his status as a saint; and another scholar, James MacKenzie, for the border See of Cashien. Since the elections exactly paralleled the recommendations Kelson had made to Cardiel, and the three were already bishops, they had been seated immediately in their new capacities, thus filling all twelve titled sees. Arilan had no doubt that the king would approve the actual elections.

And that had brought the synod to its next phase—an intermediate process to interview candidates for the five itinerant bishoprics subsequently vacant or vacant before—the task in which they had been engaged the day before, when Duncan's arrival pulled Arilan temporarily from the evaluations. A second such set of deliberations would follow after the disposition of five more itinerant bishops under suspension, whose fate had yet to be decided, but who certainly would be deprived of office, even if allowed to return to parish work as simple priests on a probationary basis. At least the first phase of the selection process promised to go moderately quickly, for the findings of a similar set of in-

terviews not two years past had already been refined and
studied during the past winter.

Thus it was that Arilan was able to daydream a little as
Bishop Siward of Cardosa questioned a priest named Jodoc
d'Armaine, wondering what reaction his letters would bring
when they reached Dhugal and the king in the next day or
so.

The king, meanwhile, was happily engrossed in one of the
more whimsical aspects of his quest for Saint Camber. The
royal party had slept at Saint Bearand's Abbey the previous
night, and would sleep there again before heading out, for
the next day promised an arduous climb to the pass leading
out to the plain of Iomaire, and Saer wanted the pack animals, in particular, well rested.

The day was sunny and fine, however, far too beautiful
for young knights to remain cooped up indoors, so Sir Jatham
and Jass MacArdry organized a hunting expedition on the
abbey lands, while a few, like Conall, preferred merely to
sleep late and relax. Kelson declined both options, he and
Dhugal choosing to ride ahead shortly after dawn with Saer
de Traherne, Dolfin, and a man-at-arms to inspect the ruins
of Caerrorie.

It was a place once intimately associated with Saint Camber. Until confiscated by the Crown, after the institution of
the Statutes of Ramos, Caerrorie had been the favored seat
of the MacRorie family outside the titular lands of Culdi,
convenient to the then-capital of Valoret. Unfortunately,
anti-Deryni reaction following in the wake of Camber's
demotion from saintly status had led to the wholesale
demolition of the old castle, with a new manor house being
constructed elsewhere on the estate for the new master of
Caerrorie. The land had passed through two families since
then, and was now held of the Crown by Thomas, Earl of
Carcashale, though said earl had his principal seat farther
west, near Dolban. Kelson had dined with him earlier in the
week, and had been assured that little remained of the old
demesne buildings.

The allure of Caerrorie, however, was not necessarily that
Camber had lived there, but that it had been Camber's original burial place. Though most of the vast pile of the earlier

castle had been dismantled to build the new manor house, the cellars and family burial vaults were said to remain, though in deplorable condition. Kelson did not tell Earl Thomas, of course, but he hoped that Haldane or Deryni powers still might sift some information of import from the ruins, despite the ravages of time and the destroyers.

Thus noon found Kelson quite happily immersed in Camberiana as he, Dhugal, Saer, and the squire Dolfin clambered over the ruins of old Caerrorie keep, working their way down to the lower levels to gain access to the MacRorie burial vaults—for, in the decade immediately following Camber's canonization, an active cult of Saint Camber was said to have flourished around a now-ruined shrine there. A monk from the local village church, one Brother Arnold, had kilted up his habit to guide them, but he clearly was dubious as Dhugal, Dolfin, and the king tried to shift a fallen beam that blocked the way.

"I don't really understand why you want to go down there, Sire," the man said, wringing his hands together as Saer joined in and the beam shifted. "It will be full of water, after all this rain. And I understand that no effort was ever made to restore the graves that were desecrated."

"Why, for shame, Brother," Kelson murmured, grunting and straining at the slowly shifting beam. "Even if you hold with those who took away Camber's sainthood, surely his kin before him did no harm, that they should deserve such treatment."

"Why, no one would argue that, Sire," Brother Arnold said. Able to stand it no longer, he pitched in on the beam and helped move it far enough aside that a boy or a slender man could slip through, but not one of his own size, or even of Saer's. "People did strange things in those days, though. They say that one of Camber's sons used to be buried down in my churchyard, too, but the mob didn't spare him when they sacked the castle, either; and he died long before all the rest of this happened. Local tradition has it that *he* should have been the saint, not his father."

"Indeed?"

Kelson peered down into the opening and considered whether he really wanted to get his feet as wet as it looked to be down there.

"How deep is it?" Dhugal murmured, craning to see over his shoulder.

Saer took a torch from Dolfin and shoved it into the opening, but the resultant smoke obscured anything the increased light might have revealed.

"Hmmm, that's no good," Kelson muttered. "Dhugal, do you want to do the honors? Brother Arnold, if you're likely to be offended by a little Deryni assistance here, I suggest you leave now."

Arnold gulped audibly, but he did not back off.

"I'll—stay, my lord. You'll—need someone to direct you to where the crypts were."

"Suit yourself." Kelson took Dhugal's hand as Dhugal lowered himself through the opening and dropped with a splash and a muffled oath.

"Are you all right?" Kelson called.

Silvery light filtered upward from the opening, and Brother Arnold blanched and crossed himself furtively.

"Aye. Let me have a look around here. Wouldn't you know I'd find the only pit in the place? The rest seems to be only ankle deep—except for the spot I picked."

"And how deep is *that?*" Kelson called, chuckling as he and Saer exchanged glances and Dolfin tried not to laugh behind his torch.

"Oh, a little past my knees—just high enough to slosh over my boot tops when I landed. I just *love* wet feet. Try to aim a little farther to your right. I'll guide you. And Saer had better stay up there, in case we need help getting out. You might send Dolfin for a rope, too."

Still chuckling, Kelson vaulted his legs over the edge of the opening and supported himself with his hands until he could lower himself enough to feel Dhugal's hands on his boots, pushing him farther to the right.

"All right, come on."

Smoothly he let himself drop, missing the hole but almost sprawling on his hands and knees instead, for the footing was uneven under the shallow water. Dhugal caught him, though, and steadied him as he straightened in the silver-lit gloom.

"Creepy, isn't it?" Dhugal murmured, as Kelson scanned the close-ceilinged chamber by the handfire hovering near Dhugal's head.

Kelson shivered, though as much from cold as from anything else. The place stank of stagnant water and the musty, slightly sweet odor of the charnel house, though perhaps that last was as much imagination as any real scent, for Kelson felt sure there could have been no burials down here for at least a hundred years. He motioned for Dhugal to take his handfire in hand again as he glanced up at the opening where the silhouettes of Saer and Brother Arnold blocked out most of the daylight.

"Brother, you can come down if you want, but I fear it may be a tight squeeze for you to join us," Kelson called. "Not to mention that it's a goodly drop, and the only way out is back up a rope. You might prefer to direct us from there."

A nervous cough came from the side of the opening that was not Saer's.

"Ah, if you please, my lord, I think I *would* prefer to stay. I haven't been down there in years and I'm not as thin as I used to be. But if you'll turn so that a carved doorway is to your backs, you should be facing toward the length of the vault. Move straight ahead, as best you can, until you can't go any farther, and you ought to be near the place where it's said the Earl Camber was interred."

"And that's where his shrine was?" Kelson asked.

"Yes, Sire. But there's really nothing left. They burned it, you know. That's what brought down part of the roof."

"Bluidy fond of burning, they were," Dhugal muttered darkly, his border accent oddly noticeable.

Kelson flashed his foster brother a speculative glance.

"All right, Saer, we're going on in. We shouldn't be too long."

"Aye, Kelson," came Saer's low reply.

Kelson conjured more handfire as he followed Dhugal farther into the ruin, crimson to Dhugal's silver, and set it to floating just above head level behind him. The footing continued to be very uneven under the water. Marauders had been thorough in their destruction of the place, and the passage of time had not improved on the state of things.

"Look here," Dhugal called, bending over a broken slab of marble just ahead. "*Ballard MacRorie, Sextus Comes*—Sixth Earl of Culdi. I can't quite make out the dates, but it looks like 808 to 871. Would that make him Camber's father?''

Shuffling his feet to keep from splashing, Kelson moved closer to see what Dhugal had found, bending to pick up gingerly a piece of jawbone gleaming just under the surface of the water beside it.

"I should think so," he said. "Wasn't Camber the seventh earl? Look at this."

"Hmmm, good teeth," Dhugal observed, turning his attention back to another piece of slab jutting from the water beyond the first one. "This one says *Ballard MacRorie*, too, but it's a later date: 877 to 888. Why, he was just a boy. And here's another set of dates, 876 to 888, but the part with the first name's broken off. Why in God's name did they have to destroy the tombs of children?"

Kelson shook his head. "Mankind has done a lot of stupid, wasteful things in God's name, Dhugal. When has any of this sort of thing made sense?"

He moved on past the spot where Dhugal was scrubbing at a film of moss growing on another marker stone and nearly fell as his boot slipped on a step going down. He must be very close to where the Camberian shrine once had been, for he was almost at the end of the chamber. But the water was deeper ahead, at least half a dozen steps leading down to the lower level of the final section of the crypt. He sent his handfire ahead, but there was little to see. Burned-out stubs of beams and ancient chapel furniture jutted from the water, interspersed with broken slabs of marble, and several tomb niches yawned wide and empty in the back wall. He thought he might be able to work his way a little closer by balancing on some of the underwater debris, but there seemed little point.

"What do you think?" Dhugal asked, sloshing to his side. "Do you really want to get even wetter than you are?"

Kelson wrinkled his nose in distaste. "Not particularly. It's at least waist deep down there, and one can see from here that the tombs are all empty. Besides, whether one believes that Camber's body was assumed into heaven from here or that his son moved it to another resting place, it hasn't been here for over two hundred years."

"Well, we knew that before we came."

"True. But I wanted to see for myself. I might try one

other thing before we leave, though," Kelson added, picking his way carefully to the left until he could lean against a rough, slanted chunk of granite that had fallen from the arch. "Come and give me a little support. I'm going to try to cast for psychic impressions that may still be lingering."

Dhugal frowned, though he came dutifully, if soggily, to stand beside the king.

"You'll be opening yourself up to a lot of garbage besides Camber, if you're not careful. And all of this mayhem is a lot more recent than anything that might remain of *him*."

"True," Kelson conceded. "None of it is likely to be very powerful after so long, though. I ought to be able to separate the wheat from the chaff without too much trouble."

"Well, you know your own abilities. What do you want me to do?"

"Just give me your hand and stand by to brace my shields," Kelson said. "One way or another, this isn't going to take long."

Dhugal's hand was cold in his as Kelson closed his eyes and let himself slip easily into trance, bolstered by Dhugal's support. He went cautiously at first, only gradually slipping his shields to let impressions from his surroundings begin filtering through.

Intimations of lingering violence came through most strongly, of course, just as expected, but he was able to shift that aside with relative ease. Actual images of what had happened here were harder to divert—the sacrilege of the shrine's destruction, the tombs broken open and plundered, and bones, half-decomposed bodies, and even partially mummified remains dumped unceremoniously into the pyre whose fire eventually had brought down part of the roof.

Kelson winced at the intensity of it, letting a little of it spill over for Dhugal's reading. But there was nothing of the presence he had come to associate with Saint Camber. It was almost as if the saint had never been here. He was shaking his head as he came out of trance.

"No luck?" Dhugal asked, blinking himself back to full awareness as well.

"Not really." Kelson gave the ruined chamber another visual scan, then called his handfire back. "Maybe we'll have better luck at Iomaire, where he died. We'll be there next week. Did you want to look at anything else?"

"No, I just want to get my feet dry," Dhugal quipped, lifting one wet boot clear of the water. "I could also use some food. Even the Lenten fare of our hosts at Saint Bearand's will be welcome, with the empty pit I've got in my stomach."

The remark reminded Kelson that he was hungry, too, and the two of them jested about food as they made their way back to the entry hole and called for Saer and Dolfin to let down a rope.

The king had not yet returned to Saint Bearand's when Arilan's courier finally caught up with the king's party there at midafternoon. He was not expected back much before dusk. Earl Roger and a few of the men-at-arms had gone out for a gallop after the noon meal, and Jass and many of the others were still hunting, so Conall was the ranking knight present when the courier arrived.

Hence, it was he to whom the courier reported, when he had made himself known to the Haldane lancer on duty at the abbey gate; and since Conall was the king's cousin and at least a few of the letters were addressed to him in particular, the courier turned over the dispatch pouch without demur and went on to the refectory to sup on the sparse abbey fare of a Lenten Friday.

Conall's stomach tried to tie itself into knots as he took the pouch into the room he had been assigned. His squire was there, mending a strap on a breast collar off one of the sumpter horses, but Conall put him deeply and somewhat precipitously to sleep before upending the pouch on the rug in front of the fireplace and sorting quickly through the letters. Those addressed to himself, one each from his mother and his two brothers, he put aside immediately, for he could deal with them later, after Kelson returned; but those addressed to the king he scanned without opening, using the talent Tiercel had taught him for reading a sealed letter.

Not unexpectedly, most were from Nigel and dealt with the day-to-day running of the kingdom—the usual sorts of dispatches sent to a king while away from his capital, to keep him generally informed as to what was occurring in his absence. A few were in Duncan's hand, either in a clerical capacity for the prince regent, signed by Nigel, or else his own analysis of certain items. Those, too, were innocuous enough.

One was from Duncan to Dhugal, however, with instructions to share it with Kelson, and it made Conall almost dizzy with fear, for it detailed Duncan's discovery of Tiercel's body in the secret passageway.

Blast! It *would* have to have been Duncan who found the body!

Another was from Arilan to Dhugal, inquiring as to any knowledge he might have of what transpired to bring about Tiercel's death. The Deryni bishop had written a similar letter to Kelson, asking him to be certain that Dhugal responded to Arilan's inquiry immediately.

These last three frightened Conall, both singularly and in their combined implications. He had known that Tiercel's body eventually must be found, but it was one thing to learn that the expected had happened and another to know that Duncan had found it—the one man in Rhemuth who might have been expected to recognize the dead man.

And by now, not only Arilan but very likely all the other powerful and mysterious members of the Camberian Council had applied their not inconsiderable Deryni talents to probe Tiercel's death further. And while none of the letters even hinted that Arilan suspected Tiercel's death had not been accidental, much less mentioned Conall, Conall's guilt gnawed at him like a hungry wolf; already extant jealousy began almost immediately to color the guilt.

Conall found that the thought of Dhugal being questioned in the matter terrified him. If Arilan or Duncan or one of the others had been able to pin down a precise time for Tiercel's death, Conall knew that Dhugal's alibi was iron-clad. Conall had an alibi, too, for Jowan, his squire, could swear honestly under oath that his master had been abed early that night; but close questioning of the boy *might* reveal that his memory had been tampered with, and by whom.

That, in itself, could be damning enough to press the inquiries further, for Conall had no business knowing how to do such things. And who knew but that Dhugal, under intensive interrogation, might remember hearing something connected with Conall's wary approach to the doorway into his chambers, when Conall had tried to return through the palace after arranging Tiercel's body on the landing? What if he could make a connection to Conall? After all, Conall *had* pushed Tiercel, even though he had not meant to do him serious harm. . . .

But suppose, on the other hand, that evidence somehow could be contrived to implicate Dhugal in the matter? Now, *there* was an attractive proposition. Perhaps Dhugal could even be framed, thereby eliminating not only a dangerous potential betrayer, but also a troublesome rival. Of course, steps would have to be taken to ensure that Dhugal could not defend himself. . . .

Conall thought about the notion as he restored all the letters to the dispatch pouch saving his own and the three dealing with Tiercel's death. He had brought Tiercel's drug satchel with him, for he dared not leave it behind and risk it being found. Perhaps something from that could be put to good use. He did not know the purpose of all the drugs in Tiercel's pharmacopia, but he knew some of them—enough to ensure, if he could figure out a way to administer them, that Dhugal should not survive the next day.

And not by a mere poison or overdose, either, for they rode through some very rugged country tomorrow. A more subtle solution was required—something sufficient only to blur the victim's judgment or perceptions, or perhaps to lull him into a false sense of security. According to the monk who would guide them, there were ample opportunities for an unwary rider to meet a fatal accident.

But Conall could do nothing to further his developing plan until the others returned, in any case, and he needed the time to decide exactly what he was going to do. After closing the courier pouch, he took it next door, into the room Kelson and Dhugal shared, and left it beside the snoring Ciard O Ruane. Then he went back to his own quarters to let Jowan wake up, to read his own letters, and to firm up his plans for later in the evening.

Kelson and his companions returned just in time to hear Vespers, and Conall watched fearfully and jealously as Dhugal walked into the abbey, arm in arm with the king. The prince did not even try to pray as he knelt not far from them, though he mouthed the responses dutifully enough and bowed his head at the appropriate times.

Afterwards, at supper, Conall was as merry as any in the refectory, at least within the bounds of Lenten propriety. He even stayed a while to listen to the ballads one of the lay brothers sang when the royal party had retired to the abbot's quarters for another casual hour by the fire.

No one tarried late, though, for Saer meant them to get an early start, to be well through the pass before any chance of failing light. And so, when the king and his favorite retired even before Compline, Conall, too, made his devoirs to the abbot and repaired to his bed.

He dared not sleep, however. Not much later, when all the abbey slept in those deeply silent hours between Compline and Matins, Conall made his way without challenge to the abbey stables, where harness and equipment was already assembled, ready for an early departure after Mass in the morning. There he located Dhugal's belongings without difficulty, and slipped the stopper from a shoulder flask already filled with wine for the next day's journey. He sniffed of the contents before adding the contents of the earthenware vial he had concealed on his person since late afternoon, to ensure that the scent and taste would cover what he had added. He need not worry if Dolfin or Ciard or one of the other servants had a nip from the flask, for Tiercel had told Conall that the drugs only affected those of Deryni blood.

Then, apprehensive but at the same time thrilled, Conall quickly returned to his own bed and lay down, though he did not sleep much in what remained of the night.

CHAPTER TWELVE

The way of a fool is right in his own eyes.
—Proverbs 12:15

The next morning dawned still and damp, pregnant with the probability of more rain, though none was yet falling. The local monks, when questioned about the outlook, avowed that the weather *should* clear by noon—but the time of year was capricious. Even snow was not unheard of in the passes, well into March. Given the present aspect of the sky, either storm, snow, or a clear day were equal possibilities.

After Mass and over a far more leisurely breakfast than originally planned, Kelson considered what to do. It still was not raining. Nor did they even need to worry about getting all the way through the pass today, for there was a small abbey at the summit that could surely provide them a dry place to sleep, if it came to that. Saer declared himself half of a mind to delay another day, in hopes that more definite signs of clearing weather might prevail over the clouds scudding along the eastern horizon, but Kelson was impatient to be gone, fired by the prospect of what he might learn at Iomaire—for a shrine once had graced the spot where Camber fell in battle, and the king hoped he might learn more there of Camber than he had at Caerrorie.

So Kelson ordered the company to assemble in the abbey yard as planned, if a few hours later than he would have wished. And, as if in answer to his optimism, sunshine did break through the clouds just as he signaled the column forward to ride out the gates of Saint Bearand's.

An unexpectedly welcome addition to their number was the monk who accompanied them to point out the way— one Brother Gelric, a garrulous, almost comically thin individual mounted on a shaggy piebald pony, who soon had everyone in his vicinity laughing at his assessments of the court life he had known in Llannedd before his profession as a monk. His good humor, added to the clearing weather, soon lifted the spirits of the entire expedition. It was not long before young Jass MacArdry had half the knights, all his borderers, and most of the Haldane lancers joining in the refrain of a jaunty border ballad that told how the bonnie Earl of Kilshane once had ridden day and night, night and day, for near on a week, to warn an earlier chief of Clan MacArdry of a terrible sea invasion.

They made good time for the first hour or so, easily climbing the smooth, gentle grade that was the approach to the proper ascent to the pass. The weather remained cold but clear, though it became more overcast as they climbed higher. The going got harder, too. Gradually, as they turned along the bank of a wide, fast-running mountain stream, swollen with rain and early runoff from the mountains whose slopes they climbed, the footing and the grade got worse. On a rocky plateau, close beside the icy-cold spill pool of a spectacular waterfall cascading down the mountainside to their left, Brother Gelric called a short halt to let men and horses rest.

"You'd best have everyone check their girths and other equipment before we move on, Sire," he told Kelson, as the king and Dhugal walked the kinks out of their legs, and Dolfin took their horses over to the pool to drink. "Make sure everything is well strapped down. The footing gets far worse before it gets better. This is the last reasonably flat spot until we reach the summit, and it will be single file very shortly."

"How much farther is it?" Kelson asked.

"Another hour and a half," the monk replied. "Perhaps a little less, if it doesn't start raining again."

From a little farther along the bank, Conall watched and listened nervously, giving his sword to Jowan to strap to his saddle as he sprawled on a sun-warmed rock and tried to pretend that he was not interested in whether or not Dhugal drank from the flask slung across his chest. With the sun shining, albeit weakly, and the exertion of the past hour, Conall was sweating a little in his riding leathers. In addition, he had begun to have second thoughts about what he had done. While Dhugal and Kelson fiddled with their equipment, dutifully shifting loads and tightening down straps with Dolfin, Conall unlaced the throat of his tunic and bade Jowan bring him a cupful of the cold, sweet water coming off the mountainside. If Dhugal did drink, Conall would need a cool head to make sure no shadow of suspicion was turned on himself.

But like most of the party, Dhugal, too, chose to slake his thirst from the stream, stretching out on his stomach on a flat rock to drink from one hand, like any common peasant. Conall found himself becoming annoyed all over again when Kelson also followed suit, in most unkingly fashion. It almost made Conall wish that both his rivals would go ahead and drink from the flask. That would solve even more problems, for no one else in the royal party was in a position even to recognize the effects of the drugs in the wine, much less to counteract them, and fate might well run its course in the next few hours.

And if neither drank through the day and Conall could retrieve the flask tonight, he would do that, he decided. No harm would be done, and Conall could pretend he had never even thought of doing anything wrong.

The greatest danger to Conall accrued if only Dhugal drank and Kelson intervened before Dhugal could meet a mishap. For, while there was nothing to link Conall with the drugs in the flask, their discovery *would* alert the king that someone with access to such substances was up to no good. Kelson had no reason to suspect Conall, but the fact that Conall had purloined the letters about Tiercel's death eventually would have to lead to uncomfortable inquiries—and Conall did not think he could withstand a direct Truth-Read, if brought to the question.

On the other hand, far rougher terrain was coming up. Perhaps, if he rode close to Dhugal, Conall could simply nudge Dhugal's horse over the edge at a crucial point, claiming that his own mount had spooked at something. And he could *make* the big grey spook. No one would ever think to ask him directly whether he had done it deliberately. And with Dhugal would go the telltale flask of wine as well as a dangerous rival.

Ahead, the trail did become more difficult, and narrower, climbing slowly above the level of the flood-swollen streambed. As he had hoped, Conall managed to get behind Dhugal when they funneled down to single file. The footing, never good, changed from muddy to sandy, but any improvement in consistency was canceled out by an increase in the number of sharp, hoof-bruising rocks that might provide a fatal stumble. The farther they went, the more Conall began to wonder whether he would dare to do anything untoward, for fear of following his intended victim over the edge. A sheer cliff face loomed hard on their right—mostly rock, but slick in spots with mud and tiny rivulets of runoff from the days of rain. The embankment on their left sloped down in an increasingly steep and treacherous drop to rocky rapids below. The higher they climbed, the faster the stream ran, deeper and narrower, studded with massive, stream-scoured boulders and more jagged rocks jutting out of rushing, seething white water.

Then the rain began again, perhaps half an hour out of the last rest stop. At first, light sprinkles only prompted men to glance around suspiciously and wonder whether the droplets had come from the raging stream; but then came large, splattering drops that demanded that hoods be pulled over heads ducked down in collars. And the large drops quickly became a downpour.

Conall hunched down in his cloak and muttered to himself as he squinted against the rain. Even if the trail had been wide enough to turn around, which it was not and had not been for some time, he would not have relished the thought of retracing the route they had already come, and especially not going downhill. Nor did he particularly want to make the climb again, tomorrow or the next day. They had almost lost a pack horse a little way back, and the trail here was worse than it had been there. Besides, they surely must be at or near the halfway mark. Silly, to go back.

Not that the going looked appreciably better ahead— what little Conall could see ahead for the pelting rain. Dhugal's red dun was directly in front of him, with Dolfin between Dhugal and Kelson, who followed close on the heels of their guide. The rest of the company was strung out behind

Conall, Jowan immediately behind. Just before a curve in
the trail would have put the monk out of sight, Conall saw
him pull up his piebald pony and turn to mouth something
to Kelson in the rain; but then the man and Kelson were
moving on, and Conall supposed they had decided not to
turn back.

Very well. That was fine with him. They could hardly get
wetter than they were, he supposed. And even if what lay
ahead was worse than what they had already passed, there
was the promise of the abbey at the top, warm fires, dry
clothes, and hot food . . .

He daydreamed about hot mulled wine as he hunched
down in his saddle and prayed for it all to end, concentrating
only on the even *plop-plop* of his horse's hooves as it followed Dhugal's, nose to tail, wincing occasionally when his
mount would falter, trying not to look at what lay so very
close at their left. The rain washed down the trail in torrents,
so that, in spots, the horses were fetlock-deep in muddy
water. On the opposite side of the canyon cut by the stream,
several tributary streams tumbled down in smaller versions
of the waterfall they had already passed. Their din, plus the
roar of the rapids below them, drowned out all possibility of
verbal communication, and Conall dared not use what he
knew of mind-speech, so he had to content himself with
trying to read the hand signals and facial clues that he could
note on the riders ahead. Kelson, he was pleased to note,
did not appear to be at all happy, and Dhugal looked down-
right worried.

The rain finally began to slack off, at least. Conall supposed that was something of an improvement. The footing
ahead looked no firmer or less muddy, but the trail seemed
to be slightly wider. Conall even had the impression that it
was not quite as steep as it had been, though he was to decide
later that it had been an optical illusion. Whatever the true
state of the slope ahead, so far as steepness was concerned,
the forces of nature at work chose that moment to precipitate
disaster.

The piebald pony was the first animal to founder, suddenly up to its knees in shifting, rain-sodden mud and starting
a chain reaction that soon had the horses of Kelson, Dolfin,
and Dhugal mired to the belly as well, squealing and thrash-

ing as that entire section of the trail began to dissolve under them.

Then Conall's mount lost its footing under the near foreleg and nearly pitched him off over its head as he tried to recover. Squire Jowan, riding directly behind his master, crowded closer to reach out a hand to Conall, in case he had to get off, but that set Jowan's bay to slipping and sliding, its entire hindquarters suddenly over the edge and scrambling wildly to regain decent footing while Jowan tried to crawl up its neck.

Conall grabbed instinctively at the animal's reins, trying at the same time to steady his own beast, but it soon became obvious that he might not even be able to get himself out of this alive. The whole cliff face seemed to be disintegrating, too long waterlogged and then subjected to too many horses and too much weight.

He heard someone go over the edge ahead—whether man or beast or both together, he had no time to find out, because he was fighting to keep from following. Dhugal's horse, whinnying and plunging ever more wildly for footing, pitched Dhugal over its near shoulder and managed to put a hind leg through the reins of Conall's, jerking the poor animal's head down flat against the muddy trail. Conall could not see where Dhugal landed, because his own mount's gyrations jerked Jowan's reins out of his hand, and he twisted in the saddle to see the consequences.

Jowan screamed. Conall saw him and his mount beginning to slide slowly over the edge, but his own straits were desperate, and he dared not make any more aggressive attempt to try to save Jowan, or he would overbalance and both of them would go over. As it was, his horse was slipping and scrambling past the point of no return and making matters no better by trying to break free from the leg Dhugal's horse had through its reins.

Some of the horses were going to go over the edge. Up ahead, at least one already had done so. Conall heard its scream and the muted splash its body made as it hit the rapids far below, but he was too busy scrambling for firmer ground to look and see whose it was—Kelson's or Dolfin's, most likely. And he could not see either of them.

But his own horse was about to follow. Seeking any feeble chance to save himself, he launched himself from the saddle to hug the cliff face, twisting his gloved fingers around a few spindly tree roots and bushes exposed by the rain and praying that they would hold his weight. Mercifully, they did, though his grey, relieved of the extra weight in the saddle, reared up in a desperate attempt to break free of Dhugal's red dun and went over backwards, taking the dun with it.

Conall was quick enough to see his and Dhugal's horses disappear over the edge and could only assume that Jowan had gone over, too. And ahead, a tangle of russet and mud, equine and human, slid and tumbled down the face of the embankment—Dhugal, surely—followed by the flailing figure of Dolfin, all into roiling white water below. Of Kelson he could see no sign.

Then, suddenly, his Uncle Saer was at his side, edging along the cliff face on foot and passing a rope around his waist, sobbing—and Conall dared to look over the side again, where a frantically struggling red dun horse was disappearing around a bend, toward the waterfall that raged beyond. His own horse lay battered on the rocks below, not moving, several of its legs at impossible angles, and a little farther along, he spotted the body of the piebald pony floating belly-up, temporarily wedged against some rocks. It appeared that a few of the sumpter horses had gone over, too.

Afterward, Conall never quite remembered just how Saer got him back down to the rest area near the falls, or precisely when it stopped raining. But he would remember, for the rest of his days, the looks on the faces of the survivors gathered there, gradually retrieving bodies of men and beasts from the pool of stiller water that lay a little beyond the waterfall's crashing spillway. The only living things to come from that pool of flood-wrack were the plucky Squire Dolfin, half-drowned and with a broken wrist and several cracked ribs, not to mention bruises over most of his body, and Dhugal's horse, shuddering and heaving, one leg dragging pitifully as it made a game try to follow the servant leading it away from the water.

Dolfin, at least, would mend. No so the red dun, who had to be put down. Once they had gotten Dolfin to cough up the water he had swallowed, Father Lael bound up the boy's wrist and ribs, poured a hot posset down his throat, and pronounced his survival a miracle.

No such miracle had attended the other lost squire, how-

ever. Conall was among those who found Jowan's body
wedged in rocks at the far edge of the pool—drowned, even
if his skull had not been fatally split open by collision with
a jagged rock. And as they watched, Conall still a little dazed
from his own near brush with death, the body of the unfortunate Brother Gelric bobbed out of the roiling rapids at the
base of the waterfall, swirled around for several minutes,
then was sucked under, never to emerge again, as was the
feebly struggling form of Jowan's bay.

Within the next few hours, the carcasses of Dolfin's
chestnut, Conall's grey, two sumpter horses, and the piebald
pony also came over the falls, long drowned and battered to
death. And later, farther downstream, they recovered the
drowned and broken body of Kelson's grey, with the Haldane sword still strapped to its saddle. But of the king and
his foster brother they found no trace, though they kept looking as long as the light held, and by torchlight thereafter, for
several hours more.

Even after Saer had called off the search until morning,
the MacArdry men kept their own vigil at the edge of the
pool, old Ciard O Ruane keening softly as he rocked back
and forth in his grief—for Ciard had regarded his young chief
almost as a son of his own. Taking a cue from the old gillie,
Father Lael assembled the entire company nearby and led
them all in prayers for Jowan's soul, with added supplications for the safe return of the king and Dhugal. Afterward,
while the servants threw together a makeshift supper, Jass
and the other MacArdry men remained with Ciard, Dhugal's
sword thrust into the ground like a cross, Jass with his hands
on the quillons and forehead bowed against the pommel, as
he had watched with his chief and their king during their
knights' vigil not three weeks before, weeping as if his heart
would break.

It was not until well after dark, huddled under a borrowed
cloak beside one of the fires of their miserable campsite, that
it suddenly struck Conall, through the numb shock of the
entire afternoon's events, that they were not likely to find
Kelson or Dhugal—not alive, at any rate. And that made
Conall's father king, and Conall himself heir to the throne!
Nor need Conall suffer any pangs of guilt over his shift

in fortune, for it honestly had been none of his doing. Forget about the fact that, but for the accident, Dhugal and even Kelson might have drunk from the flask that Conall had drugged. That flask was now gone forever into whatever watery grave had claimed Dhugal and the king.

Chapter Thirteen

Behold, my terror shall not make thee afraid,
neither shall my hand be heavy upon thee.

—Job 33:7

Dhugal fought his way feebly back to consciousness with the certain conviction that he was dying. Or perhaps he was dead already. Even though he struggled to open his eyes, it was pitch dark, and he certainly was cold and wet—though, if he were truly dead, why could he hear this roaring in his ears?

Besides, he hurt too much to be dead. Every part of his body ached, where it was not numb from the cold. He was lying on his stomach, water lapping at his face, and he managed to lift his head enough to draw a ragged breath, but his lungs burned with the water he had already inhaled. All at once, his entire body convulsed in violent spasms that curled him hard on his side, coughing and choking. Water spewed from his mouth, from his nose, and it was all he could do to keep his head high enough to avoid breathing it in again.

Somehow, he managed to haul himself to hands and knees—or, rather, to elbows and knees, for his left wrist twinged with a terrible pain whenever he tried to put any weight on it. But then he could only cough up more water, gagging and retching helplessly until he was sure that either his guts or his lungs must come up.

Finally, though, his body seemed satisfied. His chest ached as if a giant had been sitting on it, and he did not even want to think about how badly he might have damaged his wrist, but at least he was alive. He let himself collapse down on his calves and forearms, bracing his forehead against his good wrist to keep from breathing water again—for he was awash in it, several fingers deep—and made himself take a slow, steadying breath while he willed his pounding heart to subside to something approaching normal rate and blinked the sand out of his eyes, trying to pierce the darkness of his surroundings. The roaring sound behind him continued to be a mystery—until suddenly, without preamble or further prompting, memory came flooding back.

The river! Good God, where was Kelson? The cliff had collapsed under their horses, and they had gone over the edge, into the rapids.

Dhugal whimpered as he struggled to a sitting position, for the pain of his wrist was almost enough to make him faint, even though he tried to brace it with his good hand. If he did pass out again, and he fell face-down, there was a very good chance that he might truly drown, this time. And Kelson—

Kelson surely had been in the water, too. Dhugal remembered throwing himself clear of his horse as he fell, trying to angle his body so he would not hit squarely on any of the rocks rushing up to meet him—but even as he fell, he had been aware of Kelson already in the water not far away, looking dazed and scared.

He had hit the water hard, narrowly missing collision with a massive boulder, and he went deep. Somehow he managed to push something and surfaced almost immediately, wildly shaking water from his eyes and searching for Kelson. He saw the flash of a crimson-clad arm not far away and struck out for it, yelping as he slammed one knee against a submerged rock, but he dared not spare too much attention for where he was going or he would lose sight of the king.

Things got a little hazy after that, but he knew he had managed to reach Kelson, and that the two of them had clung together as long as they could, while the water buffeted them along—and then he remembered the waterfall, and *knowing* that there was nothing he could do to prevent them going over. Kelson was hurt already, far more than himself. Both of them had screamed weakly as they were swept over the edge.

He had held onto Kelson all the way to the bottom of the falls, but, after that, he was not sure. A quick, tentative sweep of the darkness around him with his good arm confirmed that Kelson was not within reach, at least.

He knew they had still been together when a current sucked them under, however—deep, deeper, until Dhugal was sure his lungs would burst. In the end, though, he had had to surrender to the pain and the cold, breathing in water and letting go.

That realization set him coughing again, but it was not as bad as before—though a different kind of pain in his chest told him that he might have cracked another rib or two, in addition to whatever he had done to his wrist. His braced his good hand against his ribs for a few seconds while he caught his breath again, trying once more to pierce the darkness that pressed close around him, and was surprised to find that his wine flask somehow was still slung across his chest.

Well, thank heaven for very small favors. If the stopper had not come out—which it had not, his questing fingers soon discovered—wine might help ease the pain, or at least warm him a little, when he had gotten his bearings better.

But first he needed light, and he dared not move from where he was without it, for suddenly he realized the full implications of the roaring sound behind him—the river from which he must have dragged himself, with some vestige of semiconsciousness. If he was not careful, he would be back in it—and he knew he could not survive another like buffeting.

Very well, then, his light must be handfire. He should be able to manage that much magic, even with his head still full of water. But when, without thinking, he tried to flex the fingers of his injured hand in the proper configuration for the spell, pain shot all the way up his arm, making him suck in his breath between clenched teeth and nearly setting him to coughing again.

Jesu, was the blasted thing broken?

Subsequent examination, feeling gingerly with his right hand, convinced him that perhaps it was not broken after all, but only badly sprained; but the distinction made little difference just now, other than the fact that he would not be able to do this as easily as he had hoped. Under normal circumstances, he had no doubt that he could conjure handfire with either hand; but his circumstances were anything but normal just now, and he had never done it except with his left. Not for the first time in his life, being corrie-fisted had become a distinct disadvantage—though he supposed that, if he had been right-handed, it would have been *that* wrist that was injured, for he suspected he probably had sustained the injury while trying to fend himself off a rock with his stronger hand.

Very well, then, he would have to do it right-handed, but light he must have—to look for Kelson, as well as for his own survival. Taking a slow, careful breath, he cupped his right hand and shifted his usual mode of concentration from left to right, bending the power in his mind. The resultant glow in his right palm grew a little unsteadily at first, but then it swiftly took on its usual, robust silver gleam.

Thank God!

Not that the light did much good. As Dhugal lifted his hand to look around him, he saw at once why he had been choking when he first regained consciousness. He was sitting in water, on a very shallow shelf of rock just at the edge of what obviously had become an underground stream—or river, at this point, for it was too wide for him to even see the other bank of the roiling water that continued to rush past at such a furious pace.

Sand gritted under him as he shifted to take it all in, and his teeth began to chatter from the cold, but he noticed piles of driftwood and other flood wrack caught along the embankment and looming darker against the sides of the cavern, farther from the water. Perhaps some of it was even dry.

Very well. Perhaps he could build a fire. He was going to have to do something to get dry and warm, and soon, or he might as well have drowned. He was a well enough trained battle surgeon to recognize the signs of shock in his own body—and God knew what he might have to contend with when he found Kelson.

If Kelson was still alive, of course. The very thought that he might not be sobered Dhugal fast and lent him strength he did not know he had, to get his feet under him and wobble slowly to a standing position. The effort made him dizzy, and from more than cold and shock, he suddenly realized. He had been too dazed to notice it before, but his head hurt from more than just his long submersion, right at the back of the skull. A quick inspection with his good hand revealed a sizable lump, where he must have cracked it against a rock. He could only hope he did not have a concussion.

His right ankle twinged, too, when he tried to shuffle to higher ground, swelling already in his soggy boot, but he dared not think yet about whether it might be broken. It didn't hurt as much as his wrist; but if it was broken and he took off the boot, he might not get it on again. At least the leather would give him a little support while he tried to search for Kelson. And he could sense no grinding of broken bone as he hobbled as far as a pile of branches and contrived to break off a piece of wood for a crutch, though the ankle did hurt.

He had best shed his waterlogged cloak, at least for the present. The sodden leather and fur must weigh nearly as much as he did; and wet, whatever warmth it might have provided was more than canceled out by the energy he would have to consume, dragging it around. Besides, now that he was thinking a little more clearly, he realized that the air itself probably was not terribly cold down here, even though the water had been, and he was shivering from that. He seemed to recall that underground caverns generally maintained a more or less constant temperature year-round, rather like a wine cellar. If he could get dry, the cold probably would become one of his less important considerations. So if he shed a few layers of his wet clothing—

He nudged his handfire up to hover beside his head and was unlacing his tunic one-handed, anxiously peering into the darkness all around him, when all at once he spied a darker, more regular shape than the piles of flood wrack, lying at the water's edge just a little upstream from where he had come aground. He froze, his head twinging as he concentrated his powers in that direction, but then he was shoving aside the pain of head, wrist, and ankle to hobble in that direction as fast as he could go.

"*Kelson!*" he cried.

He got no response as he approached, but he knew it was the king. The solid silhouette became a lumpy something under a soggy crimson cloak as his handfire drew nearer; and as Dhugal collapsed to his knees beside it in panicked apprehension and began clawing at the wool, he found the prone, scarcely breathing form of Kelson.

"He's alive! Praise God!" Dhugal whispered, though

Kelson was not breathing well at all, his head awash on the river bank where he apparently had managed to drag himself, much as Dhugal had done.

Hoping he was not adding to any injuries Kelson already had, Dhugal carefully lifted the king's head clear of the water and, after some little juggling to spare his injured wrist, unfastened the clasp that bound Kelson to the water-logged crimson cloak—which must be at least as heavy as his own had been. That done, he could slide two fingers into the neck of Kelson's tunic and feel for a pulse, though he was not happy at what he read. He tried to get a look at Kelson's pupils, but the angle was all wrong. In any case, Kelson was already in shock, in addition to whatever injuries he might have.

"Got to get him out of the water, get him warm," Dhugal muttered to himself, dragging the rest of the soggy cloak aside so he could shift Kelson partially onto his side. Thank *God* they had not been wearing mail or even jazerants in the foul weather!

"C'mon, Dhugal, you can do it!" he grunted. "You've got to, or he'll die! Come *on!*"

Bracing himself against the pain he knew it would cost him and determined not to succumb to it, Dhugal shifted Kelson's torso upright enough to grasp him under his arms from behind, slipping his left arm past the injured wrist to hook at the elbow in Kelson's armpit and spare his wrist as much as possible. It still hurt terribly, and Dhugal thought his ankle surely must collapse under him as well, but somehow he managed to drag the unconscious king as far as the cavern wall, perhaps a dozen paces away. Just as they got there, Kelson stirred feebly and began to gasp and choke, coughing up water explosively from his mouth and nose much as Dhugal had done when he first came to. All Dhugal could do was hold him close until it passed, trying to warm him and praying that, rid of the water in his lungs and stomach, Kelson soon would come around.

But Kelson did not regain consciousness when the spasms ceased, though he did breathe easier, and his pulse seemed stronger. Dhugal laid him on his back and loosened his clothing at the neck, cushioning his head with the wet overtunic he pulled off over his own head, then quickly ran his good hand over the rest of Kelson's body to check superficially for broken bones. There was a fair-sized rip in the right leg of Kelson's leather breeches, with a massive bruise already purpling the thigh underneath, and doubtless he would develop other bruises elsewhere—Dhugal knew *he* was going to have a savage crop of them—but nothing appeared to be broken.

Nothing below the neck, at least, but how about above? Dhugal could already see a lump swelling beneath a raw, bloody scrape above Kelson's right eyebrow, and a graze along the left side of his jaw promised another bruise, at least. He prodded both spots lightly with a fingertip, but neither seemed serious enough to cause too much worry.

But when Dhugal again lifted Kelson's eyelids to check his pupils, only the left reacted immediately to light. The right was dilated, and closed down only sluggishly when Dhugal beckoned his handfire closer.

Urgently, Dhugal ran his fingers under the wet black hair to hunt for fractures he had missed the first time, probing with his mind as well as his hand—and found, to his utter horror, that what he had judged, at first inspection, to be a matte of mud in the hair above Kelson's left ear concealed not only a slowly seeping wound, now clotting, but a depressed skull fracture that was nearly the size of a small walnut.

Fear clutched at Dhugal's throat as he found it, and tears came to his eyes. He made himself take a closer look, praying that he was wrong, but he had seen such injuries too often before. The prognosis generally was not good, even with a skilled surgeon's services and adequate facilities. If Kelson regained consciousness soon, there was reason for guarded optimism—*if* the wound above the depression was only superficial, and no infection penetrated the skull—but his chances decreased for every minute he remained unconscious.

Nor were the signs any better as Dhugal tried to use his powers to rouse the king. The shields that should have guarded Kelson's mind were almost nonexistent—intact all around, but shell-thin, breachable by anyone with even a modicum of power—but Dhugal did not want to risk destroying what little defense the shields might afford. His mental nudge at the centers that controlled respiration did seem to ease Kelson's breathing a little, however. That was not so very different from the monitoring he had begun to learn, while Kelson or his father went into deep trancing.

"Shock's the worst threat, right now," Dhugal told himself, bending to begin stripping off the outermost layers of Kelson's wet clothes—for that, unlike the head injury, was something he *could* do something about. "Gotta get these wet things off him and keep him warm. I'll build a fire, somehow. The air's not that cold—but, God, I am!"

The exertion helped Dhugal get warm, though, even if Kelson looked no better, stripped to a soggy singlet, than he had before. Dhugal was light-headed by the time he was ready to go gather kindling to get a fire started, and his wrist was throbbing, so he decided to take time out to wrap it before he went. With his teeth and his good hand, he managed to tear strips from the lining of the overtunic he had taken off Kelson; and though he was clumsy, trying to bandage his injury with his off hand, it did feel better when he had finished. He considered making a closer inspection of his ankle as well, but discarded the notion immediately when he realized that the swelling now had immobilized his foot in the boot far better than he could have done on his own. And a more careful probe with his powers confirmed that, if anything was broken, it was also being held in place by the boot, so he had best not mess with it for now.

Dealing with both his injuries left him a little weaker in the knees than he had hoped, however, so he decided to have a drink from the hitherto forgotten wine flask, to fortify himself before tackling the task of dragging wood back to Kelson. Later, after he got the fire going, he would have to think about what they were going to eat, while Kelson recovered enough for them to worry about getting out of here in some other manner than the way they had come in, so he knew he needed to hoard what he had; but he did not know whether he could go out looking for wood without at least a swallow or two.

Dhugal's hands shook as he hugged the flask against his chest with his bandaged arm and tried to work the stopper out of the flask with his right hand. He thought with pleasure of the taste of the good Fianna wine he knew Ciard had packed.

But before he could raise it to his lips, Kelson stirred,

moaning aloud as he tossed his head from one side to the other and shifted his legs, eyelids fluttering.

"Kelson! Thank God!" Dhugal murmured, wincing as he laid the fingertips of his injured wrist against the king's forehead. "Kelson, are you all right? Can you hear me, Kel?"

With another groan, Kelson opened his eyes, focusing only slowly on Dhugal's face bent anxiously over him.

"Where do you hurt worst?" Dhugal demanded. "Can you tell me?"

"Thirsty—"

Though the swollen lips shaped the word but awkwardly, Dhugal rejoiced in even that glimmer of returning function.

"You're thirsty. Yes, of course. Here, let me help you sit up a little."

"So thirsty . . ." Kelson repeated drowsily.

Elated, Dhugal slipped his injured arm under Kelson's head to raise it, cradling it carefully in the crook of his elbow as he held the flask's opening to his mouth.

"It's wine. Is that all right?" he whispered. "You've probably had enough water for a while."

Kelson did not answer, but only drank greedily, taking four or five deep swallows before pushing the flask aside.

"'S good," he murmured. "God, it feels like fire in m'stomach, though. Have we got any food?"

"Afraid not. Not right now, at any rate. I was going to build us a fire, but I was afraid to leave you unconscious. If you think you'll be all right alone for a few minutes, I'll get some wood and see if I can get it started."

"'M not a baby," Kelson said muzzily. "I'll probably just go back to sleep."

"Sorry, but I can't let you do that," Dhugal replied. "You were unconscious, Kelson, I don't know for how long, but you've got a concussion. I—don't know how bad it is, but I want you to try to stay awake for a while. You were practically comatose."

Kelson blinked, a vague look shadowing the grey eyes. "Comatose?"

"In a coma, unconscious," Dhugal replied, suddenly wary. "Kelson, are you all right?" He paused a beat. "Do you remember what happened?"

Kelson swallowed with difficulty and shook his head, but the movement made him wince.

"I—have the feeling I should know what you're talking about, but I—"

Suddenly, he went white as the singlet he wore, one hand shooting up to grasp the front of Dhugal's shirt in a death-grip.

"Dear God, everything's blurring. I can't breathe! And my head—"

Even as Kelson said it, Dhugal guessed the cause, thrusting a mental probe into the flask still in his hand and then flinging it across the cavern in rage.

How had he not noticed it? There was *merasha* in the flask—not as high a concentration as what they had drunk with Arilan, but high enough—and something else besides. He did not know what the rest was, but it seemed to be choking Kelson. Already, the *merasha* was eroding what had remained of Kelson's shields in the wake of his head injury, and his breathing—

Desperately, Dhugal yanked the failing Kelson to a sitting position and rammed two fingers down his throat, holding them there relentlessly while Kelson gagged and retched and vomited up what he had drunk, giving Dhugal's fingers a fairly savage chewing in the process. At the same time, he forced the full strength of his powers past Kelson's already tattered shields and seized control of his respiration center, forcing him to keep breathing.

Dhugal dared not hope that was sufficient, though, for whatever had been in the wine was already in Kelson's system—though hopefully not in fatal concentration—and its effects would get worse before they got better. While the *merasha* might be slept off with only a fairly predictable discomfort—though he had no idea how Kelson would weather the experience with his head injury—Dhugal had no notion what the other substance or substances might do. He might not even be doing the right thing to make Kelson vomit— but he knew nothing else to do, under the circumstances.

And so, drawing strength from he knew not where, Dhugal dragged a weakly gasping Kelson back to the water's edge again and poured water down his throat from cupped hands, using physical strength, his skills as a battle surgeon, and even his Deryni powers to force the king to swallow, then repeated the process with the fingers down the throat. He did this over and over again, each time forcing the king to swallow more water, each time getting weaker and weaker resistance—whether from his own man-handling or from the effect of the drugged wine, he had no way of knowing—until finally he sensed that further repetitions would only weaken his patient far more than any slight gain from continued treatment might warrant.

He sobbed as he held Kelson close, himself gasping for breath in harmony with Kelson's labored breathing—which would cease altogether if Dhugal relaxed his control at all. With the part of his mind that was not occupied with keeping Kelson breathing and avoiding the *merasha* disruption as much as he could—which was achieved only by teeth-gritting single-mindedness—Dhugal scanned for other, less obvious wrongnesses that he might have missed in the horror of dealing with the immediate emergency of getting the drugged wine out of Kelson's stomach; but there seemed to be nothing.

Nothing besides the concussion damage, of course, which could not have been improved by the buffeting Dhugal had been forced to give his patient to flush out his stomach. Since they were back by the water again, and whatever drying out Kelson might have managed before the crisis was obviously undone—both he and Kelson were drenched—Dhugal gently bathed the wound above Kelson's left ear. He might as well find out the worst of the news.

But in the first piece of luck since he had opened his eyes in this Godforsaken place, Dhugal found the cut a superficial one—not the skull-splitting gash he had feared. Most of the clotted blood washed away easily to reveal only a badly bruised lump over what he could sense, with powers and with fingertips, was the skull depression he had found before. Nor was it quite as deep as he had first feared, though it was a serious injury. For if Kelson's brain was swelling on the inside of the skull, the way his scalp was swelling on the outside—

Dhugal did not want to think about that. Later, if there was absolutely no other choice, he might try to use his powers to gently lift the depressed bit of bone back into place; but he had seen too many head injuries as a result of battle not to know how risky it was to tamper with them physically. He wished he had his father's healing talent; but, unfortunately, he had found no sign of such a blessing in the short tenure of his discovery of his powers. He even considered trying to contact his father, the way he had contacted Kelson after last summer's terrible battle at Dorna; but he knew it was futile, alone and unsupported as he was, and so far from Rhemuth.

Besides, he did not even know if he could maintain what he was doing to keep Kelson breathing. He would have to sleep eventually, after all. He knew how to stave that off for a while, but not indefinitely. And even the cost of delay was high, after too long.

What if Kelson was not yet breathing on his own again by then? And even if he was, how long might that take? What were they going to eat? How were they going to get out of this place? He had no idea where they were, for he had no idea how long they had been in the water or how long he had been unconscious. They had started this mad episode in rugged country, from which it might take days to get a rescue party to them, even if they could find a way to make their whereabouts known. Surely *everyone* could not have gone over the cliff with them—though he was certain that Dolfin and the monk had, and perhaps Conall and his squire as well.

But thinking about the others raised an interesting question: How had his wine gotten drugged? For it was he who obviously had been the target of whomever it was who had decided to wreak mischief on this expedition. Ciard, who had charge of Dhugal's things, was above suspicion—but who? *Merasha* was a Deryni drug, generally available only to other Deryni, and not even to all of them, else Morgan would have been able to obtain some during the winter, and they would not have had to subject themselves to Arilan's harsh testing. And no one else in the expedition was Deryni or had close contact with Deryni.

Of course, that had not stopped Edmund Loris and Gorony from obtaining *merasha*—so there must be human sources for it. But who, in the expedition, would have a reason to want Dhugal dead or incapacitated? And surely whoever had done it would have known that Kelson, too, might drink from Dhugal's flask. It was a horrifying parallel to what had happened to Kelson's father—but who would have been poised to take advantage of their helplessness?

Thinking about it helped keep Dhugal alert when, after a

few more minutes to rest from his and Kelson's mutual exertions, he dragged the unconscious king back against the cavern wall, near to where they had been before, though closer to a pile of flood wrack that looked as if it might make a suitable fire to get them warm. He dared not break physical contact with Kelson to build the fire, for fear of losing his hold on the respiration control, but he was able—with much concentration, and at the expense of extinguishing his hand-fire for a while—finally to get a small fire going. It would only burn for as long as he could feed it with wood he could reach from where he and Kelson lay, but at least it was blessed warmth.

He held Kelson close against him and tried to think warm thoughts for both of them as he mused on what had happened and tried to think who could have done it. And whenever he started to doze off and Kelson's breathing faltered, he would jerk himself back to awareness and resolve not to do that again. He could not tell, as the hours crawled by, whether Kelson's breathing was easing or not.

CHAPTER FOURTEEN

Yea, his soul draweth near unto the grave.

—Job 33:22

The sun shone brightly on the mountains the next morning, as if in apology for the disaster of the day before. But though the survivors camped by the waterfall began searching again at first light, and even found another drowned sumpter horse a few hundred yards downstream, they found no sign of Kelson or of Dhugal. Men-at-arms from Saint Bearand's joined in the search, fetched by a messenger sent scurrying down the treacherous descent the previous afternoon, but the outlook for the king's survival grew dimmer by the hour; by late afternoon, Saer reluctantly called off the search.

Nor, with the king lost, was there any question of continuing on to Iomaire and thence to Cardosa, by this or any other route. Once Saer and his party got safely off the mountain and gained Saint Bearand's again, the terrible news must be taken back to Nigel in Rhemuth, and a messenger would be dispatched to inform the Earl of Eastmarch that no royal party would be joining him.

Beyond that, Saer had no plans. The new king must decide the course of future policy regarding Torenth. Since Saer was kin to Nigel by marriage and already a valued royal advisor, he had a fair idea what Nigel probably would do, but he would not presume to try to second-guess his brother-in-law at a time such as this.

It was going to be difficult enough to tell Nigel that his

much-loved nephew was dead—for dead Kelson surely must be, and Dhugal and the missing monk as well. The abbey men told Saer that part of the river went underground just past the pool by the waterfall, and no one knew where or whether it surfaced. Even the chances of finding the king's body were virtually nil, if the waters had not given it up by now.

Thus it was that a grieving and much diminished company descended the rugged mountain trail that afternoon, though Ciard, Jass, and the other MacArdry men remained, determined to keep looking at least through the rest of the week, in hope that eventually they might find some tangible clue as to the fate of their chief and their king. The rest straggled into Saint Bearand's yard just after dark, there to take a much-appreciated hot meal and snatch at least some semblance of a full night's sleep in proper beds before riding out the next morning, to return to Rhemuth via Valoret. The monks sang a solemn Mass for the king's safety before Saer led out and promised constant prayers until Kelson's fate was known for certain.

Saer and those with him rode fast all day, pausing only to change horses, and entered the walled city just at dusk. The bishops were at Vespers, the newly elected auxiliary of Valoret, Benoit d'Evering, leading the devotion. The rich counterpoint of the sung Office ascended joyously among the roofbeams as Saer wrenched open the postern door in the great west facade of the cathedral, but it dwindled to hushed surprise and apprehension as Saer led Conall, Earl Roger, and Father Lael down the center aisle and into the choir. A buzz of consternation murmured among the assembled clergy as the four paused just before the altar steps to make a ragged genuflection. Saer remained on one knee for a few seconds longer than the others before rising to turn and face the questioning faces.

"My Lord Bishops," he said, his voice uncharacteristically tremulous with emotion, "I regret to have to inform you that the king is dead."

They had been prepared for any of a number of announcements, but never that. A gasp swept universally among them, and almost to a man, they came to their feet,

questions bursting unwieldy and incoherently from their lips
as Saer held up both hands for silence.

"There was an accident half a day's ride north of Saint
Bearand's Abbey, above Caerrorie and Dolban," Saer said
dully. "We were climbing to take the High Grelder Pass
down to the plain of Iomaire. One of the monks from Saint
Bearand's was our guide. We almost didn't go that day, because it looked like rain and the monk warned us the trail
might be treacherous, but Kelson wanted to go."

He paused to swallow, obviously seeing it all again in
memory, and Archbishop Bradene crossed himself heavily.

"What day was that, my lord?"

"Friday? No, Saturday," Saer replied. "The days have
run together, I'm afraid. What day is it today?"

"Monday," Arilan said quietly. "Tell us what happened,
my lord." His face was ashen, and he longed to get Father
Lael aside for a fuller explanation.

Saer nodded, obviously pulling himself together only with
great effort.

"A—rain-soaked embankment collapsed under the front
of the party. Kelson was lost in the rapids below, along with
Dhugal MacArdry, the monk who was guiding us, Prince
Conall's squire, and many horses. The whole cliff side began
to crumble. The king's squire also went into the water, but
we recovered him alive. And Conall almost went in. I managed to get a rope around him just in time."

Archbishop Cardiel, his face etched by grief, slowly
shook his head.

"Thanks be to God for that, at least."

He and most of the other bishops crossed themselves at
that, several of them murmuring, "Amen," and Conall
bowed his head.

"You *did* recover the bodies?" Arilan asked, suddenly
guessing that they had not yet heard the full extent of the
tragedy.

Saer shook his head. "Only the dead squire's and some
of the horses. We searched for the rest of that day, until we
lost the light, and most of the next day, but—"

His voice broke, and he had to bow his head into a shaking
hand for a few seconds, but then he went on.

"Forgive me, my lords. The local people tell us that there is virtually no chance of recovering any more bodies after this long. Nonetheless, we left a party to continue the search, just on the chance that they're wrong. If—if anything is found, they'll send word. In the meantime, we—must ride to Rhemuth and tell N—the new king." He swallowed again. "Bishop Duncan will also have to be told—and young Jowan's family. I suppose it would be a wise idea if some of you accompanied us back to Rhemuth. Archbishops Cardiel and Bradene, in particular. There will be—arrangements to be made."

They surged up to surround him after that, asking questions all at once, unable to believe the enormity of the tragedy. In the confusion, Arilan drew Father Lael aside and shuffled him into the ambulatory aisle that led around behind the high altar.

"Tell me what *you* saw, Lael," he said softly, catching and holding the priest with his eyes, but not yet exerting any obvious control.

Lael's eyes filled with tears, and Arilan could read his deep grief so poignantly, without any further extension of his powers, that he knew there was no question in Lael's mind that the king was, indeed, dead.

"It—it was as de Traherne said, Excellency," Lael whispered. "No one could do anything to prevent it. I—watched them slip over the edge, one by one, and there was nothing— I could do." A sob caught in his throat. "I—think he managed to miss the rocks when he first hit the water, but he—"

When it became obvious that Lael could not go on, Arilan gently laid his hands on the priest's shoulders and drew him close, outwardly giving comfort while he sent his mind into Lael's to read the full horror of what had happened. He saw Kelson thrashing in the water, Dhugal flailing about to try to reach him, the horses struggling, one smashed pitifully on the rocks where it first hit.

And then Kelson, Dhugal, the monk, two squires, were being swept away. And later, beside a raging waterfall, men were pulling out the drowned body of one of the squires, and miraculously, the living body of the other. But of the others, there was no trace. And surely, the king, Dhugal, and the monk *were* dead.

Nor could even Arilan bear to read any more of the tragedy. Though he and Kelson often had disagreed on matters that meant a great deal to both of them, and he had only just begun to get to know Dhugal, the depth of Arilan's sense of loss over Kelson represented almost the same magnitude of grief for him as Dhugal's would for Duncan, when he heard the news. For indeed, Arilan had been Kelson's spiritual father, before Duncan came to take on that role—and long before anyone knew that Duncan was Dhugal's father in fact as well as in spirit.

Only by the greatest of acts of will was the Deryni bishop able to distance his grief enough to cover what he had just done with Lael, carefully burying any fleeting awareness Lael might have had that his mind, at least for a few minutes, had not been his own. In all compassion, he let Lael weep in his arms, considering what must be done next.

Obviously, he must go back to Rhemuth with Saer, Conall, and the two archbishops, for Nigel would need him—far more than any of those four might suspect, with the possible exception of Conall. And with Nigel to be king, there was Conall himself to be considered—a new heir to be molded in the proper form to succeed *Nigel* eventually—and Conall was not the same sort of clay as Kelson, or even Nigel.

But just as obviously, Arilan also knew he should notify the Camberian Council of what had happened. Another change of kings, not yet five years after King Brion's death, would alter many factors in how the Council dealt with its self-appointed duties to safeguard the welfare of the Eleven Kingdoms.

However, notifying the Council presented its own problems. Arilan could gain immediate access to the Council chamber via the Portal in the sacristy, only steps away from where he stood consoling the grieving Lael; but summoning the Councilors from their residences scattered all across the Eleven Kingdoms would take time—more time than he dared be missed. Furthermore, the energy cost would be enormous. Summoning the Council when they were not expecting it was never easy; and Arilan had already done it once in the past week to inform them of Tiercel's death. To do it again so soon, and still have any reserve available to deal with the ride to Rhemuth and what might be required once he got there, almost required that Arilan have assistance to amplify his power.

Nor was there anyone here in Valoret who could serve that purpose, without themselves being missed. After reading Lael, Arilan felt certain he could call on the surgeon priest if he had to, and he knew Cardiel would cooperate without demur, and Saer as well—but Arilan also knew that it was Saer's intention for them to ride for Rhemuth tonight, as soon as everyone had a hot meal and fresh horses could be procured; Arilan and Cardiel must be among them when they did.

And so, for the first time in his adult life, Arilan decided that his duty to the Haldanes came before any duty he might owe to the Council, so far as priorities for notification were concerned. Nor, considering the news to be carried, dared he use the Portal to return to Rhemuth ahead of the others, for such action would shatter whatever cover he still possessed in the wake of the many things that had been happening over the last six months.

No, he must ride with the others. The news was dire, but it could wait another two or three days to reach Rhemuth and the man who, even now, was king, though he did not know it yet. And then, when Arilan had helped cushion the first shock to Duncan, he must send the hapless bishop on to notify Morgan—for both of them would be essential in doing what must be done to bring Nigel to his full Haldane power as soon as possible. *That* was the highest priority.

And all of this must be done before Gwynedd's enemies learned that her king was dead and tried to take advantage of the instability—inevitable whenever a crown changed hands—that would unman even Nigel for a time and perhaps make him vulnerable.

They were under saddle and away before Compline, riding by torchlight down the good, firm road that skirted the river, blessed, at least, with clear weather, each man alone with his thoughts as the hoofbeats drummed out the refrain, *he is dead—he is dead—he is dead*, heading for the first of

the way castles where they would change horses and begin
the next of several dozen legs of the sad journey home.
  He is dead—he is dead—he is dead . . .

But deep in the bowels of the earth, miles from where
loyal MacArdry men kept their ceaseless vigil over the
waters that had claimed their young lords, Dhugal rejoiced
in the knowledge that Kelson was *not* dead. Further, the
king finally seemed able to breathe again on his own.

It was a slender victory, for Kelson still had not regained
consciousness; but to Dhugal, gone without sleep for nearly
three days now, it was the closest thing to a miracle he had
yet seen, since discovering that both he and Kelson had survived the initial catastrophe.

He worried about the skull fracture, though. The useful-
ness of his ability to probe the injury with his powers was
somewhat limited, for he had only a vague idea what his
perceptions meant in medical terms; but he did not like what
he *thought* they meant. The depression was putting pressure
on Kelson's brain, and there was some swelling. He could
not tell for certain whether there was bleeding as well. Dhugal had heard of surgical procedures to relieve such pressure,
involving drilling a hole in the skull and trying to lift the part
that was pressing, but he had no instruments, even if he were
fool enough to think he had the ability.

He pondered the problem while he left Kelson alone long
enough to retrieve the wine flask he had hurled aside in such
haste—he had no idea how long ago. He rinsed it long and
carefully while he kept a wary eye on the scarcely breathing
form wrapped in a cloak now only damp, not soggy, then
filled it and hobbled back to Kelson's side, there to raise his
patient's head and let a little trickle down Kelson's throat.
He used his powers to trigger the reflex to swallow, for he
had learned a great deal about the centers that controlled
such functions while he kept his lonely watch.

He was going to have to do something about food, too.
Nothing had passed Kelson's lips since whatever he might
have eaten at their last rest stop before the accident, other
than the tainted wine, soon regurgitated, and a little water
Dhugal had managed to bring to Kelson in his own mouth,
when the danger of dehydration became greater than the dan-

ger that Kelson might stop breathing again if Dhugal left him for more than a minute or two. Dhugal had no idea how long ago that might have been, but his own growling stomach told him it had been far too long. And while a healthy man might survive for weeks on water only, if he had to, such a diet was not conducive to mending injuries. He had no idea what he might find down here that was edible—perhaps there were fish in the underground river—but now that Kelson seemed to be past the most immediate crisis of his hurts, Dhugal would have to take steps to find *something*.

Meanwhile, though, there was the skull fracture to consider—and Dhugal was in an agony over what to do. If he did nothing, and the swelling continued, Kelson likely would die despite everything he had already been through and survived. And if Dhugal did the wrong thing—not that his options for actual treatment were many—Kelson might die anyway.

Sighing, Dhugal dragged more driftwood nearer the fire he had been nursing for so long, hobbling painfully on his swollen ankle and trying to spare his wrist as much as possible. After placing a few branches on the fire, he settled against the cavern wall next to Kelson and turned the raven head away from him, so he could brush his fingertips lightly over the lump behind Kelson's left ear. The wound was closing nicely in whatever time had passed and seemed to be healing cleanly, but he could sense the walnut-sized piece of bone depressed just beneath the skin—and the pressure under that.

If only there were some way to raise the depression, other than by surgery. Not that he was about to attempt to prise the bone back into place with the little stiletto in his boot—which was the only metal implement or weapon that seemed to have made it through their tumbling in the river.

But perhaps there *was* another way! He had moved things before, just with the power of his mind. One of the first things his father had shown him, after they knew Dhugal was Deryni, was how to work a lock without a key. If Dhugal could move the tumblers of a lock without seeing them, was it possible he could do the same to lift this bit of bone back into place in Kelson's skull?

It was not a healing function, in the Deryni sense. It certainly did not sound like what his father and Morgan had described about the healing process—visualizing the damaged area as it ought to be and having the healing take place under one's hands. But was there not a physical side to surgery, as well as a biological one? Provided that no irreversible damage had been done to the tissue beneath the skull, relief of Kelson's condition might come simply by restoring the bit of bone to its proper place and letting natural healing take its course.

It certainly was worth a careful try. Dhugal did not see how he could do much further harm, for Kelson's condition, though stabilizing, was not getting better from Dhugal doing nothing. He made himself take several deep, steadying breaths as he gently shifted Kelson to lie against his chest, supporting the lolling head against his right hand, just at shoulder level, while he brought his left to touch the lump behind the ear lightly. His sprained wrist gave a twinge, but he was able to shift his position slightly and relieve that.

But it was going to be a tricky balancing act to keep a part of his mind attuned to Kelson's breathing and heart rate while he turned his main attention to the other task at hand— for he knew that, when he relieved the pressure under the lump, he also was likely to upset the tenuous autonomic rhythm so recently reestablished. As he closed his eyes and settled into that rhythm, he wished he were better rested himself, for the few hours' sleep he had snatched were not nearly adequate to make up for the exertion of the past few days. But wishes were useless at this point. It was determination that would triumph now, if anything would, and a little luck on their side—or maybe a miracle or two.

Slowly Dhugal pushed himself deeper into trance, at first simply letting the shallow whisper of his and Kelson's breathing carry him gradually into rapport. It was not comfortable at first, for even with the *merasha* mostly gone out of Kelson's system, his shields were still irregular, distorted—intact in some areas, but utterly gone in others, not at all in balance. The condition probably was at least partially a function of the concussion Kelson had suffered, either from the injury under Dhugal's fingers or the other one above his eye; but whatever its source, it made for a rather jerky descent to the level of rapport that Dhugal felt he needed in order to risk what he was about to do.

Not daring to think too much more about it, Dhugal extended his Deryni senses into the body beneath his hands, centering on the circle of bone that lay beneath his fingertips. All at once he could see it in his mind, as if it were exposed by a surgeon's knife—a rounded triangle of bone, one edge still neatly in place and the opposite angle depressed almost to the depth of the tip of a man's little finger.

Gently, gingerly, he eased his powers around it and lifted. It moved more easily than he had expected, smoothly pivoting on the edge still in place until all three sides were flush again. Nor was there any disruption of Kelson's breathing.

He spent a few more seconds inspecting what he had done, wondering whether it would be enough, then withdrew mind and controls and opened his eyes to look at Kelson again. The king appeared unchanged. When, after Dhugal judged an hour or so had passed and Kelson still seemed unimproved—though neither was he any worse—Dhugal decided it was time to do something about the food situation. Whatever happened, he could be no help to Kelson or himself if he starved to death.

It was late on Wednesday, Lady Day, the Feast of the Annunciation, when what remained of the king's party reached Rhemuth. Some intimation of the news apparently had run ahead even of that fast-riding band, so that Nigel, Meraude, Duncan, and Jehana were already waiting anxiously in the privy council chamber. Saer and Earl Roger broke the news, Conall prudently keeping a very low profile, suitably subdued and decorous, and the three bishops then gave what comfort they could, though Father Lael had to be called to lend his physician's services when Jehana finally began weeping hysterically and had to be escorted from the room. Roger left with them, leaving only the bereaved families and clergy.

Nigel, too, wept briefly, comfortless and forlorn in his wife's arms, and Duncan withdrew into himself, moving to gaze unseeing out a window. Arilan wavered uncertainly between him and Nigel as Cardiel and Bradene tried to give the new king more immediate attention, and even Conall could be seen to blink back tears.

"God strike me dead if I ever wanted to be king," Nigel

said, shaking his head disbelievingly as he mastered his grief and looked up, still bleary-eyed, at Cardiel. "This can't be happening, Thomas. I'm not ready. I wanted never to *have* to be ready. Isn't there some chance he's still alive?"

"Not within reason, no," Cardiel said softly, himself almost in tears again—for he, too, had wept at the news in Valoret, three days before. "They tell us that there's little chance the bodies will even be recovered, after this long."

Saer, trying to comfort his sister, now that Nigel seemed to be in control again, shook his head, too.

"We did everything we could, Nigel," he whispered, "but we didn't find a trace. Not a trace! The river goes underground, just past where they were lost. We never found the monk's body, either. The local folk say the river never gives up its dead, after that long."

Speechless, Nigel only shook his head, his grief almost palpable in the silence of the old room. Arilan, still hesitating between Nigel and Duncan, turned his attention on Nigel.

"There are things that must be done—Your Majesty," he said quietly.

Nigel looked up in shock, dread in his eyes.

"Don't call me that. Please."

"You *are* the king, however," Arilan insisted, "regardless what you are called. And by tomorrow, you will have to be proclaimed as such. Gwynedd cannot go without a king for long."

Nigel looked away. "I'll continue as regent, until we're sure. But I don't want the title—not yet; not while there's still hope."

"Hope of what?" Arilan replied. "Hope of finding Kelson's body? That doesn't change things. And after this long, I'm afraid there's virtually no chance of his being found alive, much as I wish I could tell you different. Meanwhile, you have responsibilities that *must* be fulfilled."

"I'll fulfill them."

"*Haldane* responsibilities, Nigel," Arilan said softly.

Even Duncan looked up at that, as Nigel blanched and quickly looked away.

"I shall exercise the customary responsibilities of the crown," he whispered, "as I have as regent. But unless Kelson's body is found, I shall not be crowned until a year and a day have passed. That decision is not open to negotiation."

Even through his own grief, Duncan knew that neither Nigel nor Arilan was talking about merely human functions of royal responsibility. But while Nigel apparently had assumed that his full assumption of the Haldane powers would be contingent upon his crowning, as Kelson's was, Duncan knew that no such contingency existed and that, if Kelson truly was dead, and Dhugal—*God, let it not be true!*—then the power must be brought to full fruition in Nigel as soon as possible. But he dared not speak openly about it in front of Bradene, for Arilan's sake.

"I see no difficulty in delaying the coronation, if that is what His Highness wishes," Duncan said quietly, deliberately using the more neutral royal title to which Nigel was entitled as a prince of Gwynedd, but that also applied to a king. "Once a suitable period of mourning has passed, however, and we can all think more clearly, His Highness may wish to amend that decision. For now, however, I suggest that no date be set at all.

"In the meantime, I would recommend that Your Highness summon the rest of the privy council to return to Rhemuth immediately, along with those other lords whose opinion Your Highness values. If I may be of service, I would offer to take the news to Duke Alaric myself. He—would take it best coming from me, I think."

Arilan, flashing Duncan a look that confirmed he knew precisely what Duncan was about, gave a nod of agreement.

"I concur, Your Highness. But, Duncan, you are doubly bereaved—not that we all do not mourn the loss of your son. Do you think it wise to attempt such a long and grueling journey?"

Duncan swallowed painfully. "I shall value the time alone to remember both my sons," Duncan murmured. "In the meantime, Excellency, I wonder if you would pray with me a while before I leave."

The request startled Arilan, but only until he had followed Duncan up to the apartment that once had been Dhugal's, where Duncan, rather than praying, began stripping off his cassock to change into more suitable attire for riding—the courier's garb he had worn to Valoret.

"Have you told the Council yet?" Duncan asked.

Arilan shook his head. "No, there was no time before we

left Valoret. I'll do it as soon as I've seen you off. Cardiel will cover my absence until morning."

"Fine. Then you won't be missed if you spend a little additional time to take me to Dhassa—unless there's a Portal closer to Coroth, that is."

Arilan scowled as he watched Duncan pull on leather breeches and a shirt of soft black suede.

"I don't recall having told you there was a Portal there."

"You didn't; but if there wasn't one before, I can't imagine that you and some of your Council brethren wouldn't have put one in, once you became Bishop of Dhassa."

"It was already there," Arilan said sourly. "But you're asking a great deal."

"I'm asking you to save me at least a week's riding, between here and Coroth," Duncan replied. He plopped on a stool to begin tugging on stout leather boots that came well over the knee. "Even from Dhassa, I'll still have a solid day's ride each way. And I'll need a horse to get out of Dhassa, if you can manage it. I'd rather not steal one."

Arilan could not control a wry smile as the younger man strapped on plain, blackened steel spurs such as any man-at-arms might wear.

"You would, too, wouldn't you?"

"I've had to do worse," Duncan said, rising to take up a quilted leather vest, heavy with metal plates sewn between the layers. "Will you or won't you help me? If you won't, I'll go directly to the stables from here. I haven't the time or the inclination to argue with you."

"I'll help," Arilan said, also helping him into the jazerant. "May I ask one favor, however?"

Duncan gave the other Deryni bishop a warning look before bending to the buckles that closed the front of the vest.

"As a condition for your assistance?"

"Of course not. As a point of information that may benefit both of us. Will you and Alaric be able to convince Nigel he must assume the full Haldane power before the year is out?"

"I don't see that that's any of your business," Duncan replied coolly, tucking the last strap of the jazerant under its keeper. "Just now, I don't give a bloody damn about the

Haldane power. I just want to try to find out whether my son and my king might still be alive."

"Do you really think they are?" Arilan asked softly, refusing to take offense.

A sob threatened to well up in Duncan's throat, but he managed to stifle it. He knew he would not be able to do that much longer. But by concentrating on picking up his sword, unwinding the belt from around the scabbard, and buckling it around his waist, he managed to keep the tears from blurring his vision worse than it already was.

"I want to believe they are," he whispered. "As long as no bodies turn up, it's all too tempting to let myself keep hoping for a miracle. Besides, I can't shake the feeling that I'd *know* somehow, if they were dead—especially Dhugal, He's my *son*, Denis. And I've been Kelson's confessor for nearly seven years. You know what kind of bond that can put between two people—especially two Deryni."

As Duncan jammed a fur-lined leather cap on his head and snatched up a pair of riding gloves, slipping them under his belt, Arilan picked up the black leather travel cloak Duncan obviously planned to wear and flung it over his arm, moving with Duncan toward the fireplace.

"Yes, I know what kind of bond that can mean," he said. "Have you tried yet to invoke it, or the bond of father and son?"

Duncan shook his head. "It's too far away to try on my own. Besides, there hasn't been time; you know that. You've been with me every minute."

"It's even farther from Coroth."

"Yes, but not from Dhassa." Duncan leaned the heels of both hands against the mantel, watching the firelight play in the amethyst of his bishop's ring—the only concession he had allowed himself to his true identity. It would just barely fit under his glove.

"Well, what's it to be? Will you take me to Dhassa, or must I go down to the stable yard and do this the hard way?"

"What about the Haldane power for Nigel?" Arilan countered. "What if he needs it before you get back?"

"I suppose," said Duncan, "that he'll just have to cope as best he can—or do you think I could bring him to power by myself?"

"Could you?"

"I don't know. I'd rather not find out. And I'd especially rather not find out until after I'm more certain that Kelson—really is dead." He swallowed and half turned his face to glance over his shoulder at Arilan. "And Dhugal. Do you think they *are* dead, Denis?"

Arilan sighed wearily. "I fear they very well may be, son," he whispered. "Now, do you have any preference which Portal we use at this end? I think I would recommend the one in your study."

A quarter hour later, they were stepping into the compartment that concealed the study Portal, Duncan gathering his cloak close around him to make room for Arilan behind him. Silvery handfire followed Arilan in, and he dimmed it almost to nothing as Duncan pulled the door closed.

"We aren't going to surprise anyone at the other end, are we?" Duncan asked.

Arilan gave a soft snort as he set his hands on Duncan's shoulders. "It isn't likely, since the Portal's in my private chapel, but who knows what may have been going on while I'm away? Father Nivard, my chaplain, has permission to say Mass there, but it's late for that. Anyway, he—ah—knows about me."

"In other words, you have him controlled," Duncan said, smiling a little despite the numb sense of loss churning just at the edge of awareness. "Not that I have any room to sermonize, after what I've done to Father Shandon on occasion. Suppose someone else is there, though?"

"If there should be, I'll bounce you back, return to Dhassa to deal with the situation, then come back for you again," Arilan said, drawing Duncan close against him, his voice very near Duncan's right ear. "Close your eyes and relax now, and we'll go. Don't fight me, or I swear I'll make you take a horse next time. If we *should* have to do any to-and-froing, that's going to waste enough energy as it is; and I've got other things to do after I've seen you safely on your way to Dhassa."

"How far *is* it to where the Camberian Council meets?" Duncan whispered, expecting no answer as the last of the handfire's glow died away behind his closed eyelids.

From Rhemuth or from Dhassa? came Arilan's bemused

reply, just before his mind wrapped around Duncan's like a blanket of fog, dense and almost physical, and closed out everything with a soft, numbing greyness.

Duncan felt the vague, stomach-wrenching shift of the jump, subtly blunted by Arilan's silken control, and an instant of suspended *not-ness* into which not even the grief penetrated, almost as if Duncan had managed to leave it behind in Rhemuth. But then the soul-numbing sense of loss was back, and Duncan opened his eyes to near darkness again, though they were not where they had been.

"Well, we're in luck," Arilan whispered. "Even Nivard's elsewhere, though I'm going to have to go find him, if he's to be any help to you."

"How much are you going to tell him?" Duncan asked.

They had appeared in a tiny side chapel, hardly more than an oratory, opening off the left of the main chapel—Duncan presumed it was in Dhassa. A rack of votive candles in clear glass holders illumined an odd, tight expression on Arilan's face just before he moved out of range, heading into the chapel proper.

"Well, you're hardly a private figure, after all," Arilan murmured. "Don't worry, you can trust him. Take a few minutes to learn this Portal while I try to fetch him up. And it might be a good idea at least to look like you're praying, in case anyone should happen by. Nor would a true prayer be out of order, I think. I shan't be long."

He was gone before Duncan could ask any more questions, leaving the door to the chapel a little ajar. Duncan stared after him for a few seconds, a little uneasy, then shifted his attention to the tingle of the Portal beneath his feet. A vaguely circular pattern in the mosaic of the floor tiles marked the Portal's location visually, but he needed more than that to make it his for all time.

Kneeling, he dropped both hands to brush the floor on either side of him, bowing his head and closing his eyes as he extended his senses to discern the peculiar features that made this Portal unique. Within a dozen heartbeats, he knew that he could reach out and link it with the power of any of the other four Portals he knew. It was a reassuring feeling that helped blunt the enormity of the physical effort he would have to exert in the next few days, though it did little to blunt the emotional beating he had taken in the past hour.

He had doffed his cap and was praying in fact, begging God that his son and Kelson might yet be found alive, when he heard the chapel door open again. He kept his head bowed, pretending to be yet in prayer as two sets of footsteps started down the center aisle.

"Come and meet Father John Nivard," Arilan's low voice said, releasing Duncan from his taut listening and apprehension.

Duncan rose and turned to face them, expecting a staid and dignified older man, and was surprised to find that Father Nivard was young. In fact, he looked hardly old enough even to be a priest, much less chaplain to a bishop of Arilan's stature—pink-cheeked and still a little soft with puppy fat, the top of his head barely reaching Arilan's shoulder, dark curls springing crisply from around his tonsure like the halo on some pagan godling.

Duncan could not see whether the eyes matched the imagery, for the young priest kept them modestly averted as he and Arilan approached, but the hands were squared and sturdy, hard with honest work, as he knelt to kiss Duncan's ring—for Arilan introduced Duncan by his true name and rank. What surprised Duncan even more than Nivard's youth was the quickly damped flare of shields as their hands touched.

Good God, could this be one of Arilan's other Deryni priests?

"I am honored to meet you, Excellency," Nivard murmured, awe touching voice and demeanor as he raised seagreen eyes to meet Duncan's. "Bishop Denis tells me you require very discreet assistance. How may I be of service?"

Awed himself, Duncan raised the young man up and glanced at Arilan, though he did not release Nivard's hand.

"One of ours?" he breathed.

Arilan smiled and nodded.

"Go ahead and test his shields. I think you'll be pleasantly surprised. When I found John, nearly four years ago, he was a seminarian having a crisis of conscience because he was just beginning to discover what he was and was sure he would have to abandon his vocation. I fancy he's done rather well since then, all things considered. I ordained him last fall."

"Ah, then, you're still quite a new priest, too, aren't you?" Duncan murmured, turning his attention back to Nivard.

"Yes, Excellency."

"Do you mind?"

Nivard swallowed and shook his head.

"No, sir."

Duncan started to flick a tendril of thought against Nivard's shields, then paused as the sea-pale eyes flinched a little at his mere glance.

"Are you sure you don't mind, Father?" Duncan repeated. "I don't have to do this. And you don't have to let me."

Nivard's hand was trembling under his now, but the young man only shook his head again, glancing furtively at Arilan for reassurance.

"I'm not afraid, Excellency," he whispered. "I just—"

"He's just unaccustomed to having anyone else probe beyond his shields yet," Arilan explained. "Other than myself, you're the first of our kind that he's ever met, who knew what he was. And I think, perhaps, that our young Father John is a little in awe of you, Duncan. John, I can play the intermediary, if you wish, but I really think you're ready to try it on your own. I assure you, Father Duncan has a very gentle touch—probably gentler than mine, if the truth be known."

"Perhaps it's best if we just wait," Duncan said. "I can't guarantee that my touch will be that gentle, in the state I'm in."

"No," Arilan said, "it's time he learned this; and I want the two of you to be able to work together, at least on a general level, in case you need his help when you come back. John, show him the physical layout of the cathedral complex. That's a specific topic that isn't at all threatening, and one that will benefit Duncan as well."

Trembling still, Nivard drew a deep breath and let it out as he had been taught, slipping into a light trance before Duncan could raise any further objection. Duncan sensed the surfaces of the other's shields clearing, and on impulse, raised his free hand to touch fingertips lightly to the young priest's eyelids. The additional physical contact, plus not having to look at Duncan anymore, was the catalyst to let Nivard roll back his shields with near-perfect control. The trembling stopped as he laid out everything Arilan had ordered for Duncan's inspection, shyly inviting deeper contact when Duncan's tentative penetration of his shields did not produce discomfort.

Duncan took it all in in an instant, assimilating it without hesitation and then following as Nivard allowed an even deeper probe, gaining confidence when contact with the legendary Duncan McLain turned out to be not nearly as frightening as he had feared it might. Duncan did not push the probe, but he followed where Nivard allowed it to go. When he surfaced, just a heartbeat after Nivard, and let his hand fall away from the young man's face, releasing his hand as well, he found Arilan staring at him, Nivard with a sheepish grin on his face.

"Now, was that so bad?" Arilan asked dryly. "I do suspect that the contact involved somewhat more than a showing of the cathedral plans, but I gather no one has any complaints."

Duncan shook his head. "My compliments to your prize student, Denis. Father, we must try that again when I'm not so distracted. Meanwhile, I think I must be off, if you don't mind. I'll need a good horse, instructions to the post houses for changes of mounts, and provisions for a full day on the road. I want to be in Coroth by this time tomorrow."

"To bring Duke Alaric back here?" Nivard breathed.

"Aye. Can you arrange to be wherever you leave me tonight, two days hence, so we can get back here safely and without anyone knowing who we are?"

"Yes, Excellency, of course."

"On that note, then," Arilan said wryly, moving onto the Portal circle behind them, "I shall bid you both adieu and be off about my business. Father Nivard, if anyone should ask, I've not been here, and you know nothing about the news Duncan has brought."

"Yes, Excellency."

With that, Arilan simply disappeared, so far as the two left standing in the chapel were concerned. And half an hour later, mounted on a sturdy mountain pony and lightly provisioned for the dash down the mountains and across the plain to Coroth, Duncan was on his way as well, leaving a starry-eyed young priest to muse on what he had experienced.

CHAPTER FIFTEEN

I am clean without transgression, I am innocent.
—Job 33:9

In Alaric Morgan's capital city of Coroth, a very hard day's ride southeast of Dhassa, nothing was yet known of the news Duncan McLain brought. Indeed, even the news of Tiercel's death had not yet arrived, for the messenger Duncan had sent at the beginning of the week was only now disembarking from a ship in Coroth Bay and counting himself fortunate to have reached his destination at all, given the unseasonal spring storms. The monk in the forest green mantle and cassock of a canon regular of Saint George's Cathedral drew some consolation in learning that the weather had been no better in Coroth for the past week, since the duke's return. Today was the first day it had not rained in nearly a month.

Nor, snug in his solarium at Coroth Castle, did Corwyn's duke have any inkling of a messenger's approach, either the man in the harbor or the one riding pell-mell from Dhassa. In truth, events of the outside world were far from his mind at that moment. A cold, damp wind blew off Coroth Bay, wailing around the parapets and whistling shrill and bleak around the window fittings, but it was cozy and warm where Morgan pored over a table covered with tally sticks and counters.

Warm physically, at least. A fire burned cheerily in the fireplace across the narrow room, and a charcoal brazier warmed his booted feet, propped on a green leather foot-

224

stool. But psychic frost in the air made Morgan glad of the heavy, fur-lined court robe he wore this morning, though it was a poor substitute for snuggling next to the sultry warmth of his wife on such a morning, back in their great canopied bed.

Not that such a pleasant pastime was likely, with Richenda in her present state of agitation, even if official duties would not call him from her within the hour. While he had been reviewing revenues for an assizes court to convene shortly in the ducal hall— a tedious task, at best, that was made no more pleasant by his wife's ill humor—Richenda had been pacing back and forth before his table and arguing.

Or rather, Richenda was arguing and Morgan was allowing himself to be preoccupied by the counting board and the tally sticks spread out before him, only half listening, for he had heard all these arguments before. Stacks of markers dotted the checkered cloth covering the counting table, each representing the income of a particular manor in the east of Coroth over the past year—incomes in knights' services as well as cash and kind, the former a vital ingredient for the defense of the eastern borders with Torenth, with which Kelson had charged Corwyn's duke.

And then there was the baby to consider—far more attractive a proposition than Richenda's arguments or manorial incomes, so far as Morgan was concerned. He and Richenda had already chosen Kelric as the boy's first name, to honor Kelson as well as Alaric; and Richenda favored Alain as a second—the name Morgan himself had borne the first time he and Richenda met, outside the Shrine of Saint Torin—while Morgan preferred Richard. Perhaps the lad would end up with both.

But as Morgan mused on the joy of soon having a son in addition to the little daughter with which Richenda had presented him two years before, his attention to the mother of those children strayed beyond even her forbearance.

"Alaric, have you heard a word I've said?" Richenda asked, suddenly stopping to rest both hands on the table opposite him, blue eyes flashing.

Morgan, checking a tally stick for the newly refortified manor of the Sieur de Vali, looked up in surprise. In the sweeping blue robe she had donned upon rising—for she had announced her adamant intention to attend court with him, despite the advice of Master Randolph, her physician—he could almost forget that in less than a month, she would present him with his first son.

"My dear, I've heard every word. The problem is, I've heard them all before—and there really isn't time to go into all of this again, with court convening in a quarter hour."

"There's *never* time," she murmured, twisting angrily at the marriage ring on her left hand. "You've been home for a week, after nearly a month's absence and most of a winter's procrastination about dealing with this, and I still can't get you to give me an honest answer. Do I have to Truth-Read to find out what's bothering you, Alaric?"

"I've told you, I don't want to talk about it anymore," he murmured, returning his attention to the counters representing the de Vali incomes and dipping his quill to make a notation. "You shouldn't be concerning yourself with serious matters when your time is so near."

"Ah, I see," she said softly. "So a breeding woman's judgment is not to be taken seriously, is it? You think this is just a hysterical reaction?"

"Not hysterical, dear. But you really needn't worry your pretty head about it. In a few months, after the baby's born and you're yourself again, we'll talk about it."

The next thing Morgan knew, Richenda was yanking the checkered counting cloth off the table in front of him, upsetting ink across his assize roll and sending tally sticks and counters flying in every direction as he watched in helpless horror. He lunged to try to save the inkwell from smashing on the floor, but realized only just in time that to do so would have added his hands and possibly his court robe to the list of casualties. The sound of shattering glass only punctuated Richenda's continuing tirade.

"*Listen* to me, damn you!" she screamed. "I am *not* just a ducal brood mare! Nor am I just an ornament for your court! And I am not even mistress of my own house!"

"Richenda!"

He caught her wrist as she swung at him halfheartedly and burst into tears. Even though he was very angry—for the counters now scattered over the carpet represented hours of work undone, not to mention the ruined assize roll—he tried to draw her closer to calm her.

"Richenda, you're overwrought," he murmured. "It's your condition."

"It is *not* my condition! There's nothing *wrong* with my condition. And if I'm overwrought, it's because of *you!* I'm not sick and I'm not a child. Why do you persist in treating me like one?"

"Because you're acting like one, and a spoiled one at that! Look at what you've done!"

"Aren't you going to hit me?" she taunted. "That's what one does to a spoiled child, isn't it? I've upset your precious tallies. They obviously mean more to you than I do!"

"*Hit* you?" Morgan released her instantly. "When have I ever hit you, or even been unkind to you? Why would you even *think* such a thing?"

Drawing herself up with dignity, Richenda half turned away from him.

"I do believe I've finally engaged your attention," she said coolly.

"My attention?" Morgan set his fists on his hips in amazement. "Richenda, you almost always have my attention. You are never far from my thoughts."

Tears started to well in her eyes again, and she lowered her head to stare at her hands, twisting a fold of her gown in agitation.

"Alaric, I know you love me in your way," she said softly. "But your heart is in Rhemuth with the king and Duncan, even when your body is not."

"That isn't true."

"It is, and you know it. I don't begrudge you that, for they were your family long before I came into your life— and even if I didn't know how much you love them both, your simple duty as a duke and privy councillor would require that you spend a certain amount of time at court each year."

"Much of which you, too, have spent at court with me," Morgan replied. "Our separations have not been that great, I think."

"Perhaps not," she conceded. "But *this* is my home now, Alaric."

"Well, haven't you been here at home for the past six months? And haven't I been with you most of that time?"

She sighed. "Even when you are here, I am not mistress

of my own house, for the master's wishes take precedence.
And when you are gone. . . ."

Morgan folded his arms at that, for they had come back
to an old, old bone of contention that he had never been able
to bring himself to explain.

"*Why* will you not make me regent in your absence,
Alaric?" she asked. "And why will you never answer me
that question? Surely, after three years of marriage, you can
trust that I know the affairs of Corwyn well enough to govern
in your place when you're away. I'm the granddaughter of
a sovereign prince, for goodness' sake! I learned statecraft
at his knee. Do you think I didn't run Bran's estates for him
when he was away? Have I been that bad a manager of Brendan's lands?"

Agonizing inside, Morgan came and took her hand,
though he kept his mind tightly shielded from any attempt
she might have made to pry.

"No," he said softly, "you've done very well. And I'm
sure you would do as well for Corwyn, if I made you regent.
Better, because you are here, while you govern Marley
mostly *in absentia*."

"Then, why?"

"Come and sit down with me, and I'll try to tell you,"
he said, starting to draw her toward the benches facing one
another in the window embrasure. "Or would you and our
son be more comfortable in bed?"

"Our son is perfectly content where he is," Richenda
replied, pulling back when he would have changed direction
to draw her toward their sleeping chamber, though she did
manage a sheepish smile. "And his mother knows better than
to get into bed with his father when she hopes to learn anything of serious import."

Morgan smiled halfheartedly. "Now, would I try to se-
duce a woman who's eight months gone with child?"

"I'm sure we could find some mutually satisfying dalli-
ance," she replied coyly, now drawing *him* into the window
embrasure. "However, I suspect that such diversion, pleasant though it undoubtedly would be, might also divert a certain gentleman from revealing what he has promised."

"I didn't precisely promise," Morgan said, as she settled
on one of the benches and braced a pillow against the small
of her back.

"You said you would tell me why you haven't let me be your regent," Richenda said. "As far as I'm concerned, that's a promise."

"Very well."

Morgan sighed and sat opposite her, twisting at his gryphon signet as he rested his forearms on his knees.

"You said earlier that you aren't even mistress of this house," he said after a few seconds' pause. "In a sense, that's true, though the problem lies in a totally different quadrant from what you might think."

"What do you mean?"

"Well, it didn't take long for the servants to accept you, when I brought you home as my wife. They're paid to do their jobs, and—no slight intended toward you, but—I suspect they would have accepted almost anyone that their bachelor duke brought home to be his duchess."

Richenda nodded carefully. "It took a while, even so, but we were hardly here that first year or so, what with one thing and another."

"True. The problem isn't with my officers, either. Hillary adores you, and I think Hamilton looks upon you almost as the daughter he never had. Nor need I justify Master Randolph or Father Tagas, I think."

"But there *are* those who are opposed to me," Richenda guessed. "Alaric, what in the world *for?* I've never done anything to any of your people. I've never been anything but loyal to you and your interests."

"Ah, there's a key word—loyalty," Morgan said. "And it's apparently a subject of concern among the junior officers and the men."

"*My* loyalty?" Richenda asked, astonished.

Morgan turned his face toward the window, wishing the sun warming his face could warm his soul, for he did not want to tell Richenda this.

"Your loyalty," he repeated. "Because of Bran."

He watched her in his peripheral vision. At first he thought she would not catch what he was driving at—and he did not want to say it. But though she went white, one hand clenching into a fist down in the folds of her skirt, where she thought he could not see it, she only closed her eyes briefly and then herself turned her face toward the sun streaming in through the window.

"Because my first husband was a traitor, they fear that I will be, too," she said after a moment.

"In a word, yes."

She swallowed audibly, but she did not break her numb staring into the sunlight.

"I won't speak against him, Alaric," she said softly. "I know he died in dishonor, at Kelson's hand—and Kelson had not only the right but the duty to do what he did. It was a mercy, in the long reckoning. But Bran Coris was my husband and the father of my first-born, and he loved me in his way. Nor do I think he chose a traitor's part willingly. I shall believe until the day I die that Wencit of Torenth seduced him into treason."

"Seduced or not, that does not absolve him of the responsibility for his actions."

"Of course it doesn't. Bran had a taste for power that was not being satisfied as a fairly minor earl of King Brion's court. I knew that and accepted it, for the sake of peace between us and the hope of raising Brendan to a better life one day.

"But to suggest that I would follow Bran in treason—that's preposterous! Why, even if they suspected me of the most base and mercenary motives imaginable, what more could I possibly hope to gain than what I already have? I am wife to the most powerful man in all the Eleven Kingdoms, after the king himself—unless, of course, they fear I will seek the crown." She laid a hand on his arm in horror. "Alaric, they don't think *that,* do they?"

Morgan chuckled mirthlessly. "Oddly enough, it doesn't seem to be your loyalty to *Kelson* that's in question—except indirectly, perhaps."

"But loyalty *is* the issue?"

"Yes."

"But, if not to Kelson, then, to *whom?*"

"To me."

"To *you?*"

Morgan turned to look at her as he nodded.

"To me."

"But—*why?* Have I ever given you any cause to doubt me?"

"Of course not. Now perhaps you understand why I've been so reluctant to tell you about this."

"But, what possible reason could they have to think me disloyal?"

"As near as I can determine, the main reason is called Brendan," Morgan said.

"*Brendan?*"

"Darling, I never pretended you were going to *like* what I had to say. I'd hoped I'd never have to tell you, it's all so insane."

"But he's only a little boy—"

"He's your son by another marriage," Morgan said bluntly, cutting her off. "When our first child was a girl, they feared you might eventually try to push her aside and give Brendan the precedence in Corwyn that should be reserved for *our* son. I'm hoping that once Kelric is born, and it's known that I have no intention of allowing the two boys' inheritances to mingle, or to cut either one out of what is rightfully his, the objections will finally die down. They'll both be *your* sons, after all—each with a sizable fortune to inherit in his own right."

"And your people actually believe this?" she asked, still unable to believe it herself.

"Not necessarily the people, but the men," Morgan replied. "Or so I'm told. And certainly not all of them, though apparently there are enough that Hillary has been fearful of precipitating a general mutiny, if you were put in charge and anything were to happen in my absence—whether or not it was your fault. My men are rather fiercely loyal, in case you hadn't noticed."

"And they expect that your wife is not, simply because her first husband betrayed his overlord? Alaric, that isn't fair."

"I didn't say it was fair; I'm simply reporting what I've been told. And with everything else I've had on my mind, there simply hasn't been time to track down the truth of the matter."

"Well, you could have told me before this," she pouted. "I wonder if you have any idea the kinds of things I was imagining for why you wouldn't give me my wife's due. I—"

A knock at the outer door cut her off in mid-statement, and Morgan gave her an apologetic shrug as he rose and stepped into the opening of the window embrasure, where he could be seen from the doorway.

"Come."

An entire contingent was waiting to enter: Lord Rathold, his chamberlain and master of wardrobe, carrying a state coronet he had brought up from the ducal treasury; Lord Hamilton and the chancellor, Lord Robert of Tendall, the latter robed to assist at the coming assizes court; and bringing up the rear, Sean Lord Derry, Morgan's former military aide and now his lieutenant for Corwyn, escorting a messenger wearing the deep green cloak and cassock of the monastic chapter at Rhemuth. But before Derry could edge the messenger past the others, Lord Robert let out a gasp as he saw the tally sticks and counters scattered over the carpet before the counting table.

"Your Grace, what has happened?" Robert asked. "The tallies—"

"I have the necessary figures in my head, Robert," Morgan said, coming down out of the embrasure. "Don't worry yourself about it. One of the jewels on this damned sleeve caught in the cloth and pulled everything off before I realized what was happening. Rathold, you'd better check the settings after court. In the meantime, please have someone clean up the mess. There's ink spilled, too."

As he took his coronet from a dismayed Rathold and set it on his head, the old man was shaking his head.

"I don't see how that could have happened, Your Grace. I always check so carefully—"

"Yes, well—I probably snagged it on something else first. Anyway, it doesn't matter now. Just see to the mess," Morgan said, easing past him toward the messenger waiting with Derry. "Brother, you have something for me?"

The monk bowed respectfully, handing over a pair of sealed missives from his scrip.

"Correspondence from Bishop McLain and the Prince Regent, Your Grace."

"Thank you."

The monk's use of Duncan's proper title assured him that the news was not of Duncan's deposition or other ill fate at the hands of the synod meeting in Valoret—at least not yet, or so far as the monk knew—and the physical contact as the missives changed hands conveyed no other apprehension about Duncan, so Morgan opened Nigel's letter first, turning slightly and lifting his arms to read it so that Rathold could buckle on his sword belt and make last-minute adjustments to his attire. Nor was Duncan's status the subject of Nigel's missive, though what Morgan read instead made him go a little cold, all the same. He had only met Tiercel de Claron twice, but the death of any member of the Camberian Council could not but affect him and those close to him.

"Bad news, m'lord?" Derry asked.

"A death," Morgan murmured, scanning the rest of Nigel's letter but learning little beyond a superficial report of Duncan's finding of the body. "More an acquaintance than an actual friend, but he wielded a great deal of influence in some circles."

Derry nodded. "Anyone I might know?"

"No," Morgan said quietly, "I don't think so." He looked up at the others waiting on him and decided that Duncan's letter was best read in private. "Please go ahead to the great hall, gentlemen. I'll join you directly, when I've read the other letter. And see that this good brother is given a hot meal and a decent bed, would you, Derry?"

"Right away, sir. This way, if you please, brother."

As they were filing out, Morgan turned back into the room, easing loose the outer seal on Duncan's letter. He had thought it might contain a hidden message, discernible only to Deryni senses, but it did not—though the one at the bottom of the page, next to Duncan's signature, did. Richenda had come to the opening of the window embrasure at his words about a death and she came down the rest of the way when she saw Morgan scanning the written part of the message.

"Who died?" she asked.

Morgan did not look up as he continued reading Duncan's letter, but he held out Nigel's, which she took.

"Tiercel de Claron. Apparently he fell down a flight of stairs and broke his neck—though what he was doing in that secret passage that leads out of Kelson's old rooms, I have no idea. Duncan pretty much reiterates what Nigel's said—at least there's no bad news about the bishops. But there's an extra message in his seal."

He touched his fingertips to the seal and closed his eyes for several seconds, taking a deep breath to trigger the light trance state necessary to read the message beyond the words penned on the single sheet of vellum. Duncan's synopsis was short and concise, telling of the finding and initial examination of the body, bringing Nigel back to look at it as well, the grueling ride to Valoret to inform Arilan, Arilan's reaction, and of Arilan's bringing both of them back to Rhemuth through a Portal in the sacristy at the Cathedral of All Saints, to which Duncan now had access. Tiercel's body had been taken to the Camberian Council, but Duncan, to his immense relief, had not been obliged to go and testify before them in person concerning his finding of the body, though he *had* allowed Arilan a deep reading of his memories surrounding the event. No action was required on Morgan's part, for all the evidence pointed to accidental death, but Duncan had felt he should know.

Morgan let out a weary sigh as he came out of trance, allowing Richenda to read what he had learned from the seal as he handed her Duncan's letter and let her retain his hand a moment longer. Tiercel's death brought the number of councillors down to six— an event that could not but send them into an even greater state of disfocus than was their usual wont, so far as Morgan's experience could tell. But perhaps this would shift their attention away from Kelson, Duncan, and himself for a while. He had no idea whether they, through Arilan, had been trying to influence the proceedings in Valoret—he knew Arilan was *very* unhappy about Duncan confirming his Deryni status in front of the entire court— but perhaps they would concentrate on finding new councillors for a while now and leave Duncan alone.

He was thinking about the Council chamber, remembering the one time he had been there, and trying to envision it, as he took a subdued Richenda on his arm and went into the great hall for court a few minutes later.

And in a domed chamber atop a remote mountain many miles away, the six remaining members of the Camberian Council were, indeed, discussing Duncan, Morgan, and the king—but it was not the same king Morgan had in mind.

"Denis, the fact remains—King Kelson is dead, and Nigel must be the new king," Vivienne was saying. "This presents us with a unique opportunity to reassert our influence over the House of Haldane."

"Oh, must you be so cold-blooded about it?" Barrett murmured, uncharacteristically snappish. "Unlike the rest of us, Denis was close to Kelson. Let him have a decent interval of mourning."

"If he observes a 'decent' interval of mourning," Kyri said, "the moment may pass before we can seize it. Of the four persons designated to assist in bringing Nigel to his full Haldane potential, three are safely occupied, for at least another two or three days. That leaves the initiative with you, Denis. The question is, can you bring Nigel to full potential alone?"

Arilan, still exhausted by the monumental effort it had taken to assemble the Council a few hours before, leaned his dark head against the back of his chair and closed his eyes.

"I don't know," he whispered. "I'm not sure it's wise, in any case. What's wrong with waiting for Morgan and Duncan?"

"Don't be naïve," Kyri said. "This is our chance to break the hold that Morgan has had on the last two Haldane kings. If we can't control him, and you won't allow us to eliminate him permanently, then pushing him out of the facilitation is at least a reasonable alternative."

"Must it really come to that?" Arilan said.

Barrett bowed his hairless head, shaking it sadly.

"We know how you feel about them, Denis," he said. "But Kyri is right. Having you trigger Nigel's Haldane potential wouldn't exactly give us any more control over him than we had over Kelson, God rest his soul." He crossed himself halfheartedly—a motion copied by most of the others, with varying degrees of impatience—"But at least we would know more about the process, so that when the time comes to bring Conall or one of his brothers along, we'll be in a position of greater influence."

"I don't know whether I can do it alone," Arilan repeated. "I'm sure things were set, even in me, that were supposed to trigger at the appropriate time, but Nigel's in no state right now, even if I were."

"But he was prepared to become king, if anything had happened to Kelson in battle last summer," Sofiana said neutrally.

Arilan nodded. "Yes, but that was last summer. Who

would have thought Kelson would meet his end on his
knight's quest, falling off a goddamn embankment? After all
he's survived, to go that way——''

"Then, is Nigel despondent?" Vivienne asked impatiently.

"No, but he's very deeply grieving and stunned. I
wouldn't know how to begin to approach him about such a
thing."

Laran pursed his lips thoughtfully. "Perhaps some medical intervention might be appropriate," he ventured. "We
have medications that can ease the process. You used some
of them on Nigel before. I suggest that such assistance is
definitely indicated now, if you're to try to trigger the reaction alone. You shouldn't have to worry about physical
or even psychological resistance while you're juggling more
esoteric balances."

Choking back a sob, Arilan folded his arms on the table
before him and laid his forehead against his sleeve.

"I can't think about it right now, Laran. Why can't I make
you understand that? All of you."

His shoulders shook as he surrendered to his own grief
and shock, for the first time since passing his terrible news
on to Duncan, hours before. Only Sofiana, realizing that he
was weeping silently, had the presence of mind to clear the
chamber and leave him in peace for a while, grieving with
him as she led the others downstairs to the ritual chamber
known as the *keeill*, there to guide them in a silent meditation
for the repose of the dead king's soul.

CHAPTER SIXTEEN

*Chasten thy son while there is hope, and let not thy
soul spare for his crying.*

—Proverbs 19:18

Dhugal fought down an urge to gag as he made himself
gnaw on a charred chunk of rank, stringy horsemeat, washing down each bite with water because he knew he had to
eat or starve.

He had never been partial to horse, even properly prepared—though, when times were lean, he had sometimes
eaten it in the borders, of necessity—and he hated over-
cooked meat. This was neither properly prepared nor rare
the way he liked it—and starting to go bad besides. Not bad
enough to make him sick, but bad enough that he hardly
cared that this was the last of it that was at all edible. At
least partially burning it did help to disguise the flavor.

Unfortunately, the bloated carcass had already been half-
ripe when he found it, perhaps a day earlier—though day
and night had no meaning in this cavern of perpetual darkness.
His nose had led him to it. It had been wedged in a tangle
of flood wrack, held fast by the savage current not far downstream of where he still kept hopeful vigil beside the unconscious Kelson. It had been Jowan's horse. He had
watched horse and rider go over the edge, what seemed like
half a lifetime ago. He wondered whether young Jowan had
met a kinder fate.

Their hapless guide had not. Dhugal had found his body,
too, not far from the drowned horse, skull fatally breached
in at least two places, brain matter protruding, and both arms

and both legs shattered beyond mending, even if death had not been likely instantaneous from the head injuries.

There was nothing Dhugal could do for the monk besides offer a brief prayer for his soul, which he did, but there *was* one final service the monk might do for him—or rather, for Kelson. The man's clerical habit under the still soggy cloak was woven of a fine wool, warm and light. It wanted a good washing, for Brother Gelric's body also had begun to go the way of the dead horse, but when rinsed out and dried before the fire, the loose-fitting garment would be far more comfortable for Kelson than the soiled clothing in which he now had been lying for however long he had been unconscious. Dhugal was doing the best he could to keep his patient clean and dry and at least getting water down him on a regular basis, but unless Kelson stirred soon, Dhugal held little hope for his survival.

The horse also had proven useful, beyond the few pieces of tainted meat that Dhugal managed to salvage before dumping the decaying carcass back into the river, for its saddle-bags somehow had managed not to be separated from the animal's saddle or even burst open. Most of what Dhugal found in the one side was of little value to anyone but the presumably drowned Jowan, but he did find flint and steel, an extra belt, and a few spare leather straps, all potentially useful. And the other side, wonder of wonders, had yielded a hard winter apple, much bruised, and a soggy piece of journey bread, starting to mold.

The latter Dhugal had fed meticulously to Kelson, picking off the mold as best he could and easing small, semi-liquid amounts of the bread past Kelson's lips, washing it down with sips of water which he made Kelson swallow. He tried to pulverize bits of the apple and feed them to Kelson, too, but finally had to give that up and eat the apple himself, for he dared not risk having Kelson choke while unconscious.

He had just finished bathing Kelson, as he had done for his foster father during the old man's last years, and was gently easing the dead monk's habit over Kelson's head and down around his waist, when the king gave a moan, stronger than he had yet managed, and opened his eyes.

"What're you doing?" he managed to croak, his voice thready and weak from disuse.

"Kelson! Thank God, you're awake!"

"M'head hurts," Kelson whispered. "I think I'm going to be sick."

"Oh, no you don't," Dhugal murmured, easing Kelson onto his side, one hand on his forehead and one on his throat, easily forcing his mind past Kelson's almost nonexistent shields to push down the nausea that was threatening to expel what little food Dhugal had gotten down him. "I can't have you wasting energy on that kind of nonsense. Just relax, and the nausea will pass. It's from your concussion. Close your eyes and let me hold the control for you. You'll be all right in a minute or two."

It was a near-run thing for something longer than a minute or two, but at last Kelson seemed to rally a little on his own, finally rolling weakly onto his back again to look up at Dhugal. He seemed to be having trouble focusing.

"Dhugal?" he breathed.

"Aye, who else, my prince?" Dhugal murmured, grinning as he brushed both hands tenderly over Kelson's forehead. "Just rest you easy. You're going to be fine. How do you feel?"

"Terrible. And starved," Kelson croaked. "And parched. Where are we? What happened?"

"We're somewhere underground." Dhugal unstoppered his flask and raised Kelson by the shoulders far enough to set the flask against his lips and gently support his head. "We went down an embankment into a river, and that sucked us under. Don't you remember the accident?"

Kelson grunted in the negative, still guzzling water greedily, and Dhugal sighed.

"Well, I'm not surprised. You took several nasty whacks on the head. What's the last thing you *do* remember?"

Kelson pushed the flask away at last, turning his face slightly to belch weakly, then glanced uncertainly back at Dhugal.

"You *are* Dhugal MacArdry, aren't you?" he asked. "God, it's been so long. . ."

A chill went through Dhugal's heart.

"Kelson, don't you know me?" he whispered.

"Of course I know you. But you look so much older." The king's eyes darted to Dhugal's waist. "And you're wearing a white belt. You can't be old enough for that. Who knighted you?"

"Don't you remember? *You* did."

"*I* did? But—"

Kelson closed his eyes tightly for several seconds, then opened them again as Dhugal watched anxiously.

"Dhugal, what year is it?"

Dhugal swallowed carefully. "What year do you *think* it is, Kel?"

Kelson thought a moment, then said gravely, "To the best of my recollection, it's 1123."

Compressing his lips grimly, Dhugal shook his head. "Wrong by two years," he murmured. "It's March of 1125. When's the last time you remember seeing me?"

Kelson screwed up his face in concentration, then shook his head bewilderedly. "When you left court, after your brother died, I suppose. I know you weren't at my coronation."

"No, blasted luck. I'd broken my leg a few weeks before and couldn't travel. But at least you remember that you're king. That's something. You obviously have some amnesia from your concussion, though." He laid one hand lightly on Kelson's forehead again. "Let me have a look, and we'll see what the gaps are. God, your shields are—"

"You can sense my shields?" Kelson said. "But—"

"I'm Deryni, too, Kelson," Dhugal said. "*Jesu*, I suppose you don't remember that, either—or that Duncan is my real father."

"Duncan?" Kelson said weakly. "But, how—"

"God, we're going to have some catching up to do," Dhugal murmured, half to himself. "Just relax, and I'll see what I can do."

"Conall, I'd like a word with you, please."

Arilan caught at Conall's sleeve as he and the new crown prince filed out of the withdrawing room at the end of the great hall at Rhemuth, leaving Nigel in privacy with Meraude and Saer de Traherne. Archbishops Bradene and Cardiel had already gone on ahead, to be stopped and questioned by a few of the lesser lords beginning to flock to court as news spread of Kelson's demise.

It had not been much of a privy council meeting—just the seven of them, for Jehana had kept to her rooms since receiving the news of her son's death, and Duncan was en route to Coroth, while other messengers carried the news to seek out the rest of the crown's senior advisers. Nigel had presided, but he was still numb at his change of status, and seemed unwilling or unable to take much initiative yet on his own.

Thus it had fallen to Bradene, assuming nominal leadership in Ewan's absence and Nigel's reluctance, to draft the official proclamation naming Nigel as king to succeed Kelson. That, at least, had finally sparked a reaction from Nigel—though all he had done was reiterate his refusal to be crowned until a year and a day had passed, or until proof should be presented that Kelson was, in fact, dead. Conall had kept his peace for the most part, wisely judging that now was not the time to draw any unnecessary attention to himself, when the crown was finally within his grasp, if only he should wait—*if* nothing went awry.

"Let's go out into the garden, shall we?" Arilan went on, shifting his hold to Conall's elbow. The Deryni bishop's touch made Conall's heart pound in apprehension, though he found he was able to keep it hidden more closely than ever, behind shields that seemed to have grown stronger since his return from Valoret. Conall wondered whether it had to do with the fact that Kelson was dead, and Conall's own Haldane powers were beginning to manifest in earnest, now that he was first in line for the throne. Perhaps both Tiercel *and* the Camberian Council had been right about Haldanes.

"Is something wrong, Excellency?" Conall asked, managing to keep his voice low and even.

"No, just something I'd like to ask you about," Arilan replied.

Glancing easily around him to see who might be watching, the Deryni bishop opened a door into the garden beyond the hall and drew Conall outside, not saying anything else until they had walked slowly into the center, where no one might approach too closely without being seen over the hedges. A few figures moved at the far end of the garden, hardly visible behind the trees only just beginning to green again after the long winter, but otherwise it was deserted. And though the sun was shining brightly, drying up the last puddles of the previous days' rain, it was also chilly. Conall wrapped his black cloak more closely around him as he and Arilan paused by a leaf-clogged fountain.

"I suppose you may have gathered," Arilan said quietly, without further preamble, "that I had something to do with setting your father's Haldane potential last spring, before Kelson went off on campaign. Likewise, I suspect you will not be surprised when I tell you that I have noticed your own gradual development along these lines. Shields and the like, which seem to have strengthened considerably since Kelson's death—not altogether surprising, since Nigel now is king and you are his heir."

Conall felt the cool, velvet touch of the other's mind against those shields, but it did not penetrate, even though the pressure grew considerably before slacking off.

"Yes, indeed. A spontaneous Haldane manifestation developing," Arilan murmured, smiling. "I've been told that Kelson had also developed a few spontaneous talents, before Brion's death. Perhaps Tiercel was right all along."

"I—beg your pardon?" Conall managed to murmur, fear rising in his throat, though he knew Arilan could not have read that from his mind.

"Oh, no one you would know," Arilan replied. "A friend who once believed that more than one Haldane could hold the power at a time. We all thought him mad. But, no matter. What matters is that because you *are* manifesting some of the Haldane gifts on your own, perhaps from so much contact with Deryni, you may be able to assist me in a very important matter."

Conall swallowed uneasily.

"Assist *you*?" he breathed.

"Only indirectly," Arilan allowed. "But I've been given an assignment by—" He sighed. "This is silly. I'm not supposed to say the name of the Camberian Council to outsiders, but you know very well what group I mean, even if you don't know names of individuals. I'm sure Morgan and Duncan have had no compunctions about mentioning it, though I would hope they continue to respect the identity of its members. They *have* mentioned the Council to you, haven't they?"

Almost holding his breath, Conall nodded. Could it be that he had escaped any further mention of Tiercel so easily?

"Anyway," Arilan went on, "I was one of four who participated in Nigel's patterning last spring. The other three, as you may have guessed, were Morgan, Duncan, and Richenda. They're all in Coroth right now, and at least a couple of days from being able to get back here—and Richenda not at all, with her time approaching—so I've been asked to trigger Nigel's final power assumption myself."

"And not wait for Duncan and Morgan?" Conall asked.

Arilan smiled sardonically. "The Council—ah—does not precisely trust Duncan and Morgan just now. I can't go into details why. Personally, I have no compunctions about waiting for them, but I am—not entirely my own master in this matter."

"You follow the Council's orders," Conall said, nodding carefully.

"For the most part, yes."

Uneasy still, Conall turned half-away, setting one booted foot on the edge of the fountain and pretending to study some leaves.

"I don't think I follow," he said after a moment. "Where do I come into this? I'm not Deryni. I don't know anything that would be useful to you for something like that."

"No, but you're Nigel's son and heir."

"Which only means that, once he's come to full power, someone will have to worry about setting *my* potential," Conall replied. "What does my father say?"

Arilan twined his fingers before him at waist level and gazed blindly at his bishop's ring.

"I've spoken to him about it in passing, but he wants to delay until the coronation."

"Until the coronation? But that isn't for a year, if he has *his* way."

And the longer the delay, Conall thought to himself, the greater chance that his own enhanced powers would come under closer scrutiny than they could bear, and his connection with Tiercel be discovered.

"I know," Arilan said. "And do you think that the King of Gwynedd can survive that long, without full power, knowing some of the enemies he'll be facing, once word gets out of Kelson's death?"

"Against Morag and her Arjenol duke?" Conall said contemptuously. "Hardly."

"Which exactly echoes the Council's sentiments," Arilan

agreed. "That is precisely why I need you to help me convince Nigel that his power assumption should go ahead as soon as possible."

"Without Duncan and Morgan?"

Arilan raised an eyebrow. "Don't I recall hearing you complain once that Morgan and Duncan had too much power in Gwynedd, too much influence over the king?"

Conall pursed his lips thoughtfully. "I sometimes said things without thinking, when I was young and foolish. But what's to prevent *you* from gaining 'too much influence,' if you're the one who engineers my father's power assumption?"

"Ve-ry astute," Arilan said, nodding approvingly. "I won't lie to you and say that isn't possible, because there *is* a certain link between the king and the person or persons who assist him to power. However, I think you know that I honor my oaths; and I swear to you, Conall, that my aim is only to make King Nigel more independent of Morgan and Duncan than King Kelson was."

They spoke a little longer of what arguments Conall might use to change Nigel's mind, and then Arilan left. Conall stood there in the garden for several more minutes, thinking about all the ramifications and wondering how he could turn the situation to his own best advantage, then began strolling slowly toward the other end of the garden, turning a dead rose stem between his fingers and testing one fingertip against a thorn, letting the slight pain keep him tuned to the subject at hand.

But then, as he rounded a turn in the garden path, he saw another possibility to turn recent events to his own advantage. Rothana was sitting alone on a garden bench, blue-coifed head bowed over an open breviary on her lap, one hand spread flat on the right-hand page. He almost had not recognized her at first, however, for her habit was black this afternoon, not the usual pale blue of her coif. He hoped the change of habit did not mean she had somehow taken more binding vows, for now that Kelson was out of the way, Conall intended to make Rothana of Nur Hallaj his wife.

"Good afternoon, my lady," he said softly.

She started as she looked up, apparently taken by surprise, and started to stand, but he stayed her with a gesture and sat down beside her instead. She had been crying, and she wiped self-consciously at her tears with her free hand.

"I note a change of habit," he said, running his eyes over her attire. "Does this indicate a change of status as well?"

She shook her head hastily. "We wear black for the king," she whispered. "All of us in my order. I—cannot believe that he is dead."

Conall lowered his eyes, pretending to study his own black attire, though his was broken by a crimson badge of the Haldane heir on the breast of his tunic.

"I wish I could tell you otherwise, my lady," he said after a moment. "Unfortunately, I saw him fall. No one could have survived, after this long."

"I know," she answered, her voice very small.

He ventured a very, very gentle probe, no more than might be expected of a Haldane heir beginning to come into his powers, if she should detect it, but she did not seem to notice. Her shields were all but down, and he sensed the guilt associated with what she hid beneath her hand, though he could not tell exactly what it was. But perhaps he could use that guilt, and turn it to make her do his will.

"Would that I had died, instead of Kelson," he said quietly, turning his glance out to the dead garden, though he continued to watch her out of the corner of his eye. "Then this burden would not have fallen on my father. Not yet, at least."

He felt her quick intake of breath psychically as well as physically, and knew he was taking exactly the right approach.

"He never expected or wanted the burden of the crown," Conall went on. "Nor did I, though now it will be mine some day as well."

She swallowed noisily, on the verge of tears again, but Conall did not relent.

"The burden is a lonely one, my lady," he whispered. "My father has my mother at his side, but I have no one. I—will need a queen to stand beside me some day. Perhaps this is not the time to ask, but may I dare to hope it might be you?"

"Me?"

Her voice squeaked as she glanced up at him in dull shock.

"Please don't refuse me outright, my lady," Conall pleaded. "Consider carefully what I'm asking. I—know that you are under vows. But the vows are temporary. And I—also know that you—were considering giving them up for another Haldane prince."

"Who told you that?" she demanded.

He could feel her probing at his shields, but he only stiffened them and met her searching eyes, though he pretended to shrink a little from the pressure.

"Please don't," he whispered, relaxing a little as she backed off without further attempt to pry. "I'm still learning what I am."

"Forgive me," she replied. "I never would have pressed you against your will."

"I know that."

"But—who told you?" she insisted.

"Why, who do you think told me? Kelson was my cousin. We often talked. I—know about your leave-taking, and—by what little margin he spared your virtue that last night before we left."

And that was all literally true, as far as it went—just in case she should be able to Truth-Read him without his knowledge. She blanched and glanced down guiltily at her hand, still laid flat on the page of her breviary, and suddenly Conall guessed what lay beneath.

Then her resistance seemed to crumple, her shoulders slumping as she slowly picked up what lay beneath her hand and then exposed it on her open palm. It was the ring Kelson had given to Sidana on their wedding day, threaded on a thin white silken cord crumpled around it.

"I did not think he would tell anyone, my lord," she whispered. "Nor did I think you and he were that close. Dhugal, perhaps, but—"

"I have told no one else, my lady," Conall said gently. "Your honor is safe with me."

"I do not doubt that, sir."

She turned the ring in her fingers a few times, then glanced up at him wistfully, sniffling back tears.

"Do you believe in magic, my lord?" she asked softly.

He nodded, not daring to speak.

"Of course you do," she whispered, answering her own

question. "You are a Haldane, your own peculiar form of magic already manifesting. How could you not believe?"

She glanced at the ring in her hand and slowly shook her head.

"But the magic can go awry, sometimes," she went on. "Sometimes, when we wish too hard, we can jinx the very thing we most desire. It is not uncommon. I should have known better. But I allowed myself to dream, before the magic was accomplished. And I shall pay for my presumption for the rest of my life."

He cocked his head at her, not sure he understood what she was trying to say.

"Your presumption?" he murmured.

She shook her head. "The ring was not given in pledge. He made that quite clear, before he even gave it to me. It was meant only as a token that he had put the past aside, that he was ready to start considering the future. He was only just beginning to let himself release his own guilt over the Princess Sidana's death—though no one blamed him, surely. We—spoke about the possibility of—marriage, when he returned, after both of us had had time to think. But he asked me not to wear the ring, for it was tainted with *her* blood."

"Then, what presumption was there on your part?" Conall asked.

She shook her head sadly. "Sometimes, my lord, a woman lets herself dream on what might be. And sometimes, even the magic of an ordinary woman is strong enough to make it actually happen. For one of *us,* however—"

A stifled sob escaped her lips, and it was several seconds before she could go on.

"A week ago—it must have been just before the accident—I let myself imagine what it would be like, to wed him. There was no harm in that, alone. Nor was it the first time I had fantasized thus, though my abbess would be shocked to learn of it—and Father Ambros *was* shocked, at first.

"But then I dared to put Sidana's ring on my finger— poor, doomed princess—imagining that it was the king who gave it. Only, it was the giver of the ring who perished this time—not the recipient. The king must have—met his accident very shortly after that."

"But, surely you don't think *you* caused the accident," Conall said. "That's nonsense."

"Is it?" She glanced down at the ring, then closed it in her palm. "My mind tells me you are right, my lord," she whispered, "but my heart will never be certain. I know too well how great our power can be—sometimes when we least expect it. Now that—now that you have moved closer to the throne, you will be discovering that for yourself, I think. Indeed, by your shields, I think you already are. God grant that it may be long before you must face the full power of what you are—and that you may never need to face the uncertainty, as I must do, of wondering whether your powers destroyed the very thing you most desired."

"Then, you did intend to marry Kelson," Conall breathed.

She nodded slowly.

"The letter requesting dispensation from my vows had already been sent to Archbishop Cardiel—though I doubt not that it has gone astray between here and Valoret, what with His Excellency now returned to Rhemuth. It will find him eventually, however. And when it does, I shall ask that he not act upon it."

"I see," Conall murmured, hope sinking in his breast as he realized she meant to continue in religious life. "But, will they take you back? Won't the mere act of asking for dispensation cast doubt upon your vocation?"

She bowed her head. "I did not tell my abbess that I wrote to the archbishop," she said. "Father Ambros knows, for he has lately been my confessor. I discussed the matter fully with him. But he is bound under the seal of the confessional—and I shall ask Archbishop Cardiel to destroy the letter when it arrives, preferably without reading it first."

"Please don't," Conall whispered.

"And why should I not? In retrospect, I must wonder whether all that has happened is not God's way of telling me He still desires me for His bride. They say He is a jealous lover."

"And I, too, can be a jealous lover, Rothana," Conall said. "Be *my* bride."

"Thou shalt not mock the Lord thy God," she murmured.

"I do not mock Him. But I do not think a god of the spirit has great need of things of the flesh. I have never favored the practice of cloistering young virgins to spend their youth and beauty in service to a God Who cannot appreciate their charms.''

"You must not blaspheme, my lord," she managed to whisper, not daring to look at him. And she gasped and closed her eyes as Conall brushed two tentative fingertips against the back of her hand that clasped Sidana's ring.

"You and I are flesh, Rothana," Conall said softly. "How can I make you understand what your very presence does to me? You are everything a man could possibly desire. I think I have wanted you from the first time I set eyes on you. I only held back asking because of Kelson. But he's dead now, and one day I'll be king. And this Haldane has no less need for you as queen than he did. Gwynedd needs you as well, Rothana."

Her face flamed, and she bowed her head into her empty hand to hide it as she clutched the other, with Sidana's ring, closer to her breast.

"Do not lay *that* upon me as well, my lord," she whispered. "I was bred to duty. I know full well what Gwynedd's queen must be, to rule beside a Haldane king. How can you ask it, knowing what I've told you?"

Conall smiled, for Rothana herself had just shown him how he must shape his argument, so that in the end, she could not refuse.

"I can ask because now, more than ever, I know how much love you have to give—to Gwynedd as well as the man you wed. With God's help, perhaps I may one day win a portion of that love for myself. But meanwhile, Gwynedd needs you, as much as Kelson ever did, and *I* need you—for many of the same reasons. You need not answer me now, my lady, but promise that you'll think about it. Be the queen Gwynedd needs, to balance a Haldane king. And, if you truly think that Kelson's death lies partly at your feet, then make expiation by doing what you dreamed—only, with me rather than Kelson. I swear to you, only the name of your king will change."

He knew he gambled much on so emotional an appeal, and prayed she would not refuse outright and force him to resort to blackmail—for as a last recourse, he knew he could tell her what he had seen between her and Kelson, and threaten to reveal it to her superiors, suitably embellished.

It would end any hope she might have of being permitted to continue in a religious vocation.

But she neither accepted nor refused him, in the few more minutes they spent together there in the garden, and he sensed she was considering, as he had asked. The interview ended when her abbess, Father Ambros, and several other sisters of Rothana's order came into the other end of the garden, the priest apparently leading the others in devotions while they walked. Rothana excused herself immediately, promising, when pressed, to continue considering what he had offered.

Conall watched her thoughtfully as she hurried to join the others. His head ached with the strain of the encounter, but he was sure she had not pierced his façade. Now he could only wait for his next opportunity to broach the subject and pray that Father Ambros was discreet and Rothana herself would not dare to speak further of the matter to anyone else until Cardiel should release her from her vows.

And Rothana's letter to the archbishop must be investigated, too, to see how specific she had been. From what he was learning of her way of thinking, Conall guessed she would have been circumspect in her exact reasons for requesting dispensation; but Conall stood a far better chance of accomplishing their marriage if Cardiel thought her motive a questioning of her vocation rather than an intention to marry a specific individual.

Fortunately, Cardiel was human. Conall could manipulate him, if he had to. In fact, other than Arilan himself—and Morgan and Duncan, when they eventually returned—Conall doubted there was anyone at court that he could *not* manipulate, with the possible exception of his father. And if Conall could make himself a part of Nigel's power assumption—as was certainly possible, now being the heir—there might be ways to circumvent Nigel's abilities as well, even after he was brought to full potential.

Conall could feel his own power stirring within him as he stood and began making his leisurely way back into the residence wing of the castle, heading for his father's apartments to deal with the request Arilan had made of him. Nigel must be persuaded to accept his Haldane power as soon as possible, so that Conall could be confirmed as the heir and his own growing powers not be so noticeable.

They *were* growing, too—no doubt as a result of Kelson's death and Conall's subsequent nearer proximity to the throne. Growth of any kind often produced growing pains, however—headaches, in Conall's case, becoming more and more frequent. He had one now. Though Tiercel might have set his Haldane potential in motion early—and Conall's reading of Tiercel's memories undoubtedly had given him increased abilities even over what he had gained to that point—Conall was now eligible for more orthodox assistance to come into his inheritance. Once Nigel was confirmed in full power, they would have to confirm Conall as the heir—delicious anticipation!

His head continued to ache as he climbed the stairs, but he pushed the pain down with relative ease, now that he did not have to be on guard against Rothana. Nor need he be too concerned about his father's powers. So far as he could tell, Nigel was far behind Conall in ability, for all that he had been prepared to assume Kelson's legacy of magic as well as blood.

He found his father at a writing table built into a window of his parents' sleeping chamber, gazing out across the river, a quill forgotten in his fingers. The funereal black of the prince regent's raiment was relieved only by his still, winterpale face and hands and the silver threading his temples, the latter glinting in the sunlight as Nigel turned his head to see who had entered. The new King of Gwynedd smiled and laid aside the pen as his eldest son approached, pushing aside the sheaf of parchment rectangles with an immense sigh of relief.

"Thank God, Conall. You've rescued me from an interminable stack of correspondence that needs to be signed and sealed. The scribes must have worked all through the night—dozens of them. Arilan is an even worse taskmaster than Duncan. I don't suppose you'd care to lend a hand?"

Conall smiled thinly in return and detoured to the fireplace to fetch a lighted candle before joining his father at the cluttered table, setting the candlestick in a space Nigel cleared hastily at the end exposed to the room. Conall wanted to talk about only one of the two bishops his father had just named. Helping seal the documents would give his hands something to do while he chose his words with care.

"They *have* left you with a stack, haven't they?" he said,

pulling a coil of scarlet sealing wax from the clutter and straightening out the wick end to light it from the candle. "I fear I shan't be much help with the signing, but I can dribble sealing wax with the best of them. Which seal are you going to use?"

Nigel twisted his personal signet off his finger and set it before Conall with a sigh.

"Regardless of what they say, I'm not the king *yet*, son," he said. "And I don't mind telling you, I hoped never to have to send these."

He pulled the first letter from its stack and laid it on the table before Conall, holding it steady as the red drops made a growing mound of molten wax on the parchment below his signature—to which Nigel had added *P.* for *Princeps,* rather than *R.* for *Rex.*

Conall said nothing as his father set the seal into the hot wax, leaving the imprint of Nigel's personal arms rather than the undifferenced Haldane lion that was now his due, but it was obvious Nigel was aware of his son's scrutiny. He gave Conall a tight, strained smile as he set the letter aside and drew the next one into position, deliberately averting his grey Haldane gaze.

"I know," Nigel said softly, watching the wax pool on the next letter. "I'm probably being foolish still to hold out hope that Kelson might yet live. But I don't *want* to be king. If I thought I dared, I'd seriously consider abdicating in your favor. You wouldn't mind, either, would you? You're young enough for the responsibility to seem like adventure. But of course the great lords would never stand for it. There's no place but the grave for a man who once was king."

As Nigel applied seal to wax again, Conall felt a stir of anger at how little his own father understood his yearnings, but he forced himself to put it aside dispassionately, in the same way he put aside the second letter. In many respects, Nigel was absolutely correct. There was no room for two kings in any land.

"God grant that day may be long in coming, Father," he murmured. "For now, I'm perfectly content to continue learning statecraft at your side. In the meantime, however, there's other craft we both must learn. And you, in particular, dare not delay that overlong."

"Ah, I see Arilan's been at you," Nigel said.

"Only casually," Conall replied, focusing all his outward attention on the next seal, though his shields had firmed instinctively at his father's faint rebuke. "He's right in warning that our enemies will be testing, as soon as they learn of Kelson's death, hoping for just such a delay in confirming your powers."

He sent a cautious tendril of thought against the shields he expected to be already in place, but it slithered unimpaired and undetected past defenses only barely maintained, and never intended to stop his own son. Nigel only shook his head in response to Conall's words as he switched a sealed letter for an unsealed one.

"I don't see that they'll be testing all that soon. They can't even know yet, in Torenth. Even Morgan will only be finding out in the next day or so—and Duncan didn't have to ride the distance from here to Dhassa. It will take far longer for conventional couriers to cross the Torenthi border."

"From here, perhaps," Conall agreed, "but not from the north, where it happened. We took four days to ride from Saint Bearand's via Valoret, but one must take into account that the news will have spread directly from there as well. All the monks at Saint Bearand's certainly knew, as soon as anyone outside our immediate party. And we ourselves sent a messenger directly to the Earl of Eastmarch, to name only one. He'll have sent word on to Cardosa. And once the news reaches Cardosa, it can be all over Torenth within a matter of hours, as soon as some Torenthi agent with Deryni connections can make it to the nearest Portal."

"You paint rather bleak prospects," Nigel replied, exchanging another sealed letter for an unsealed one. "Still, I think we can delay making any binding decisions until Duncan and Morgan return."

"Why not let Arilan handle it and be done?" Conall asked. "He says he was keyed to your power ritual, the same as Duncan and Morgan. And he isn't emotionally involved over Kelson's death in the same way that the rest of us are. He might be a better bet, all the way around."

Nigel sighed and laid aside his seal, setting one fist on his hip to turn and gaze at Conall.

"Did he tell you that, son, or did you figure it out for yourself?"

Suddenly uneasy, for no clear reason he could immediately discern, Conall straightened and blew out the flame on the coil of sealing wax, setting it carefully beside his father's discarded ring.

"What do you mean? He *is* less emotionally involved."

"Less involved over the immediate matter of Kelson's death, perhaps," Nigel conceded, "but I'd hardly call him disinterested. He *is* a member of the Camberian Council, after all."

"What does that have to do with anything?"

Nigel shrugged, then folded his arms on his chest. "I'm not sure. Nothing I can exactly put my finger on. But they were already in turmoil themselves, over Tiercel's death. Kelson *did* tell you that one of the councillors had been found dead, right here in the castle, didn't he?"

Conall felt like a cold hand was closing around his heart and he had to avert his eyes to keep from telegraphing his consternation to his father. He hoped Nigel had not seen his momentary start of panic as the words first registered. He had not expected the conversation to turn to the dead Tiercel de Claron.

"He mentioned that *someone* important had been found dead, but he never said whom—only that it was no one I would know."

"No, you wouldn't have," Nigel murmured.

But an odd flicker of confusion rippled across his mind. Conall still had a probe set deep within his father's shields and could read no sign of real suspicion—yet—but he could follow connections being made as Nigel tried, mostly just below the surface levels of real awareness, to reconcile Conall's words of denial with the momentary start. Conall feared he might have underestimated his father and wondered whether it was too late to turn the light of doubt on Dhugal.

"Kelson really didn't say much else about it," Conall went on. "I got the impression it was something that needn't concern me, so I didn't pry. I do seem to recall a letter to Dhugal, however. In fact, Dhugal seemed very upset about it. Did he know the man?"

"We don't know," Nigel replied. "Duncan didn't think so. But the body was found in the secret passageway that leads from Dhugal's room out to the yard by the basilica. Only a few people knew about it."

"Well, obviously Tiercel de Claron did," Conall said. "How do you suppose he found out?"

Too late, he realized what he had said, and watched with a sick churning in the pit of his stomach as Nigel's face changed.

"I never mentioned Tiercel's full name, son," Nigel whispered. "How did you know it?"

"Well, I—suppose Kelson told me," Conall lied, trying frantically to retrace and cover his tracks. "Or maybe Arilan mentioned it."

"No, Arilan never would have said it to you, and you told me Kelson had never given you the dead man's name, since you wouldn't have known him. Conall, do you know more about this than you're telling me? Don't lie to me, son."

All at once, Conall knew that Nigel was aware of his probe, appalled to find it already past his shields. A part of the invaded mind tensed to repulse the intruder, but Conall could sense his father also trying to tap into the Truth-Reading ability he had been authorized to use.

Conall dared not let that happen. But even as he squelched the attempt, wrapping a part of his mind around that section of Nigel's and reaching for more emphatic controls, he knew that Nigel knew.

"Conall, what are you doing?" Nigel managed to gasp, clutching at the edges of the table for support as he quailed before his son's intrusion, grey eyes hurt and confused. "Oh, God, you *did* know him. And he gave you power, didn't he? Sweet *Jesu*, he gave you power, and you killed him!"

Conall was never sure just where the knowledge or the power came from—only that he could feel it welling from somewhere deep within him, coiling to strike, he helpless to stop it. Later, he was to reflect that it might have been triggered by reading the dead Tiercel's memories, for he experienced a rapid succession of mental images that were not in his own experience, but that seemed to hint that he had done battle with his mind before.

But guessing the source of his new-found power gave him no control over it. It was a survival reflex, untempered by reason or mercy or even by the knowledge that it was his own father he was about to strike and almost certainly slay. And though he thought he managed, in the very last instant, to deflect a portion of the lethal blast he loosed in his father's mind, he had no idea whether his efforts had been enough.

He watched in horror as the assault ran its course, Nigel's open hands uplifted in a futile warding-off gesture as he tried to stand, his handsome face contorted in a rictus of pain, hands clutching at both silvered temples in silent agony. It seemed to last for hours, though in fact no more than thirty heartbeats passed, and rapid ones at that, for Conall knew his heart was racing.

When, at last, he felt the power wane, still by no command that he himself had given, Nigel crumpled slowly like a felled tree. Conall watched, spellbound, until his father's limp body had sunk to the floor in a tangle of faintly twitching limbs and overturned chair, the handsome face drained of color, grey eyes blank and etched still with the echo of unspeakable pain.

CHAPTER SEVENTEEN

*And they shall mourn for him, as one mourneth for
his only son.*

—Zechariah 12:10

Kelric was kicking. Morgan, with his cheek laid against
the bulge that was his unborn son, glanced up at Richenda
in wonder, grinning as the baby kicked again and she winced.

"Our son is active this morning," he murmured.

"He's been active most of the night, Richenda countered.
"I think he's turning. It must get very cramped for a baby,
just before the end. At this rate, he may not wait another
three weeks to be born."

Morgan sat up in alarm.

"Is it time? Shall I send for Master Randolph?"

"Alaric—"

She laughed and set her hands to either side of his face
as she shook her head, dispelling his anxiety and coaxing
him by gesture and mind to worm higher in the bed, so she
could kiss him. He sighed contentedly as he snuggled down
beside her and buried his face against her shoulder, one arm
now draped protectively above her swollen abdomen.

"I know," he murmured, gazing beyond her at the cur-
tains enclosing the bed. "I worry too much. But I wonder
if you realize how frightening it is for a man to know what
his wife is going to have to go through to give him a child,
and worry whether she'll survive it."

"Dearest heart, I've done it twice before—" she protested.

"Yes, and I wasn't there either time," he said, rubbing

his unshaven cheek against her arm and raising his head to grin wickedly when she protested. "Well, you didn't wait until I could get home, the last time," he went on. "And it isn't *my* fault you had your first baby with the wrong husband. If you'd been sensible and married me first, things would have been much different."

"You didn't ask," Richenda retorted. "Besides, Brendan wouldn't be Brendan, if he'd had you for a father. He'd be very nice, I'm sure, and quite extraordinary—but he'd be someone else."

Morgan raised one eyebrow in agreement. "Aye, that's true. Well, little Kelric will be someone else, that's for certain—and undoubtedly extraordinary, just like his mother." He glanced thoughtfully at her stomach again. "I wonder what he's thinking right now. I wonder if babies think, before they're born."

"Well, if he does, I hope he's thinking how sorry he ought to be that he's giving his mother such a difficult time this morning," she replied sourly. "I doubt I slept more than a few hours. At least he seems to be settling down now. Maybe you can wheedle Lord Rathold into having Cook send breakfast up, and then I'll let *you* wrangle with your precious officers while I spend the morning napping. They won't miss me anyway. Besides, it's hard to take a woman seriously who looks as if she might explode at any moment."

"Darling! You do not," Morgan said indignantly, sitting up to look at her again.

"Well, I *feel* as if I might. Alaric, you have no idea how—"

"Hush a moment, love," Morgan murmured, touching fingertips to her lips as he cocked his ear to the sound of feet pounding up the staircase outside their door. And as fists hammered on it, he reached for a night robe.

"Your Grace! Oh, please. Morgan, come at once!"

It was Derry's voice, agitated and edged with heavy emotion, and Morgan was out of bed and dashing to the door, pulling on his robe, before the next set of pounding ceased.

"I'm coming, Derry. What is it?" He threw the bolt and flung open the door and was stunned to see Duncan standing at Derry's side, travel-stained, smelling of horse, and looking as if his entire world had ceased to exist.

"Duncan?"

"It's Kelson," Duncan managed to choke out. "And Dhugal. There's been an accident."

My God, what have I done?

Fists pressed to his temples in disbelief, Conall stared at his father's motionless body in shock for nearly a dozen heartbeats before he could move himself to kneel beside him.

He did not know what had come over him. He had not meant to do Nigel any harm. The power he had tapped, which he had channeled into an attack on his own father, had risen all unbidden and uncontrollable in response to his panic. It had been like the bolt of energy that Kelson loosed at Charissa in that terrible battle in the cathedral on Kelson's coronation day. Conall had *wanted* the full power of his Haldane potential and had gone to considerable lengths to get it, but he had never thought to pay *this* price for it.

But by some miracle which Conall could not begin to explain, Nigel still lived, despite the frightful blast of energy he had taken, all unprepared for an attack by his own son. His breathing was shallow and erratic, his skin clammy, and he did not respond to any of Conall's attempts to rouse him, but a pulse throbbed weakly in his throat. There was blood in Nigel's mouth, too, from biting his tongue while he convulsed; and Conall had to close the unseeing eyes, for they would not close of their own accord.

But though the pulsebeat steadied after a minute or two, nothing else of Nigel's condition seemed to change. And a fearful venture back into his mind encountered only the fog of unconsciousness, the irregular shadows of vast trauma done to body as well as mind—though even Conall, knowing what to look for, could detect no sign of how it had occurred, or by whose action.

Conall's own pounding heart began to slow down as he realized that he, at least, could not be blamed, and a detached, unfamiliar part of him began quite coolly developing a story to explain the condition without casting blame upon himself. Some of the reasoning, he knew with a frightening and puzzled certainty, came from the memories of the dead Tiercel de Claron.

He had seen men in a similar state before—usually older men than Nigel, who was not yet forty—but it sometimes happened that young men suffered a like fate. Physicians differed as to whether the heart or the brain was to blame. In any case, the effects were very similar to what Conall now observed in his father. Recovery, if it came, was always slow and laborious, and the victim might lie unconscious for days, weeks, or even months and be paralyzed and speechless for some time after that—perhaps indefinitely.

Except that, in this case, Conall knew that the victim would *not* get better unless someone could reverse what he had done. He himself did not know how, for he did not know how he had done it; and if anyone else discovered the true reason for Nigel's condition, they would surely make the eventual conclusion that Conall was responsible.

He dared not let his part in it be known, then. His guilt was multiplying with every new, terrible thing that happened, but he dared not confess—not with the crown at last within his reach.

For with Kelson dead and Nigel indefinitely incapacitated, Conall was now the most powerful man in Gwynedd. Perhaps he was not king yet in fact, for Nigel was rightful king so long as he lived, and Conall did not wish his father dead; but Conall certainly was the logical choice for regent, in his father's incapacity—king in everything but name.

The idea had a delicious feel to it—King Conall. And even *Regent* Conall was not without its charms. All that remained was to weather the discovery of his father's condition without giving clue that he had had any part of it.

He thanked God for the care Tiercel had taken in helping him sequester off a part of his mind from even Deryni probing, for Arilan was the one Deryni he would have to deal with immediately; but even Arilan did not scare him anymore. He required only a few seconds to seal away this newest guilt with the several others, where Arilan would never see it. Then, drawing a deep breath, he ran to the door and wrenched it open, calling down the spiral stair.

"Guards? Guards! Fetch a physician at once. My father's had some sort of a seizure!"

Morgan sat numbly on the edge of the hearth in his sleeping chamber, Richenda crowded close beside him, holding his hand mutely, watching him with wide, frightened eyes as both of them listened to Duncan repeat the details of his news one more time. Derry had taken a stool across from them, and Duncan slouched in Morgan's carved armchair, sipping halfheartedly at a cup of mulled wine a page had brought.

"That's all I know, Alaric. God help me, I can't believe it either, but it must be true. I questioned all the eyewitnesses before I left—and I do mean *questioned*. At least one of them saw Kelson slam into a rock, almost as soon as he hit the water. They say Dhugal seemed to be swimming, the last time anyone saw him, but both of them went over the waterfall—hell, *everyone* who went into the water went over the waterfall! And if, by sheerest luck, anyone survived *that*, apparently most of the river goes underground just past the spillway. So you either dash your brains out on a rock or you get sucked under and drown—or both."

"But you said one man did survive," Richenda ventured.

"Aye, but only barely," Duncan replied. "That little squire of Kelson's—Dolfin. They left him behind at Saint Bearand's until he's recovered enough to travel, but that could be weeks. Father Lael says the boy could be crippled for the rest of his life."

"They did find other bodies, though," Morgan said.

Duncan nodded. "One—and a couple of dead horses. But no sign of the monk who was guiding them, and no sign of Kelson or Dhugal."

Morgan closed his eyes, rubbing Richenda's hand gently along his cheek for creature comfort but not allowing her mind to touch his. He must keep himself detached from what had happened. If he gave up and let himself admit that Kelson was dead, his grief would overwhelm him, and he would be no good to anyone until it ran its course. Given the circumstances Duncan had reported, Kelson probably *was* dead—though, as had been the case with Brion, Morgan felt he should have sensed some sign of such a momentous passing. But as long as no one found Kelson's body, at least a part of him might still hold enough hope to sustain him through the rest of what must be done, to keep the reins of Gwynedd's government in capable hands.

And if Kelson *was* dead—in which case, neither Morgan nor Duncan nor anyone else could do anything for him now—there was a new king in Rhemuth who would need their help. Stabilizing Nigel and the transition of government must be their first priority. Only when that was accomplished might they indulge in mourning those lost—both of them.

"This must be especially difficult for you," Morgan said to Duncan, looking up at last. "In my concern over Kelson, I fear I'd almost let it pass that you've lost a son as well as a king. I'm sorry, Duncan."

Duncan shrugged forlornly. "It's a natural omission. I know you didn't mean to slight Dhugal. Do you think there's any chance they *are* somehow alive?"

"Do you want me to answer with my heart or my head?" Morgan countered.

"Why don't we try not to answer it at all, just for now, then?" Duncan said. "We both know our first priority. We have to get back to Nigel."

"Aye. On the other hand, we can't just stand by and assume that Kelson and Dhugal are dead. Too much depends on it. We need proof, one way or the other."

"I hoped you'd feel that way," Duncan whispered, after swallowing painfully. "What do you want to do?"

"A deep link, to see whether we can reach them."

"I'll help," Richenda said.

Smiling gratefully, Morgan shook his head, patting her held hand with his other one.

"Not from here, darling. It's too far, even if they *are* alive. No, I had in mind from Dhassa."

"Then, I'll come with you to Dhassa."

"Don't be ridiculous. You're in no condition to travel."

"And neither of you is in any condition to attempt such a working without help," Richenda countered. "It's still a long way from Dhassa to the area of Saint Bearand's. And if they're injured—"

"You're not coming, and that's final," Morgan said, releasing her hand as he rose. "Besides, someone Deryni has to stay here because of Morag. That's asking a great deal of you, as it is, with your time so near."

Richenda's face grew petulant. "I've told you, that isn't nearly as big a factor as you insist upon making it," she said. "A pregnant woman isn't *sick*, for God's sake. Even when the birthing starts, I'll only be thoroughly distracted for a few hours. And we've already made provisions for Morag. Derry knows what to do, when the time comes."

"Aye, well, that's one thing if you're here. It's quite another if you go gallivanting off with me to Dhassa—which is no place for a pregnant Deryni woman to be, in any case, among a bunch of intolerant clerics."

"There *is* another Deryni there, Alaric," Duncan interjected. "He's young and hasn't a great deal of training, so I don't know how much use he'll be, but he should be able to hold a passive link well enough."

Morgan blinked once, digesting the information, then shook his head.

"I won't ask more about him now. But his presence makes it even less necessary for Richenda to come along."

"I beg to differ!" Richenda said. "If you think I'm going to let you trust your safety to some ill-trained Deryni sprat who, with the best intentions in the world, could let you slip too deep and—"

"Richenda, I've said 'enough.' We won't discuss it further."

"Then, let *me* come with you, m'lord," Derry said. "I'm not Deryni, but I know what to watch for. Or you could draw on me for extra power. I'm not afraid."

"And leave Richenda to the wolves, Derry?" Morgan said archly. "I'm *going* to make her regent before I go, but I'd hoped you'd stay with her, to give her a hand."

As Richenda looked up in surprise, uncertain whether to be pleased or stubborn still, Duncan glanced among the three of them in bewilderment.

"It's a long story, Duncan," Morgan murmured. "I'll tell you on the way. In the meantime, can I trust that my beloved wife and my lieutenant can handle things in my absence?"

"Well, of course, but—"

"Good, then. Duncan, do you want a bath and a change of clothes before we head out? And maybe even a nap? You've got time. If—the worst *has* happened, we may be gone for quite a while, so I'll need a few hours to set things up."

As Morgan set about the business of getting ready to leave for Dhassa, Kelson's face was before him in his mind's eye.

Meanwhile, Kelson's face was before Dhugal in the flesh as he touched a fingertip to the forehead of the sleeping king and released him from sleep. The aroma of roasting fish wafted past Kelson's nostrils, and he came to with a start.

"Food," Kelson murmured, as he struggled blearily onto his elbows and blinked. "Thank God! I'm so hungry, I could eat a horse."

"You wouldn't want to eat the one *I* was eating," Dhugal said, helping the king sit up. "That's fish you smell."

"Well, I know that," Kelson muttered, giving Dhugal a sour glance. "Where'd you get a fish?"

Dhugal chuckled and held up his hands, wiggling his fingers in display. "I charmed him right into my clutches. Marvelous, the things one can do, if one's Deryni. He hadn't any eyes, either."

"No eyes?" Kelson glanced at the fish spitted on a stick above the fire. "What do you mean, no eyes?"

Shrugging, Dhugal fetched the fish on the stick and handed it to Kelson.

"He hasn't got any. Here, see for yourself. He's ready to eat, anyway. I guess they don't need eyes, living down here in the dark and all."

Looking a little queasy, Kelson handed the fish back.

"I don't know if I want to eat a fish that doesn't have eyes. It isn't—natural."

"Well, I think it's natural down here," Dhugal said, as he slipped the fish off the stick and onto a clean-washed depression in the stone floor of the cavern, breaking it open so it could cool a little. "Besides, there's nothing else to eat, now that the horsemeat's gone bad. This is the fifth or sixth one I've caught, and none of them had eyes. I threw the first few back, because of that, but they're all the same."

He licked a fingertip and raised an appreciative eyebrow. "They taste good, at least. And they're certainly proper Lenten fare. My father would approve."

Kelson sighed, nibbling halfheartedly at a morsel of fish after Dhugal had broken off a more sizable chunk and fallen to.

"Do you think Duncan and Alaric will come looking for us, Dhugal?" the king asked. "Or will they think we're dead?"

Dhugal, hungrily wolfing down another bite of fish, shook his head.

"I dunno," he said, when he had swallowed. "I have the

feeling we're pretty far underground, so I'm not sure they'd know where to look. I'm hoping there's a way out of here by following the stream bank in the direction the water's flowing. We certainly can't get out the way we came in.''

He picked up another chunk of fish. "We were tumbled along for quite a while before we beached in this cavern, though. We could have come miles. I'm sure they'll *try* to look, but—"

As Dhugal shrugged again, Kelson sighed and glanced toward the darkness in the direction the stream was flowing.

"God, I wish I could remember more about what happened," he whispered. "My memory's starting to come back, but—"

"How about your powers?" Dhugal asked quietly.

"Nothing." Kelson shook his head forlornly. "I keep trying to focus—on *anything*—but nothing happens that my head hurts worse. Do you think they'll come back?"

"You're asking *me?*" Dhugal said.

"Well, you're the battle surgeon," Kelson replied. "How long do the effects of head injuries last?"

"With a concussion like you've had—weeks, maybe. But I don't know about your powers being affected, Kel. I've never had a Deryni patient with a concussion before—at least not that I was aware of."

Kelson sighed explosively. "Well, you've got one now. Besides, *you're* Deryni."

"Yes, but only recently—recently discovered, that is. You know my training is marginal."

"Maybe you're a healer, like Duncan," Kelson said. "Maybe you could heal me."

"Kelson, I wouldn't dare."

"But, you already said you'd healed my head, where the skull was pressed in."

"No, I did a physical manipulation with my mind, like opening a lock without a key. There's a big difference between that and healing."

"I suppose."

"Anyway, now that you're getting back on your feet again, we need to start moving downstream. We can't stay here indefinitely."

Kelson looked doubtfully at Dhugal's boot, strapped with strips of fabric wound round the ankle.

"Can you walk on that?"

"I'll manage." Dhugal grimaced as he got to his feet, leaning heavily on his staff. "I'm pretty sure it isn't broken. It does hurt, though."

"You mean, you haven't looked at it?"

"I didn't dare take off the boot," Dhugal replied, giving Kelson a hand up as he braced himself against his staff. "I'm getting pretty good at sensing through leather, though. I tore some ligaments, but they're mending. It's less swollen than it was."

As Dhugal thrust a stick of driftwood into the fire for a torch, Kelson shook his head gingerly and picked up another stout piece of branch that would serve as a walking stick. Dhugal slung the saddlebags across his shoulder, and Kelson carried the flask.

Even that soon proved too great a burden for the king, however. Although Kelson thought they had been walking for several hours by the time they took their first rest break, Dhugal knew it had been far less time than that. Regardless of how long it had been, the king was exhausted. Dhugal had to let him sleep for several hours before he could summon up the strength to go on. Dhugal wondered how long they could keep this up.

It went on for several relays of hobbling on along the rushing riverbank and then falling into exhausted sleep, the roar of the water lulling them almost immediately into deep, dreamless slumber; but finally the roof above them widened and opened out into a vast cavern, so high they could not see the ceiling, even when Dhugal sent a sphere of handfire as high as he could make it go. The darkness seemed to press closer around them the farther they followed the river across the cavern, and pieces of driftwood for torches became fewer and fewer, so that Dhugal finally had to begin picking up suitable branches whenever he could find them and packing them along in the tops of the saddlebags.

CHAPTER EIGHTEEN

*The way of the wicked is as darkness: they know not
at what they stumble.*

—Proverbs 4:19

In Rhemuth, Conall's luck continued to hold. Nigel's
"seizure" was taken as exactly that, as first guards and servants, then a distraught Meraude, and finally a coterie of
physicians flocked into the royal suite to attend the stricken
king. Beyond initial, hurried inquiries regarding what had
happened, no one paid much attention to the apparently dev-
astated Conall; and he made a point to stay out of their way.

Arilan came, too, a little while later, but he was no physician; and by then, Conall had fixed a stunned façade of
innocence in the outer halls of his mind, so that the Deryni
bishop was unable to detect any hint of what *really* had happened to Nigel—and certainly, no one else was astute
enough to discern the truth. By dusk, Nigel's condition had
stabilized, but he did not regain consciousness.

"He's been working too hard since we brought back word
of Kelson's death," Conall said to Father Lael, when the
latter had withdrawn from the royal bedside at last, the first
to think seriously of seeing how the king's heir fared. "I told
him he should rest more. He was distressed about having to
send out those letters to the barons, too."

He gestured toward the table in the window, where the
letters lay temporarily forgotten, and Lael followed his
glance.

"He was working on those when he had his seizure?"
Lael asked.

Conall nodded. "They're the letters proclaiming his accession. He'd already signed them when I came in, and I was helping him seal them. It all went against the grain, though. He never really wanted or expected to be king. Archbishop Cardiel's probably told you what the privy council went through, just to gain his consent to be proclaimed right away. If he'd had his way, he would have made them wait a year and a day for *that*, as well as for the coronation. He was complaining about it when he—"

He broke off in a choked sob and buried his face in one hand, feigning overwhelming sorrow as Lael laid a sympathetic hand on his shoulder.

"It's been hard on you, too, hasn't it, son?" Lael murmured. "Don't you think you should get some sleep, though? There's nothing you can do for your father right now. I or one of the other physicians will stay with him through the night."

Conall sniffled back tears and looked up, shaking his head. In the event that anyone started to get suspicious, he wanted to be awake—just in case he needed to defend himself.

"I don't think I could sleep."

"I'll give you a sedative."

"But, what if he needs me?"

"Nonsense," Lael said. "Even if he does regain consciousness during the night—which I doubt he'll do—there's nothing you could do for him. Besides, I think you're still a bit in shock yourself."

Conall started to protest, but then he cut himself off and shook his head, for he had begun to weigh the merits of having people at least *think* he was asleep, thereby putting him beyond possibly dangerous questioning. Bed might, indeed, be the best place for him through the night, but he was not certain about Lael's sedative—just in case he did need to function at his best on short notice.

"I—perhaps you're right, Father," he said softly, all diffidence and subdued Haldane charm. "Undoubtedly you're right. I haven't had a proper night's sleep since it all happened."

"Well, then, let's see what we can do to ensure that you get one tonight," Lael replied. "In the morning, we'll have a much better idea how your father's condition is going to progress, and it will be far more important for you to be clear-headed and rested then. In case it hasn't yet dawned on you, you'll be king if Nigel dies. And even if he lives, you'll be regent until he recovers—if he recovers."

"You mean, he could be this way forever?" Conall asked softly.

"He could. Until he dies, at any rate. I'm sorry, Conall. I wish I could give you a more encouraging prognosis."

A quick pang of guilt stabbed at Conall's conscience, but it was quickly overshadowed by satisfaction. He had never really wished his father ill, but neither had he been prepared to accept the consequences of being blamed for Tiercel's death. He had intended neither, but he could not bring himself to regret either one, given the alternatives otherwise. Besides, what was done was done now; and the prospect of being regent and eventually king was far too tantalizing not to thrill him.

"I think I *will* have that sedative you mentioned, Father," he whispered, making himself look up at Lael in sad resignation.

"Fine," Lael replied. "Let's get you into bed first, though. You'll rest best in your own room, I think."

Without further discussion, an apparently dutiful Conall led Lael to his chambers and undressed in silence as the priest mixed a potion from his medical satchel. But instead of getting into bed immediately, the prince drew on a night robe and went to the prie-dieu set against the wall near the door, feigning restlessness.

"Set it on the nightstand there beside the bed, if you will, Father," Conall murmured, resting one hand on the armrest of the prie-dieu as he glanced back at the priest. "I think I'd like to pray a little while before retiring."

"Of course," Lael murmured, complying. "Would you like me to pray with you, or would you rather be alone?"

Conall bowed his head. "I think I'd prefer to be alone, Father, if you don't mind. This has all been—very difficult."

"Of course, Your Highness."

Conall thrilled to the title of address as Lael made him a bow and left the room, but as soon as the priest had gone, he went to the nightstand and emptied the contents of the cup into the chamber pot under the bed. He poured fresh wine into the cup after that and sat sipping at it in a window for nearly an hour, gazing lazily down into the darkening garden. Just at sunset, before it got too dark to see, he was pleased to observe Rothana among a group of other nuns and ladies of the court whom Father Ambros was leading back from the basilica, returning from evening prayers.

Soon after that, he did go to bed, and his dreams that night were of Rothana, as they had been several times since his return from Valoret, and of making love to her. He woke in a sweat more than once, determined to make the dream a reality as soon as possible.

"Once," said Morgan, "just once, before I die, I'd like to ride into Dhassa without having to resort to subterfuge."

"If you don't keep your voice down, we'll be doing it this time," Duncan murmured, "possibly with consequences that are at least inconvenient. Act like a monk, now."

"*Dominus vobiscum,*" Morgan muttered, bowing in the saddle of his little mountain pony as a merchant passed by.

He and Duncan were making the final approach to the city gates from the northeast shore of the lake, mail and leather concealed under the ubiquitous black habits and cowls of lay brothers attached to the cathedral chapter there. As courier monks, they were even entitled to the swords strapped beneath their knees—though Morgan had wrapped the hilt of his with leather to hide the gold wire and gemstones that adorned it, and sheathed it in a plain black scabbard.

The disguises had been Father Nivard's idea, before sending Duncan on his way three days before. The two also wore the pilgrim badges of both Dhassa's patron saints, though Saint Torin's had burned to the ground the last time these two particular Deryni passed through Dhassa territory. Both Morgan and Duncan had made substantial donations to cover the cost of rebuilding the shrine, so discovery of their true identities would not invite their murder, as it once might have. Nor were they any longer under episcopal Interdict and excommunication, and therefore to be incarcerated for canonical trial and execution. Still, their presence in Dhassa might raise awkward questions for Arilan as well as the two of them, if it were learned that they had come there to use a Deryni Transfer Portal.

But the delicacy of their situation, as well as any Deryni aspect of it all, paled almost to insignificance beside the very human ache of Kelson's loss. Morgan had been trying, all during the long, hard ride from Coroth, to make himself accept that Kelson and Dhugal were, indeed, dead, but his heart refused to countenance the notion with any real seriousness; and when, occasionally, it did, the dull, heavy weight in his chest far surpassed the grief he had felt even at Brion's death—and at least at the time, he had thought he could never grieve for anyone as he had for his dead friend and king. Duncan's grief he dared not touch at all.

And so, in clergy masquerade, Morgan followed his cousin through the gates of Dhassa and up toward the market square before the entrance to the bishop's palace. On this Lenten Sunday afternoon, the square was mostly deserted, but Duncan headed immediately toward the public well, where several black-cowled monks were watering half a dozen milk cows. A young man whom Duncan greeted as Father Nivard stepped out of their midst at the two's approach and bade one of the monks take their ponies, waiting while they unstrapped swords from saddles before leading them briskly into an inner chamber of the palace, not far from the chapel. Duncan had told Morgan about Nivard, during one of their infrequent rest stops on the way, but Morgan was still surprised to see how young the Deryni priest looked. Morgan's light, tentative probe confirmed that in shielding, at least, the priest knew what he was about. Still, he seemed very young and vulnerable as he closed the double doors and turned toward them, awe lighting his face now that they were alone.

"We shan't be disturbed here, my lords," Nivard said, crossing self-consciously to add wood to the fire burning on the hearth. "Bishop Denis has instructed me to give you every cooperation I can."

"I see," Morgan replied cautiously. "Our mutual benefactor," he gestured to indicate the room, with the arms of the Bishop of Dhassa above the fireplace, "neglected to mention that he'd been—ah—recruiting. Is it safe to talk here?"

"Or to do anything else that you might deem needful," Nivard said. "Bishop Denis said you'd want to try for a long range contact with the king or Lord Dhugal, before you go on to Rhemuth, and that you might want to use me to augment the link. I haven't a great deal of experience in that particular kind of working—none, in fact," he added with a fleeting, sheepish grin, "but he assured me that it wasn't necessary, and that you'd know what to do with me."

As he glanced expectantly between the two men, Morgan exchanged a skeptical glance with Duncan.

"Are you sure he's up to our needs, Duncan?" Morgan asked. "Sometimes a little knowledge is worse than none at all. Humans might be better, for our purposes."

"But not as potentially powerful," Duncan replied, giving Nivard a kindly smile. "Arilan had him make a light link with me, before I left for Coroth, and he was steady as a rock. Besides, he'll be worth three or four humans who don't know what they're doing, even if he doesn't either."

"Very well," Morgan murmured.

He had no idea how broad Nivard's experience might have been with Arilan, but as he and Duncan made the physical arrangements necessary for what must be done, drawing three chairs into a tight circle so that knees could touch when they were seated, Nivard seemed to take it all in stride, not batting an eye when Morgan pulled out the red leather box containing his ward cubes and began placing the black and white cubes in the proper configuration on the floor at their feet.

He could sense Nivard centering and relaxing, his psychic presence smoothing out, as minute adjustments were made to the positions of the black cubes, set at the corners of the white square formed by the four white ones. By the time Morgan was ready to touch his forefinger to the first white cube and name it, Nivard was as steady as Duncan, his leashed potential already settling into a light guidance by Duncan—who drew both of them back just a fraction as Morgan activated the first cube.

"*Prime*."

Nivard hardly batted an eye as the first cube began to glow—if anything, seeming to center even deeper. When the speaking of the next cube's name—"*Seconde*"—brought hardly any more reaction, Morgan put Nivard almost totally from his mind and concentrated on the cubes exclusively. Nivard was not likely to bolt from ward cubes, at any rate.

"*Tierce*" and "*Quarte*" followed close on, giving four

white-glowing cubes. And as Morgan straightened momentarily to take a deep breath and get the cricks out of his back, shifting the polarities in his mind before tackling the black cubes, Nivard closed his eyes and bent to lay his forehead against his crossed forearms, supported by his slightly splayed knees, his shields now wholly transparent and quiescent.

Any further apprehensions Morgan might have had about the young priest vanished in that instant, for to disregard the setting of wards so unflappably was an accomplishment, indeed. Nivard obviously was far more skilled than he had let on—or perhaps he was not aware of how good he was, having had only Arilan by which to measure himself before. Quickly Morgan named the black cubes—*"Quinte,"* *"Sixte,"* *"Septime,"* *"Octave"*—then began matching black and white counterparts to form the four pillars of the wards.

"Primus.

"Secundus.

"Tertius.

"Quartus."

Nivard straightened as Morgan and Duncan began putting the pillars into position outside the circle of their chairs, placing the one behind his own himself. And it was his energy as well as that of Morgan and Duncan that raised the ward itself, as Morgan spread his arms to either side and threw back his head, speaking the final ritual words that would seal their safety while they cast for some sign of Kelson or Dhugal.

"Primus, Secundus, Tertius, et Quartus, fiat lux!"

As the faintly glowing canopy of silvery light sprang up above them, Morgan lowered his arms to take hands with both Duncan and Nivard. The physical link reinforced the rapport that had already been bridged astonishingly well while the wards were being set, and Morgan found it easier to speak directly into the minds of his two associates than to try to say verbally what he planned to do.

I'll direct the first cast and try to link with Kelson, he sent. *If, after a suitable interval of trying, we're unsuccessful, we'll shift the cast to Dhugal. Duncan, you'll direct that one. Nivard, you're to back up the inactive partner in both instances and simply hold yourself ready to be tapped for additional power, if it's required. Any questions?*

There were none. Morgan ceased to worry about Nivard after the first few seconds, as he sent out his call to the missing king. Before the working was complete, he drew deeply on the young priest, too.

But though they cast in the direction of Saint Bearand's for nearly an hour, searching first for Kelson and then for Dhugal, and alternating between the two, no sign of either was forthcoming. By the time they dismantled the link and dispelled the wards, all three of them were drained and exhausted, and both Morgan and Duncan were forced to admit that further attempts were probably futile.

"I kept hoping," Morgan murmured, his voice hoarse and unsteady as he ran a spell to banish fatigue. "I still can't believe they both could be dead, and us not have known. But to find no sign. . ."

He and Duncan were very subdued as they followed Nivard quietly into the chapel to make the long Portal jump back to Rhemuth.

Nor were their spirits raised by the news awaiting them at the capital. That Nigel should have succumbed to so human a weakness as a seizure was ironic, after everything else that had happened; but the evidence was there before their eyes as they visited the royal bedside with Arilan, shortly after their arrival, and heard the physicians' opinion when they had withdrawn to another room.

"He hasn't gotten any worse," Father Lael told them, "but he's made absolutely no improvement, either. Usually, if they're going to recover, there's been some change after this long."

"He isn't responsive at all?" Duncan asked.

Lael shook his head. "Not really. His heartbeat is strong, his breathing is regular and even, and we do get some of the standard reflexes you might expect, but he's deep in coma. We're getting clear soups and broths down him, so he's taking some sustenance, but that's a losing proposition, in the long run. He's lost weight already. If nothing else happens to change things, he'll last a few months, at best."

Morgan sighed and glanced down at his boots. He had

managed to isolate a great deal of the emotion he felt at learning of Nigel's illness, for hope still remained as long as Nigel was not actually dead, but its weight, on top of Kelson's and Dhugal's loss, had pushed him even nearer the brink of sheer exhaustion. He palmed both hands across his eyes while he ran through his fatigue banishing spell again, aware that there must come an end to that soon, then glanced blearily at Duncan, who was hardly the better for wear. Both of them knew they had things to discuss with Arilan now that were not for human ears.

"Thank you for briefing us, Father," Duncan said to Lael, dismissing him with a nod. "You probably ought to get back to your patient."

"Of course. If you need me, you have only to call."

When he had gone, Duncan turned his focus on Arilan. He had a feeling Arilan knew precisely what the next topic was going to be.

"Well, what now?" Duncan asked softly. "Obviously, this raises difficult questions vis-a-vis the Haldane inheritance. Denis, when we returned, we were prepared to bring Nigel to power. Obviously, that won't be possible now, if ever. Does the Council have an opinion about this?"

Before Arilan could answer, Morgan snorted and folded his arms across his chest. "Of course they have an opinion on it. When have you ever known the Council not to have an opinion on any given topic, whether it concerns them or not?"

"Rudeness is hardly called for, I think," Arilan said evenly. "I'll forgive it because I know the strain under which you've been operating. As it happens, the transfer of the Haldane power is of vital concern to the Council—and yes, they do have an opinion. They want Conall confirmed as the Haldane heir, and his powers fully activated, even if he can't be crowned as long as Nigel lives."

Duncan gasped. "But can that be done, with Nigel still alive? Besides, Nigel was already partially confirmed in the powers."

"Yes, but he's now incapable of succeeding to Kelson's powers and incapable of passing on what he does have. It will be tricky, I'll grant you, but we estimate that it should be possible to strip away what was given to Nigel and confer it all on Conall. Of course, that would preclude Nigel ever taking up the crown, if he *should* recover; but you heard Lael. This isn't really likely."

Morgan snorted. "I'm half surprised they don't just remedy the situation, if it's a problem," he muttered. "A convenient pillow held to a helpless invalid's face or something—that's just about their style. And it would make all their job's easier, wouldn't it?"

"Don't you think you're being a little harsh?" Arilan countered.

"Not really." Morgan turned half-away, his hands clasped behind his back, and gazed out a nearby window. "How does Conall feel about the whole situation? Is he ready to write off his father, just to satisfy the noble Council's notions of what constitutes appropriate transmission of the Haldane power?"

"As a matter of fact," Arilan said, setting both fists on his waist, "Prince Conall is far more of a realist than either of you seem to be. It's nearly April, after all. There's an entire season of fighting weather ahead of us, if Gwynedd's enemies should decide to take advantage of the fact that the throne is currently unstable. And as regent, he's the one who's going to have to take the consequences of what men like the three of us decide in the next few days."

"Conall as king in all but name," Morgan breathed, shaking his head as he rubbed again at his eyes. "The mind boggles."

"He *is* Nigel's son," Duncan reminded him, "and King Donal Blaine's grandson."

"He's also very immature," Morgan replied. "I know. He was with Kelson and me for the first part of the campaign last summer. Nor have I seen any particular evidence that he's grown up much, since. Fathering a child does not necessarily make a boy a man."

"A child?" Arilan frowned. "I've heard nothing of a child."

Duncan sighed and shook his head. "It isn't born yet, so far as I know," he murmured. "Court gossip had it due around the end of the summer. The mother's a country maid. He keeps her in a cottage about an hour's ride outside the city."

"Hmmm," Arilan said, stroking his narrow chin. "He hasn't gone and married the girl or anything stupid, has he?"

"No." Duncan laced his fingers together. "She's just a royal mistress—has been for close on a year, from what I hear. He may be immature, Denis, but he isn't stupid. He's saved his hand in marriage for a princess worthy of his blood."

"Which he'll need to find, as soon as possible, if he has a bastard about to be born. We can't have the succession disputed, once he's king in name as well as in fact."

"Good God, Nigel isn't even dead yet!" Morgan breathed. "Can't you let the poor boy be? There's time enough for him to find a wife. We were content to let Kelson take his time. Isn't it bad enough that he's going to have to assume the power while Nigel's still alive?"

"The matter of the heir is an important one," Arilan said icily. "However, if you would prefer, steps can be taken to ensure that Conall's bastard is never born."

The threat brought Morgan up short, for he knew Arilan could and would do it, if pressed. Nor, glancing at the astonished-looking Duncan, was there any doubt that Duncan believed Arilan would do it.

Further resistance was futile. Morgan knew that neither he nor Duncan was in any shape to resist both Arilan and the rest of the Council. Sighing, he spread both hands in a gesture of acquiescence.

"Very well, Bishop. You win."

CHAPTER NINETEEN

*Stolen waters are sweet, and bread eaten in secret
is pleasant.*

—Proverbs 9:17

Four days later, Conall learned what his fate would be.
Arilan briefed him in a private interview in Archbishop Cardiel's study, setting the time of Conall's power ritual for two
nights hence.

"Morgan and Duncan will preside, as originally intended
for Nigel," Arilan told him, "but I shall be in attendance as
well. The procedure will be a little more complicated than
usual, since your father is still alive, but you should weather
it without undue difficulty."

Arilan's assurances did little to allay Conall's uneasiness,
however, for he was fully aware how vulnerable he must
make himself, in order to let the full potential of the Haldanes
be realized within him. A careful perusal of the knowledge
he had gained from Tiercel indicated that participating in
the power ritual mainly would augment and expand what he
had already developed on his own and from Tiercel's tutoring, but he must be able to make the expected responses.
The overwhelming question, which he dared ask no one,
was whether or not he could keep his present achievements
under wraps long enough to let them be assimilated in the
new powers. Once the power ritual was complete—even if
nothing further happened—he would be able to explain
everything he now had as a part of the Haldane legacy;
and Haldanes rarely had to explain, in any case.

In the meantime, however, he had nearly two days to get

through. And aside from the preparations of the actual day—meditation and fasting, for the most part—no further demands would be made upon him.

Aside from dynastic ones. Apparently Vanissa's pregnancy had precipitated that. Arilan had made no bones about the fact that Conall, now the active Haldane heir, would be expected to contract a suitable marriage as quickly as possible, to provide a legitimate heir of his own. The bishop had not actually threatened, but it was clear to Conall that any delay on his part might result in danger to Vanissa and her unborn child.

Not that Conall was particularly concerned about that, though he did care for the girl, in his way. The reason he was not concerned was that his chosen bride was all but locked in promise already, whether or not she was consciously aware of it. His agent finally had intercepted Rothana's letter to Archbishop Cardiel only the day before and had inserted it in a stack of documents awaiting the archbishop's attention.

Thus, when Conall had concluded his interview with Arilan, he asked to see the archbishop privately. Arilan went out, and very shortly Cardiel came in, a little curious as to why the prince wanted to see him. Conall kissed the prelate's ring dutifully, taking the opportunity of physical contact to establish an undetected control link between himself and the archbishop that persisted even when Conall released Cardiel's hand.

"You wished a word with me, Your Highness?" Cardiel asked, sitting behind his desk and gesturing for Conall to take a seat opposite.

"I did, Excellency." Conall sat gingerly, on only the front edge of the chair. "I—ah—believe you should have received a letter from the Lady Rothana by now. Have you?"

"From Rothana?" Cardiel's brow furrowed in surprise. "Not that I'm aware of. Does it concern you?"

Feigning nervousness, Conall twined his fingers together, twisting at the golden signet on his left hand.

"I—ah—yes, it does, Archbishop. She—" He broke off, as if embarrassed, then looked up at Cardiel hopefully.

"She said she was going to ask for a dispensation from her vows, Excellency," he whispered. "I thought surely you would have received it by now."

"A dispensation?"

Cardiel riffled through the pile of letters on his desk, then froze briefly before pulling out a single sheet.

"Good heavens, she *has*." His blue eyes widened as he scanned over the text. "Uncertain in my vocation . . . release from my vows, which are but temporary, in any case . . . dispensation from the religious state. . . ."

He looked up at Conall in pleased surprise, unaware that his pleasure at the notion, with all its implications, was being encouraged and reinforced by Conall himself.

"Good heavens, this *is* a surprise. She makes no mention of her reasons for such a request, but am I to assume, since you have interested yourself in this matter, that you and she—"

Conall ducked his head in sheepish acknowledgement. "I know it will come as a surprise to many, Excellency, but the foundations for this match were laid nearly a year ago, when I escorted her back from Saint Brigid's. She has been loath to talk about it since my return, feeling it unseemly to be discussing such things when we are in mourning for Kelson, but I believe I have persuaded her that no time ought to be lost. As regent now—and, alas, likely to be king before the year is out—it is my duty to provide Gwynedd with an heir as soon as possible."

"Ah, yes," Cardiel said, raising an eyebrow in mild reproach. "A *legitimate* heir."

Conall had the grace to at least feign a blush. "Oh. You've heard about Vanissa."

At Cardiel's rather curt nod, Conall decided he had best put this to rest once and for all.

"I made her no promises, Archbishop," he said quietly, "if that's what you're worried about. I'll provide for her and the child, of course, but I'm totally free to marry Rothana."

Fortunately, Cardiel's reaction mellowed enough at this reassurance of responsibility that Conall did not have to intervene further.

"I see," Cardiel said. "Well, I suppose most princes sow a few wild oats before they settle down. Kelson was an exception. But I'll expect no repeats of this sort of behavior after you're married, my son. I cannot stress enough the importance of an undisputed succession."

"I know my duty, Excellency," Conall murmured, eyes

downcast. "There will be no more Vanissas. In the meantime, however, I should like the marriage to take place as soon as possible. I—believe my father would wish it."

"Of course," Cardiel agreed. "Lent will be over in little more than a fortnight, so—"

"I'd prefer not to wait that long, Archbishop," Conall interrupted, again insinuating subtle controls. "My enemies will be upon me before we realize. My right to the crown must be established beyond doubt. It needn't be a lavish ceremony. In fact, under the circumstances, a small, quiet ceremony is wholly appropriate—immediate family only. You can grant the necessary dispensations."

"Yes, of course."

"In the meantime, I'd appreciate it if you would approve Rothana's request for release from her vows," Conall said, pushing the letter back in front of Cardiel and putting a quill in his hand. "A simple *Placet* at the bottom will suffice for now, with your seal and a note that official approval will be forthcoming. I'll take that back to her today, and you can have a formal writ drawn up after I've gone."

Without even a blink of resistance, Cardiel set pen to parchment, scrawling the words, *Placet*, "It pleases," and then *Mandatum diliget*—"An order will follow." After that, he signed the note and set his seal beneath his signature, sitting back placidly while Conall blew on the wax to cool it before folding it to stash inside his tunic.

"I'll also ask your discretion in this matter," Conall went on, as he prepared to take his leave. "Other than any necessary communications with Rothana's abbess, I'd prefer that you discuss this matter with no one until after I've had a chance to make my own announcement to the privy council. That will be sometime after the weekend, when my full assumption of power has been accomplished."

Reinforced by magical insistence, Conall's request had the force of a command, but it was not at all an unusual requirement, given the delicacy of the situation. Nor was Cardiel's reaction entirely out of character, even though guided by Conall's will in the matter. The subject of the next heir's speedy marriage already was or would be a topic of concern to nearly every high-ranking official at court, especially now that he had been confirmed as regent.

The only point that might have raised questions was the

apparent suddenness of Rothana's request; and Conall, with a brief touch to Cardiel's brow and the merest flick of thought, inserted vivid memories of a confession given him by Conall before his knighting—wholly in keeping with what was expected of a royal candidate for knighthood—in which Conall had stated his most tender and devoted love for Rothana and asked Cardiel's guidance in winning her hand.

And Cardiel—as he would have done, had he been asked in fact—would remember only that he had advised circumspection for the present, because of the lady's temporary vows to the Church, and assured Conall of his wholehearted support, should the lady request dispensation of him.

As Conall left Cardiel's study, after receiving the archbishop's blessing on his enterprise, he fancied that even Arilan would not be able to penetrate the truth of what had just transpired. Nor should the Deryni bishop have cause to question, in the first place. Conall was whistling under his breath as he rode back to the castle with Squire Ivo, whose services he had appropriated upon his return, along with the crown he hoped soon to wear and the bride he hoped soon to wed, the archbishop's imprimatur secure at his breast.

Once safely ensconced at the castle again, however, the prince decided to waste no time confirming Rothana's part of what he had just set in motion. He must see her at once—and determined to have her summoned to see *him* this time, to ensure that they would not be interrupted or disturbed. After checking on his father and taking a leisurely lunch with his mother, Conall retired to the withdrawing room behind the dais in the main hall and sent Ivo to ask Rothana to attend him. She came half an hour later, clad still in the black habit of mourning, thinner than Conall remembered her, leaving one of the sisters to wait outside the door, for appearances' sake.

"You wished to see me, my lord?" Rothana said, cocking her blue-coiffed head at him in mild curiosity as she made him a curtsey.

"I did," he replied, gesturing for her to be seated beside him on a bench before the fire. "Please, sit down."

She folded her hands inside her sleeve openings as she obeyed, keeping her eyes modestly downcast as he stretched his booted feet out on the hearth, closer to the fire, and sighed wearily.

"A great deal has changed since we last spoke, my lady," Conall said after a moment. "No doubt you've heard about my father's seizure."

"Yes, I have, my lord," she replied. "We pray for him daily, but I have heard—"

"What you have heard is undoubtedly true," Conall said quietly. "The prognosis is not good. I thank you for your prayers, but—"

He shrugged, letting a tremor of grief pass through his body as he lowered his head into one hand.

"Forgive me, my lady. It's just that I feel so helpless. First Kelson, and now Father, slipping away. . ."

She turned her face in profile to him, gazing unseeing at the fire beyond his boots.

"They say he will not last the summer," she said softly. "You will be king, when he is gone. And they say you are regent already."

He nodded carefully, hardly daring to believe that she had led into precisely the topic he wanted to discuss.

"I am, my lady; and I will be. Nor do I feel myself ready to shoulder such an enormous burden. Have you—considered what we discussed before?"

As she turned her head to look at him, all wide, frightened eyes, he uncoiled from the bench to kneel at her feet, seizing the edge of her hem to press it fervently to his lips, shaking, for all that he had believed he was in control.

"I love you, Rothana," he murmured. "And what's at least as important, for a king, I *need* you. I need you by my side to help me rule Gwynedd. Without your support and guidance, I don't know that I can bear the weight."

"You could learn to love another," Rothana whispered, extracting her hem from his grasp only to have him take her hand and press a kiss to her knuckles. "There are—many princesses who would be honored to give you their hand in marriage."

"But none to compare with you, my lady," Conall replied. He turned her hand to kiss the palm. "I am a Haldane, but I was never trained to be a king. I *am* king now, in everything except name. In the space of a few days, I will be master of all the power that being a Haldane king implies— and I don't know the first thing about using it properly. But you're Deryni. You could teach me. And our children—"

"My children—"

A sob caught in Rothana's throat, and she bowed her head in her free hand.

She was weeping for Kelson. Conall felt a sharp stab of envy, but he made himself put it aside as useless. Kelson was dead, and he, Conall, was alive, to reap the Haldane benefits. He could afford to be indulgent.

"You loved Kelson, didn't you, Rothana?" Conall said quietly, "and you thought your children would be his children, too." He paused a beat. "I think I know how much you wanted that, but it can never be, now. What *can* be is similar, however—a chance for most things to be almost exactly the way they would have been, if he had lived."

"It can never be the same," she managed to whisper.

"Of course it can," he crooned. "You had plans, Rothana—and there's no reason most of those plans can't go forward, with me as your husband instead of Kelson. You'd be the Deryni Queen of Gwynedd, with all that implies, with an unassailable position from which to improve the lot of your people—*our* people. You could found religious institutions, explore the extra spiritual dimensions the Deryni seem to have, maybe even restore the cult of Saint Camber, as Kelson wanted. And you'd be the mother of Haldane princes and princesses—and I do want lots of children, my darling. Even if you don't love me now, do you not think you might learn to love me?"

As he pressed a kiss to her palm again, then let his tongue linger for just an instant to caress the smooth skin, teasing, he felt her shudder. And a very cautious probe, out from under his double shields, found her own shields in chaos, as she apparently found no reason to be on guard against his mind.

Her body was a different story, however. He knew that she was responding to him and that it disturbed her. She was not afraid that he might try to take advantage—though she should have been—but her own body was only barely held in check. He was annoyed to find that she compared his touch to Kelson's, but reassured to note that the comparison was favorable.

"Ah, I'd forgotten something," he said, releasing her hand to reach into his tunic and withdraw the parchment he had just had Cardiel sign. "I saw Archbishop Cardiel this morning, and he thought you might like to have this now, rather than waiting for the official writ in a day or two.''

As he handed it to her, she blanched, her hands trembling as she opened the stiff parchment and scanned the few words Cardiel had penned.

"I'll be released," she whispered dully. "Why did he give this to you?"

"Because I told him I want to marry you."

"You—told him."

Slowly she crumpled the parchment against her breast, staring into the fire, tears welling in her eyes, not resisting when he took the parchment from her hands and set it beside her on the bench. Nor did she pull back when he took her hand again, cradling it between his two as he stared up at her longingly.

"Marry me, Rothana," he whispered, conveying all the yearning he dared, with mind as well as with voice and body. "Be my queen and my love. There's nothing to stop you now. You're free to do as you choose."

Sadly, she shook her head. "No, not free, my lord. I am as much a prisoner of duty as you are. More, perhaps, for I have been bred to what I am, while your duty is new-come."

"And is Gwynedd so unpleasant a prison?" he asked. "Would you find me so abhorrent a jailer?"

"It—isn't that, my lord, as you must surely know. It is only that—it is so *soon*."

"I share your despair at that, dear heart," he agreed. "It is far too soon for the burdens being laid upon *me,* but sometimes we have no choice. If you will share those burdens, we can make of our prison a palace, I promise. We shall be the fairest king and queen ever to rule this noble kingdom, and I shall be your lord and love, and live only to make you happy."

He laid his head in her lap as he spoke, slipping his arms around her waist, and after a few seconds, when she did not pull back, he raised his head to graze his lips against her breasts. She moaned at that, closing her eyes, and even through the stiff wool of her habit, he could feel her response.

That realization brought him to his feet, drawing her after him, to enfold her in his arms and press his mouth to hers.

After a few seconds, as her lips parted beneath his, he swept the coif from her night-black hair, releasing its braid to tumble wantonly down her back and graze her buttocks, as one of his hands was doing. She made a tiny, whimpering sound, deep in her throat, but he did not relent, drawing her with him to ever increasing depths of arousal as his kiss lingered.

Pulling back, as Kelson had done that night Conall watched them in the garden, was almost more than he could manage, for Conall wanted her more than ever; but the value of a royal and virgin bride was almost beyond price for a king—or a future king—and he did not want to risk her denunciation, if he took her here and now, in her present state of vulnerability, and she later regretted it.

So he did pull back, still hardly daring to believe that, without coercion, she had agreed to marry him. But it was only then that it occurred to him that, indeed, she had not yet said she would.

"*Will* you marry me, Rothana?" he whispered.

But when uncertainty showed in her eyes, spilling over from her churning shields, he kissed her again, soundly, thrusting his tongue lingeringly past her lips until he thought he must explode from that alone. He was shaking as he drew back again, to gaze into her eyes, and she was shaking, too. But this time, she did not shrink from his gaze as he held her there, gazing down into her teary brown eyes.

"Marry me, Rothana," he repeated. "You can't deny there's *something* between us."

Shuddering again, as if exerting all her strength to pull herself together, Rothana nodded.

"I will," she mouthed, so silently he could not hear her.

"Say it louder," he demanded, grinning with wonder. "Say, Conall Haldane, I will marry you!"

She managed a ghost of a smile and gave him a little nod.

"Conall Haldane, I—will marry you," she said.

He crushed her hard against him for several seconds then, breathing of the heady perfume of her hair but refraining from any further intimacies, now that he had her promise; and after a while he let her go, with a scarce-breathed murmur of his thanks. He used the time it took her to tidy her person and put her coif back on to bring his own emotions back into order, bridling his elation and commanding his body to quiescence with several deep, well-disciplined breaths.

He would pay for that later, when he tried to sleep, but it was worth it, for the present. All his dreams and desires were now within his grasp, could he but contain his impatience. He had only to endure the power ritual planned for him the next night, without betraying himself, and he would have all the Haldane power validly confirmed. As soon as the banns could be read after that, he and Rothana would be wed.

For now, though, and until that time came, he must keep his ambitions in check a while longer. Enjoining her not to speak of their betrothal to anyone save Cardiel, if she must—and for the same reasons he had given the archbishop—he gave her leave to go, waiting a few minutes after she had gone, to lessen the likelihood that anyone would note that she had spent time alone with him.

Thus Conall Haldane was smug and quite pleased with himself as he returned to his quarters to adopt at least the semblance of meditation and fasting required for the next twenty-four hours; for with Rothana wedded to him and the Haldane power officially confirmed in him by Morgan and Duncan themselves, no one could defy him. In fact, he doubted that even a resurrected Kelson would be able to stand against him!

Not that he believed, for even a moment, that Kelson was still alive. . .

Kelson *was* still alive, of course, but still not really himself. Though he had recovered enough to maintain a reasonable pace, as he and Dhugal hiked through seemingly endless caverns, he complained almost constantly of headaches, and his memory of how to use his powers did not come back. He was strong enough to walk mostly under his own power—which was more than Dhugal could say, at times, as his ankle continued to pain with every step—and he ate what Dhugal put before him; but the king seemed to have lost focus and sometimes went for hours without uttering a word, as he and Dhugal trekked on.

The days passed—or so Dhugal presumed, for he had lost all notion of time as the hours stretched on, unmarked by any day or night—and Dhugal wondered with less and less hope whether anyone was still looking for them. Several times, just before he sank into exhausted sleep, when he and Kelson would stop to eat and rest, he tried to send his mind out beyond the confines of their underground prison; but he never got any impression that his calls had been heard.

CHAPTER TWENTY

The getting of treasures by a lying tongue is a
vanity tossed to and fro of them that seek death.
                                        —Proverbs 21:6

"Why did we let ourselves be talked into this?" Morgan
asked, as dusk bore the room into ever-deeper shadow and
he and Duncan finished putting the final touches to preparations for the rite to empower Conall.

Duncan gave his cousin a forbearing look as he carefully
laid another log on the fire, but both knew the question was
rhetorical. It had been asked too many times during the past
week, as they debated the final form the ritual would take,
exploring various options and methods of approach—for
nothing was predetermined for the unprimed Conall, whom
no one had ever expected to be king. Unfortunately, the only
consistent answer was that they had no choice.

For Nigel certainly was dying. He might last weeks or
even months, but his general condition was deteriorating
with every passing day, the once-powerful body slowly wasting away, the mists growing thicker behind what shields had
survived his seizure. They had set up in his room this afternoon, deeming it only fitting that the uncrowned king
should be present, at least in body, as the Haldane legacy
was confirmed in his son—and to permit at least a form of
withdrawing the mandate of Haldane power from him before
beginning its facilitation in Conall, though nothing but his
lingering shields remained to show that even rudimentary
Haldane gifts had ever been conferred.

The last had been Arilan's suggestion, at the behest of

the Council—formally withdrawing the mandate, just in case the prohibition against more than one Haldane holding the power at a time should interfere when the time came to bring Conall into his inheritance. No Haldane king or regent had ever been so endowed while his predecessor still lived—not that Nigel lived in anything but physical form.

That brought them to another point which neither Morgan nor Duncan had yet dared to voice but which plagued both of them—for, if power *was* manifested in Conall, then it would be nearly incontrovertible proof that Kelson was, indeed, dead.

Nearby, the object of their concern waited somewhat nervously to be fetched, doggedly schooling his thoughts in the appropriate directions to survive what was to come. Conall was hungry from fasting, and his knees ached from kneeling at the prie-dieu, but he put these discomforts of body aside as he reviewed his precautionary measures one final time—for someone would be here soon.

Odd, but he felt a curious detachment from what was about to happen to him. He had been given little hint of what physical trial might await him, but he believed he could face that, so long as his psychic defenses did not fail him.

Nor had he any real concerns in that regard, for he knew that the defenses with which Tiercel had endowed him would stand against a great deal. He had reinforced his shields by several levels, doubly shielding the guarded portions of his mind so that he felt certain he could withstand anything short of total *merasha* disruption—and he did not think tonight's ordeal would involve *merasha*, judging by what he had gleaned from Tiercel's memories on the subject. For the most part, the respect of trained Deryni for the drug put it outside normal use, except for learning how to cope with it and occasionally using it to prevent the use of powers.

Of course, there were other substances aplenty that might put him through dire experiences, totally at the mercy of Morgan and Duncan—and Arilan, who truly frightened him, because the Deryni bishop was so highly trained—but Conall knew about most of the possibilities through his contact with Tiercel, either from firsthand experience during his training or from the forbidden knowledge he had gained in final reading. And while there was nothing he could do to stop a reaction to medication, he was confident he could ride out its effects with minimal risk of exposing his true power—and its source.

He started, though, as a soft knock at the door announced the arrival of his escort, and ducked his head reflexively in a rote childhood prayer for protection.

It would be one of the two bishops come to fetch him, either Arilan or Duncan; and the locked door would stop neither man for more than a few seconds. Like his father, Conall ordinarily did not put much stock in outward religious observances, but now that the moment had come, hypothetical bravery wavered just a little before realistic apprehension about the unknown, and a prayer seemed in order. Besides, Conall as king would be expected to pay at least lip service to the appropriate minimal forms—so it surely could not hurt to let his priestly escort observe at least an outward semblance of piety.

After a few seconds, the formerly locked door swung softly inward on its hinges; and a moment later, Conall felt a hand on his shoulder.

"It's time, Conall," Arilan said softly. "Or do you need a little longer?"

Squaring his shoulders, Conall raised his head to meet the bishop's gaze unflinchingly.

"I've prayed enough, Excellency—but I'd welcome your blessing before we go."

He stayed kneeling as Arilan laid a hand briefly on his head in benediction, echoing the bishop's movement as the sign of the cross was sketched above his head.

Then he was rising to let Arilan lay a dark cloak around his shoulders, drawing the hood close around his face at Arilan's gesture. He kept his face averted as Arilan led him out into the corridor and finally up the narrow stair that led to his father's rooms, his heart pounding in his chest.

Standing opposite Duncan, on the right-hand side of the bed where Nigel lay, Morgan waited, arms crossed on his breast in a ritual posture of readiness, of receptivity, fingertips brushing opposite shoulders. Like Duncan, he wore a cowled black cassock girdled in scarlet, hood pulled low over his forehead to block out distractions. Though his gryphon signet adorned his right hand, he had taken off that of the King's Champion and put it on a leather thong around his neck, for now he was champion of neither Kelson, nor the uncrowned Nigel, lying motionless before him, nor of Nigel's regent son, yet to be crowned. But he would keep Kelson's ring until the day he died, in loving memory of the king who was lost.

And Nigel, the king who now would never be, lay in state in the center of the canopied bed, robed in the lion-charged crimson of his royal line, the Haldane sword laid atop the length of his body with the hilt beneath his crossed hands, one of the Haldane state crowns set on a pillow above his head—a crown Nigel would never wear. Bearded now, since his illness, he looked even more like his dead brother Brion—and Morgan had a terrible foreshadowing of some future time when Nigel would lie thus arrayed on his funeral bier, with funeral tapers guttering at the corners of his catafalque and the noblest knights in the land keeping watch to do him honor before his final journey, deep into the royal crypts of Rhemuth Cathedral. In a sense, Nigel was dead already; Morgan mourned him as a friend and brother, though the true time of mourning was yet to come.

And yet, it was fitting that Nigel should be here; for Nigel twice had witnessed rituals similar to what would be worked here tonight, first for Brion's coming to power, half a lifetime ago, and then his own potentializing. He had not been present at Kelson's enabling, only a handful of years ago, though Duncan had been. What was about to transpire tonight would be a melding of elements from all three rituals, with additional details added according to tonight's peculiar circumstances. If only a successful outcome would not also confirm that Kelson was truly gone. . .

Morgan tensed as the click of the door latch announced the arrival of Arilan and Conall, but neither he nor Duncan looked up as the Deryni bishop took Conall's cloak from him, guided Conall to a prie-dieu set against the foot of the canopied bed, and bade him kneel before returning to secure the door. Conall bowed his head without prompting, impassive behind smooth-layered shields, then crossed himself piously and looked up at his father's still form, the shallow breathing hardly stirring the sword laid along the shrouding Haldane crimson. Arilan moved directly behind the kneeling prince, a scarlet cope now covering most of his black cassock, hands joined in an attitude of prayer.

"If you have any misgivings concerning what we are about to do," Morgan said softly, still not looking directly at Conall, "now is the time to voice them. We expect everything to go smoothly, but the procedure we have decided upon is not without its dangers, especially since we have had to improvise, to some extent.

"I therefore must ask you, formally, and as designated Master of this ritual, whether you are willing to place yourself unreservedly in our hands, body and soul, to do with as we deem necessary for the purpose of raising the Haldane power within you."

"I am willing," Conall replied, as he had been told to answer.

"Before we proceed, then," Duncan said, taking up the thread of formal narrative in a flat, emotionless voice, "it behooves me to read the formal declaration outlining the reasons for this ritual. For, in the normal course of things, a prince ought not to usurp the office of his father while the father still lives."

He drew a flat sheet of parchment before him, from a small stand set beside the bed, and read from it in a steady voice.

"Whereas our late lamented and beloved lord, King Kelson Cinhil Rhys Anthony Haldane, by the Grace of God, King of Gwynedd, Prince of Meara, and Lord of the Purple March, has departed this realm without leaving an heir of his body;

"And whereas said King Kelson did designate his beloved uncle, the High and Mighty Prince Nigel Cluim Gwydion Rhys Haldane, as his heir both in law and in magic, should the said King Kelson die before engendering such an heir;

"And whereas said Prince Nigel, before he could be crowned or his Haldane powers confirmed, has been rendered incompetent to reign, by virtue of physical illness rapidly drawing him toward death of the body;

"And whereas the High and Mighty Prince Conall Blaine Cluim Uthyr Haldane, firstborn son and heir of Prince Nigel, has been recognized as Regent and future King by the Lords of State, both temporal and spiritual;

"And whereas our late lamented and beloved King Kelson did designate as executors of the passing of his Haldane powers The Most High, Potent, and Noble His Grace The Duke of Corwyn, General Sir Alaric Anthony Morgan; The Most High, Potent, and Noble His Grace The Duke of Cassan, Sir Duncan Howard McLain, Priest and Bishop; and The Most Reverend His Excellency The Bishop of Dhassa, Lord Denis Michael Arilan;

"So, therefore, do said executors agree that, inasmuch as Gwynedd has urgent need of a ruler with the full faculties of the Haldane legacy intact and functioning;

"And inasmuch as said Prince Nigel is not now able, nor is he likely to be able in the future, to assume these Haldane faculties, the temporal authority of his office already having been vested in his son and heir, Prince Conall;

"Therefore, the spiritual and magical authority of that office ought also to be vested in said son and heir.

"To which purpose, the aforesaid Duke Alaric, Duke Duncan, and Bishop Denis have gathered together, in the presence of the aforesaid Prince Nigel, to perform such rites as are necessary to see the transfer of such authority to His Royal Highness, The Most High, Most Mighty, and Most Illustrious Prince Conall Blaine Cluim Uthyr Haldane.

"Attest: Morgan, Duke of Corwyn; McLain, Duke of Cassan; Arilan, Bishop of Dhassa."

The three of them had already signed and sealed it. Now Arilan brought Conall to add his signature to the document, setting a quill in his hand as Duncan spread the parchment on the side table. Conall traced the letters carefully—*Conall Interrex*—finishing with the flourished paraph, almost impossible to forge, that made the signature unique. But when he set the pen aside and glanced at Duncan in question regarding the matter of a seal, Arilan drew him back to kneel again at the foot of the bed, cautioning silence with a forefinger held to lips. Morgan, with a quick glance at Conall, drew a thin stiletto blade from inside his cassock and gently unwound Nigel's right thumb from around the hilt of the sword.

"It's traditional," Arilan murmured in Conall's ear, "that such documents be sealed in the blood of the principals."

Morgan's deft pricking of Nigel's thumb with the point of the stiletto produced a glistening drop of scarlet that Duncan caught at the bottom of the parchment and set with Nigel's thumbprint as seal. Then, while Morgan cleaned the wounded thumb with a cloth Duncan gave him, and briefly enclosed it in his hand to heal it, Duncan passed the document to Arilan, who laid it on the armrest before Conall.

"Your sealing will be done a little differently," Arilan said, as Duncan brought a small glass tray from the side table and Morgan came to hold it. On the tray were Kelson's Ring of Fire, an earring set with a blue star sapphire, a needle threaded through a scrap of white silk, and a small glass vial with a tuft of cotton wool stuck into its neck. This last Duncan took from the tray and upturned once, holding the wool in place with a forefinger, as Arilan moved closer to straddle the kneeling Conall and brace his head lightly from either side.

"The Eye of Rom was lost with Kelson," Morgan explained, watching as Duncan swabbed Conall's right earlobe with the moistened cotton wool and then began cleaning the needle and the wire of the earring. "That's doubly unfortunate, because we are of the impression that it has always played some part in the setting of the Haldane potential in Haldane heirs. I know for a fact that it was used in Kelson's and Nigel's rituals; but I have reason to believe that Brion was invested with it as a boy, with a ten-to-fifteen-year gap between the two parts of his ritual.

"On the positive side, however, that particular jewel does not seem to be essential to the power transfer. The Ring of Fire may be another matter, but we have that. In any case, Duncan and I have attempted to endow this replacement jewel with the kind of psychic energy we've perceived in the Eye of Rom—which should be sufficient for our purposes. The essential element of the conferring seems to be tied up with the shedding of blood, rather than the stone itself— which makes it useful for sealing the document you've just signed: a necessary item, since you were never given any official recognition prior to now. The Ring of Fire also needs to be primed by your blood, so we'll do that at the same time. Don't worry; you only get stabbed once."

He watched Conall close his eyes as Duncan brought the needle close, though the prince did not flinch as Duncan thrust it briskly through. Arilan lifted the parchment so that Duncan could catch Conall's blood on it, when the needle had been withdrawn, but Conall looked up of his own accord as that was done, and without prompting set his thumb deftly against the blood to seal it. The prince said nothing as Duncan touched the Ring of Fire to the blood welling from his earlobe, not seeming to notice how the large, cabochon-cut garnet in the center had darkened with something more than blood-color, when Duncan laid it back on the tray, but he flinched a little when Duncan threaded the wire of the star sapphire through his still-raw flesh.

"I'll heal this, if you can relax your shields a little," Duncan murmured, lightly enclosing the jewel and earlobe between his fingers. "There's no sense enduring any more discomfort than you must."

Conall let out a heavy sigh at that, looking much relieved when, after a few seconds, Duncan drew back. Arilan withdrew to lay the sealed document on a small table set against the opposite wall, bringing the whole into the center of the room before returning to stand at Conall's back, and Duncan resumed his place at Nigel's left side, once more taking up his ritual pose with arms crossed on his breast as Morgan spoke.

"I now charge and require you, Conall Blaine Cluim Uthyr, as the true-born heir of Nigel Cluim Gwydion Rhys, to witness the lawful withdrawing of the Haldane mandate from this Nigel Cluim Gwydion Rhys."

Morgan closed his eyes and held up his open palms at shoulder level, like a priest invoking the Divine Presence, as he went on.

"To that end do I now summon, stir, and call up invisible witnesses to approve and ratify this act. May we be protected from all dangers and adversity approaching from the East, in the name of Ra-pha-el."

He chanted the archangelic name, and as the final note faded, Duncan and Arilan sang, "Amen."

"So, likewise, may we be protected from all dangers and adversity approaching from the South, in the name of Mi-cha-el."

"Amen," the two priests sang.

"May we also be protected from all dangers and adversity approaching from the West, in the name of Ga-bri-el."

"Amen."

"And finally, may we be protected from all dangers and

adversity approaching from the North, in the name of Auri-el.''

"Amen, Amen, Amen, and with open hearts may we proceed," the priests responded.

And as Morgan again crossed his arms on his breast and bowed his head, Arilan let his left hand rest on the back of Conall's neck, pressing him to bow his head against his folded hands, while his right hand was raised palm-outward toward Nigel, as if in benediction.

"Blessed be the Creator, Yesterday and Today," Arilan said, tracing a cross the full length of Nigel's motionless body, "the Beginning and the End, the Alpha and the Omega." As his hand moved on to trace the Greek letters at Nigel's head and feet and the signs of the elements in the quadrants of the cross, he went on.

"His are the seasons and the ages, to Him glory and dominion through all the ages of eternity."

The words, though Morgan had heard them in a magical context before, were those normally used to bless the Paschal candle and perhaps had an added connotation of acknowledging Nigel as the sacrificial victim—as, indeed, were all Sacred Kings for their people.

"Blessed be the Lord," Arilan concluded. "Blessed be His Holy Name."

As he finished, he released Conall's neck and folded his hands on his breast as Morgan and Duncan had done, and Morgan, with a quick glance at Duncan, extended his hands to lay the left one on Nigel's brow, the right on the naked blade of the Haldane sword beneath Nigel's hands. Duncan followed suit, but in reverse, right hand on Nigel's brow and left on blade, fingertips overlapping with Morgan's.

"Now, in sorrow," Morgan whispered, "do we withdraw that which was given, Nigel Cluim Gwydion Rhys, that in the fullness of time, all that is encompassed by Haldane blood and right may be vested in thy son and heir, Conall Blaine Cluim Uthyr. So be it."

"So be it," Duncan murmured, as Arilan said, "Amen."

Morgan let himself plummet into deep rapport with Duncan then, taking nearly a full minute to mesh the linkage before beginning a symbolic visualization of power being withdrawn from Nigel. He was never certain, afterwards, whether Nigel, indeed, lost anything in the operation; but when he and Duncan had ended the link, stiffly pulling back from the physical exertion of the contact, he seemed to feel a new power pulsing in the sword, beyond that usually associated with the magical blade.

Gently he disengaged the weapon from Nigel's further grasp, waiting until Duncan had rearranged the unconscious prince's hands crossed on his breast before lightly touching the cross hilt of the sword to Nigel's lips. Then he was taking the blade into the center of the room, hand closed firmly around the blade just below the quillons, and turning to face east, waiting while Duncan and Arilan brought Conall to stand directly behind him.

Arilan picked up an aspergillum and moved ahead of Morgan to bow to the East and begin tracing a circle clockwise around them, sprinkling holy water to define its perimeter, the circumference of the room. Duncan lit candles on the little table Arilan had moved into place earlier, then touched flame to the document they had signed and sealed, laying it in a small clay bowl when it had caught and was burning well.

"May this offering blessed by Thee ascend to Thee, O Lord," Duncan said, signing it with a cross, "and may Thy mercy descend upon Thy servants, both present and to come." He then traced a similar cross over an incense boat before sprinkling a few grains on charcoal glowing in a thurible.

"Be thou blessed by Him in Whose honor thou shalt be burnt," he said, taking it up by its chains and setting it to swinging gently. "Welcome as incense smoke, let our prayers rise up before Thee, O Lord. When we lift our hands, may it be acceptable as the evening sacrifice."

The stench of the burning parchment and blood was quickly covered by the sweeter smell of incense as Duncan moved to the East and bowed, swinging the thurible, then proceeded to follow Arilan in the second casting of their protective circle.

And when Duncan had gotten as far as the southern quadrant, Morgan reversed the Haldane sword in his hands to salute the East, then began cutting the third circumambulation, the tip of the blade seeming to extrude a shimmering ribbon of deep orange flame at chest level, where it passed. When the third circle was complete, Morgan returned to the center to face Duncan and Arilan, both of whom had returned to flank Conall.

"Now we are met," Arilan said softly, as Morgan extended the sword horizontally across his body, the tip braced against his left hand, and raised the sword to shoulder level between himself and the other three, throwing back his head to summon the psychic triggers to extend the wards. The fire of the circle rose with his arms, closing in a glowing dome above their heads; and when he swept the sword and his empty left hand downward, to end with the tip grounded at his feet and both hands resting on the quillons, the fire closed downward to floor level, completing the wards.

"Now, we are One with the Light," Arilan continued, head bowed. "Regard the ancient ways. We shall not walk this path again."

"Augeatur in nobis, quaesumus, Domine," Duncan went on in Latin, *"tua virtutis operatio."* May the working of Thy power, O Lord, be intensified within us.

"So be it. *Selah.* Amen," Morgan responded. And Arilan lifted his hands in one final blessing, all of them tracing the sacred symbol as he did.

"Et mentis nostri tenebras, gratia tuae visitationis, illustra, Qui vivus. Amen." By the grace of Thy coming, light up the darkness of our minds, Thou Who Art.

Conall looked wary but not at all frightened as Morgan glanced up at him, and Morgan did not know whether he liked that or not.

"Very well, we're fully warded now. Do you have any questions, before we proceed?"

Conall shook his head carefully, but did not seem inclined to speak. At Morgan's gesture, the prince turned to follow Arilan around to the other side of the altar table, where Duncan pulled out a small stool that had been concealed beneath it and Arilan sat, his back to the altar. While Arilan unfolded a linen cloth across his lap—for Conall would next receive a form of anointing, since he was not yet king in fact—Duncan loosed the prince's shirt strings and bared his breast, then signed for him to kneel at Arilan's feet. As Morgan moved in closer behind Conall, straddling Conall's calves and setting the sword between his feet so that the blade lay close along Conall's spine, the prince bowed his head and rested folded hands on Arilan's knees. Duncan took up an ampule of holy oil and also knelt at Arilan's right to hold it for him.

"'Zadok the priest and Nathan the prophet anointed Solomon king,'" Arilan said, quoting from scripture. "Prince Conall Blaine Cluim Uthyr Haldane, thou art not yet crowned or anointed; yet the acknowledgement of a Haldane sovereign doth customarily involve a sacring. Therefore, as senior bishop present here as witness, I hereby anoint and bless thee, as a foreshadowing of the blessing and anointing to come when thou art become king in fact."

The bishop dipped the first two fingers of his right hand into the oil Duncan held and anointed the palms Conall opened on his linen-draped lap, tracing from right thumb to left forefinger, left thumb to right forefinger, then making individual crosses on right and left palms.

"Be thy hands anointed with holy oil, that thou mayest achieve glory."

Dipping again, Arilan set the sacred sign on Conall's breast.

"Be thy breast anointed with holy oil, that valor and courage may be ever in thy heart."

And finally, on the crown of Conall's bowed head.

"Be thy head anointed with holy oil, as kings, priests, and prophets were anointed, that thou mayest receive knowledge."

Arilan closed Conall's hands then, binding them lightly together with a strip of linen before carefully cleansing his own fingers. The oil was indeed holy oil, but it also contained a substance to lower resistance and induce mild relaxation. It had no observable effect on Arilan, whose exposure had been brief, but Conall continued to absorb the drug through hands, breast, and scalp, swaying a little on his knees. As Duncan exchanged the ampule of oil for the bowl containing the ashes of the burned document, Morgan steadied Conall with his right hand on a shoulder, while his left continued to press the flat of the Haldane blade against their subject's spine.

Morgan sensed a mellowing in Conall's previously rigid shields as Duncan dipped his thumb into the ashes, signed the prince between the eyes, and read a gentle wash of warmth and faint disorientation as he briefly touched what lay beyond.

"Conall Blaine Cluim Uthyr," Duncan said, "I seal thee Haldane and confirm thee as Heir."

While Duncan took up a pinch of the ash between thumb and forefinger, Morgan slid his right hand under and around Conall's jaw as cue for him to open his mouth. Conall complied without resistance.

"Taste of the ashes of mingled Haldane blood," Duncan murmured, sprinkling some of the ash onto Conall's tongue, "thine own and thy father's, in unbroken line. By blood art thou consecrated to the Haldane legacy and acknowledged as The Haldane, that the power may come upon thee in its fullness."

But the actual channeling of power would not come from the ash. Nor would it come from the Ring of Fire that Arilan slipped onto Conall's left hand, after he had unbound Conall's hands and cleansed them of the oil. As for Kelson's ritual, hardly more than four years before, Morgan and Duncan had set the catalyst for the descent of power in a physical vessel associated before with Haldane magic—the heavy, fist-sized brooch that Duncan brought out from under a linen cloth, last seen at Kelson's knighting—golden Haldane lion inlaid in a crimson enamel field.

And on the back, which Duncan had carefully prepared during the afternoon, was the pin that normally clasped the brooch—three inches of gleaming gold, very sharp, which Conall, like Kelson before him, would be required to stab through his left hand. The golden shaft also carried a second, stronger drug that would further reinforce the lowering of any possible resistance to the forces about to be focused in Conall.

Arilan stood to Conall's right as Duncan put the opened brooch in Conall's right hand, and Morgan prepared to step back—for none of them must touch Conall at the actual moment of his ordeal. In turn, each of the priest-bishops offered a prayer for the health and prosperity of this latest Haldane heir, Morgan leading Conall in the response of "Amen" at the appropriate moments—for Conall's eyes were dilated now, and he was sinking deeper into thrall of the first drug.

And then, as Morgan stepped back to kneel directly behind Conall, the Haldane sword held beneath the quillons like a cross between them, Arilan also knelt at Conall's right and Duncan, still standing, placed both hands lightly on Conall's head, careful not to touch the oil still glistening there.

"Conall Blaine Cluim Uthyr Haldane. Though the cords of the nether world enmesh thee, though the snares of death surge about thee, thou shalt fear no evil. With His pinions the Lord will cover thee, and under His wings thou shalt take refuge." He lifted his hands and made the sign of the cross over Conall's bowed head. *"In Nomine Patris et Fils et Spiritus Sancti, Amen."*

And then, kneeling at Conall's left, Duncan lifted his hands in final entreaty, as he had lifted them similarly for Kelson, what seemed a lifetime ago.

"Domine, fiat voluntas tuas." Lord, let it be done according to Thy will.

Drawing only a single, final breath to brace himself for what he was about to do, Conall shifted the lion brooch slightly in his right hand to steady his grip, poised the point of the clasp against the center of the left palm, and thrust the metal home.

CHAPTER TWENTY-ONE

They have pierced my hand.

—Psalms 22:16

It hurt far more than Conall had expected. The impaling pin seared like molten metal as it slid between the bones of his hand. The pain took his breath away, doubling him up like a kick in the stomach, hardly even able to gasp, much less cry out.

And yet, there was something besides the pain—something besides his awareness, gently blurred by medication, of the power that was already his. Through the burning that centered in his palm, he could feel it like the buzz of a trapped insect, beating to be released—only mildly distracting at first, but increasingly irritating, for his inability to focus on it. Gritting his teeth against the pain, he pressed the heel of his good hand harder against the cool sleekness of the brooch, as if the added pressure might capture whatever it was between his hands, might pinion it the same way the brooch pinioned his hand.

The second medication was having its effects, too. He could feel the new drug reinforcing the first, but he knew them both from his times with Tiercel—and knew that he could ride their effects; that they would not force him into betrayal, but only facilitate his mastering of whatever else was stirring with increasing insistence inside him.

That something else was rising like a gale within his mind, but it did not precisely threaten—though he was far from comfortable. Power there was—even more than had been within his grasp before, and that had not been inconsiderable—but this new and different sort of power was there for *his* using, not to be ordered by any other living soul. The clasp of the brooch burned in his hand, almost as if the very metal were growing hotter, but he knew that to be but a reaction of his physical body. The power was another thing, apart and alien, yet at the same time known and now completely controllable. He could feel it pulsing stronger with every heartbeat, filling up the empty spots, bringing new knowledge into being and casting old, only half-understood knowledge into sharper focus, so that even the jumbled material he had gained from Tiercel became accessible in its fullness, so far as it went.

He reveled in it. He floated on the tide of the ecstasy of knowledge and let himself flow with it—though he kept his pressure on the brooch so that the pain in his hand would keep him firmly anchored in his body. For, though it would have been tempting to surrender wholly to the power coiling within him, he worried that if he opened himself too fully, his shielding might slip to the point that the others could read him and know that he was not what he had seemed.

So he slumped even lower over his clasped hands, his breathing still a little ragged in response to the white heat concentrated in his left hand, and set his mind to assimilating all that had been brought to conscious levels and was still surfacing.

Not all of it was pleasant. There was a brief, thorny moment when the ghosts of what he had done rose up to threaten him—first Tiercel's face, frozen with horrified incomprehension as he went over backwards on the stair that claimed his life; and then his father, hands lifted in futile warding off as Conall's flare of guilt-spurred anger, powered by forbidden magic, enfolded him in death within life and left only a slowly dying shell.

That latter almost set Conall to sobbing, for he truly had not wanted to harm his own father. It simply had—happened—and he still was not sure how or why. Trembling, he tried to regain his equilibrium—but the newly stirred forces churning within were not yet finished with him.

Any of the other three kneeling around him would have understood what happened next, but Conall did not. As he banished the accusing face of his father from his mind's eye, another began slowly to take its place—and this one also looked little pleased with what it saw.

A pale, roundish face framed by a cap of quicksilver hair, sensitive mouth set in mute, stern contemplation, grey eyes like a Haldane's, that seemed to have nothing behind them but the darker grey of the cowl pushed back slightly from the head. The eyes caught and held Conall, so that he felt they must draw his very soul out of his body. He whimpered once and cringed harder into a ball as hands joined the face, reaching toward him.

But then, from somewhere, he was drawing the strength to resist that compulsion, raising a barrier of crimson light between himself and that other presence, banishing it at last from all contact. It was not easy, but he finally succeeded.

He huddled motionless for a little while after that, gradually regaining equilibrium, and finally even his breathing steadied as the pain in his hand began to be controllable with his new-found mastery of his power. Tiercel's memories, too, seemed to have settled into orderly stability, the knowledge gained now totally accessible.

He spent a few minutes confirming and testing, aware that the drugs in his body had reached maximum effect and he was still able to exercise his own will. Then he drew a deep, careful breath and slowly straightened, sitting back on his heels and cradling what was now just a brooch in his left hand.

"Conall?" he heard Morgan murmur, just barely audible.

Though he tried to be careful, Conall jarred the end of the clasp protruding from the back of his hand and he sucked in breath between his teeth at the new pain. But Duncan was already scrambling closer, Morgan gently prising loose his right hand while Duncan uncurled the left fingers so he could remove the brooch. Even though the metal pin was polished smooth, it hurt coming out, and Conall let the pain show, rather than damping it down, for it had occurred to him that perhaps he was not reacting enough to account for what supposedly had happened. His father had reported losing consciousness after even the abbreviated working to set the Haldane potential, and Conall had the impression that Kelson, too, had swooned away at the collective effect of his assumption of power. Perhaps Conall should pretend to faint.

But Arilan was kneeling eagerly before him and watching

with keen interest, apparently well pleased with his reaction. And Duncan, though he cleaned the wounds in Conall's hand with something that stung ferociously, back and palm, soon took away pain and wound and all with a firm healer's touch, with nothing apparently amiss in his assessment of Conall's reaction. Conall flexed the hand in wonder when Duncan had done, for there was not even a drop of blood to show for his ordeal, though blood still stained the pin of the brooch Morgan held.

"How do you feel?" Morgan asked, searching the grey Haldane eyes.

Cautiously Conall nodded, allowing a faint hint of dazedness to color his movement.

"All right, I think. It—"

He swallowed and shook his head, truly unable to articulate what had just happened to him, even if he had dared, with what was on his conscience. And he did *not* want to talk about that unfamiliar face he had seen.

"I'm very tired," he whispered, instinctively knowing that to be the safest response.

"It's amazing that you're even conscious," Arilan murmured, wiping the oil from Conall's breast and then scrubbing at what remained on his head. "In fact, I don't think you ever really lost consciousness, did you?"

Conall decided immediately that a slightly embellished truth was safer than an outright lie.

"Well, I—think I did," he whispered. "It was sort of like—drifting in and out. I don't remember much, though."

"Well, that's standard enough," Duncan murmured. "I don't think Kelson was ever able to tell us much about what *he* experienced, though he did report seeming to see his father."

Arilan snorted. "Hardly to be expected in this instance, since Nigel's still alive. It seems certain something happened, though. Conall, do you feel up to flexing your Haldane powers yet? Maybe making some demonstration, since you're in pretty good shape?"

Conall swallowed uneasily, considering what harmless thing he might do that would not seem too pretentious after so short a time, from someone previously unschooled. Then, pretending to concentrate very hard, he held out his right hand and cupped it, summoning handfire. He feigned awe as it appeared, flickering crimson in his palm, but Arilan only smiled, and Duncan and then Morgan nodded slowly.

"Handfire," Arilan said. "Well, that's certainly a start." He glanced at the other two Deryni. "Will you need my help dismantling, or shall I take him back to his room?"

"We can manage," Duncan said, as Morgan got slowly to his feet with the Haldane sword.

Later, when they had dismissed the wards and Arilan had gone with Conall, and the two of them had gathered up most of the paraphernalia of the night's work, Morgan, with a weary sigh, sank down on the floor with his back to the side of Nigel's bed, still toying restlessly with the hilt of the now-sheathed sword.

"I suppose we—have to accept that Kelson is dead, then," he whispered, as Duncan knelt beside him in question. "I didn't want to believe it before, but—"

His voice broke, and he bowed his head in one hand as the grief, held back for so many days, became a force no longer to be denied. He indulged it for a little while, taking comfort from the circle of Duncan's arms and the gentle brush of his mind as the other drew him into soothing rapport, though Duncan's grief was surely no less than his own, for having lost a son as well as a king. But oddly, the hard, despairing grief abated fairly quickly, gradually being replaced by a growing certainty that they must somehow confirm for themselves that Kelson and Dhugal were, indeed, dead.

"Do you mean, go to the place where they were lost and keep looking for bodies?" Duncan asked aloud, when either of them could speak again.

Morgan nodded woodenly. "We have to, Duncan. Until we can see the evidence for ourselves and accept that they're gone, we'll be little use to anyone. I'm not even certain how much we had to do with what happened here tonight."

"Odd that you should mention that," Duncan said. "I was thinking myself how different tonight was from what I'd expected. Almost a little hollow, as if we were only going through the motions. It certainly wasn't anything like Kelson's."

"Well, I'll grant you that the sequence was jumbled by the standards of what we've seen before," Morgan said, jarred more deeply than he wanted to admit by Duncan's confirmation of the—*oddness* of the night's experience. "That alone would have made it seem different. And maybe other things felt different because we didn't have the Eye of Rom—though I'd certainly have to say that the end result was successful. *Something* certainly happened when he impaled his hand on that brooch—though I'll grant you, everything felt very different from when Kelson did the same thing."

Sighing, Duncan sat back against the side of the bed beside Morgan and ran a hand over his face, off in his own thoughts for a few seconds, before shaking his head.

"We're tilting at shadows, Alaric," he murmured, "and unfortunately, the source of those shadows is far more likely to be our own unresolved grief than anything truly odd that happened here tonight—not that Haldane magic can ever really be considered other than odd by Deryni standards, I suppose."

"Aye, that's true."

"Which brings us to another interesting point," Duncan went on. "Conall is *only* Haldane. He doesn't have Jehana for a mother—which will make for a far duller sort of power exercise than we've become accustomed to with Kelson, I'm afraid."

"Unless there's Deryni blood in the Haldanes already, even before Jehana," Morgan said. "There has been, in the past—though I daresay it's pretty well diluted by now." He sighed. "But you're right. Conall is not going to be the king that Kelson was—or Brion. Which is a pity, for its own sake."

He dragged himself slowly to his knees to turn and gaze at Nigel, now divested of his Haldane regalia, even paler against the stark white of the sheets than he had been when swathed in Haldane crimson.

"And what a pity that Nigel will never get to reign," he went on, laying a hand regretfully on one of Nigel's still ones. "God, he would have made a wonderful king, Duncan! He isn't a Kelson, I'll grant you, but in many ways, he had all the best attributes of Brion—without the weaknesses. Poor, dear Nigel. He wouldn't have wanted to go this way, either. Why couldn't he have had a clean, honest death in battle?"

Duncan looked away, fighting for composure. "We aren't

doing ourselves any service by dwelling on this, Alaric. You know that."

"I know."

With a sigh, Morgan rose and laid the sheathed Haldane sword across a pair of pegs above the head of the bed.

"Duncan, let's go tonight, shall we?" he said then, turning to face his cousin squarely. "I know it's ridiculous to suppose that they could be alive after so long, and with Conall now in possession of the Haldane powers, but even if all we ever find is battered, waterlogged bodies, at least we'll *know*."

Duncan kept his eyes averted as he, too, rose, head bowed, restless fingertips twisting at a fold of blanket he had started to pull over Nigel.

"Do you really think we ought to go so soon? What if Conall needs us?"

"Why should he need us?" Morgan replied. "He's never needed us before. And if he does need a Deryni, Arilan will be here. We can check in at regular intervals, if that will make you feel any better. Besides, Conall's The Haldane now and king in everything but name." He glanced sadly at Nigel. "And I don't know that I necessarily want to be here to see this wind to its end. I said all my good-byes while we were waiting for Conall to arrive."

Duncan nodded slowly. "I think I told you that Ciard and Jass and a few of Dhugal's other men stayed at the campsite to continue looking. If we take the Portal as far as Valoret, I'm told one can get from there to the Saint Bearand campsite in just under two days, given reasonable weather and adequate changes of horses."

"Shall we do it, then?" Morgan asked.

"I think so."

"Tonight?"

"No, in the morning. We can hardly just go, without even a by-your-leave."

"And suppose Conall won't give us leave?"

Duncan snorted. "Do you really think he wants us hanging around here, any more than we want to be here? He's got his power now, Alaric. He's going to be king. The old order changeth—and you and I, unfortunately, are no longer a part of it."

While they were gathering up the accoutrements of the

ceremony and setting things right in the room, Arilan returned and they told him of their decision. The bishop was sorry to hear it, but understood their reasons for wanting to go, and readily consented to setting up prearranged times for contact, so that the two might stay abreast of events in the capital.

"You're wrong about Conall not needing you, though, you know," Arilan said. "Oh, right now, in the first flush of being The Haldane, and preoccupied by his father's declining condition, he's even less gracious than his usual wont. But I'm extremely hopeful that he'll be making some changes for the better. He's getting married, you know; and a good woman can do a great deal to smooth out the rough edges, I'm told."

"He's *what?*" Morgan said.

"Well, don't act so surprised," Arilan replied. "Look what marriage did for you."

"But—"

"Be glad that he's making such dynastic considerations already," Arilan went on, drawing himself up in episcopal indignation. "I understand that Cardiel will be publishing the banns on Monday, after Conall has made the announcement to the privy council. I would have made you wait until then to find out, but since you're leaving—"

Duncan only shook his head in disbelief.

"Who's he marrying? Not the little village maid he got pregnant?"

"Good heavens, no," Arilan said. "She's a proper princess, and Deryni, to boot. I'm sure you'll both approve. He's marrying Rothana of Nur Hallaj."

"Rothana!" Morgan gasped.

"But, she's under vows!" Duncan added.

Arilan shrugged. "According to Thomas Cardiel, not any more. Apparently she made formal application to be dispensed from her vows—which were only temporary, in any case—some time ago, after discussing the possibility with him under the seal of the confessional. Conall's very keen to get a legitimate heir, so the wedding's being held even before Lent is over—a small, quiet affair, due to the tragedies of the past month or so—a week from today, I believe."

Shaking his head, Morgan could only be amazed.

"I had no idea. I always thought it was Kelson who had his cap set for her—though it certainly wouldn't have been easy sailing. I'll never forget how shaken he was, the first day he met her." He smiled sadly, remembering. "He asked me if I'd ever raped a woman."

"He what?" Arilan said. "Good God, you don't mean that *he*—"

"Oh, good heavens, no," Morgan replied. "So far as I know, Kelson's still a virgin—or was," he added lamely. "I don't think he ever laid a hand on a woman with other than respect."

"Well, what happened between him and Rothana, then?" Arilan asked.

Morgan sighed wistfully, forcing himself to concentrate only on answering the question.

"He was after the man who'd raped the Princess Janniver. He wanted to read Janniver's memory of the attack, to see whether he could identify her assailant, but Rothana wouldn't hear of it. Then *she* read Janniver and gave the information to Kelson—only, she also gave him a taste of what it feels like to be a woman under those circumstances. I daresay it was a useful thing for him to learn, but maybe it made more of a negative impression than I'd thought. I wonder if Richenda knows about this."

Arilan shrugged. "I can't answer that, of course. I'm glad, however, to hear that there was nothing between her and Kelson. I should hate to have to get involved with questions of consanguinity and such. She'll make the perfect queen for Gwynedd. And Conall *does* need a legitimate heir, no less than Kelson did."

"Well, if that's what Rothana wants," Duncan murmured. "And at least Gwynedd will still have a Deryni queen, which is certainly to the good. You don't think Conall will be offended if we aren't here for the wedding, do you?"

"Oh, I shouldn't think so," Arilan said. "It will be a very small ceremony, under the circumstances. And it will probably do Conall good to be out from under the scrutiny of both of you for a few weeks, while he finds his stride—no offense intended."

"None taken," Morgan said dryly, mentally signaling Duncan that it was time to go. "It will certainly do *us* good to get away and work out our grief, once and for all—and

I doubt anything will crop up militarily that Ewan and Saer can't handle for Conall. Please present our apologies to him and his mother for leaving so precipitously, but I understand it's safest to use the Valoret Portal in the early morning hours, and we'd rather not delay until tomorrow night."

"A wise precaution," Arilan agreed.

"Just one other question," Morgan said, before turning to go.

"Yes?"

"What will the Camberian Council think of all this?"

"Of Conall marrying Rothana?" Arilan smiled. "I should imagine they'll be delighted. Her parents are well known to us and have always been in sympathy with our aims. She'll make a fine and biddable queen."

"Biddable, indeed!" Duncan muttered under his breath, when they were safely outside and heading toward Dhugal's rooms to change. "Biddable, indeed!"

Meanwhile, he who should have had Rothana for his queen continued to trudge along an apparently endless corridor deep underground, going steadily deeper, watched and assisted with growing concern by an ever more exhausted Dhugal.

His royal patient had made some progress. Kelson's memory was returning with each passing day, so that he now could recall most of what had happened up to the time of the accident, but he still tired easily and was plagued by headaches if he pushed himself too hard; and his ability to tap into his powers was still very weak and chancy. Periodically, he made game attempts to link with Dhugal, in hopes of enhancing the latter's strength enough to cast beyond their rocky prison and make contact with the outside world, but even the mildest exertion along these lines set the king's head to throbbing again. The only Deryni ability working with any real reliability was that of lowering his shields so that Dhugal could block his pain for a time and help him sleep.

And so he did sleep each time they stopped, deeply and without dreams. That, at least, enabled him to go on afterwards. But neither of them was growing any stronger on the limited diet of fish and water that was all the caverns could provide. And the time finally came when the caverns continued on in one direction and the river went deeper underground, disappearing into a deep pool whose bottom Dhugal could not sense.

After Dhugal had tried and worn himself out in the trying, the two of them slept beside the pool, huddled together for warmth beside only a meager fire, for less and less driftwood could be found as they went deeper into the earth. Dhugal caught more fish and cooked them when he woke; and while he and Kelson ate their fill of it, he tried his best to set out the situation as he saw it.

"We've come to the end of the river, Kel," he said. "I've probed as deep as I can in the pool, but it dives underground, and there's no indication how far it might go before it surfaces again. Maybe it *never* surfaces. In any case, it doesn't appear that our escape lies in that direction unless it's by way of death."

Kelson shivered, pulling his cloak more closely around his shoulders. He chilled more easily than had been his usual wont before their accident and he had lost far more weight than pleased Dhugal. He had resumed wearing his riding leathers in preference to Brother Gelric's habit once he regained some of his strength, but they hung on him, as Dhugal's did on him. The passing days had also endowed the king with a sparse but silky beard, which he rubbed at distractedly as he huddled closer to the fire.

"I want out—but not *that* way," Kelson said. "If we'd wanted to die by drowning, we could have managed that when this all began—however long ago *that's* been."

"I thought you'd say that," Dhugal said, threading another fish on a stick for roasting. "That being the case, our only option is to push on through the caverns and hope we'll find an escape before our food and water run out. I caught a couple of extra fish, so we can cook them and take them with us, but water is restricted to what we can carry in the flask—which won't last long once we've left the river, I'm afraid."

Kelson shrugged. "So, it's a choice of staying here, where we've got fish and water enough to keep us alive sort of indefinitely—but not getting any stronger or any closer to a way out—or else taking the gamble," he said, rubbing between his eyes. "There *has* to be some kind of opening, though—eventually. The air is always fresh. And if there isn't a way out, at least we'll have tried.''

Solemnly Dhugal nodded. "I wish you were strong enough for us to try really punching through a contact with outside, just once. I can't believe Father and Alaric aren't searching for us. Of course, after this long, I suppose everyone thinks we're dead.''

After a moment, Kelson asked, "How long do you think it's been, Dhugal? Several weeks? A month?''

But Dhugal honestly had no idea. Nor did they talk about it any more, after they had cooked up the last of their fish, packed it for travel, gorged themselves on water, and gathered up as much driftwood as they could carry to keep them in torches for as long as possible.

By the time they were far enough from the river that its roar was only a soft murmur—welcome silence, after so long on its shore—the character of the cavern changed very quickly. At first, their way lay through a succession of damp, rough-walled corridors connecting larger chambers, like beads strung on a necklace, irregularly spaced, some of them blank and featureless, but others fairylands of grotesque rock formations and mineral encrustations. But increasingly, they were forced to pick their way through cathedral-like caverns almost clogged with stalactites and stalagmites studding ceilings and floors. Sometimes, such places yielded pools of standing water; but it was stagnant and mineral-laden and cramped the bowels. They soon learned not to try to drink it.

After the first few hours, they had to rely exclusively on Dhugal's handfire for light, too, because there was no more wood for torches. The added exertion did nothing for Dhugal's already dwindling energy levels; and Kelson could not help, doing well just to stay on his feet and keep plodding ahead. They stopped and slept several times in the next few "days," each time eating and drinking sparingly from their now limited provisions. Nor did they have a fire anymore to keep them warm while they slept.

As a consequence, they slept badly and derived less renewal from their rest than they had before. Dhugal judged it well into the third day after they left the pool, and near the end of their supplies, when their hopes were brought up short. The cavern simply ended. A despairing sob escaped

Dhugal's throat as he completed most of his circuit of this final chamber and sank to a sitting position, his back against the stone.

"There's no way out?" Kelson called, from the mouth of the corridor by which they had entered.

Dhugal made a strangled sound of negation as he shook his head and buried his face in his hands, his handfire dimming until he wept in total darkness. Stunned, Kelson groped a few steps in that direction until his hand encountered the wall that would lead him to the other. But then he, too, sank to the ground, laying his cheek and both hands against the stone and merely concentrating on his breathing for several minutes, unable to do more, praying for some reprieve from their apparent death sentence.

They could not go back. Oh, they could start back—but with what provisions they had left, they would never make it as far as the pool. And even if they could, nothing awaited them there except a slower, more wasting death.

But as Kelson knelt there in darkness, himself on the verge of despair, he became aware of something he had not noticed before. There was a regularity beneath his questing fingertips—a smooth horizontal line which, as he ran his hands farther afield, was echoed in other lines running parallel—and others perpendicular. An artificial pattern, like—

Bricks? Good God, could the wall be man-made?

"Dhugal!" Kelson murmured, hardly able to believe what he was feeling. "Dhugal, it's a wall!"

"I know that," came Dhugal's listless reply, through muffling hands.

"No, I mean it's man-made. Bricks or something. Someone built it. Feel it, Dhugal. You can feel the lines of the joins. Bring back your handfire and have a look!"

Dhugal snuffled in the darkness, presumably making his own tactile inspection of the wall, then gasped.

"Sweet *Jesu,* you're right!" he breathed, as his handfire flared again to show him frantically running his hands over the wall. "It's bricks and mortar. Kelson, we *are* going to get out of here! If someone built this, then they have to have done it from the other side. All we have to do is find a way to break through."

But finding a way through was going to prove more difficult than their first exuberant optimism indicated, for they had no tools except Dhugal's dagger and their hands. The mortar binding the bricks might be dug out, but it was slow, maddeningly painstaking work that quickly ruined the blade for any other purpose and made a disaster of fingernails—but at least they made progress.

It took them several hours to get the first brick out. Behind it was another, slightly offset from the first. Several more hours were required to remove enough other bricks from the first layer to expose a full brick in the second, though the work went a little easier, with the first one out. They worked far past the time when, ordinarily, they would have stopped to sleep, even though Kelson was starting to droop with exhaustion.

Eventually, however, they were able to push a single brick of the next layer through to the other side, rejoicing that the wall had proven only two layers thick. It hit with a dull, solid thud, but something tinkled metallically as Dhugal's questing fingers dislodged more mortar in reaching through.

"It's smooth on the other side," he said, feeling around the opening. "A plaster finish, maybe."

"Can you see anything?" Kelson asked.

But only darkness lay beyond, as the two of them pressed their faces to the opening to peer through; and even when Dhugal jockeyed his handfire through to illuminate the other side, they could see nothing. But the breach was made now; and the wall's very existence was proof that others had been there before them to build it—and that, therefore, a way out must lie beyond.

Thus spurred by new hope, they rested for a short while, eating the last of their increasingly unpalatable fish and taking meager sips of water from the nearly empty flask. Kelson slept a little then, while Dhugal continued to dig and pry at the bricks, though both knew it would be at least a day's work to enlarge the hole enough to wriggle through.

At the campsite above Saint Bearand's, Morgan stood with Duncan and Ciard O Ruane on a rocky outcropping overlooking the plunge of the waterfall, spray rainbow-sparkling around them in the bright midmorning sunlight.

"And you say Kelson's squire went over this waterfall

and survived?'' Morgan asked the old gillie, shaking his head in disbelief as he craned his neck to see farther over the edge.

"Aye, but ye can see there, at the edge of the pool, how the rocks ring it. I dinnae know how the lad managed not to hit 'em. Or maybe he did. The t'other squire did. But the rocks before the falls are treacherous enough.''

Heartsick, Morgan glanced back at the white water rapids leading down to the drop. Kelson and Dhugal would have gone into the water considerably farther upriver. He and Duncan had ridden up there at first light with the monk who had guided them from Saint Bearand's. The man was waiting in the campsite below with Jass MacArdry and the other MacArdry retainers who had kept a hopeful vigil here for nearly three weeks now.

Much remained to question, but the outlook did not look good. It was now fairly well confirmed that Dhugal and Kelson both had survived the initial fall, for several people had seen Dhugal swimming toward the weakly struggling king as the water swept them out of sight around a curve in the river. But whether either or both of them could have survived going over the waterfall was another question entirely. The fall had been young Jowan's death and presumably that of the monk who had led them. Certainly, nothing that went over that drop had escaped without some sort of damage.

Added to that was the treachery of the river plunging underground, just when one might have thought himself safe, after surviving the ordeal of the falls. From where he was, Morgan could detect no hint of where that occurred, but it was certain that the part of the river that continued on down the canyon was not large enough to account for the volume of water going over the falls.

"Where do you think the river goes underground, Ciard?'' Morgan asked, after a minute or two.

"Just there,'' Ciard said, sighting along an outstretched arm and finger. "If ye follow a line straight doon from that cleft in the cliff face, there where yon branch sticks out— d'ye see th' patch that looks aye stiller than the rest?''

"Yes.''

"Now watch th' wee branch comin' toward it,'' the gillie directed, pointing slightly to the right. "It happens without much fuss, but—there't goes! One o' the squires ridin' at the end o' the line actually saw a horse get sucked under.''

Morgan saw Duncan grimace and look away and he, too, turned from the sight.

"Let's go have a closer look at that part of the river from the campsite," Morgan said, starting to scramble down the steep path that had brought them to their vantage point.

Closer scrutiny brought no reassurance, however. Morgan stood for a long time on the bank, staring at the spot and trying to send his mind into the abyss where that part of the river plunged downward, but he touched nothing.

"You're not thinking of trying to follow them, are you?" Duncan murmured, coming to stand at his elbow after a few minutes.

Morgan shook his head. "Despondent I may be, but I'm not suicidal," he said. "That river bottom's like a funnel at this point. The water must come out somewhere, but I can't get any feel for how far away that might be. For all we know, it could drain into an underground cistern—though one would think that would have to feed something too, or at least fill up eventually."

"Suppose it doesn't go into a cistern, then," Duncan said. "Suppose the river continues as a river, but underground. It must come out *somewhere*. This is high country here, but eventually, there are lowlands all around."

Morgan nodded. "That's what I've been thinking, too. But no one seems to know where."

Ciard, listening to their conversation, cocked his head thoughtfully.

"Now, *there's* a thought, sairs," he said. "These monks dinnae know anything o'mountains, fer all that they live in 'em—an' mayhap they'd wrinkle their long noses at what I'm a-thinkin'—but we folk o' th' borders hae the second sight, sometimes. Hae ye ever heard o' dowsin' tae find water?"

"Dowsing?" Morgan murmured.

But Duncan nodded enthusiastically, giving Ciard his full attention.

"I've heard of it, Ciard. But, we already know where the water is. Do you think it's possible to focus on a particular body of water, with all this surface water around?"

"Weel, I dinnae know that *I* could focus it that fine—but Deryni like yerselves. . ."

"We can't end up any worse off than we are," Morgan

said impatiently. "*I'm* willing to try. Ciard, is there *any* chance they might have missed the funnel and been swept farther downriver?"

Ciard shook his head. "Th' lads an' I hae been a full day's ride downstream, sair. None o' th' bodies we did find got even half that far—an' most were just here, caught in th' rocks around th' edges o' this pool. Nah, puir Dhugal an' th' king must've gone under, all right—God rest 'em."

The old gillie's assessment was harsh, but after Morgan and Duncan had exchanged quick, silent queries, they agreed that the suggestion to dowse for the course of the river certainly could do no harm. They watched with honest curiosity as Ciard picked through the piles of driftwood at the edge of the pool until, after inspecting and rejecting nearly a dozen, he found a forked branch that suited him. Quickly he trimmed it to the shape of a short-tailed Y and peeled it, pausing often to pare away a knot or test the proportions of the arms. When he had sheathed his dirk, he held out his work for their inspection.

"Now, why did you pick this particular bit of wood, Ciard?" Morgan asked.

"Why, because it spoke t'me, sair. Some o' them hae th' yen tae bend tae water, an' others dinnae. Feel th' life in this one—not th' life o' the tree it came from, exactly, but a—a vitality, if ye will."

As the two Deryni ran their fingers along the smooth, pale wood, Duncan nodded, opening his perceptions to Morgan as well.

"I think I see what you mean," he said. "Now, how do you use it?"

A little more tentative now, Ciard took the two arms of the forked branch lightly in his fingers and turned so that the tail of the Y pointed toward the water. After a few seconds, the tail dipped a little between his hands.

"Are you doing that?" Morgan asked.

Duncan shook his head at the same time Ciard shook his.

"No, sair," the gillie murmured, his seamed face very still, eyes a little unfocused on the end of the stick. "I— cannae exactly explain what I'm doin', but. . ."

As his voice trailed off and the tail of the Y jerked more strongly between his hands, Duncan moved enough closer to touch his forearm gently.

"Try not to pay any attention to me, Ciard," Duncan said, pushing a tentative probe toward the gillie's mind. "You've worked with Dhugal, so you know a mind touch won't hurt. I just want to see if I can figure out how you're doing that."

He closed his eyes then, reading all the nuances of energy flow that went into what Ciard was doing.

"We'll have to make our own dowsing sticks," he said, when he looked up at last and let his hand fall away. "Each one has to be chosen by and for the user. But I think I've got the general idea."

An hour later, forked sticks in hands, both of them were focusing on the pool where the river went underground, gradually beginning to pick up impressions of where the river went next.

"It's going to be slow going," Duncan said, "and God knows whether it will lead us anywhere useful, but at least it's better than doing nothing. We need to get to the other side of the river, though. Ciard, is that possible, without going all the way down to the valley of Saint Bearand's?"

"Aye, but it'll be tricky with th' horses. There's a ford o' sorts a few miles farther up, above where the bank gave way."

"Let's go, then," Duncan said. "Unless you think we're wasting our time, Alaric," he added.

Morgan, who was not yet as adept with his dowsing stick as Duncan, could only shake his head and follow Duncan and Ciard back to the campsite so preparations could be made.

CHAPTER TWENTY-TWO

If I wait, the grave is my house.

—Job 17:13

Dhugal chipped loose another shard of mortar—hopefully the last he would have to remove to loosen the brick it held—then smacked the brick with the heel of his hand. It gave, tumbling into the chamber beyond before he could catch it, and hit the floor with a muffled clatter. The sound roused Kelson, who had been dozing on their heaped-up cloaks, close beside the pile of bricks that had grown from their exertions.

Dhugal had been at it for what must be nearly twenty-four hours now, with only short breaks to catch his breath and snatch a few fitful minutes' nap. The last of their water was gone. Kelson had tried to help with the digging, but he could not work for long before he must lie down and rest or else swoon. He rose now, however, wobbling closer to peer over Dhugal's shoulder as the latter conjured a second, smaller sphere of handfire and sent it through the opening.

"Is that one going to make the difference?" the king asked, as Dhugal stuck his head and one arm through and began inching his shoulders past the uneven edges.

"I certainly hope so," came Dhugal's somewhat muffled reply. "We should have made the opening lower, though. Give me a boost, can you?"

Though it made his head reel a little, Kelson bent to set his interlaced fingers under Dhugal's knee, as if giving him a leg up onto a horse. Dhugal's contortions as he wormed his way through the opening nearly knocked Kelson off balance, but he braced his shoulder against the wall and somehow managed to keep the other's legs steady until Dhugal had gotten both hands safely on the floor beyond and could drag his torso and legs the rest of the way through.

They already knew that no immediate escape lay on the other side. Hoping to break through into the open, they instead had found themselves working to enter a burial chamber, dank and decaying, very likely but the first in a long series of similar tombs set beadlike on the string that was the long cavern they had been following. The tomb's occupant apparently lay in a coffin hewn from a tree trunk, set lengthwise across the room on a raised bier of piled stones. A pall or banner shrouded most of it, though too mildewed and moisture-rotted to be read any longer, at least from their limited vantage point, and the floor around it was littered with the long-decayed remains of floral tributes, mostly gone to mulch.

But the acrid, musty odor of ancient death was not Dhugal's primary concern, as he picked himself up and dusted debris from his hands and knees. It was the distinct possibility that his and Kelson's deaths might follow all too soon. For hardly half a dozen paces beyond the coffin lay another wall very like the one he had just breached, though plastered and painted with a fresco now cracked and peeling from the damp. And though a substantial-looking wooden door pierced the wall at its center, it was tightly closed and ominously latchless. Nor would it yield when Dhugal came and set his shoulder against it, first tentatively and then with a lunge whose impact reverberated in the close confines of the chamber.

"Is it latched from the other side?" came Kelson's fearful query, from where he bent to peer through the hole in the first wall.

"Seems to be," Dhugal replied, returning. "But we'll worry about that after we've gotten you through. I wonder whose tomb this is. It looks really old."

Kelson, who had been stuffing their cloaks through the hole, passed Dhugal the empty flask and saddlebags, then bent to stick his right arm and head through the hole.

"Right now, I don't care how old it looks," he said, as he began the contortion process to get his upper body through. "The question is, am I going to be able to get through here?"

"You should," Dhugal replied, taking Kelson's right arm. "You're a bit broader through the shoulders than I am, so it's going to be a little tight—and unfortunately, there's no way to give you a boost from behind, but—that's it. Good. Can you push yourself off now, and I'll pull?"

"'Push yourself off,' he says," Kelson muttered, as he tried to suit action to words. With his legs now dangling free, he took his full weight across his middle and one trapped arm and bit back a gasp. "God, I'm about to amputate my arm!"

"No you're not."

"It isn't *your* arm that's being amputated!"

"That's true."

Shifting his grip beneath Kelson's arm that was through, Dhugal began twisting and pulling.

"Arch your back a little, if you can. Shift more to your right. We don't want to have to spend another few hours making the hole bigger."

"We're going to have to," Kelson gasped. "I'm stuck."

"You're not stuck."

"Dhugal, I'm leaving skin behind!"

"That's all right. You're nearly through. Easy now—I've nearly got your other arm free. Try to squirm a little to your left, if you can, and—there we go!"

Kelson cried out as Dhugal drew him the rest of the way through, almost sobbing as both of them fell in a tangle of flailing limbs, fortunately cushioned by the heap of their cloaks. Dhugal rolled to a sitting position at once and scrambled to help Kelson, but the king only shook his head and curled into a ball, clutching at his groin and sucking in breath between clenched teeth.

"Are you all right?" Dhugal demanded.

"I will be, in a minute," Kelson grunted, white-faced, as Dhugal helped him to sit, "though I don't know if I can say the same about future Haldane heirs."

Dhugal did his best not to chuckle.

"Sorry, but it was a little late to push you back through and start over. You aren't really hurt, are you?"

"Only my pride." Shakily, Kelson eased to his knees and

then to his feet with Dhugal's help. "Let's have a closer look at what we've stumbled into."

In addition to the fresco on the wall with the door, there was one where they had just broken through, though unknown years of moisture had rendered the subject matter unrecognizable.

Of more immediate interest, however, was the body. The fabric covering it fell away in shreds at Dhugal's tentative touch, and he leaned closer to peer inside as its disintegration revealed that the coffin had no lid.

"Well, would you look at this?" he murmured, as Kelson staggered closer.

The remains were skeletal, though the leather and metal of the brigandine in which the man had been buried were still intact. The wool of his arming coat and breeches crumbled almost at a breath to show yellowed bone beneath. The skull was encased in a crested helm whose like had not been seen in Gwynedd in several centuries.

But what had arrested Dhugal's attention was not the armor, Kelson saw as he laid his hands on the coffin edge to inspect its contents more closely, but a regular pattern of scarlet threads laid over the entire body like a net, the openings perhaps a hand's breadth wide. And each intersection of the threads was knotted with what appeared to be a small, greyish stone, drilled through the center to take the thread.

"What is it?" Kelson whispered, glancing up at Dhugal in question.

Dhugal shook his head and held a hand close over one of the stones.

"I dunno. Something magical, I should think. A protective charm of some sort? It's all dissipated now, so far as I can tell, but there's a residue of some sort of energy."

"Deryni?"

"You're asking *me*?"

"Well, it's a cinch *I* can't tell, right now," Kelson replied. "What do you think it's made of?"

Dhugal fingered one of the threads cautiously. "Silk? And some of the stones have traces of *shiral,* unless I miss my guess. It's all awfully old, though. I've never seen anything like it. I wish Father and Duke Alaric were here."

Kelson sighed, glancing around the rest of the room. Now that they had satisfied their immediate curiosity about its

occupant, the priorities of escape and survival began to resume their former places of prominence in his mind. The
door to which Dhugal was returning remained the immediate
barrier to the former, but Kelson was startled to realize that
the chamber's two end walls, defined by the natural stone
of the cavern, were stacked knee-high with the vague hulk
of funerary offerings—pottery jars, rotted baskets, mold-
ering wooden caskets—and food and wine were among the
items traditionally included in such offerings. Even as he
turned to say something to Dhugal, the other was circling
back in that direction, picking up what was left of his dagger
as he passed the heap of their cloaks.

"Do you think any of these are still good?" Kelson asked,
as Dhugal began prising at the stopper in the nearest one.

"We'll soon see," Dhugal replied. "I certainly hope so."

The stopper popped out, and Dhugal peered inside. After
a few seconds' scrutiny, he dipped into the jar, bringing up
a handful of musty looking grain.

"Well, we're on the right track—though I don't think I'm
quite hungry enough to try munching on moldy grain just
yet. I was hoping for some wine. The temperature's probably
pretty constant down here, so wine could have aged rather
well, if it was properly sealed. We might end up working a
little tipsy, but it's nourishing—and our water's gone."

They did find a jar of wine, after a few more tries. It was
sour but drinkable. After a few swallows, Dhugal went back
to the blank door and knelt down to lay his hands flat against
the wood where a latch ought to be. Kelson watched as his
foster brother's eyes closed and his breathing slowed, wishing he were not so helpless. But even thinking seriously
about trying to use his own powers made his head hurt.

"It's just a sliding bar across the other side," Dhugal said,
after a minute or two, not opening his eyes. "I think I can
move it, but it's awfully heavy. I'm going to need your help."

"I don't know how much help I can be," Kelson said,
coming to stand beside Dhugal, "but I'll do what I can."

"Sit down against the door and try to open your mind for
a link, so I can draw energy," Dhugal murmured, slipping
his right hand around the back of Kelson's neck as the king
complied. "I'll try not to push you too hard."

Kelson closed his eyes and did his best to relax, but there
was little reservoir from which to draw, and the very drawing

caused him a great deal of discomfort. Nonetheless, the sound of wood against wood came from the other side of the door after a seemingly endless time of that discomfort; and then the door moved behind him. He snapped out of his trance with a groan and a nearly blinding headache, barely able to make his eyes focus as he turned on hands and knees to look when Dhugal swung the door outward.

Beyond lay another chamber very like the one they were in, with another door in the opposite wall and another tree-trunk coffin set across the floor, the rotting funeral pall festooning it in shreds. Dhugal got slowly to his feet and circled haltingly to the next door, but it, too, was barred from the other side. He made a fist and started to slam it against the wood, then pulled the blow at the last moment and merely set his fist against the door, briefly bowing his forehead against it. He tried to smile as he turned at last to look at Kelson, but the hollow dullness of despair was in his eyes.

"Well, it's clear this place wasn't designed with us in mind," he said softly. "Who would have thought anyone would be trying to get out, once these doors were closed?"

"Do you think this one's the same as the other?" Kelson asked, as he hauled himself groggily to his feet by the first door's latch.

"Probably," Dhugal replied. "And there's simply no way to get a physical purchase from the locked side, except the way I just did it. Nor is there any way of knowing how many more of these burial chambers there might be. If these two are as old as they seem, and the caverns have continued in use, there could be dozens—even scores."

Kelson closed his eyes briefly, swaying on his feet even with the support of the door, then swallowed hard and started toward Dhugal.

"We'd better get busy, then. I'd like to sleep in a bed in the next day or two. *I'm all right*," he added, as Dhugal caught him under an arm and helped him sit against the second door. "Pull the energy you need to get the job done. I'll keep up with you if I have to crawl to do it."

Dhugal went back to get their cloaks and the flask, filling the latter from the wine jar they had opened, then returned to kneel beside Kelson again and set his hands against the new door. The latch moved a little more easily this time, since he knew what he was doing, but it still took a lot out of Kelson—and Dhugal still could not do it on his own.

Another burial chamber lay beyond the second door, with another closed door opposite. The two of them half stumbled and half crawled to reach it and rested for nearly an hour before tackling its opening—to yet another doored burial chamber.

And while Kelson and Dhugal continued to make their slow, disheartened way through chamber after chamber—though at least the burials began to look more recent, when they had gone through nearly a dozen—Morgan and Duncan were equally disheartened, if not as hungry. They had left the two MacArdry retainers behind at the campsite by the waterfall, to continue keeping the watch there, and proceeded with only Ciard and Jass as they dowsed the course of the underground river. As the four of them sat by their campfire, sharing a rabbit that Jass had caught and roasted, Morgan wondered yet again whether they were wasting their time, prolonging the agony of finally having to admit that Kelson and Dhugal were dead.

"D'ye really think there's any hope?" Ciard murmured, setting his bewhiskered chin on one upraised knee as he tossed the leavings of his portion of rabbit into the fire.

Morgan looked up sharply, almost wondering whether the old gillie had picked up his thought. One day, he really must try to find out more about the second sight that Ciard blamed for many of his otherwise unexplainable perceptions.

"Why, are you ready to give up, Ciard?" he replied softly, as Duncan looked up at him in surprise.

Ciard shook his head and sighed, clasping his arms around his knees for the comfort that Morgan's words—or any other's—could not give.

"Nah, I'm wit' ye until th' end, sair. It's just that I dinnae know that we're goin' t' like th' end, when we find it. The thought o' layin' th' puir lad in th' ground, at his tender years—sure an' ye cannae think they're still alive, after this long."

"I can't give up until there's absolutely no hope!" Morgan said.

The fire flared up briefly as he tossed the dregs of his cup into it, and he lurched to his feet to stagger away to the edge of the circle of firelight. After a few seconds, Duncan came to join him.

"Are you all right?"

"No, I'm *not* all right; and I won't *be* all right until we know," Morgan snapped, though he instantly regretted his sharp tone. "I'm sorry, Duncan," he went on. "I guess it's finally beginning to get to me—knowing that we've done everything we can and it hasn't helped, that we're going to have to admit, eventually, that they *are* dead."

"Well, we haven't reached that point yet!" Duncan said fiercely. "And we aren't *going* to reach that point, so long as we have faith that we're going to find them."

"Faith." Morgan quirked a bitter smile in Duncan's direction. "That's easy enough for you to say. My faith's a little shaky right now, though, Duncan. How could God do this to us? How could He let this happen?"

"Maybe He's testing us."

"Well, if He is, then I'm failing."

"No you aren't," Duncan said, "because I'm not going to let you. Come on, let's put out another Call to Kelson and Dhugal. If they're alive, they could really need us."

Back at the campfire, directed by the two Deryni, Ciard and Jass settled into their passive link with ease, for the four of them had performed this ritual morning and night, every day since leaving the waterfall campsite. When it was done, with no more success than any of the times before, the two humans were allowed to slip gently and naturally into normal sleep. Morgan and Duncan, still lightly in rapport, lay awake for nearly an hour afterwards, refreshing themselves with memories of the two they sought.

The two, meanwhile, continued to work their way through tomb after tomb. Each burial was more recent than the one before, but each had yet another closed door barring their way out. They tried not to disturb anything more than was necessary, for they truly meant no disrespect to the dead they must disturb in their attempt to survive.

They did arm themselves at the first opportunity, however, lest their eventual emergence should produce hostility before explanations could be given—for their very presence in the tombs likely would be viewed as sacrilege and a desecration of sacred ground. They also continued to forage for edibles in each new tomb—for Kelson's strength, in particular, was being drained without renewal by the constant demands Dhugal must make on him for help in opening the doors. The sour wine gave them some sustenance, but it also kept them both gently buzzed until Dhugal discovered how to use his powers to counteract the effect, at least in himself. For Kelson, it seemed a greater kindness to let him constantly stay a little drunk, to dull the fuzzy edge of headache that had been his constant companion since regaining consciousness. Dhugal would have given a great deal to find grain that was not insect-infested or moldy, or a crust of bread not reduced to the consistency of the mortar they had chipped from the first wall.

But only the wine remained generally palatable. Dhugal's one cautious attempt to chew on a handful of grain resulted in horrible stomach and bowel cramping, and then a frightening bout with hallucinations that rendered him unable to continue for what could have been as much as a day. During the worst throes of the reaction, it even disrupted his powers to the point that he could not maintain handfire, so that a desperate Kelson was driven to breaking up some of the wooden coffers for torches—for he must have light to tend Dhugal.

The episode taught them a valuable lesson, not only about the dangers of contaminated food, but about the amount of energy Dhugal had been using to maintain the handfire on a constant basis, other than while they slept. Consequently, they continued to use torches in preference to handfire, though they tried not to destroy anything other than the boxes. Indeed, the first time one of them had needed to relieve himself, they had pondered for some time to choose the least offensive place—for they truly did not wish to profane sacred ground. And Dhugal still grimaced every time he had to empty out another coffer and break it up for more torches. Some of the boxes were beautifully made.

Thus, it was by torchlight that they swung back the door to enter the most recent tomb of their discovery—and it was very recent, indeed. Evergreen boughs scattered on the floor around the bier were barely gone brown; and the tomb's occupant obviously had not been dead more than a week or two.

Nor had he been much older than themselves at the time of his death—certainly no more than twenty-five or thirty. He lay, not in a log coffin like all but the most recent of his predecessors, but directly on a pall draping the bier of piled stones, all but his face muffled in a cloak and under-robe of fine, dark grey wool, rather than in armor. The familiar, wide-meshed net of scarlet shrouded him from head to toe, but this one seemed to be woven of rough-spun wool rather than silk; and the drilled stones at the junctures were only stone, not *shiral*. Even Kelson, his normal perceptions blurred by wine and with his powers still reduced to only a fraction of their former levels, could tell that no power was stored in the net.

Of more immediate interest, however, were the funerary tributes left on a small table near the head of the bier; flat rounds of bread, very stale but not yet even gone moldy, with sealed flasks that proved to contain ale which, far from being merely adequate, tasted almost like ambrosia to the two famished youths. Their arrangement reminded Kelson of the bread and wine presented at the Offertory during Mass, and he pointed this out after he and Dhugal had wolfed down their first few, hurried bites—for with the discovery of palatable food, the first to pass their lips in many, many days, the urgency to see what lay beyond the ubiquitous next door had temporarily disappeared.

"Well, whatever the reason they left it," Dhugal said, wiping his mouth with the back of his sleeve after taking a long pull at one of the flasks, "I'm glad they did. They may just have saved our lives in the bargain."

"*I'll* say," Kelson mumbled around a mouthful of bread, as Dhugal leaned closer over the still, waxen face of the corpse. "What do you think killed this chap? He's awfully young. And more important, how long do you think he's been here?"

Dhugal shook his head. "I dunno. A week? Two, at the outside. Look at those evergreen boughs," he added, poking at some of the debris beside the bier with his toe. "They're hardly brown at all, so they can't have been here long."

"No, I suppose not."

When they had eaten and drunk their fill, replenishing

their flask with ale and wrapping up the last two bread roundels in a corner of Dhugal's cloak hitched under his belt, they approached the door. Kelson was still a little unsteady on his feet, but he was feeling stronger than he had since regaining consciousness and he held the torch as Dhugal laid his hands on the door opposite where the bar must be, his free hand resting lightly on the back of Dhugal's neck to facilitate the link through which the other must draw.

He tolerated the drain far better than he had in the past, too, and was still standing when the door gave under Dhugal's hands and swung gently outwards. This time, the room beyond was empty, though the door in the opposite wall was just as tightly closed as any of the others. Kelson crouched down against it as Dhugal again laid his hands on the door, for though another drain of energy so quickly, without time for even partial recovery, would be hard on both of them, they knew this might spell an end to it all. Beyond this last door could lie freedom.

Kelson breathed a deep sigh of relief when it was done, breathing in again, deeply, of fresh, cool air tinged with the scent of pine and wood-smoke, as the door swung slowly outward and he drew himself shakily to his feet by an edge of Dhugal's cloak. More corridor lay beyond, with live torches stuck into the walls on either side—certain sign that they had regained civilization—and the air was no longer the still, moist atmosphere of the tomb cavern, though they could not yet see the outside.

"Thank God!" Kelson whispered, as he and Dhugal hobbled toward the source of the breeze, gulping in deep lungfuls gratefully. "Dhugal, we did it! We're free!"

But before they could get their bearings or go more than a dozen paces, they burst from the mouth of the cave into a clearing peopled by a score of shocked, startled men lounging around a bonfire. Both groups simply froze and looked at one another for an interminable instant, one of the men by the fire surreptitiously crossing himself. The motion freed at least the voice of another man, who started backing off, murmuring, "*An spiorad!* The dead walk!"

"They aren't spirits!" another snapped. "They're brigands. They've tried to rob the *tuam coisrigte!* Take them!"

"Robbers! Sacrilege!" the others took up the cry, as suddenly all of them were drawing weapons and swarming toward the two.

Kelson never had time to do more than wonder why they were under attack, too stunned even to draw the odd short sword at his belt—if, indeed, he had had the physical strength. Dhugal had the presence of mind to draw his weapon, at the same time shouting for their attackers to hold off, that this was the king—but no one seemed to be listening.

Kelson struggled weakly as they were overrun, trying to tell them that he was no robber but their king—for surely the river could not have swept them all the way out of Gwynedd—but he was overshouted by frenzied orders to secure and bind them, not to listen to the words of blasphemers and perpetrators of sacrilege.

As they bore him to the ground, some of them babbling in a dialect Kelson did not understand, he caught a brief glimpse of a flailing Dhugal disappearing under a heap of at least six men, one of them with a choke-hold on him from behind, and Dhugal's freckled face going red.

But then, as Kelson continued fighting for his own life, already disarmed and his pounding head threatening to do him in, even if his captors did not, he saw the flash of a dagger in a burly fist, coming toward his head.

He tried to avoid it, to at least fend it off, but he could not move fast enough or far enough. Pain exploded through his head, in the same area he had hit his head before, and everything immediately went black.

Chapter Twenty-Three

*Fear not the sentence of death, remember them that
have been before thee, and that come after.*
> —Ecclesiasticus 41:3

Dhugal, too, was roughly handled, but he never lost consciousness during his capture—though he came close, when one of the men bore him backwards in a choke-hold, with others pinning his arms. In hopes of curtailing any further violence to his person—for it was clear he could not hope to escape, at least for now—he made his body go limp and feigned unconsciousness. The hands searching him were no less thorough after that, stripping off his cloak and belt after they had spread-eagled him on the ground, but at least the arm across his throat was released, and he was struck no more.

Even so, it was one of the most difficult shams Dhugal had ever had to maintain—for he had seen the king go down, and the deadly glitter of a dirk above him. He had not been able to see what part of the weapon touched Kelson, or where, but the king had ceased struggling immediately.

Heartsick, Dhugal prayed that they had not killed him and concentrated all his energy on trying not to react to the tears scalding behind his closed eyelids. Though he longed to explode in one last burst of defiance, he knew it would not help Kelson—if anything could—and would only get him roughed up more and possibly killed. Alive, Dhugal might eventually be able to talk his way out—though the men's shouts of sacrilege and thievery did not bode at all well for their willingness to listen.

Nonetheless, Dhugal managed to maintain the charade of unconsciousness while they continued to search him. Thinking him oblivious made his captors garrulous, too, though they spoke a quick, oddly inflected dialect of which he could understand hardly one word in ten. A word that he did catch was, *"Rightire,"* as they discovered his golden spurs—surely a close cognate to the border word for *knight.* They removed the spurs, as he had known they must—for spurs could be used as a weapon, aside from the value of this particular pair—and then, apparently as an after-thought, they started on the boots themselves.

Removing the boots, with no care for his injured ankle, nearly made Dhugal swoon in earnest, but he knew it was reasonable from their viewpoint to reduce the likelihood of his escape. Barefoot and unarmed in what must be rugged mountain country, they would know he could not go far. They also stripped off his leather jerkin, leaving him with only shirt and breeches against the cold.

That enabled them to find his Saint Camber medal and the *shiral* crystal that had been his mother's, both of which they took. They had already divested him of his MacArdry signet. After that, they rolled him onto his stomach and drew his arms high behind him.

In this, too, they knew what they were doing, for they lashed his wrists with the hands back to back and took an extra turn around his thumbs, so that it would be impossible for him to lower them even to waist-level, much less use them to untie his bonds. The manhandling made his wrist ache, even though he had thought it nearly healed, but he was able to bear that pain. It was his ankle that made him groan, as they bound his legs at ankles and knees and pulled his feet toward the small of his back, passing an end of the rope from his feet, under his wrist bonds, and around his neck, so that if he tried too hard to move he would choke himself. And when, at length, two of them rolled him on his side and hoisted under his back to carry him off, the rope tightened across his throat and he did pass out.

The distant, muffled murmur of voices pricked Dhugal back to awareness. Groggy, still half choking from the rope around his neck, he came to his senses in a small, semidarkened room, lying on his left side and with his face pressed against a mat of woven rushes, fresh and fragrant. A gag bit across his cheeks, not making it any easier to breathe, and his left shoulder was so numb from pressure on the unnatural angle caused by his bonds that he whimpered a little in the back of his throat from the movement it cost to ease the rope—though at least his head cleared after a few seconds.

And his next thought, with his own immediate condition stabilizing, was for Kelson. The room was not totally dark—a little light leaked in from under a door not far away, beyond which the voices continued to converse—but Dhugal could see little else from his present angle. He nearly choked himself again, trying to rear up on his hip for a look around, and had to arch his back and roll on his stomach in the end, so that he could twist his head to see the rest of his surroundings.

A similarly trussed Kelson was lying on his side not far away, however, eyes closed but breathing shallowly.

Thank God!

Immensely relieved, Dhugal eased his chin back down to rest on the matting and closed his eyes, his feet in the air, giving himself as much slack as possible on the rope around his throat. He must evaluate their new situation.

First of all, and on the positive side, he seemed no worse injured than he had been since this whole misadventure began—though he did not know whether he could say the same for Kelson. The king appeared to be unconscious, and being hit on the head again would not have done his original concussion any good.

Also on the positive side was the fact that the two of them had gorged on the bread and ale they found in the last tomb. That would not make them any more popular with their captors, who already believed them to be tomb robbers and desecrators of sacred ground, but Dhugal could feel new strength coursing in his veins already, as his body greedily took nourishment from what he had eaten. He would have preferred something with more substance than bread—like a haunch of venison, or a brace of partridges, or at least a pigeon pie or something else to stick to the ribs. But after days of nothing but water, fish, and wine—and only wine, recently—the bread had been like manna from heaven. Nor had the ale fuzzied his perceptions, soaked up by all the bread, so he would not have to use precious energy to neutralize the effect of the alcohol.

Another effect of the ale, more annoying than really troublesome—and one for which he had no realistic solution, at least for now—was that his bladder was filling. Nor was there any way to relieve himself in a genteel manner, trussed as he was like a spring lamb ready for slaughter—an apt imagery for Lent, he supposed, if indeed Lent was not already past, for he had no idea how long he and Kelson had wandered underground. His condition was not yet urgent, but it would become more and more of a distraction as the hours wore on.

Very well, then, he must get free—though to tend the injured Kelson and get them both out of here, rather than for any point of false vanity. Escape just might be possible, if he were given the time to work on the problem—for the sounds outside the room were winding down, their captors apparently getting ready to turn in for the night. Dhugal judged that it must have been early evening when they were captured and so guessed that no disposition would be made of them until morning—though he did not want to think about what that disposition might be, if they could not convince their captors of their benign intentions.

So, which to try first? To get free of his own bonds or somehow to worm his way to Kelson's side and see whether he could do anything to ease him?

He had decided to run a fatigue-banishing spell first, then see if he could summon enough power to work his bonds loose. He was working on the former when the door opened, laying a stripe of golden light across him from behind, quickly blocked by several silhouettes. He stiffened minutely, immediately realizing he could hardly feign to be unconscious still, with his feet in the air above his back, then rolled awkwardly onto his side with a muffled grunt of pain to see who had come in. Two of the men looked familiar from the altercation outside the tombs—grey-cloaked minions who only followed the orders of others—but the third was of a different sort.

He reminded Dhugal of old Caulay in his prime—sunbrowned and bandy-legged from years in the saddle, forearms corded with muscle where they emerged from a soft, full-sleeved saffron shirt, and trews of an unfamiliar greyblack tweed. Over the shirt, a pale grey jerkin of quilted leather was laced close to the man's body, with quilted leather boots coming nearly to his knees and a silver-mounted dirk hanging close along the right thigh. He had a full beard of rich chestnut, the moustaches frosted with grey, like a cat's whiskers, and his thick mane, also threaded with silver, was bound in a clout not unlike Dhugal's border braid. A silver chief's torc gleamed at his throat.

"So, then," the man said very softly, not taking his eyes from Dhugal's, "these be the villains as sacked Sagart's tomb, eh?"

"Aye, an' profaned the holy places, Bened-Cyann," one of his henchmen replied. "We willnae know th' full extent o' their sacrilege until th' morrow. Brethairs be lookin' o' th' damage."

The other man, glum and aloof in a grey cloak that fell from shoulder to ankle, muttered something quick and impassioned in the dialect that Dhugal could not understand, for all its similarity to several other border dialects he knew, and the first man went tight-jawed, his glance flicking briefly to the still-unconscious Kelson before returning to Dhugal.

"Yer partner in perfidy has th' better part, young brigand," he said softly, "for when we burn th' both o' ye fer yer blasphemy, methinks he willnae feel th' flames. *Ye*, on t'other hand—"

With a contemptuous snort, he turned and left, the other two measuring Dhugal with their own hard looks before turning to follow, closing the door behind them. Dhugal's heart sank as he heard a bar drop in place with a hollow thunk, and he arched his back to take the strain off his throat as he tried to find a more comfortable position on his side.

Flames. Their captors were going to burn them, apparently with no chance to speak in their own defense. He had no idea who this Sagart was whose tomb they had profaned, but apparently he had been a man of some import locally. And the sentence smacked not of fanaticism, but of simple logic. A crime had been committed by two strangers—never mind any extenuating circumstances—and burning was the penalty for that crime.

The sheer unfairness of it made Dhugal angry, and he lay there fuming for several minutes before he was able to turn his anger to something more constructive—like getting loose. Adrenaline fueled his body while anger fueled his mind, so that within a few minutes more, he had loosed the

knots with his powers and was easing his wrists from their
bonds, unlooping the choking rope from around his neck,
removing his gag and the ropes binding his legs.

Before even checking on Kelson, Dhugal crept silently to
the door and crouched down to try and peer beneath. The
light was dimmer now, and whatever chamber lay beyond
had begun to reverberate to the sound of snoring. Praying
that no one would come to look in on them again, Dhugal
eased to his feet and started back to Kelson, pausing in a
corner to relieve himself, then knelt beside the motionless
king to free him. He conjured a faint sphere of handfire to
see by, and Kelson stirred in his arms as Dhugal finished.

Don't speak aloud, Dhugal spoke in Kelson's mind as the
grey eyes fluttered open, laying his finger across Kelson's
lips to underline the order. *I think we're going to be left alone
for the rest of the night, but it sounds like there's a whole
hall full of guards sleeping just outside.*

Kelson nodded weakly as Dhugal took his finger away,
but Dhugal could see by the light of his handfire that the
king's pupils were reacting unequally again. A new bruise
purpled his temple, not far from where Dhugal had lifted the
first skull fracture, and Kelson nearly gasped aloud as Dhugal touched it lightly with a fingertip.

It's bad, isn't it? Kelson managed to send, though only
when he had taken Dhugal's hand for close physical contact.

Swallowing with difficulty, Dhugal nodded. *That isn't the
worst of it, either,* he replied. *Kelson, they think we broke
into the tombs and deliberately desecrated them. They're
threatening to burn us tomorrow.*

Burn us—

Kelson closed his eyes, but then his thought came
stronger in Dhugal's mind than Dhugal had thought possible,
with such an injury.

*Promise me two things, then, Dhugal—not as king, but
by the love you bear for me and as you value our blood oath
as brothers.*

Anything, Kelson—I swear it! came Dhugal's fervent response.

*First, promise that, if nothing else can be done, you'll
help your king to die before the flames reach him.*

You mean—kill you?

Yes.

Kelson, I—

Promise it, Dhugal. The grey eyes opened, calm as a fog-shrouded sea. *Of all things on this earth and beyond, perhaps, I fear that death the most. You know what your father went through—and that was only a foretaste. Promise me, Dhugal!*

Tears brimming in his eyes, Dhugal nodded.

I promise, he said, mouthing the words as his mind also shaped them for Kelson's.

And now for the second promise, Kelson went on, a faint smile curving his mouth.

Dhugal nodded, bowing his head over the king's hand and brushing its back with his lips.

I promise.

Don't you want to know what the second promise is?

What does it matter? Dhugal replied, looking up with a bitter smile. *What could you possibly ask me to do that would be more difficult than what you've already asked?*

I could ask you to save me, Kelson returned. *And, indeed, that's precisely what I'm going to ask—because I'm not ready to die yet, by any means.*

Save you? Aghast, Dhugal searched the grey eyes for some further clue of what the king was talking about. *Kelson, you know that when they come for us in the morning, I'll do my best to save both of us, but—*

Heal me, Dhugal. Kelson's thought cut through Dhugal's like a knife. *You come from Healer stock. You're Duncan's son in every other way—why not that? You fixed my skull fracture, after all.*

That was a physical manipulation, Dhugal protested. *It isn't the same. I wasn't able to touch the injury inside.*

Did you try?

No, I didn't dare.

Well, now it's time to dare, Kelson returned. *When Morgan heals, he says he has to lay hands on the part to be healed—and then he—sort of visualizes how it should be when it's well.* He rubbed distractedly between his eyes. *It probably wouldn't hurt to invoke Saint Camber, either. Both Morgan and your father have had—what to call them? Visitations?—while they're healing, by some non-physical entity who fits Camber's description. And Morgan says he gets an impression of another pair of hands on top of his.*

Dhugal knelt there for several seconds, stunned, blinking back to normal consciousness only as Kelson's thought flicked gently against his mind once again.

I know it's frightening, came the king's reassurance, seductively tempting. *If it makes it any less frightening, try healing yourself before you tackle me. You're going to need two good legs to get us out of here, in any case—so work on your ankle first. You've got a sound one to use for comparisons. And you can draw on me for additional power, as we did for the doors.*

But—even if I could do it, is it wise to drain you like that? Dhugal asked.

Dhugal, if you can't heal me, you may very well have to kill me! came Kelson's response, brutally honest. *Now, how much more of both our time and energy are you going to waste arguing? We don't know that we won't be interrupted, after all.*

The stark horror of that very real possibility dispelled whatever other notions Dhugal might have had of continuing to argue the point. He had no idea whether he could, in fact, do what Kelson obviously believed he could, but not even to try made no sense at all. To protect them from at least casual inspection by anyone looking in on them during the night, he put Kelson's gag back on him, albeit more loosely than before, and had him lie on his side as he had before, presumably still unconscious, hands and feet wrapped only loosely in their former bonds—though that fact would not be obvious to anyone standing in the doorway, since Kelson's body blocked any clear view.

Dhugal himself lay on his side and at right angles to Kelson, their heads touching, as if he had wormed his way closer after their captors' last inspection and then succumbed to exhaustion—though his gag also was only loosely applied, and his unbound hands and feet also were shielded behind his body, so long as no one came too close.

From that position, making himself as comfortable as possible under the circumstances, Dhugal quenched his handfire and triggered the first stages of deep Deryni trancing, stretching his mind confidently across the link with Kelson that now was never very far away, after the psychic intimacy of their last few weeks. The rapport steadied almost immediately, giving Dhugal access to the last dram of Kelson's energy—though he would not tap it unless absolutely necessary—and he let himself slip to deeper depths of trance to probe his own body.

He had never done anything of this sort before, other than simple exercises to relax, limb by limb. His first perception had to do with the cramps already achingly persistent in his shoulders, because of the angle at which he had to hold his arms behind him. Once he managed to put that discomfort aside, however, he very quickly began to sense more subtle functions—the blood pumping through his veins to the rhythm of his heartbeat, slow and steady, and the spring-potential in sinews and muscles as he flexed his fingers.

He shifted his arms so that he could clasp each wrist with the opposite hand and detected a subtle difference between the uninjured right one and the nearly healed left, but he found it confusing to filter his perceptions across opposite sides, so he switched, after a few more seconds, directly to his legs, rolling farther onto his stomach to ease his shoulders and sliding his hands quietly down to cup his ankles.

Here, the difference between the sound one and the injured was immediately apparent, the one coolly potent, if chafed from the ropes, the other warmer beneath his touch, tender when he pressed harder with his fingertips, seeking out the injuries his hands had sensed through his boot before, but had not dared to inspect more closely for fear of not being able to get the boot back on again.

When his captors had taken his boots, however, the ankle had been released to do what it would have done days before, had he not kept it bound, and had swollen a little even in the short time since then. He could feel the irregular line of a crack in one of the bones—not precisely by the touch of his fingers, but just as surely as if his fingers *had* stroked the bare bone, with no tissue to intervene between. And as he let himself slip to a deeper level of consciousness, wondering how to catalyze a healing, he suddenly was *in* the bone, sensing on a wholly different level what needed to be done to make it right.

It took far less energy than he had thought it would; and he hardly needed to draw energy from Kelson at all. When he sensed wholeness in that bone, he moved on to the next, mended it, went on to check the others, and then shifted into the tissue surrounding them, feeling the torn sinews, cartilage, and muscles knit beneath the binding of his will.

A soothing warmth seemed to prickle through his hands, and he used it like a balm to ease away the pain and stiffness and to reduce the swelling, increasing circulation and willing all to be as it had been before the injury. He could feel the swelling shrink beneath his hand; and his ankle, when he flexed it experimentally, was capable of a full range of movement, with nary a twinge of pain.

He was a little breathless as he came up out of his trance, hardly able to believe he had actually done it. But in his first elation, just as he opened his eyes—and just at the very fringes of his field of vision—he thought he caught a glimpse of a tall, silver-haired man robed in grey, smiling. He jerked his head up to stare, but in that split second of movement— not even a blink—the man was gone. The only thing that kept Dhugal from exclaiming aloud was the gag in his mouth; and he had remembered why he must be silent by the time he pulled it off and sat up.

"*Jesu Christe*, what was that?" he breathed, keeping his voice very, very low as he continued to look around in awe.

What was what? came Kelson's reply, as the king struggled back to awareness and seized his arm.

No matter. Dhugal conjured very pale handfire and bent to inspect his ankles, again flexing the right one experimentally—and without pain. Nor was there any discoloration or even swelling any longer.

Kelson, I did it!

Kelson's soft, careful sigh conveyed more than words or even thoughts could have, as he closed his eyes briefly.

I rather expected you could, once you knew you had to try, Kelson sent, after a few seconds. *I hate to dampen your confidence, but I fear I may present a bit more of a challenge—and we're apt to run out of time, if we delay very long. Do you think you're ready to try me, now?*

Not as ready as I'd like, but I don't think we have much choice, Dhugal responded, summoning his handfire to hover over Kelson. *Forget about looking as if you're tied up any more. I'm going to need some very deep control.*

He removed Kelson's gag and helped the king to lie flat, arms no longer cramped beneath him.

Are you going to keep that handfire lit while you work?

Kelson asked. *If anyone looks in, it's a dead giveaway of what we are.*

Smiling weakly, Dhugal settled on his heels and laid both hands over the half-healed laceration at the side of Kelson's head.

I need to see what I'm doing, at least to get started. And if they look in and see that we're not tied up anymore, we're in big trouble anyway. As well be hanged for a sheep as a lamb. Besides, maybe they like Deryni.

And maybe Saint Camber will intervene directly to get us out of this, Kelson returned.

Dhugal almost snorted at that, for judging by what he had experienced as he came out of trance the first time, Camber might be doing just that. And Kelson obviously was not aware of any of it.

Let's settle for some honest work of our own, he responded tersely, beginning to reach out for rapport again. *Just let yourself go into trance again and relax. Give everything over to me. I don't think I'll need your energy, as such, but I will need complete control, once your shields start coming back. If I've kenned this right, the first part, at least, will come easy. The rest is going to require deeper work, but we'll worry about that after the first part's done. And if you know any prayers to Saint Camber,* he added, *this is the time to say them.*

No specific ones, came Kelson's already vague, gently unfocused reply, *but I'll do my best to improvise.*

Good, because I have the feeling he's more than a little interested in what's happening here tonight.

He felt Kelson's stir of inquiry, but his own control was already more than the king could resist, as both of them settled into deeper levels. Gently he pushed Kelson into soft, easy slumber, at the same time taking them both deeper. Even as they continued sinking, Dhugal sent his will into the laceration beneath his fingertips—and felt the tissue warm beneath his touch, then grow cool, as the scabs fell away from clean, scarless skin.

Smiling, Dhugal spared a quick visual glance by handfire light, then moved his hands above the fracture he had manipulated before. He thought he sensed other hands superimposed on his own, as he reached his mind into this more challenging injury, but he resisted the impulse to look with his eyes. The Presence behind him, arms circling his to lay on hands he knew he could not see with physical sight, elicited no fear, but only calm and strength and love.

The physical healing came more easily this time, as Dhugal let the power channel through him. The line of the old fracture blurred in his mind's eye and then disappeared as new, clean bone bridged the break, the healed line finally indistinguishable from any part of the skull never breached. Underneath, the slight swelling still impeding function presented a greater challenge, but Dhugal dealt with that, too, almost the same way he had dealt with his ankle, bidding the blood carry warmth and healing to the site of injury and wash damaged tissue away—though function was not restored, and he must deal with that in a moment.

No bone was actually damaged over the third site, though there was bruising both above and below the level of the skull, and a tiny laceration that quickly yielded to his power. Dhugal took care of the bruising in what had now become the usual manner, but something yet remained to be done— for here, too, there was damage beyond the grossly physical that must be mended before function could be restored.

But suddenly it came to him that something else was required—and that he had the ability to do it. So when he had done with the external healing, he summoned all his courage and slipped beyond the merely physical of what lay inside Kelson Haldane's skull and forged a mind meld. But it was much, much more.

It was something like that very first, joyous rapport he had shared with his father, only focused through the lens of his newfound ability and amplified by the nearly lifelong friendship he and Kelson had shared. Though Dhugal controlled it, it drew him, too, into a profound sharing that shivered through the length, breadth, height, and depth of him and of Kelson, forging a bond that, at least for a time, intertwined their very souls—an ecstatic melding of all that either of them had been or hoped to be, shared to a depth that neither could even have imagined before.

It was a union that seemed to have no limit and no need for one, giving each the fullness of the other; an intimacy so profound that it went beyond the physical and at the same time encompassed it, so that Dhugal knew, in that instant, why only a Deryni woman would do for either of them, thereafter, when each went to take a wife. His amazement was complete when Kelson shared the knowledge that he had already chosen such a woman in Rothana, and that he and the fiery Deryni princess, even now shedding her vows of religion for Kelson's sake, planned to wed when Kelson returned.

When Kelson returned. Awareness of their situation flooded back like a dash of cold water, both of them suddenly mindful of the need to return to normal consciousness, now that healing was complete—for there was no doubt that that was the case, as they surfaced simultaneously, resplendent in bright Deryni auras, intermingled scarlet and silver, as Dhugal raised his head from where it had lain on Kelson's chest.

But then Kelson froze, raising his head to look at something beyond Dhugal, his aura quickly drawing in. And as Dhugal turned, half expecting to see the apparition of his earlier vision, he, too, damped his aura.

For it was not Saint Camber who had just seen them thus. The room was still awash with the ruddy light of a torch, held aloft by the border chief who had looked in on them earlier. An elderly woman in a grey robe and wimple stood at his right elbow, perhaps a religious of some sort, and he was backed by half a dozen other men dressed in the same manner as himself, all well armed, their hard faces slack with awe and not a little dread.

Silver flashed in the chief's other hand, dangling by fine, glinting chains—the Saint Camber medals his men had taken from their two captives, Dhugal suddenly realized—but the chief seemed hardly to be aware of them, after what he had seen.

"Who are you?" the woman demanded, quietly, but in a voice obviously accustomed to obedience.

CHAPTER TWENTY-FOUR

*And his brightness was as the light . . . and there
was the hiding of his powers.*

—Habakkuk 3:4

"Who are you, and *what* are you?" the woman repeated.
"You're Deryni aren't you?"

Query flashed between Dhugal and Kelson too quickly
for mere words, but other than for sheer physical weakness
from going so long without proper food, there was no question that Kelson was sufficiently recovered to take the lead
in dealing with their captors, as he clearly intended to do.
Nor was it necessarily a good idea to admit to their true
identity yet. The woman's tone did not suggest that being
Deryni was necessarily a good thing, in her eyes.

"We are *not* brigands or grave robbers, Lady," the king
said carefully, starting to ease to a sitting position, as Dhugal
did the same.

"That remains t' be seen," the man interjected. "Stay
where ye are!"

Beyond the open door, the scuffle of booted feet skidded
to a stop, and the man took the woman's arm and quickly
urged her to one side, his companions shifting to the other,
so that two bowmen could fill the doorway, arrows already
nocked and coming to full draw. Two more knelt behind
them from the sides to train their arrows into the room. Kelson and Dhugal froze.

"Now," the man continued, "ye will get up slowly, one
at a time, and ye will allow these men t' bind ye again—else
my archers will cut ye down."

"We mean you no harm," Kelson said steadily.

"An' ye shall come t' nae harm if ye do as yer told," the man replied. "You first. Stand up and move to yer right, away from him."

Kelson stood, but he did not move away from Dhugal.

"We'll go quietly, but we won't be bound again," he said, not taking his eyes from the chief's. "If someone besides one of you is in charge, I'd like to speak to him—or perhaps to a priest. We're honest, God-fearing men."

"Honest, God-fearin' men dinnae desecrate the tombs o' the dead," the man replied. "An' we have nae priests, only *coisrigte*—consecrated brethren. We buried one o' th' best a week aye. His was one o' th' graves ye despoiled."

"Sagart," Dhugal murmured, cautiously easing to his feet as well, though he was careful to keep his hands clear of his body, in plain sight.

At the name, the man gasped and the woman's face went cold and set.

"Who has told thee that?" she demanded.

"With respect, Lady, one of his men said it, the first time Bened-Cyann came in," Dhugal replied. "*Cyann* means 'chief,' does it not? And the torc would tend to confirm that rank. Your dialect is difficult for me, but I understand a little, being border-bred myself."

As the man called Bened stared, measuring Dhugal more shrewdly, in light of what he had just heard, the woman nodded slowly.

"*Both* young men wear *g'dulae*, Bened," she murmured, "and yon *ruadh* hath recognized thy rank. And didst thou not say that both were ta'en wi' golden spurs? That means they be highborn. How art thou called, young *ruadh*?" she said to Dhugal.

She had referred to him as *ruadh*, a border term for someone with red hair, and Dhugal again exchanged a quick query with Kelson. It could do no harm to admit his name to these people, for it likely would mean nothing to them. But establishing himself as one of their kind was important. Kelson agreed.

"I, too, claim the title of *Cyann*, Lady. I am the MacArdry of Transha," Dhugal replied, "and among my own people, I too, wear the torc of chiefship. My *brathair* is an even greater chief than I. But we salute Bened-Cyann in border kinship.''

As a murmur rose up behind her, the old woman nodded.

''*Meac Ard Righ*,'' she repeated, giving his name an odd accent. ''Son o' th' high king. An' just what high king might that be?''

''I dinnae care about his lineage, Jilyan,'' Bened interrupted. ''That doesnae explain what they were doin' in Sagart's tomb an' beyond. E'en a king can be a cateran. Speak up, young MacArdry, if ye would save yerself an' yer friend.''

Dhugal nodded carefully, filing away the name Jilyan for future reference, for he sensed it was a proper name and not a title.

''We truly meant no disrespect, Bened-Cyann. We were fighting for our lives.''

''By breakin' intae *Naomha* Sagart's tomb?'' One of the men spat.

''By breaking *out* of his tomb,'' Dhugal retorted. ''That's what I've been trying to tell you. We were trying to get out— not in. We came from the other direction, from the cavern beyond the tombs.''

''Th' cavern—'' another man murmured.

''Let him speak,'' the woman said.

''Aye, *Ban-Aba*,'' the man whispered, immediately subsiding.

Dhugal recognized the old title, and made her a respectful bow of thanks, right hand to heart, as he sent the translation to Kelson.

A ban-aba's a sort of abbess. I think she may be in charge, rather than Bened.

''Thank you, *Ban-Aba*,'' he said. ''Some days ago—or perhaps it's been weeks, now—we were swept into an underground river near Saint Bearand's Abbey, northeast of Caerrorie. We nearly drowned. We have no idea how far we were carried before we came to ground in the cavern that eventually led to the end of your burial chambers. In fact, we don't even know where we are.''

He paused hopefully, but no one volunteered to clarify that point.

''In any case, we managed to dig through the wall that closed off the corridor you people have turned into a series of tombs, and then we—came through what seemed like an endless series of doors," he finished lamely, for he suddenly realized he dared not tell them how he had opened those doors.

"'Tis true, *Ban-Aba*," Kelson joined in, trying to cover Dhugal's near slip of tongue. "We only disturbed the contents of the tombs to look for food. We hadn't had anything but water and some fish for days, and it was all gone by the time we broke through into the first tomb. Fortunately, some of the wine was still good. And then, when we found the bread and ale in—in Sargart's tomb—we ate it. When we came out of there, that was our first breath of fresh air in—probably weeks."

"Yet ye escaped yer bonds, when nae man should hae been able t' do so," Bened said, gesturing toward them with the hand that still held the Camber medals on their chains and then pulling up short as he remembered what he held. "An' wi' holy fire all 'round ye when we came in just now.

"By th' Blessed One, ye made th' holy fire. An' ye wore *his* medal," he went on, his eyes widening as he stared back and forth between the two of them. "D'ye—nah, ye cannae be—"

"Wha' can we nae be?" Dhugal said, his border accent broadening as he stared back at the man, suddenly seeing a ray of hope. Could it be that Saint Camber was the "Blessed One" of whom Bened spoke with such obvious reverence? "Would we wear *his* medal if we didnae reverence his memory?"

Bened stared at them even harder. The *ban-aba* went a little white. The men began to murmur uneasily among themselves, a few crossing themselves furtively, the bowmen slightly lowering their weapons. Both Dhugal and Kelson hardly dared to breathe.

"Dost thou mock us?" one of the men whispered.

Dhugal shook his head emphatically, but he sensed it was not he but Kelson who should speak next, and glanced at the king in question.

"Say *his* name," the chief said at last, turning on Kelson to thrust the medals before his eyes.

Hardly breathing, Kelson reached one hand slowly, slowly, to cup one of the medals in his palm so he could bend to kiss it.

"We reverence the name of the Blessed Saint Camber of Culdi," he said boldly, crossing himself as he straightened. "We are his servants."

The murmur of their awed surprise rumbled into shock and confusion, and Kelson wondered whether he had gone too far.

"By what right d'ye claim to be *his* servants?" Bened finally said, his voice bringing the others to silence.

Kelson sensed that only the truth would suffice now.

"My companion and I are newly knighted," he said steadily, "and had taken as a quest of thanksgiving the recovery of some of Saint Camber's relics. It is my intention to restore his cult to its rightful place in Gwynedd."

"Thou wouldst restore Saint Camber?" the *ban-aba* gasped.

"'Tis nae possible!" one of the archers blurted, slightly lowering his bow. "Th' Church would ne'er allow it!"

"Not e'en a king could do that!" another man whispered, awe-struck.

"*This* king could," Kelson replied, "and he intends to do so."

"Ye claim t'be a king?" another said contemptuously.

"I *am* a king," Kelson answered. "I am Kelson Haldane of Gwynedd."

"Kelson?"

"A Haldane?"

Flurried questions and reactions passed among their captors for several seconds, too quick and idiomatic for Dhugal to catch much of what they said, and then, without warning, all of them withdrew, closing the door behind them. As the bar fell into place, Kelson conjured quick handfire and turned to Dhugal in question.

"Now, what the *devil* was all that about?"

Dhugal snorted. "You tell me. I suppose they've gone off to deliberate our fate. Mentioning Camber certainly seemed to get a rise out of them, though. Do you think we ought to try to escape, or wait and see what happens next?"

"Let's wait and see," Kelson replied. "Their reaction to Camber's name was far more positive than I expected, and I think they were talking about our Deryni auras when they mentioned 'holy fire.' That was positive, too, I think. If I could have been more certain of that, earlier, I might have been able to make more of it. I didn't want to tip our hand too soon, though, and get us killed. These hill people can be very touchy."

"You're telling that to a borderman?" Dhugal retorted with a grin.

Chuckling, Kelson sank down to sit on the floor, his back against the wall farthest from the door, shaking his head. After a few seconds, Dhugal joined him.

"At least you seem recovered," Dhugal said, after a few more seconds. "Whatever happens now, at least we'll have a fighting chance."

Kelson nodded, laying his head back against the wall.

"I have only you to thank for that," he said. "I'd give a lot for a square meal, but otherwise, I haven't felt this good in—longer than I care to remember. How the hell did you do it?"

"I'd ask you which part you mean, the healing or the other, but whichever part you meant, I couldn't explain it anyway," Dhugal replied. "The healing is—a miracle. I had no idea what I was doing, but it worked anyway. And that rapport was like nothing I'd ever even dreamed of, much less experienced. I gather it was new for you, too."

"I'll say." Kelson's tone was light, but respect tinged it nonetheless. "I've gone deep before, Dhugal, with Alaric and even with Duncan, but never like this. Maybe it was so intense because I'd already opened so much for the healing. My powers are completely restored—memories, too. I feel as—as if everything was refined and honed to a keener edge—as if I could do almost *anything*."

"I think I know what you mean," Dhugal replied. "All the old barriers went down. I can't tell you how I know, but I *know* that I never need to fear psychic contact again. My shields are totally under my control. It's as if what we did finished catalyzing what my father started that morning we found out what we were to one another. If I ever had any doubts about my birthright as Deryni, they're gone now."

"Aye, we're quite a team," Kelson agreed. "A true brotherhood, like Alaric and your father. I can't imagine ever feeling closer to anyone else, as long as I live."

"Not even Rothana?" Dhugal asked, with a coy smile.

Kelson actually blushed in the light of his handfire and

ducked his head as he clasped his hands between his upraised knees.

"I suppose it's silly to be embarrassed, after what we've shared. I was going to tell you, Dhugal—really, I was."

"Well, you did."

"Yes, but I hadn't meant it to be that way. I do love her, though in a totally different way from what I thought I was beginning to feel for Sidana. And even though Rothana and I haven't yet accomplished what you and I just did, that will come. I had a foretaste of it, that first time our minds touched. But, I don't need to tell you that, do I? You and I shared that, too."

Dhugal closed his eyes briefly and put that memory behind him, not eager to say what must next be said, but knowing it was necessary, for both their sakes.

"Sometimes, there's such a thing as being too honest," he said, leaning his head against the wall and looking beyond Kelson. "Believe me, I value what we've accomplished, but I think we need to have our privacy as well—an area that's set apart from *anyone*. My father does, for that part of him that's concerned with his priestly office. I would never want or expect to be privy to the confidences of the confessional, for example, and I wouldn't dream of prying into the bond between him and Morgan. I think the relationship between a man and his wife must be at least as sacred."

"Well, I hardly think we need to be concerned about that yet. It isn't as if Rothana and I have been intimate."

The awkwardness of Kelson's last words only underlined the uneasiness Dhugal himself was feeling, and he raised one eyebrow skeptically as he glanced at the king, glad for once that both he and Kelson were still virginal, at least in the physical sense.

"Oh? I suppose there was no intimacy in the taste she gave you of Janniver's rape?"

"I'll concede, that was intimate," Kelson interjected, blushing to the roots of his hair. "That's different, though."

"Ah." Dhugal nodded. "Then, are we limiting this discussion to physical intimacy? What about the two of you in the garden, the night before we left?"

"All I did was kiss her, Dhugal."

"Oh? That's not what *I* sensed, when that incident came through our rapport," Dhugal replied, sending an echo of that shared memory back to Kelson, less intense than the original, but sparing no detail of physical sensation. "You would never have actually *done* it, Kel, being who and what you are, but your body was ready to take her, right then and there. And you know she would have let you. God knows I don't begrudge you that, but it's something that should be just between the two of you, just as the intimacy of that rapport about the rape should be private between you."

Kelson closed his eyes and buried his face in one hand as his body shivered in remembrance and he knew Dhugal was right. Nor, even if it was fair to Rothana and himself, was it fair to subject Dhugal to such emotions, shared in the mind yet withheld in the flesh. As he thought about their rapport, he realized that it had, indeed, been deeper than anything he had experienced before, and it only now became evident that there were some things too precious, too intimate, to be bared to another who was not a part of them, no matter how well beloved that other.

It came to him then that this explained why he had never had any inkling of the problems between Morgan and Richenda. Morgan had sequestered that part of his life away, as a favor to Kelson as well as to Richenda—as, undoubtedly, there were things he did not share with Richenda. Despite the depth of his friendship with Morgan—indeed, his love, and for Duncan and Dhugal as well—some things remained and should remain apart.

"You're right," the king said after a moment. "It's something I'm sure neither of us ever thought about before, but there *does* have to be a separateness, even in our closeness—in *anyone's* closeness. I'm sure there will be things I ought not to share with Rothana, too, not necessarily things that I *shouldn't* tell her, but that she'd rather not know. Ah, the innocence of youth, to think that total freedom is possible or even desirable." He smiled resignedly as he looked up at Dhugal again. "Is that what you were trying to tell me?"

Dhugal grinned and nodded, turning his gaze idly back to the door. "I think so." He paused a moment, then went on. "When do you think they'll come for us?"

"I have no idea."

"Will they still want to burn us, do you think?"

Kelson sighed. "I don't know that, either. We can't allow

that, though, even if we have to kill every one of them to prevent it."

"Aye, you're right." Dhugal stretched his legs out in front of him and sighed again. "I wonder if learning who you are will make any difference."

"Do you really think they've even heard of me?" Kelson returned.

"Don't be ridiculous. Everyone's heard of Kelson of Gwynedd."

"Not if they've been cut off from the rest of civilization," Kelson replied, "and that's certainly possible, judging by what the countryside looked like, where you and I went into the river. I have no idea where we are, but I can't imagine such a devotion to Saint Camber surviving, after all these years, in any place you or I have been."

"Hmmm, that's probably true."

"And remember the armor in the tombs? Some of that looked old enough to be from Camber's time. I don't know what we're dealing with, Dhugal, but it's different from anything we've ever encountered before."

Just how different was about to be made abundantly clear, as the bar lifted on the other side of the door and both young men scrambled to their feet.

"Th' Quorial will see ye now," said Bened-Cyann. "Ye'd best come quietly."

Sunlight flooded the room beyond, also revealing the bowmen, poised as before, and men waiting with ropes to bind their hands.

And in a royally appointed tower room at Rhemuth Castle, Rothana of Nur Hallaj waited for another binding—a band of polished gold to bind her finger, rather than ropes. It was her wedding day, and at noon, she would marry Conall Haldane and become Crown Princess of Gwynedd.

It would be soon. She tipped her head backward as a tiring woman finished lacing the back of her pale damask gown, letting another put the final touches to her hair, unbound and shimmering nearly to her hips in a rich, blue-black ripple. Tears started to well in her eyes, threatening to smudge the careful lines her little Jacan maid had painted at the base of her lashes to emphasize the long almond shape of her eyes, but Rothana sternly bade the tears recede.

She had cried enough in the past three weeks. She had no tears left. She had nearly made herself ill in the beginning, though she had dared tell no one the cause of her misery. Father Ambros knew by now, of course, but he would tell no one. Even he had agreed that her decision, while not the one that would have eased her heart, gave noble tribute to a lost love as well as to royal duty.

She reminded herself again that what she was doing she did by her own choice, for the sake both of Kelson's memory and of the kingdom whose queen he had asked her to be. It helped, but only a little. The day before, witnessed by Mother Heloise, she had signed the documents necessary for Archbishop Cardiel to release her from her vows—the last such formality. Neither abbess nor archbishop had pressed her for her reasons, and she had volunteered none. It would only have served to reopen wounds she was trying very hard to close. Afterwards, with only Cardiel and Conall's mother and brothers present, she and Conall had exchanged betrothal vows, and he had given her a ruby ring.

"It's time, my lady," said Sylvie, her maid, bringing her coronet and veil.

The fragile silk was as pale as sunlight and nearly transparent, shot with fine gold, its circular hem picked out in tiny seed-pearls. Queen Meraude had worn the veil to marry Nigel, nearly twenty years ago, and had given it to Rothana the night before, tears in her eyes, with the whispered hope that Rothana's marriage with Conall might bring even half the joy that Meraude had known in her marriage with Nigel. Rothana would have preferred a less revealing veil done in the Eastern manner, such as that to which she was accustomed, but she would not have dreamed of adding to Meraude's grief by declining the gift. The veil floated almost like spider silk as Sylvie let it settle over Rothana's head, just brushing her shoulders all around. The coronet Sylvie set on her brow to hold the veil in place was the same she had worn for Kelson's knighting; but Rothana tried not to think about that. She was about to become a princess of Gwynedd and would one day be its queen. She was wedding the land as well as its future king.

"You look beautiful, my lady," Sylvie whispered, holding up a mirror. "The prince will be so proud!"

Rothana made herself smile and nod.

"Thank you, Sylvie."

She glanced down at the ruby on her finger, the only jewel she owned save her coronet, and twisted at it nervously as she raised her eyes toward the room's single window. A shaft of sunlight illuminated the prie-dieu where she had spent so many hours in the past few weeks, and she stood up slowly, folding the front of her veil back from her face.

"I'll be with you very shortly, ladies," she said, moving toward it in a rustle of damask. "Please wait for me outside."

She sank down on the kneeler and crossed herself, bowing her head over clasped hands until she was sure they were gone and she was alone. Only then did she pull the folded lump of a lace-edged handkerchief from her bosom and close it between her hands, fingertips pressed against her lips as she bowed her head again.

Dear, dear Kelson, she mused, closing her eyes to picture his face as she had seen it last, *'tis time to say good-bye. You taught me that there is a duty beyond faith and brought me to love this kingdom you had loved so well. You taught me the honor I might do it and you, by agreeing to become its queen. I set aside my own desires, and gladly, for the chance to rule at your side.*

She opened her eyes and cocked her head with a sad wistfulness as she unfolded the linen square, uncovering Sidana's ring, and laid a forefinger across its circle.

And now you are gone, as she who first wore this ring is gone; and I can never be your queen, just as she can never be your queen.

But I can still be Gwynedd's queen, Kelson, as I told you I would be, and I can be a queen for our Deryni. I think you would want that for this land. Will you mind terribly if I am also Conall's queen, as well as Gwynedd's? He needs me, Kelson. And I think he is not made of the same stuff that you were made of, though I shall try to see that he does his best.

And so, farewell, my lord and my love. I go now to wed a different Haldane than either of us had planned. And if I am to be true to him, as I know you would wish, then I must say good-bye to what might have been.

She swallowed back the last tears, then rose, dry-eyed now, to move around the prie-dieu and into the window embrasure. One of the hinged panes of the mullioned window was ajar, and she pushed it farther out. The moat sparkled far below, sunlit and still, and she paused only to press the ring to her lips a final time before tossing it out in a long, curving arc, to disappear with hardly a splash.

When it was done, she closed the shields on her mind as she closed the window of the room, for she was not ready to share that intimacy with her husband-to-be—not yet. But her head was high as she turned to go to her bridegroom, for she was a princess of Nur Hallaj, bred to her duty. There would be no more tears.

She had light, gentle words for her maids as she joined them in the corridor, indulging them while they fussed with her veil and train and straightened errant strands of hair. She was calm and resigned as she let herself be led to the chapel royal, where the marriage would take place.

Mother Heloise was waiting at the church door—all of her "family" that could be summoned on such short notice. Later, there would be a more formal ceremony, but for now, this must suffice. Rothana knelt to kiss the abbess' hand a last time and receive her blessing before taking the old woman's arm to walk down the short aisle.

Queen Meraude, her brother Saer, and Conall's younger brothers, Rory and Payne, were waiting with the archbishop, all in Haldane crimson for the affair, and Conall himself looked eerily like Kelson, just before he turned to watch her approach. He wore a sumptuous tunic of quartered crimson and gold, powdered with tiny lions, Kelson's lion brooch clasped at his throat and the Haldane sword bright and potent at his waist. Rothana smiled as she put her hand in his.

CHAPTER TWENTY-FIVE

*Do no secret thing before a stranger: for thou
knowest not what he will bring forth.*
— Ecclesiasticus 8:18

"Since it was a Haldane king who rescinded Saint Camber's canonization, and Haldane kings have allowed the persecution of *his* people to continue, you should understand
why your mere identity does little to incline us to leniency,
Kelson Haldane. Your circumstances are lamentable, but a
sacrilege still has been committed, whether or not you intended it."

The speaker was a thickset individual in his potent mid-
forties, previously identified as one Brother Michael. He was
also the spokesman for the Quorial, which Kelson and Dhugal had learned was the eight-person governing body of the
village, called Saint Kyriell's. The man had an unquestion-
able air of authority about him, dark eyes gazing unwaver-
ingly out of a fleshy but powerful face. The hands toying
with a quill pen were square and callused with hard work
and made the pen look very fragile. He bore a token ton-
suring, a small but precise shaven area no larger than two
fingers in breadth, but the rest of his hair was long and drawn
back in a thin, tightly plaited braid, untouched by grey. His
garb was the same as that of the deceased Sagart—a dark
grey hooded robe and scapular girt with a knotted cord of
red and blue—and Kelson had concluded that he, like Sagart, must be one of the priestly *coisrigte*.

One of the guards standing to either side of Kelson and

Dhugal asked a question in the quick, staccato dialect that even Dhugal could not understand, and that sparked another round of heated debate among the four men and four women of the Quorial—which also included Bened and Jilyan, who were eventually revealed to be brother and sister. An archer called Kylan, another soldier whose name neither Kelson nor Dhugal caught, and two older women, perhaps in their fifties or sixties, also sat on the Quorial, as well as a young girl called Rhidian, who looked to be barely into puberty. Like the other women, she, too, wore a grey robe, but no wimple, her straight brown hair caught in a tidy knot at the nape of her neck.

Kelson had no idea how long the interview had been going, though he knew it must be several hours by now. Since his and Dhugal's arrival, the circle of sunlight streaming through the smoke-vent above the hall's central hearth had crept some distance across the floor of beaten earth. By the angle of the beam of sunshine, he judged it must be just past noon, but the windowless hall was dark and gloomy, lit only by torches. A workmanlike lattice of well-hewn rafters supported a tightly thatched roof, low overhead to keep heat from dissipating in cold weather, and the plastered walls were whitewashed to make the most of the torchlight. Just in front of the low stools where Kelson and Dhugal sat, the members of the Quorial were ranged behind a long trestle table, raised one step on a low dais.

The folk of the village had gathered to hear the proceedings, too—some fifty or sixty strong, seated on long benches just behind the prisoners—likely most of the inhabitants of Saint Kyriell's, Kelson suspected. Nearly all of them wore at least something that was grey, and some were dressed in it exclusively. That oddity, added to Brother Michael's presidency over the Quorial, lent a religious aura to the gathering that made Kelson more than a little uneasy.

Nor were he and Dhugal really certain what was actually happening. Brother Michael had informed them that they were not precisely on trial, but it was as close to one as either king or border lord wanted to come. Much of the proceeding was carried on in the quick, slurred dialect that only Dhugal understood even vaguely, so he and Kelson had to maintain constant rapport—difficult enough without physical contact—for the king to have any notion what was being said. That was doubly disturbing, since several of the men involved in their initial capture testified at length and went on to describe the damages done to the tombs in great detail.

It sounded worse, the way they told it, than what Kelson and Dhugal remembered doing. Eventually, the two were given the opportunity to repeat their stories, but they could read nothing beyond the solemn expressions of their captors other than the impression that all of them acted in what they believed to be justice regarding the seriousness of the crimes committed. It was not until Kelson had finished his third testimony, reiterating his innocence of malicious intent, that he realized someone was Truth-Reading him.

Dhugal! Someone else in here is Deryni! he sent, just before slamming his shields fully closed.

Dhugal gave a physical start, though he covered it very well with an apparent coughing fit for diversion, and Kelson ventured a wary probe in the direction of the dais. The entire area had become vaguely blurred to his psychic sight. At least one of the Quorial was Deryni and was shielding the others.

"We are aware of what you are," the girl Rhidian said, speaking for the first time. "We have known since you entered." Her voice was lower-pitched than Kelson had expected, and her eyes were a pale amber-brown, almost straw-colored. "And now you know, because we have chosen to reveal it, that some of us are Deryni as well. That you are Deryni only makes our decision more difficult, however, because the fact remains that you have committed a crime against our people that customarily demands the death penalty. And yet, we recognize now that you intended no sacrilege in the *tuam coisrigte*."

Kelson drew a deep, careful breath. Rhidian was the source of most of the shielding he now perceived over the dais. That she and at least a few of the others were also Deryni only made his and Dhugal's decision more difficult, too—for if they must try to fight their way out of here with magic. . .

But perhaps there was another option. If Rhidian had read the truth of their statements. . .

"We therefore grant you an alternative to the stake," Rhidian went on, her eyes never wavering from Kelson's.

"A chance not only to win your freedom, but to redeem your Haldane line in the eyes of Saint Camber."

She paused, as if waiting for him to speak, but Kelson did not know what to say. When it became obvious that she was not going to speak until he did, Kelson glanced at Dhugal, taut and also waiting for him to make the next move, then coughed and returned his attention to the girl.

"Do you speak for the Quorial, my lady?" he asked softly.

She inclined her head slightly. "I do."

"May I ask if you also claim to speak for Saint Camber?"

No emotion showed on her calm, childlike face, but several of the others murmured aside to one another and shifted uneasily in their seats.

"We are the Servants of Saint Camber," Rhidian said after a short pause. "We have kept his memory and veneration in secret for nearly two hundred years. We do not claim to speak for him, but we believe that, from time to time, he speaks to those who trust in him and he makes his will known."

"I see," Kelson said. "And has he made his will known to you concerning us?"

"No, but I have undergone the *cruaidh-dheuchainn* and seen his face," Rhidian said enigmatically. "If you would be pardoned for what you have done, you must do the same."

What's a cr—whatever she said? Kelson sent to Dhugal.

I dunno and I don't think I want to find out, Dhugal returned. *Some kind of trial?*

"You have seen his face," Kelson repeated aloud, trying to buy a little time. "How, if I told you that Dhugal and I have already seen Saint Camber's face from time to time?"

The murmur of consternation that rippled through the audience and the Quorial threatened to drown him out, so Kelson did not attempt to say anything more. After a moment, the commotion died down and Rhidian looked at him again, with a disturbingly discerning gaze coming from a child.

"*If* you were so bold as to tell me such a thing," Rhidian answered, as if there had been no interruption, "I would say that you must prove your claim upon your body, by submitting to the *cruaidh-dheuchainn,* the *periculum,* the ordeal."

"And what is that?" Kelson returned.

"A ritual procedure. You will see, in due time."

Uneasy, Kelson swallowed.

"And why must we undergo this—ordeal?" he asked. "You're Deryni. You know that I'm not lying about our contacts with Camber."

"You are not lying, no," Rhidian answered. "You *believe* that you speak the truth. But the mind can deceive. Our way is surer. When you recount what you experience in the *cruaidh-dheuchainn,* we will *know* whether your contact has been genuine."

"And what if we refuse to go through the *cru*—the ordeal?"

"Not the two of you, but you alone, Kelson Haldane."

"No!" Dhugal spoke up. "If it's to be only one of us, let me go! He was badly injured. I'm stronger."

As Rhidian's glance flicked to him, then to the others of the Quorial, Brother Michael shook his head.

"No. It must be the Haldane."

"Why?" Dhugal demanded. "I've felt Camber's presence, too."

"So you believe," Michael said impatiently. "However, it is out of the question."

"And how," Kelson interjected, "if I were to refuse?"

"Then you both would burn for your crimes," Bened spoke up, "though it would grieve us to consign fellow Deryni to the fire. But the desecration of Sagart's tomb demands a sacrifice in recompense—either by the flames or by the *cruaidh-dheuchainn.*"

"He will not refuse," Rhidian broke in smoothly. "He is the *Ard Righ,* the high king, duly anointed and consecrated, oath-bound to protect his own. Honor demands that he not place his own safety over that of his vassal or allow his vassal to take a place of danger in his stead. Furthermore, if everything else is as he claims, then Kelson Haldane can, indeed, restore the Blessed Camber to his rightful veneration."

"I can and will do it, my lady," Kelson said.

Kelson, no! Dhugal sent.

The subject is closed, was all Kelson sent in return.

"Restore Saint Camber?" Jilyan asked skeptically.

"And undergo your—ordeal, if that will win our freedom. I have faith that Saint Camber will not desert me now, after all we've been through together," he added, far more confidently than he actually felt.

"So be it, then," Brother Michael said. "You will be conveyed to a place of preparation, where you may bathe and meditate. The ritual will begin at sunset."

Kelson nodded. "May Dhugal accompany me in that, at least?"

Bened started to object, but Michael shook his head and held up one hand.

"After the ritual bath, yes," he agreed. "And he may keep watch with the brethren while you are apart for the *cruaidh-dheuchainn*. That much we grant you, because you are both Deryni."

"Thank you," Kelson said. "One further request—might we, perhaps, have something to eat?"

This time, it was Jilyan who spoke up.

"A strict fast is customary, to sharpen the senses, but you may have bread and water. Personally, I would advise water only, knowing what you must endure. Young MacArdry may eat, if he wishes."

"I'll fast with my blood-brother," Dhugal said stubbornly, though Kelson murmured that it was not necessary.

"Very well, then," Brother Michael said, standing. "Kelson Haldane, have we your oath, as king and knight—" He touched the spurs lying on the table in front of him, "—that neither you nor your companion will attempt to escape until the *cruaidh-dheuchainn* is completed?"

"By Saint Camber, I swear it," Kelson said.

"And you guarantee young MacArdry?"

"Yes."

"On your oath?"

"On my oath as king and knight."

"So be it, then," Brother Michael said. "Let the candidate and his companion be escorted to the place of preparation."

The sun was sinking low on the horizon, promising an early sunset behind the mountains, as Morgan and Duncan drew rein with Ciard and Jass to make camp for the night. The air was thin and cold, and men and horses were spent. They had lost the track of the underground river around noon, and everyone's spirits had flagged as the afternoon wore on and they found no further sign.

"We're not going to find that river again," Morgan said to Duncan, after he had picked halfheartedly at the stew Ciard made and then gave up on trying to eat it. Jass was seeing to the horses and equipment, and Ciard was cleaning up the supper things.

Duncan, sipping listlessly at a cup of mulled ale, shook his head and set the cup aside, resting his chin on one knee.

"I have to agree. I don't like admitting to defeat any more than you do, but I'm afraid we've about reached the end of our resources."

Morgan sighed. "Do you think it's worth one last cast tonight, just to try once more to pick up some trace? If we could even find bodies—"

Duncan shook his head and breathed out heavily, not wanting to consider that eventuality any more than Morgan did, though even bodies were better than simply never knowing.

"I don't know, Alaric. I'm so tired, I can't think straight. This mountain air's given me a headache. They can't possibly be alive, though, after so long—can they?"

"I doubt it."

Morgan closed his eyes briefly, his gryphon signet pressed against his lips, then pulled Kelson's champion ring out of the front of his tunic and looked at it thoughtfully, dangling it on its leather thong. Duncan, watching this, raised one eyebrow.

"What is it?"

Ruefully, Morgan shrugged. "Probably nothing. I was just thinking how a person's essence permeates something closely associated with him, like this ring. *It* won't do, of course, because it's here and Kelson is—somewhere else. But maybe we could link into something one of them was wearing. At least it would be a focal point to cast for—to find their bodies."

"But if it worked, then we'd know," Duncan replied.

"Yes."

After a few seconds, Duncan scooted a little closer.

"All right. What did you have in mind?"

"I was afraid you'd ask that," Morgan replied. "It has to be something they wouldn't have lost in the accident. Maybe their Saint Camber medals."

Duncan shook his head. "I don't know if the medals would have a strong enough connection. They hadn't worn them long enough."

"Sidana's ring, then," Morgan said. "Kelson hasn't been without that for the past year. The emotional attachment ought to be strong enough."

"That's true," Duncan agreed. "Shall we cast for that, then?"

Morgan sighed. "Might as well. Do you want to call the men, or shall I?"

For answer, Duncan tossed the rest of his ale on the fire and got to his feet.

"Ciard, when you and Jass are finished, would you please join us? We have some work to do tonight."

And in Rhemuth, she who most recently had worn Sidana's ring sat at her wedding supper and listened to her new uncle toast her and her bridegroom.

"I drink to the bride, the fair Rothana," Saer de Traherne said with a grin, lifting his cup in salute. "I welcome her to our family, and I wish her and Conall many happy years, abundant good health, and a bonny son before a year has passed! *Slainte!*"

Rothana blushed and stared into her goblet as the toast was repeated and drunk, very aware of Conall's eyes upon her as he, too, drank. Archbishop Cardiel, Bishop Arilan, Mother Heloise and a few of the other Sisters of Saint Brigid's, and half a dozen of Conall's friends and some of their wives had been invited to the modest wedding supper, so that perhaps two dozen were assembled to wish the couple well. The feast was restrained, because of Nigel's mortal illness, but even Meraude had taken leave of his bedside for the afternoon and sat on Conall's other side in the queen's chair, making polite conversation with those around her.

More toasts followed Saer's, some of them increasingly ribald; but not long after that, as the sunlight turned long and slanted coming through the narrow windows, drawing toward dusk, Meraude sat forward in her chair and caught Rothana's eye, her near hand resting on Conall's forearm.

"Well, it's been a long day for your bride, my son," she said softly, smiling at Rothana, "and it promises to be a long night for both of you. Daughter, shall we bid Nigel good-night before I see you to your bed?"

"Of course, *Maman*," Rothana whispered, keeping her hands steady as she set her goblet aside and rose with Meraude. Fortified with wine, she was even able to set maidenly modesty aside enough to give Conall a nervous, self-conscious smile as she added, "I shall await your coming, my lord."

"The wait will seem like eternity, my lady," he murmured. "Until then."

But as he caught her hand and pressed his lips to her palm, lingering long enough to caress it with his tongue, she suddenly could feel the eyes of nearly everyone in the room upon them.

"Not here, my lord, I beg you," she whispered, the hot blood rising in her cheeks. "It—is not seemly."

"Not seemly, to kiss my wife's hand in farewell?" he replied softly.

"Really, Conall," Meraude chided him gently. "Have a care for your bride's feelings."

Smiling, Conall released Rothana's hand and sat back, taking up his goblet again. She could feel the power in him as his hand and then his eyes finally released her, and she was still blushing—and berating herself for it—as she let Meraude lead her gently from the room, the wedding guests all rising to drink her health again as she passed.

She thought about Conall as she followed Meraude up the stairs. She had needed no Deryni abilities to sense his ardor. That had been apparent from their first private conversation. He had not yet been fully endowed with the Haldane powers then, so he had invited no true melding of their minds. Nor, once he *was* so empowered, would she have suggested it, for such an intimacy would have been considered only marginally appropriate before they were married, despite what she and Kelson had shared.

But she had no reason not to trust Conall. Repeatedly, the reasons he had given for his suit had stood the tests of her Truth-Reading, brief and seldom though those forays had been. Conall desired her with mind and heart as well as body, and truly was determined to make her a loving, kind, and faithful husband. And she, for her part, though her heart still mourned the loss of Kelson, found that her body was coming to answer the urgings that her mind found proper, for her own sake as well as the sake of the land and the young man, so like Kelson in many ways, who soon would be its king.

"I think my son is very much in love with you," Meraude said softly, linking her arm in Rothana's as the two of them reached the top of the stair and turned along the corridor that led toward her and Nigel's apartments. "You aren't too nervous about your wedding night, are you? I know you had never intended to marry."

Rothana kept her gaze averted as Meraude opened the door to the royal suite and stood aside to let her enter.

"Marriage has no aversion for me, *Maman,*" she answered quietly. "It was not to escape marriage that I took vows with the sisters."

"And yet," Meraude said, cocking her head quizzically as she leaned against the closed door, "you chose ultimately to be Conall's bride rather than God's. Understand that the outcome pleases me more than I can say, my dear, especially with Nigel—"

She broke off, a dolorous expression shadowing her face for an instant as she glanced farther into the darkened chamber where her husband lay, and Rothana gently laid a hand on her arm in compassion.

"I am so sorry, *Maman,*" she whispered. "I will try to be a good daughter to you."

Smiling bravely, Meraude lowered her eyes. "You could never be anything but a joy to me, Rothana," she said, "though I must confess, I always thought it far more likely that you would one day be my niece rather than my daughter."

Folding her hands quietly before her, Rothana ducked her head, wishing the older woman were not so perceptive.

"Had Kelson lived, *Maman,* that might well have been," she said softly. "God did not will it so."

"Then you *were* going to marry Kelson," Meraude replied, sounding a little surprised. "Why, then, once he was gone, did you decide to marry Conall? He's my son, and I love him, but it's a poor mother indeed who does not recognize her child's faults. He may well turn out to be a fine man, but he is *not* Kelson."

"Does it matter?" Rothana said bleakly, hugging her elbows as she moved farther into the room where Nigel lay unconscious.

"I think it does."

When Rothana said nothing, Meraude went on.

"Why *did* you do it? Your vocation seemed so strong when you first came to us. To abandon that vocation for marriage, and then to have one's intended die before one could be wed—most women would take that as a sign that God did not intend to share her with any human spouse."

"Ah, but I am not 'most women,' *Maman*," Rothana murmured. "I am Deryni; and your son is Haldane, and far more than any merely human spouse. When I was contemplating marriage with Kelson—and that is all we ever did; we made no promises before he left—he made me understand that, whatever personal possibilities lay between us, he was already wedded to his land, and Gwynedd needed a Deryni queen."

"Gwynedd *had* a Deryni queen," Meraude said quietly. "Her name was—is—Jehana, and she did not even deign to come to your wedding."

"And God help me," Rothana retorted, "if I should ever be like her, at least in the matter of my race! I owe a duty to my people, as well as to my wedded lord. And if my wedded lord should—be some other than the one I first had thought, why, the duty continues."

"And so, loving Kelson, you have married Conall," Meraude breathed.

"Can you name me a more loving memorial, *Maman?*" Rothana countered. "Not that I should have married Conall—and so soon!—but that I should have married the man who eventually will be king, and make me Gwynedd's queen, Gwynedd's *Deryni* queen, to carry out the dreams the two of us shared."

After a long silence, Meraude nodded slowly.

"You are a very brave young woman, Rothana," she said. "But will you be a happy one?"

Rothana lowered her eyes. "With God's grace, I shall be content, *Maman*. I—cannot honestly say that I—*love* Conall, but I care for him. And I care for the awesome task he is being given, to rule this kingdom—and I have come to love *that*. Perhaps I shall come to love him as well. In the meantime, I think he loves me—and I know he needs me. It is more than many couples are given.''

Smiling sadly, Meraude slowly nodded. "For all our sakes, I wish it had been otherwise, child. For all our sakes.'' She glanced into the room where Nigel's canopied bed loomed in the gathering darkness, then gently took Rothana's hand.

"Come, child. We must say good-night to Nigel and then see you to your bridal bed. 'Twill soon be dark.''

Kelson, too, waited for the night, soaking neck-deep in a tub of steaming water and trying to relax. He wished Dhugal were with him, but their captors had taken the young border lord off to another bath chamber, though they had reassured Kelson that he might see Dhugal briefly, just before they were taken to Saint Camber's shrine.

At least the hot bath was soothing, a welcome palliative to the natural anxiety that was slowly building over the mysterious ordeal to come. Kelson found himself becoming drowsy, though he roused with a start every time an attendant came with a ewer of hot water to warm up his bath. The steam rising eerily from the oaken tub diffused the last rays of daylight coming through a small window set near the ceiling, oppressive but for the chill it kept at bay—for the high mountain air was cooling rapidly as sunset approached, and winter had not yet surrendered its grip on the land. The scent of herbs also mingled with the steam, sweet and pungent by turns, burned on a small brazier tended by a silent man in grey; and from somewhere out of sight, a pleasant tenor voice chanted Psalms in oddly inflected Latin.

"Sunset approaches.''

Brother Michael's voice, nearly at his right ear, startled Kelson out of what had been close to actual dozing, and water sloshed out of the tub before he stopped his reflex drawing back. The chanting had died away without his noticing, and the man tending the brazier was gone, though a rushlight now burned beside the brazier. Only Michael remained in the room, almost spectral in the steam, holding a large, thirsty-looking towel between himself and Kelson. Kelson rose and let Michael wrap him in it as he stepped from the tub, allowing himself to be guided to a stool where the monk proceeded personally to dry his hair with a second towel and then comb the tangles out of it, all in silence.

"Do you wish your hair left loose, or would you prefer the *g'dula?*" Michael asked, when it finally lay shining and damp on Kelson's shoulders. Kelson remembered hearing the term before, and guessed that it must be their term for a border braid.

"Is that what you call the braid?" Kelson asked. "A *g'dula?*"

"Yes."

"I'll have the *g'dula,* then," Kelson said. "I've worn it for several years now, but we simply call it a border braid. I notice that most of your men wear one."

Michael only bent to begin sectioning off the damp black hair for braiding, all but forbidding unnecessary conversation. Kelson ventured a faint, deft probe, but the man seemed surrounded by fog. Not precisely shields, but whatever it was seemed no more amenable to probing than shields would have been. Kelson decided it might be some side effect of the religious discipline these people apparently practiced, or that Michael was Deryni, or both—or neither.

He drew back into his own thoughts while Michael finished, standing when the monk picked up what he took to be another of the grey robes so many of the people seemed to be wearing. But it was a cloak only, hooded and voluminous, with slits in the sides for his arms to go through. Michael held out the cloak between them as he had held the towel, clearing intending to offer no further clothing.

"Those who enter the shrine of the Blessed One go as they came into this world," Michael informed him, "that no distractions of the outside world might intrude upon the encounter with the Holy."

The cloak was warm, at least. Kelson held it close around his body as Brother Michael led him from the bathhouse, for the air outside was cold. He had also been allowed a pair of sandals, but the soles were very thin. He could feel every pebble on the path from the bathhouse to the church, and the way was lined with the folk of the village bearing torches, singing a hymn he felt he should have been able to recognize but could not. They fell in behind as he passed.

The church was set hard against the side of the mountain,

and a grey-robed Dhugal was waiting for him at the door, with the rest of the Quorial all around him. Dhugal knelt to kiss Kelson's hand in homage, also using the brief contact to send a quick reassurance that could not be overheard by the others.

Try to get our medals back, and I'll do my best to use them as a focal point to maintain contact and send you power, he sent, as he looked up and also spoke words aloud. "I pray thee, Sire, a blessing."

"Fear not," Kelson replied, laying his hand briefly on Dhugal's head, and with far more conviction than he felt. "The Blessed Camber knows his own and will not forsake me. Brother Michael," he went on turning away from Dhugal, "I should like to wear my Saint Camber medal, if I may. It gives me comfort. And the earring that you took from me is a potent symbol of my kingship. I should like to wear that, too."

"That cannot be permitted," Michael said firmly.

"Then, give them into the keeping of my brother," Kelson reasoned, raising Dhugal up. "At least grant him that solace, since you will not allow him to share my ordeal."

"He may have the medals," the girl Rhidian said, "since they are of the Blessed Camber. The earring is Haldane, and abhorrent to *him,* until and unless you prove yourself *his* servant in truth."

It was also a far more potent link with himself than the medals, but Kelson was not about to dispute the point and lose what had been won. The medals, whether around both their necks or solely in Dhugal's charge, were still links and better than nothing at all.

He watched silently as the medals were brought and laid in Dhugal's cupped hands, a shining mass of silver medals and tangled chains, and sent a cautious probe for the one that had been his. Dhugal completed the link, golden eyes pale as sunlight as their gaze met, then dipped his head to kiss the medals, as if quaffing from cupped spring water.

Then the doors were opening, and Brother Michael was leading them into the church, though not before pausing to step out of his sandals.

"Take off thy shoes," Michael commanded, glancing at Kelson and Dhugal as the others around them also left their footgear by the doors, "for thou art about to walk upon holy ground."

Kelson and Dhugal obeyed, and the villagers followed, quenching their torches at the door as they left their shoes and singing a solemn hymn as they came.

It was dim inside, though the whitewashed side walls intensified what light there was. The east wall was grey and blank, and seemed at first simply to disappear in distance behind the altar, before Kelson realized it was the natural rock of the mountainside. Candles on the altar and a crucifix above it gave at least some reference point on which to focus as they moved in slow procession toward it. The roof was open-beamed like the hall, but Kelson dared not spare it more than a brief upward glance. It was too deep in shadow for him to tell whether it was also thatched.

Woven straw mats covered the wooden floor to either side of the center aisle, rather than benches or pews—though that, in itself, was not unusual, especially in a small village church. To these the villagers scattered, around and ahead of the procession, standing in their places to turn and watch the progress. Brother Michael had picked up a processional cross as they entered, beautifully carved of a local wood, and he held it like a shepherd's staff or crozier as he led them. Bened and Jilyan flanked Kelson, and Dhugal and the rest of the Quorial followed, all in grey cloaks like his own. Kelson sensed Dhugal quietly untangling the chains of the Camber medals as they walked, and slipping them around his neck; his link with Dhugal strengthened, welcome comfort.

Straight to the altar rail Michael led them and paused before it expectantly. A handclap sounded behind them—signal for all to genuflect—and Kelson and Dhugal were only a hair's breadth behind in dipping a knee to the floor in respect. They stood then, and Michael went forward to kiss the altar stone. When he had done, he shifted the processional cross to his left hand and turned to face them. His right hand traced a cross as he intoned an opening blessing.

"*In nomine Patris, et Filius, et Spiritus Sanctus.*"

"*Amen,*" the villagers responded.

"*Dominus vobiscum.*"

"*Et spiritu tuo.*"

"*Sursum corda.*"

"Habemus ad dominum."
"Laudamus Dominum Deum nostrum."
"Dignum et justum est."

Lift up your hearts. We have lifted them up unto the Lord.
Let us praise the Lord our God. It is meet and just. . . .

Brother Michael turned and knelt again then, facing the
altar, and Kelson sank down on the bottom step as everyone
around him also knelt, the whisper of movement sighing
through the dim church. Then a solo voice far behind him
began to sing a versicle in an odd minor key that gradually
was picked up and repeated, expanded, and embellished by
scores of voices in antiphon.

*"Super flumina Babylonis illic sedimus et flevimus, cum
recordaremur Sion . . . ."*

By the rivers of Babylon, there we sat down, yea, we
wept when we remembered Sion . . . .

It was the song of the Israelites in captivity, but it was
also, Kelson realized, a poignant reminder of *these* people's
self-imposed exile and the reasons for it. And *he* was one of
the reasons—or his forefathers, who had allowed the persecution of Deryni to continue for nearly two centuries. The
harmonies evoked feelings he had never felt before—of the
brotherhood he shared with these people and all the others
like them who, down through the ages, had suffered and
persevered that their heritage might survive.

The Psalmist's words ended, and the voices made a segue
into another mode, whose harmonics sent unexpected shiv-
ers down Kelson's spine, wringing at something else deep
inside him, for the new words spoke of another exile of another people, far more recent. Helpless to prevent it—nor
did he wish to—Kelson found himself being caught up in the
new lament, mourning with these people as Deryni, for all
the lost years and lost lives. Tears were streaming openly
down his cheeks by the time the song shifted yet again to a
more joyful, hopeful note.

*"Duce et regere servum tui, Domine . . . Adsum Domine.
Adsum Domine. Adsum Domine . . . ."*

Guide and guard Thy servant, Lord, from all temptation,
that honor may be spotless and my gift unstained. Here am
I, Lord. Here am I, Lord . . . .

But as the song faded softly to a close, Kelson made no
move to wipe the tears away. They were his offering to the

injustice his Deryni people had endured at the hands of his
Haldane ancestors, and he vowed again, as he had so often
in the past four years, that he would dedicate his life to right-
ing that injustice, to restoring equity to all his people, human
and Deryni.

Profound silence surrounded him when the song was
done. In the stillness, Kelson could sense Dhugal also striv-
ing to master his emotions, though he had not actually cried;
and as the entire company continued to kneel for several
minutes, Kelson could hear the occasional snuffle of others
collecting their wits in the peace that permeated the place
after the purging song.

After a few minutes more, Brother Michael rose and
turned to face him, folding his hands around the staff of his
cross. Those around Kelson rose, too, and the people behind
him, but Bened and Jilyan set their hands on his shoulders
to keep him kneeling when he, too, would have risen. Behind
him, Dhugal's guardians escorted the young border lord to
a mat set in the front row, just left of the aisle. The girl
Rhidian moved closer to stand directly behind Kelson; at
Michael's gesture, everyone else sat, leaving the king kneeling alone before Michael and the altar. In that instant, Kelson
realized that all four of those surrounding him were Deryni—
not just Michael and Rhidian—their odd shields wrapping
him like a cocoon, muffling any extended perception beyond
the normal five senses, including the link with Dhugal.

"What next transpires will seem alien to you, Kelson Haldane," Brother Michael said, addressing him directly in a
voice that carried in the stillness, though he did not speak
loudly. "Much has been lost in the years of exile, but we
have tried to keep the ancient ways as best we can. We
believe that Saint Camber himself laid down certain of the
principles that will be invoked here tonight, but we have no
specific instructions to tell you what you must do, other than
to offer yourself totally to *his* service. *His* inspiration and
your own intuition will be your best guides. You, for your
part, will be best served if, of your own volition, you attempt
to put aside all barriers that might keep you from the knowledge that may be offered you, when you meet the Blessed
One face to face. Hearing this, is there anything you wish
to say before you are conducted to *his* presence? I might
add that your ordeal will not be of the body, but of the soul."

There were a hundred things Kelson might have said, but nothing that possibly could have any bearing on what would happen to him, for it was obvious that even these people did not know for certain. A part of him was relieved that his ordeal would not be a physical one, but the alternative had implications that made him far more apprehensive.

And yet, another part of him had guessed that it might be thus, from the very start—a trial in the sense of an initiation to a higher level of consciousness, as had occurred in some degree for nearly every contact Kelson knew of regarding Saint Camber. He himself had had little such contact—but had that not been his aim all along, in setting out on a quest for the Deryni saint?

Resolutely, then, Kelson shook his head once, instinctively bowing his head as Brother Michael took two silent steps toward him to rest a hand on his hair.

"Then, may *he* vouchsafe to speak to thee, Kelson Haldane," Brother Michael said softly. "And when thou hast heard him, thou shalt speak of it and we shall know if thou speakest truth or liest—*as thou knowest we can do.* And may the Lord God keep thee in the shadow of His wings as thou facest this test of thy faith. So be it. *Selah.* And let the people say Amen."

"Amen," the congregation repeated softly.

Michael lifted his hand, and Kelson dared to look up at him.

"Art ready?" Michael asked.

"I am," Kelson said.

Without further preamble, Bened and Jilyan helped him rise. But it was Michael and Rhidian who led him to a small, low door set in the wall to the right of the altar. Their shielding still faintly distorted and blurred his link with Dhugal, but just knowing that Dhugal held and would try to hold it gave Kelson courage. He dared a final glance over his shoulder as they halted at the door, the bond of his and Dhugal's affection transcending all the magic in one final farewell and Godspeed.

The wall was of living rock, the door of wood, with an iron ring to open it. Markings that Kelson recognized as sigils of elemental power adorned the door in its four corners, and a fifth incorporating an *S* and a *C* intertwined around a cross dominated the center, all carved deeply into the pale, well-oiled wood. Bowing her head in respect, Rhidian touched fingertips to lips, then twisted the ring once in either direction before stepping back slightly to turn and look at Kelson. Michael, directly behind him, reached around his neck to undo the fastening of his cloak and lift it from his shoulders.

"Thou who wouldst be the Servant of the Blessed One, now comes the time of thy testing," Michael said, as Rhidian stepped back with head bowed over her crossed arms. "Now shalt thou go down into the earth, naked as thou camest into the world, and undergo the *cruaidh-dheuchainn*. Open the door, Kelson Haldane, and go to *him*."

Kelson obeyed, setting his hands on the iron ring and opening the door, leaving the cloak in Michael's hands as he ducked his head to pass through the narrow doorway.

CHAPTER TWENTY-SIX

*In a dream, in a vision of the night, when deep
sleep falleth upon men.*

—Job 33:15

The door closed behind Kelson with a solid finality. The
dim passageway in which he cautiously tried to straighten
was close and narrow, no higher than the door itself, and he
had to keep his head ducked as he waited for his eyes to
adjust, hands resting lightly on the walls to either side. A
damp, musty scent pervaded the place, no sound intruding
on the expectant silence save the pounding of the pulsebeat
in his temples. As he slowly began feeling his way forward,
faint illumination shone from around a bend—the feeble yellowish flicker of torchlight or rushlight, some distance ahead.

The passage appeared to be natural, though his fingertips
brushed spots where the stone had been cut away to make
the walls more regular. The floor was smooth under his bare
feet, but not as cold as he might have expected of stone. He
could feel his link with Dhugal becoming more and more
tenuous the deeper he penetrated the passageway, so that,
by the time he reached the curve, the link was not discernible at all—but there was no help for that. Another short
distance brought him around a sharper angle, opening all at
once into a fair-sized chamber that made Kelson draw in a
deep, careful breath in awe.

It was the source of the light that had been growing
stronger as he went deeper into the mountainside. Torches
guttered in bronze cressets all around the room, almost out
of reach, and banks of clay-cupped votive candles lit a life-

sized statue of what must be Saint Camber set against the
wall farthest from the entrance where Kelson stood, intrigued. The figure was carved of some pale grey stone that
glittered slightly in the shifting torchlight, the graceful hands
raised to support a metal crown of archaic design, the face
deeply shadowed by folds of a cowl frozen forever by the
sculptor's art, the features perhaps never carved at all, for
Kelson could not make them out, even though he felt he
should have been able to pierce the shadows from where he
stood.

Chilled in soul as much as in body, the king moved far
enough into the chamber to stand up straight, shivering.
Charcoal braziers ringed the room to warm it—perhaps also
the source of the odd, pungent odor tickling at his nostrils—
and a pile of sleeping furs lay in the center, not far from the
feet of the statue. The double allure of braziers and furs drew
him closer, almost without conscious thought—but only
until he unexpectedly discovered the true source of the
chamber's odd aroma—a small sunken pool to the statue's
left, clear and deep, with something faintly misty bubbling
up gently from beneath the surface and being drawn out
through a vent in the ceiling.

Even as he backed off, a grating sound of stone against
stone betrayed the closure of the vent and the updraft
ceased, the mist at once beginning to dispel into the air rather
than being drawn out. As Kelson caught a stronger whiff of
it, he experienced a fleeting touch of vertigo and he caught
his balance against the wall and staggered a little as he tried
to shake it off.

He tried not to think about what it meant. The episode
had blurred his Deryni perceptions for just an instant, though
he seemed to be all right now. He tried to tell himself that
the dizziness came of moving his head too fast, or from lack
of food, or from trying to keep his link open to Dhugal at
the same time he was walking about—but he knew better.
He had read about caves like this, though he had never
dreamed there were any in Gwynedd. The natural fumes
found in such caves could sometimes induce visions or prophetic dreams, and too much of them could kill.

For that, at least, he thought he need not worry. If his
captors had wanted him dead, there had been ample opportunity for that. Danger there might be in his present situation,

but he really did not think his captors would allow the fumes to reach lethal levels.

The fumes *could* be the trigger for an inner testing, though, he realized, as he got another whiff and felt the vertigo again, stronger than before, so that he had to shake his head several times to clear it. It was said that in ancient times, such caves often were used as places of initiation, where the candidate must lie down before the god's image and breathe narcotic gas, in hopes of receiving a prophetic dream. If the method had been sufficient for the ancients to gain communication with their gods, perhaps it also followed that the method would suffice for communication with a saint—though he had to wonder how the Christian folk of Saint Kyriell's had happened upon such an archaic practice.

But, no matter. Further speculation or resistance likely was pointless. Kelson had said he wished further knowledge of Saint Camber; this was his testing, to see if he was in earnest. On one level, it was the archetypal descent into the underworld, a symbolic death and rebirth in the power and knowledge of the god-force—in this case, cloaked in the mythology of Saint Camber. And since he could not escape the ordeal, it behooved him to make the most of it and learn as much as he could. If this was the method that Camber's Servants embraced—and they seemed to hold it in great reverence and esteem—then it must have some merit.

Breathing as shallowly as possible, lest he succumb to the fumes before he had time to prepare, Kelson staggered to the pile of sleeping furs and sank down cross-legged, almost falling, pulling one of the furs across his lower body against the chill. To protect his physical body if he lost all consciousness—which was almost certain, judging by his increasing lightheadedness—he conjured a protective circle around himself, warding it conscientiously as Morgan and Duncan had taught him. It would not keep out the fumes, but it certainly would be a deterrent to any physical entity attempting to take advantage of his helplessness—for he recalled accounts of human agents sometimes assisting the forces of the divine, priests and priestesses of the old gods often taking on the guise of heavenly messengers to guide initiates toward the desired conclusions. Kelson had no quarrel with sacred drama—for that was what it was—but if Saint Camber *did* vouchsafe a vision to him, Kelson wanted to be certain that the saint's will was untainted by that of his Servants, no matter how well meaning they might be.

And so Kelson set his hands on his thighs, cupped palms upturned in receptivity, and gazed up at the statue of the saint, breathing more deeply of the fumes now—which were also becoming more concentrated, as the minutes slipped by and no vent was opened to let them dissipate—and feeling his internal guards gently slipping away as he sank into a profound meditative state, akin to that needed for deep Deryni rapport. In an attempt to nudge any resultant vision in the desired direction, he recalled the one time he personally thought he might have had contact with Saint Camber—at his coronation, when a grey-cowled apparition, seen only by himself, Morgan, and Duncan, had appeared from nowhere to place his hands on Kelson's crown, acclaiming him a king for Deryni as well as humans.

He could feel his body relaxing more with every breath, increasingly in thrall of the vapors rising from the pool, but he kept trying to focus his increasingly muzzy concentration toward that earlier vision, seeking the saint, drifting lethargically on a tide of dreamlike expectation.

No thread of Kelson's concentration or his present circumstance penetrated the many feet of rock separating him from Dhugal, however. Brother Michael and the girl Rhidian had returned to kneel together on the altar step, and Bened and Jilyan sat on either side of Dhugal, but they no longer even bothered to interfere by shielding around him. Dhugal feared it was because the two knew he could not penetrate with his powers beyond the door where the king had disappeared.

Still, he could not abandon his brother and liege lord to the mercies of these unknown folk, simply because they claimed to reverence the same saint—and a Deryni one, at that—that Dhugal and Kelson had come seeking. Kelson might be in mortal danger even now, depending upon Dhugal to make the difference in whether or not he survived—as he had depended upon Dhugal for his physical survival earlier, when he lay so badly injured.

Huddled cross-legged and miserable on his straw mat, the hood of his grey cloak pulled far over his brow to block outside distractions, Dhugal clung to the two Camber medals like talismans against evil, one cupped in each hand, trying to use their proximity to amplify his now almost nonexistent contact beyond the closed door. Concentrating on the face on one of the medals, he tried to shape a form of the same vision that Kelson sought, drawing on everything that his father, Kelson, and even Morgan had ever shared with him about Saint Camber. And he, too, raised his heart in prayerful entreaty to the lost Deryni saint.

For Kelson, time slipped, disjointed, until eventually he had no idea how long he had been sitting at Saint Camber's feet—though he sensed a mild stiffness in his knees and back, a desire to move and stretch, after sitting cross-legged for so long. The vapor in the chamber was like thick fog now, making it far easier to envision features on the statue's face. He tried to imagine what it would be like if the statue came to life and spoke to him, visualizing the robed arms lowering—for surely they were tired after supporting the crown for all these years—picturing the head lifting just enough that Kelson could see features within the shadow of the hood.

And suddenly it was so! In Kelson's dreamlike state, now fully submerged in his own trancing as well as the effects of the narcotic mist still rising from the pool, he stared aghast as a ghost of the statute seemed to step outside itself, the stone figure still standing with arms eternally holding up the crown, but a more vital and powerful entity, spectrally transparent, freeing itself from its stone prison to float slowly toward him.

Kelson's heart was pounding as he watched the thing approach. He longed to back away from it, but he could not seem to force his limbs to move. He gasped as the apparition came up short against the barrier of his wards and spread its hands in a silent entreaty, its hood slipping back from its head to reveal a serene, beautiful face, clean-shaven and roundish in shape, crowned by a cap of silver-gilt hair. The firm, sensitive lips parted as if to speak, but Kelson could hear nothing.

The entity's desire was clear enough, however; it wanted in. And though Kelson found himself released from his immobility at last, it was only to raise his hand and open a gate in the wards—for he knew his spectral visitor could not pass without his invitation, nor did he desire any longer to withhold it.

His pulse was pounding as he traced the outline of the opening, using the edge of his hand like the blade of a sacred sword to cut the energies and seal them at the edges. And as the outline was complete, and Kelson's hand moved again to dissipate the energy bound within the outline and open the gate—an inadvertent beckoning gesture—the waiting figure crossed graceful, translucent hands briefly upon its breast in gratitude. Then suddenly it was inside the circle, the open gate clearly visible through its insubstantial body, seeming almost to swell in size rather than approach in any usual manner—though approach, it did, to Kelson's transfixed dread. The closer it came, the more Kelson had to tip his head backward to keep watching it, until it stood directly before him and he found himself falling backward, sinking into the softness of the sleeping furs on which he lay.

And even then, the dread did not cease, for the figure looming over him, terrifyingly insubstantial, leaned closer, toward his head, right hand outstretched to reach transparent fingertips toward Kelson's forehead.

He had no place to go, no way to escape it. And he fainted away as what should have been illusion proved to be a cool, solid physical touch, with a command whispered in his mind to sleep.

Dhugal, meanwhile, had no notion that the being associated with the medals in his hands had made so impressive an appearance. He had lost any thread of contact with the king some time ago. His further efforts to revive that contact seemed worse than useless, for nearly half an hour had passed since Dhugal had last been sure he was in contact.

Still, he could not give up. Dhugal had no idea what kind of ordeal Kelson might be undergoing, but if there was any chance that the king might be able to tap into the energy Dhugal was determined to make available to him, then Dhugal would keep it available until he himself passed out from exhaustion. In fact, the choice was not so drastic as that, for if the power was never tapped, then there was little drain on Dhugal. What Dhugal did not realize was that the focus of his call was broadening, with no receiver to tap it and give direction to the energy flow. And that listeners far away were beginning to scan in his direction.

Duncan, with the head of the deeply entranced Morgan in his lap and Ciard and Jass lying close beside, stirred slightly as his mind brushed just a tendril of a familiar mental touch—the touch of none of those apparently asleep around the fire. Uncertain, the Deryni bishop cast more intently in the direction he thought the touch had come from, forcing himself to extend farther than he thought he could, in hope of picking it up again. Jass moaned softly as Duncan's demand for energy became more intense, but he quieted at a touch, as Duncan shifted to a more evenly distributed draw.

For Duncan had touched something startling, unperceived even by Morgan—something he had feared never to find again. Only he was fully aware of what it had been— or what he thought it had been—and he was so surprised that he all but came out of rapport, dragging a groggy Morgan with him to half-consciousness.

Did you catch that? he asked in Morgan's mind, laying a hand across the other's eyes when Morgan would have stirred and sat up.

Still in Duncan's partial control, Morgan subsided, only his silent query sounding in Duncan's mind.

Show me what you saw, he asked.

Reverting to purely psychic activity, Duncan closed his eyes again and shared the image he had picked up—a silver medal of Saint Camber, blurred as if from double vision— or perhaps there were two medals. The design, however, was very familiar to both men.

Stirring lethargically, Morgan pulled one very like that of the shared image from inside his tunic. It had been his mother's and was the master for the ones he had cast for Kelson, Dhugal, and Duncan.

There are only the three others, that I know of, Morgan observed, opening his hand so that Duncan could close it between their two palms. *And you weren't seeing yours or mine. We'll use this as a link.*

With that instruction, he edged into a dual and equal team-ing with Duncan to take both of them much deeper, casting more powerfully now in the direction of the original contact. Both of them went dangerously deep, beginning to draw heavily on the energy resources of the humans linked with them; but just when they had about reached the end of their reserves and Ciard and Jass both began breathing unevenly, the contact came again. This time, Duncan was on it at once, dragging them all into the link and locking on it, Morgan retreating far enough to safeguard their backups while Duncan pushed the contact forward.

Dhugal! Praise God, son, is it really you?

The mixture of joy, fatigue, and fear that came through the link nearly shattered it, but it was, indeed, Dhugal.

Father!

Frantically—for the young border lord feared to lose the link at any instant, or to have his captors interfere—Dhugal sent a jumble of reassurance and basic information in telegraphic bursts of image rather than words: that both he and Kelson were alive; that the village where they lay was called Saint Kyriell's, apparently a lost stronghold of people calling themselves the Servants of Saint Camber, some of whom were Deryni; that Kelson even now was undergoing some kind of ordeal having to do with a vision-quest for Saint Camber—for the two of them had inadvertently violated local holy places when they broke through a series of tomb chambers to escape their weeks of wandering underground; how they had been swept along an underground river and beached, more drowned than not, with Kelson badly injured; and that Dhugal had discovered how to *Heal* him! Almost as an afterthought, Dhugal added that there had been *merasha* in Dhugal's flask.

The multiple information levels were staggering and bore far more investigation than was possible at this remove, but Duncan knew he dared not hold the link much longer. Morgan warned that their human energy sources were nearing the end of their endurance, and Dhugal himself was wavering, his concentration slipping.

But at least Duncan and Morgan now had a fix on the direction of the contact; and provided that nothing too untoward happened to Kelson in the next few hours, all should be well. If Duncan and Morgan had not made a physical rendezvous with the two by the following evening, they would attempt another contact then. Duncan was grinning broadly as he let the contact go and brought Morgan out of trance.

"God, do you believe it, they're alive!" Morgan blurted, struggling to a sitting position with Duncan's help. "We didn't just imagine it, did we? Reassure me that you read the same things I did, Duncan."

Duncan only sighed and nodded happily, distractedly scanning their human allies and then deepening their trances to let them recover in sleep for a little while before all must rouse themselves and ride.

"Aye, they're alive, all right," Duncan said. "For every question we've just had answered, though, several new ones arise."

The first edge of Morgan's exuberance blunted immediately, and he grimaced as he shifted to a more comfortable position.

"Aye, that's for certain," he said quietly. "And the most troubling one, beyond their immediate safety, has to do with the *merasha* in Dhugal's flask. Who could have put it there, Duncan, and why? Dhugal has no enemies, does he?"

"None that I know of."

"None that I know of, either, but—wait a minute. Try this one. Who is the single person whose fortunes took an upward turn when Kelson and Dhugal came up missing?"

Duncan drew in breath cautiously. *"Conall?"*

"Conall," Morgan agreed, "who has become king now in all but name. He has the full range of Haldane powers, too, Duncan, and he isn't going to want to give them up."

Duncan whistled low under his breath. "And we gave them to him."

"Did we?" Morgan replied. "I wonder." He paused a moment to glance into the fire, then looked back at Duncan.

"What if we *didn't* give them to him? What if he already had them? Suppose Tiercel was right—obviously he *was* right! More than one Haldane *can* hold the Haldane power at a time, since Kelson's still alive. Good God, maybe Tiercel—"

"Maybe Tiercel brought Conall to power," Duncan interjected grimly, "and then Conall killed him for his trouble. Tiercel would have had access to *merasha,* too. Or—good

Lord, you don't suppose the Council had something to do with this, do you?"

Morgan shook his head. "If they did, Arilan knew nothing of it. His grief was genuine when he thought Kelson was dead."

Duncan snorted. "That mightn't have kept him from countenancing Kelson's death. He still could have been grieving, even while he accepted the necessity for it. If the Council put Tiercel up to working with Conall and found him a more biddable king candidate than Kelson—"

"More biddable." The word triggered the ghost of an entirely different memory in Morgan, and he closed his eyes to try to capture it. The word had been Arilan's, but in reference to—

"Rothana," he murmured.

"What?"

"Sweet *Jesu*, by now he's married her. And I'll bet she *did* love Kelson! No wonder I was feeling uneasy when Arilan told us Conall was marrying her. Good Lord, could Conall somehow have done all this for jealousy, for love?"

"Jealousy of Kelson and Dhugal and love of Rothana," Duncan repeated, horror in his tone. "And Nigel. Alaric, *what about Nigel?*"

"If Conall already had the Haldane power and Nigel found out—about that, about Tiercel, about the *merasha*, you name it—" Morgan said, "Conall very well could have turned on him."

"On his own father?"

Morgan bowed his head, tight-lipped. "Knowing what you do of Conall's character, do you really think that would have made much difference?" he asked quietly. "A crown was at stake, Duncan, and a queen."

"Poor queen," Duncan whispered.

"Aye, poor queen."

In Rhemuth Castle, in the royal suite formerly belonging to Kelson, now Conall's, the woman Conall had chosen as his future queen sat huddled at the edge of the hearth in a fur-lined robe, black hair tumbled loose on her shoulders and arms hugged around her knees. The cathedral bells had tolled the passing of midnight a short time ago, rousing Rothana from a fitful doze and after futile attempts to go back to sleep, she had fled her marriage bed to take counsel of the fire, leaving Conall snoring underneath the sleeping furs. More furs were mounded before the fireplace, and she snuggled her toes deep into them for warmth.

Ah, me, and I am well and truly Conall's wife now, she thought, as she gazed resignedly into the flames. The taking of her maidenhead had not been as painful as she had feared it might be, but it was unpleasant enough for one until quite recently vowed to virginity. Conall had tried to be gentle and had told her repeatedly how much he loved her—an avowal honestly reflected in the brief, awkward rapport he allowed her when he first embraced her as husband rather than betrothed—but he was both insistent and impatient as a lover. He had apologized afterward, which was an unexpected kindness, and spent quite a while kissing away her unbidden tears, his hands caressing, until her slight discomfort was transmuted to a sharp, intense crescendo of pleasure that left her weak and trembling, long after he had drifted off to sleep.

Rothana suspected she knew why such ambivalence warred within her, as she prodded listlessly at the nearest log with an iron poker. If it were Kelson sleeping in the canopied bed behind her, she did not think she would feel this way. If it were Kelson in the bed, she would be there at his side even now, content merely to be close beside him. It was not that she disliked Conall or that he had treated her badly—for in faith, he had not—but he simply was the wrong Haldane.

Oh, she would still be Gwynedd's queen when the time came and take up her royal and Deryni duties with willingness and competence, for she had been bred to that, and it had been Kelson's wish; but how she wished that it would be at the side of a different Haldane. She was thinking about that other Haldane, dreaming of what might have been, when a hand on her shoulder brought her sharply out of her reverie.

"Why so startled, darling?" Conall whispered, bending down to do disturbing things to her ear with his tongue.

She shivered as she looked up at him, for he was naked in the firelight, his body smooth and kissed with the gold of the flames and more than ready to take his pleasure of her again.

"My lord, I though you were asleep," she managed to reply, glancing back at the fire in an effort to still her trembling. "I did not wish to disturb you with my tossing and turning."

With a low chuckle deep in his throat, Conall dropped to one knee beside her and slid his hand into her hair, tilting her head back so that he could kiss her passionately, his other hand slipping into the front of her robe.

"Then, let us toss and turn together, my love," he murmured, as he drew back a little from the kiss and bore her to the furs before the fire. "This is our wedding night. The first time was for my pleasure. The second shall be for yours. Lie down with me, Rothana, and let me show you the ways of a king with his queen."

Silhouetted against the firelight, with his black hair tousled around his face, she could almost believe he was that other king she mourned, and she let herself retreat into that fantasy as he took her again. Her body believed the lie, even if her heart did not, and took even greater pleasure in his ministrations this time, eventually lifting her to an ecstasy that carried her into sated oblivion.

The sexual tension of that bedchamber at Rhemuth found its echo in an underground chamber far north and east of there, too, where Kelson dreamed restlessly in the delirium of long exposure to the vapors of the pool. In the hours just past, his mind and soul had been spent of his passion for the vision of Saint Camber, but now his body, restored to health after so many weeks, fell prey to more primal instincts.

He dreamed of Rothana, the way she had looked in the moonlight that night in the gardens at Rhemuth. In dreambound memory, embellished by present desire, as some dark-robed cleric blessed their union and then withdrew, he drank her kisses again, once more feeling the stirring she roused in his blood. Only this time, he did not let her pull back from his embrace as he loosed the ties at the front of her gown and buried his face between her breasts. And this time, she did not try to stop him.

He could feel the delicious tightening in his groin as he lay back on a bed of fragrant grass, warm and enticing on a night changed in his dream from early spring to summer. Half in awe, he watched her standing above him, her hair unbound in the moonlight, slowly unlacing the rest of her bodice until her outer gown fell in a pale, silver-azure heap around her feet. A thin shift with moonlight behind silhouetted her body, slender but enticing, little pointed breasts emerging pert and firm above the edge of the garment as she loosed the draw-string at the neck and let it slip from her shoulders, to fall in a softer, lighter mound on the gown.

He sighed as she stepped free of the gowns, for her beauty made him ache with wanting her. Her long hair lifted on the breeze as she knelt astride him, strands of it shrouding his chest and stomach, dark veiling against pale skin, and he could not seem to see clearly as she guided him into warm ecstasy. His pleasure exploded at the top of his head in a cascade of fire and flame that did not subside but grew to ever more excruciating levels of delight as she moved with him, moved with him and carried him even higher. He groaned as she brought him to release, the intensity plummeting him near to fainting.

Then she was leaning forward on his chest to kiss him, tenderly and thoroughly, her dark hair veiling his face, slender fingers pressing warm and gentle against his throat, so that his pleasure was wrapped around in soft, velvet darkness, and he was sinking into oblivious sleep.

When he next became conscious, he was aware, without opening his eyes, that the night had passed. He had pulled more of the furs around him while he slept, and he opened gummy eyelids to see the torches burned almost to stubs in their cressets, the vapors of the pool once more being drawn upward and out through a now-open vent. The hot blood rose in his cheeks as he remembered his dream of Rothana— a dream which, he discovered, had been real enough in his body's response—and he rose stiffly to hands and knees to go to the pool and wash.

But the movement brought the rest of the night's experience back to crystal clarity at once, and he froze as his eyes sought the Saint Camber statue. It was only a statue now, and at first he thought he had dreamed that, too; but then he realized that his wards were still in place, a doorway still yawning open in his circle.

He had not dreamed that part, then. Saint Camber had, indeed, come to him—or at least Kelson had believed it sufficiently to risk much by deliberately opening a gate for the ghostly presence to come through. He could recall every detail of that series of events: the double images separating, as one stepped out of the other and moved toward him, only to be brought up short against the circle; the entity's silent entreaty for admission; his own acquiescence, totally unafraid; and then the spine-tingling, awe-ful dread as the entity suddenly was *in* the circle and reaching out to touch him.

But he could not remember what had happened after that. Something of knowledge had been imparted, he felt sure, but he could not quite grasp it in conscious memory. It had been important, too—something more than a mere approval and acceptance of him, though that certainly had been given.

More thoughtful now, Kelson stood and dispelled his circle, curiously clear-headed for all that had occurred, then went to the pool to drink and wash. He immersed his head to clear it, and water streaming down his back raised gooseflesh as he paused, still kneeling, to glance up at the statue once more, trying again to see eyes or even some expression in the shadow where the face should be.

"I hope that you'll forgive me if I don't yet fully understand," he said aloud, as if the statue had ears to hear him as well as eyes to see him kneeling there. "I think you told me things last night, and I'm afraid I can't remember. Is that also part of the plan? Will it somehow come to me when I need it, remaining hidden until then?"

When no answer came, Kelson sighed and set his fists on his hips, feeling a little exasperated.

"Very well, then. I can only go on instinct, if you won't give me any more tangible sign. I believe in you, Saint Camber of Culdi, and I think you make a worthy example and source of strength for our people. God knows, they need something to help them survive in this mad, hate-filled world. So I'm going to restore your cult, as I promised."

He rose at that, standing with his hands relaxed along his sides.

"That's not all I'm going to do, either. Shrines and other places of devotion are important, but I'm also going to rebuild the wasted places of our people and found schools to teach them what we've lost in the last two hundred years—as we find it, of course. A lot of it will have to be rediscovered, but we can do that, especially with your help. The lost

Healing gifts are particularly important—and we now have three people who seem to have them. Thank you for Dhugal's discovery, by the way, if you had anything to do with that.''

He sighed and glanced around, suddenly feeling a little silly to be talking to a statue. He did not regret any of the night's experience, but it was time to reap its further fruits. With utter dignity then, even in his nakedness, he bent his knee a final time to the statue of the Deryni saint, bowing his head in homage.

Then he was turning to make his way carefully back along the narrow passageway, fingertips trailing the wall on one side while his other hand guarded against projections from the ceiling, for the passageway was much darker, heading away from the light. The door at the end swung back effortlessly at his touch, and his appearance, as he emerged from the doorway, triggered an awed outpouring of chanted psalms.

The next hour passed in something of a blur for Kelson. They would not let Dhugal come to him at first, though the sheer joy on the young border lord's face was easy enough to read. They wrapped him in a cloak of royal blue this time and put a drink of goat's milk and honey in his hands— ancient custom, they told him, symbolic of revival as he emerged into the light of the new dawn. When he had drunk it to the dregs as required, they enthroned him before the altar in a chair that looked suspiciously like a cross between a bishop's and a king's chair.

It was also Palm Sunday, he learned, as Brother Michael proceeded to celebrate a subtly different Mass of Thanksgiving from that to which Kelson was accustomed. And Kelson's acclamation as king, in the course of the Mass, drew startling parallels to another sacred king who had entered a holy city on a like day, more than a millennium past, to the same ritual cries of, ''Hosanna! Blessed is he who cometh in the name of the Lord.''

The formal ordeal past, however, they seemed to accept Kelson's previous assurance of beneficence, even before they had heard his account of the night's events. That was to be formally tested directly after the Mass. It was not until the Kiss of Peace, just before the Communion, that Dhugal finally was able to approach him. His whispered reassurances, both verbal and mental, as the two of them embraced, served to bring Kelson rudely back to the reality outside the walls of the shrine, for it was only then he discovered that Dhugal had managed to make brief contact with Morgan and Duncan, who were heading toward them at all speed, hopefully to rendezvous before the next sunset. Little though it had crossed his mind before, struggling only to survive, Kelson suddenly remembered how his kingdom must be foundering, thinking him dead. And wondering how Nigel fared, thinking himself king, the urgency to return was suddenly upon him.

But first must come the recounting of his ordeal, to the satisfaction of their captors—though the village folk had really ceased to be that when Kelson appeared in the doorway, apparently unscathed. When the Mass had ended and they gathered at his feet like so many hopeful children, he told them everything he could remember about Camber and the form of the vision he had experienced of the Deryni saint. He did *not* mention the dream of Rothana. He endured their Truth-Reading without resistance, reiterating his vow to reestablish Deryni schools as well as restore their saint, and their enthusiasm trebled.

By the time he finished talking, he had them completely in his thrall. When he told them then that he must leave them, at least for the present—that the rest of his kingdom must surely be in mourning over his supposed loss and possibly in danger from foreign enemies—their acclamation turned to hard, practical offers of assistance. By noon, he and Dhugal had eaten a modest meal and were well mounted on shaggy, sturdy mountain ponies. They rode briskly out of the valley of Saint Kyriell's with a jubilant escort of six young mountain men to see them safely back to Rhemuth, all of them garbed in the traditional mountain attire of kilted leathers and rough-spun, tweedy plaids, fur-lined cloaks pulled close against the cold.

By dusk, they still had not made physical contact with Morgan and Duncan, so Kelson halted long enough to send out a quick but powerful call, not even bothering to dismount, but only letting Dhugal hold his reins while he slipped efficiently into deep trance. Apparently strengthened by what he had gone through, his call yielded almost immediate results. By moonrise, a few hours later, their mountain escorts were treated to the rare sight of two normally dignified dukes of the realm throwing themselves from their blooded horses to sprint across a wind-scoured clearing on foot and embrace king and border earl, two whooping bordermen galloping joyous circles around all of them.

They did not press on that night, for the news Morgan and Duncan related after their initial, exuberant reunion was grave and wanted clearer heads than would be possible if they pushed on without rest. Two adjoining camps were made—one for the king and his three closest compatriots and one for the MacArdry men and the folk of Saint Kyriell's—and after a light repast, the royal party settled around the smaller of the two campfires for a council of war. Kelson listened in silence as Morgan recounted Duncan's finding of Tiercel's body, Nigel's illness, Conall's presumed marriage by now to Rothana, and, finally, his and Duncan's suspicions about Conall himself.

"We haven't any proof yet that he's done these things," Duncan said, when Kelson had asked a few stunned questions and listened quietly to their speculations. "But who else had as much to gain as he did, under the circumstances? The fact remains that Tiercel is dead, Nigel is dying, and Conall thinks he's about to become king at any moment, with the full might of the Haldane legacy already confirmed in him. And let me tell you, he didn't waste any time suggesting *that*, as Nigel's condition deteriorated."

Dhugal scowled. "Couldn't it be argued that he was only doing the prudent thing, making sure he would have the power to defend the kingdom, since he thought Kelson was dead and his father wasn't able to govern?"

"That could be argued," Morgan agreed, "and very likely, Conall will argue it. But whether he got his powers through Tiercel or through our efforts—the latter of which I doubt, looking back—he has the full Haldane potential now. I seriously doubt he's going to want to give up the crown that's all but in his grasp, just because Kelson's come back alive. And even if he's entirely innocent in all of this, there's still the matter of his rather precipitous marriage to Rothana."

Sadly, Kelson nodded. That Conall might have betrayed him was not really surprising, given the circumstances and the jealousy increasingly between them these last few years, but Conall could be dealt with, if necessary. What shocked Kelson, in quite a different way from his concern for Nigel, was Rothana's apparent defection. Word of that had set a cold, leaden lump in his stomach; he was only just able to keep it from driving him to tears.

"Conall will be given a chance to explain himself," Kelson said quietly, after a long silence. "I don't want to believe these things of my own cousin. There *could* be some other explanation."

"I hope so," Duncan said, "for Conall's sake as well as yours."

Dhugal nodded. "If we're all lucky, maybe it will turn out that he's only been guilty of opportunism—and that isn't necessarily a crime."

When they had settled down to sleep, though, after agreeing to ride on to Valoret and its Portal in the morning, Kelson lay awake in his bedroll for some time, finally reaching out to touch Dhugal's shoulder. They were bracketed between Morgan and Duncan, with the rest of the men bedded down around the second fire except for the watch, and everyone else seemed to be asleep.

"Dhugal are you awake?" Kelson whispered.

Lifting his head briefly, Dhugal nodded and closed his hand over the king's, shifting to mind-speech.

You're worried, aren't you?

Not really worried. Even if the worst turns out to be true, I can take care of Conall. And with three of you able to function as Healers now, even Nigel may come out of this all right.

It's Rothana, then, isn't it? Dhugal returned. *Kelson, I'm so sorry. You really loved her, didn't you?*

Sighing, Kelson laid his free arm across his eyes, wishing he could blot out what he was feeling.

I dreamed about her last night, Dhugal—after I had the Camber vision. It was her wedding night, wasn't it, though I didn't know that then. We made love. It was so real that I—well, let's just say that it was very, very real. You don't suppose I was tapping into—her and Conall, do you?

Not at that distance, or behind all that rock, Dhugal replied, though with the fragments of memory that leaked across his link with Kelson—quickly blocked, for he did not want to know—another image was coming to him, of his own observation of Brother Michael and the girl Rhidian, just past midnight, going quietly through another door near the one that had closed behind Kelson, unobserved by most of the dozing congregation. Michael had returned almost immediately, but Rhidian had not—not for nearly an hour. Dhugal found himself wondering whether Kelson's "dream" might have been more real than even he suspected—some form of sexual initiation, shrouded in the oblivion of the mind-tricking fumes, perhaps even a ritual marriage of the sacred king with the land, in the person of Rhidian, as sometimes had been practiced in ancient times by the ancestors of the mountain folk sleeping beside the next fire. Kelson might not have been aware of these traditions, but Dhugal was, being closer to the land through border myth and folklore very like that of these mountain people, so long exiled and apart. Perhaps Kelson's experience had been very, very real.

But he did not say that to Kelson. It was stunning enough that so poignant a dream of Rothana should have been dashed to hopelessness by the news of her marriage to Conall. That it all might have been triggered by very real human agencies was a hurt that the king need not endure, on top of everything else.

And so Dhugal sequestered those suspicions away behind the special shields that he had constructed after healing Kelson, when he and the king both had realized the necessity for some things never to be shared. Kelson could not help being aware that something was going on behind Dhugal's shields, but he concluded that it was simply the young borderer's reluctance to intrude on the intimacy of Kelson's dream; so Kelson, too, relegated that memory to the depths where others would never go, finally lying back with a sigh.

I'm sorry about the spill-over, there at the beginning, he sent after a few more seconds. *I didn't mean to disturb you. This is something I'm simply going to have to work out for myself, when we get back. She thought I was dead, after all.*

Yes, I'm sure she did, Dhugal replied. *Do you want some help sleeping?*

No, I slept last night, far more deeply than I would have wished, came Kelson's response. *How about you, though? Shall I put you to sleep?*

The offer was the most tantalizing Dhugal had heard in

days, and he readily agreed, for it meant that he would not dream. He gave a soft, grateful sigh as Kelson's hand shifted to his forehead. The next thing he knew, sunlight was shining in his eyes and the smell of roasting meat was rousing him, truly rested for the first time in weeks.

CHAPTER TWENTY-SEVEN

Ask now the priests concerning the law.

—Haggai 2:11

Slowed by rugged terrain and another vicious spate of weather on the way back toward Valoret, Kelson and his companions were nearly four days reaching that cathedral city. Once there, Kelson decided to spend a few more days reviewing the progress of the bishops' synod before going on to Rhemuth by Portal, for the clarification of Duncan's status, at least, had become an even more important issue, given the difficulties the king expected to encounter once he returned to the capital. The delay would not endanger the element of surprise necessary to confound Conall, if that prince truly was the architect of what had been happening, for even if messengers rode night and day, word that Kelson was alive could not reach Rhemuth before Easter Monday. The king, however, would make his appearance the day before, having decided that Easter itself was a most propitious time to return from the grave, as it were. Unfortunately, the irony would probably be lost on Conall.

The bishops, meanwhile, had continued independently at the work they set out to do at the beginning of Lent, even though Cardiel and Arilan had returned to the capital to counsel Conall, and Bradene, too, had absented himself briefly to assist in the solemn proclamation of Conall as king. The primate was back in his see by Holy Week, however, and thus he was on hand to witness Kelson's astonishing ride through the city gates of Valoret on Maundy Thursday, miraculously alive and restored to his people.

The cathedral bells pealed for hours in a joyous paean of celebration, in total disregard for the usual bans on such displays at this most solemn season of the liturgical year, and by midafternoon the bishops gathered in a rapidly filled cathedral to sing a jubilant *Te Deum,* in thanksgiving for the king's safe return. For the rest of the day, the usual Lenten dietary restrictions were also relaxed to allow for moderate feasting in the archbishop's refectory that night, though Kelson and his companions chose to eat sparingly, anyway. Kelson accomplished nothing that night save to tell his story again and again to various groups of bishops and other clerics and turned in early to be fresh for the next day's tasks.

But next morning, after the obligatory ceremonies of Good Friday, when the city had recovered from its initial shock, the king convened his bishops in the chapter house where he had addressed them weeks before and asked for a report on their progress. He was pleased to learn that there had been a great deal, even after his supposed death.

First of all, nominations had been made to fill all of the previously vacant sees, with appointment awaiting only royal approval, which Kelson freely gave. Likewise, six new itinerant bishops had been elected to roam at large in the kingdom, with four positions yet to be filled, as and when suitable candidates could be found. These, too, Kelson approved. In addition, the canonization of the late Bishop of Meara, Henry Istelyn, had been approved unanimously, with formal declaration of his status set for later in the year.

But most important of all, so far as Kelson was concerned, most of the draft work on the rewriting of the Statutes of Ramos had been completed. He spent the best part of Good Friday going over the document with Morgan, Duncan, and Dhugal, making but few amendments and alterations, and by sunset had pronounced himself well satisfied with the way the material was taking shape. By the next morning, the last he planned to spend in Valoret, he was ready to tackle the most delicate negotiation.

"I cannot tell you how pleased I am with what you have accomplished in the past month, gentlemen," he told the assembled bishops, during a closed session in which only Morgan, Dhugal, and himself were not ordained priests. "I should not wish to tempt true disaster by saying it, but perhaps my 'death' was not such a terrible thing after all, if this is the kind of memorial you make to me." He silenced their faint, nervous laughter with an upraised hand.

"In all seriousness, however," he resumed, "I should like to think of your work as a living memorial, if you will—for you have served me and all of Gwynedd, both present and to come, by your earnest intentions to right the wrongs inadvertently and, alas, sometimes intentionally imposed upon loyal subjects of this land for many, many generations. Judging by what you have proposed, I hope I may assume that you believe Deryni can be a valuable part of the many and varied peoples who make up this kingdom—and not merely because four of them are sitting here before you, and one of them is your liege lord. Indeed, were it not for these three, I would not be here today."

Another ripple of faint uneasiness passed among the listening bishops, though it was not tinged with fear, as it had been so often in the past, but only with the slight apprehension natural to anyone contemplating something just a little unknown.

"Which brings us to the last item I should like to present for your consideration," Kelson went on, "and that is the full reinstatement of one of your own number, who has served me and Gwynedd in ways most of you can hardly begin to fathom. I refer, of course, to Bishop Duncan McLain, whose loyalty and service to myself and my father before me can in no way be impeached. And since that part of the Statutes of Ramos forbidding those of his blood to take holy vows is now in the process of being rescinded, I would pray that you extend him the right hand of brotherhood and forever put aside any reservations you may have had because of his Deryni blood. I believe he has proven far too often that it is just as red as anyone's and that he has always been willing to shed it to defend our crown and land."

Duncan, sitting quietly a little behind Kelson, austere and solemn in the plainest of black working cassocks, rose respectfully at the gesture of Archbishop Bradene, waiting as the archbishop glanced around the room at his colleagues. He and Bradene had conversed briefly the night before and agreed on a format for what they hoped would follow, but

its success depended upon whether the other bishops would
go along.

"Your Majesty," Bradene said quietly, still watching his
colleagues, "in the matter you have just addressed, I personally am satisfied that, in every instance save one, perhaps, Duncan McLain has acted for the honor of his God,
his king, and himself, in that order of priority. If any shadow
of a doubt remains in my mind, it concerns his personal jus-
tifications at the time he accepted ordination to the priesthood, knowing that he was Deryni and that the Church forbade him this sacrament."

A murmur of agreement rippled through the assembly,
but again, it was not hostile—only wary. Kelson allowed
himself to breathe a little as Bradene went on.

"I propose, then, that Father Duncan confess those jus-
tifications openly before this assembled company, and that
if, in our opinion, he can be absolved of wrongdoing, absolution be granted and the matter nevermore brought before
this assembly—for I should hate to lose so able a shepherd,"
he concluded, giving Duncan a faint but genuinely warm
smile. "Is anyone opposed?"

Miraculously, no one was. And so, with Kelson, Morgan,
and Dhugal watching very much as outsiders—for what was
about to transpire was under the full seal of the confessional
for the priests seated in the room—Duncan came forward
to kneel at the foot of Bradene's throne. The bishop's ring
on his right hand flashed in the torchlight as he bowed his
head and crossed himself—the ring wrought of gold that formerly had been a piece of altar plate associated with Saint
Camber—and his blue eyes were almost silver as he looked
up at the archbishop, clasping his hands before him.

"I confess that on the Feast of Easter, in the Year of Our
Lord 1113, I accepted ordination to the priesthood from
Archbishop Alexander of Rhemuth, knowing that I was Deryni and that canon law forbade my reception of this sacrament."

"And why did you do this, my son?" Bradene asked.

Duncan's vocation had never been so apparent, as he
gazed into Bradene's eyes.

"I believed and still believe that I was called by God to
be His priest and that the gifts of my Deryni inheritance

should be turned to His service, as Deryni priests had served Him in prior times."

"And what of the Church's teachings, that Deryni might no longer serve in this way?" Bradene asked.

"My decision was a matter of conscience, Excellency, formed by years of study and prayer. The Church also teaches that, once formed, not to have followed my conscience would have been a serious, grievous sin.

"And so, knowing that I was called, how could I *not* have responded to His will? His call was an ache within me that could not be satisfied save by giving myself wholly to His service—a yearning to be constantly in His presence, offering His sacraments to His people, both human and Deryni. And in offering those sacraments, I, too, become a part of them, and myself offer up all that I am upon God's altar, to use as He wills. Is there a man here among the clergy who has not heard and heeded that call?"

There was not, of course—or at least none who would admit it. One elderly itinerant bishop asked about the evil inherent in Deryni powers, but Duncan's old friend Hugh de Berry, the newly appointed Bishop of Ballymar, answered that argument before Duncan could.

"It is not power that is evil, your Excellency," Hugh said, "but the use to which evil men sometimes put their power. Surely we are more sophisticated than to believe that a valuable gift should be destroyed because someone unscrupulous once used such a gift for other than its intended purpose and brought destruction with it, rather than joy. Are we not all given certain gifts at birth, that, with proper training, make one man strong, another scholarly, another nimble of fingers, still others bound by every breath they take to give their lives in God's service? Are Father Duncan's gifts so different? How dare we say that it is not to God's glory that Duncan can ascertain whether a man speaks the truth, protect the innocent against those who would misuse their power, or heal the injured? Have you forgotten, Excellency, that Duncan McLain, like Our Lord, has the gift of *Healing* in his hands? Who better than a Deryni Healer-priest to heal the rifts and exorcise the fears that have separated us from our Deryni brothers?"

Little remained to be said after that impassioned appeal. As Hugh took his seat and Duncan continued to kneel before the archbishop, Bradene requested a period of meditation, at the end of which each bishop was to cast his written vote as to whether Duncan should be absolved. Kelson closed his eyes while the voting went on, listening to the whisper of silks and fine wools as each bishop took his ballot to a small table in the center of the chapter house, just at Duncan's back, and dropped it into a large chalice. When everyone was done, Bradene himself went to the table and began to read the ballots, Duncan raising his eyes to the crucifix above the archbishop's empty throne as the votes were read.

"*Absolvo,*" came the first vote. I absolve him.

"*Absolvo.*

"*Absolvo.*

"*Absolvo.*"

The tally went on without a single dissenting vote, a full nineteen repetitions of the healing word: "*Absolvo.*" At the end, Duncan buried his face in his hands and wept tears of joy that he made no attempt to hide. His eyes were still wet when he looked up again as Bradene came to sit once more upon the episcopal throne. The archbishop was smiling. Nor had Duncan's tears been the only ones in the ancient chapter house.

"Duncan Howard McLain, you who are called to be Christ's priest," Bradene said formally, paralleling the calling forward of a priestly candidate to be ordained as he referred to a book that Bishop Tolliver came and knelt to hold for him.

"*Adsum,*" Duncan replied softly. Here am I.

"Duncan Howard McLain," Bradene repeated. "According to the ordinal under which you were ordained these twelve years hence, you were commanded and charged, under pain of excommunication, not to come forward for ordination to God's holy priesthood under any pretext if you were irregular, excommunicate in law or by judicial sentence, under interdict or suspension, illegitimate, infamous, or in any other way disqualified. At that time, according to the letter of the law, being Deryni was not only a disqualification from the priesthood, but an automatic death sentence if you had been discovered after your ordination.

"And yet, in the spirit of the law, you came forward and accepted the yoke of God's holy priesthood, obeying a higher call than that which had prompted frightened men to make frightening laws two hundred years before, in the aftermath of a terrible tyranny—for you knew in your heart that you were called. By the letter of the law, you would have incurred the most severe penalties of Church and state had you been discovered; but in the spirit of the law, you chose to serve God despite the danger, remaining true to your conscience and your calling, in hope that God's will and man's might one day be as one again."

Bradene sighed as he closed the book and gave leave by gesture for Tolliver to return to his seat.

"I wish I could say for certain that God's will and man's are, indeed, one at last, though I believe—and your brothers obviously believe—that in this matter at least, we are reaching a little nearer that perfect reunion with His will, by the progress we have made in these latter days. But you, beloved son in Christ, are surely more aware than any of us just how far we still have to go to right what was awry as the legacy of our forebears. Still, your brothers in faith have absolved you of any further guilt in whatever technical disobedience you may have committed in the past—and your own soul has been your harshest warder, I think, so far as any recompense that might be owed for expiation. Further, canon law will soon legitimize the truth you recognized more than a decade ago.

"Therefore do I absolve you as well, in the name of the Father, and of the Son, and of the Holy Spirit." He made the sign of the cross over Duncan's upturned head. "May almighty God have mercy on you, forgive you your sins, and bring you to life everlasting."

"Amen," the bishops said together, as Duncan also mouthed the response.

"May the almighty and merciful Lord grant you pardon, absolution, and remission of your sins," Bradene said, signing Duncan again.

Again, the assembly said, "Amen."

"And finally," Bradene concluded, "may the blessing of almighty God, the Father, Son, and Holy Spirit, descend upon you and remain with you forever."

The third "Amen" positively resounded among the ceiling beams as Bradene signed Duncan a third time, then gently laid both his hands on Duncan's head.

"I ask you a special favor now," Bradene said then, bending closer to Duncan's head as he took away his hands. "Will you again promise obedience and reverence to me and my successors, according to justice and according to your grade of ministry, as you promised on your ordination day, aware from this time hence that deception no longer will be necessary?"

Smiling, tears running openly down his cheeks now, Duncan placed his hands between Bradene's and ducked his head to kiss the archbishop's ring.

"*Promitto*." I promise.

"*Ora pro me, frater*." Pray for me, brother.

"*Dominus vobis retribuat*." May the Lord reward you.

With Duncan once more restored to his episcopal purple, a proper cassock lent by Bishop Hugh, the evening meal was cause for joyous if subdued celebration—for it was still Holy Saturday, after all, and the most solemn time of Lent. The fare was simple, but Duncan sat in a place of honor at the archbishop's right hand, Kelson deliberately taking the left, out of deference to Duncan's restoration to grace. Early on Easter morning, the king and his party kept the Paschal feast with the bishops in Valoret Cathedral, raising their voices with the choir in the joyous introit.

"*Resurrexi, et adhuc tecum sum, alleluia. . . .*" I have risen and am still with thee, alleluia; Thou hast laid Thy hand upon me, alleluia. . . . Lord, Thou hast seen me put to the test; Thou hast seen my death and my resurrection. . . .

Afterwards, when the Mass was ended and all of them had received Communion, the MacArdry men and Kelson's mountain folk as well, Duncan and Morgan led them into the sacristy, especially cleared for the occasion, and began taking them through the Portal. Archbishop Bradene also came.

Their emergence from the sacristy at Rhemuth Cathedral half an hour later, just as Archbishop Cardiel's High Easter Mass was ending, nearly provoked a riot. The sudden appearance of men in the rough border and mountain garb of Kelson's escort was first taken as an attack by local belligerents who had somehow managed to pass the city gates unchallenged and infiltrate the cathedral compound, for Kelson was not recognized immediately, being similarly dressed.

But Morgan was recognized, and then Duncan and Bradene. And then, as the company parted around Kelson, anger and fear melted into astonishment and then joy. The king had returned!

"Let's not make too much fuss, though," Kelson warned them, after the initial shouting had died down, when one of the priests wanted to begin ringing the cathedral bells, and the overjoyed Squire Dolfin asked whether he ought to ride to the castle to tell Prince Conall the good news. "And if you don't mind, I'd like to tell my cousin myself."

And so, it was a subdued but barely contained assemblage that began making its way from the cathedral complex up the hill to the castle gate, picking up followers as it went and the word spread. And Kelson, now that he was nearing home, prepared himself to meet his cousin Conall and the woman who was to have been his own queen, but was now his cousin's wife.

Conall, coming out of his father's bedchamber, shuddered and pressed the back of a trembling hand to his forehead for a moment when he had closed the door softly behind him. His mother had been bathing the comatose Nigel when Conall came to make his expected daily visit to the royal bedside. Seeing the once powerful body so wasted and frail had been a shock. He had not realized how much his father had deteriorated in two weeks of unconsciousness; and that recognition, colored by his own secret pangs of regret and guilt, made Conall's own rising star seem less bright—though there was nothing he could do or say about the situation without betraying himself, even if restoring Nigel were within his power.

He had mastered his trembling, but he was still very sober when he returned to the king's solar to sit in the sunshine and review the draft of a coronation plan submitted by Duke Ewan—premature, perhaps, but it would be necessary to have one ready when Nigel inevitably died, for the semi-limbo status necessitated by a regency ought not to be prolonged overmuch once the regent was king and ready to be crowned. Conall chewed on a heel of new white manchet bread as he read the draft, elegantly booted legs propped on a footstool, enjoying the luxury of one of Kelson's silk tunics next to his skin, the front and back adorned with golden Haldane lions. He came to his feet immediately, however, as Rothana joined him in the solar, hair unbound and looking sleepy still, wrapped in a fur-lined dressing gown of deep blue velvet.

"Darling, I had thought to let you sleep," he said, coming to put his arms around her from behind and nuzzle at her neck. "I'm afraid I let you have precious little rest last night. Can you forgive me?"

Her expression, had he been able to see it, might have been read as a trifle resigned or even indulgent, but no hint of anything but proper wifely affection was reflected in her voice.

"There is nothing to forgive, my lord. But I must not sleep the morning away. 'Tis Easter, and I've already missed the early Masses."

"I'll go with you," he murmured, turning her to nibble fond kisses across her lips and eyelids. "I've been already, but I'll go again, just to be beside you that much longer."

"Such devotion will surely gain you much grace, my lord," she replied, laughing a little as he caught her double meaning and held her even closer, kissing and caressing her as if he could not get enough of her.

"Oh, God, how I adore you, Rothana!" he whispered, when he had drawn back enough to look down into her eyes again. "I want to love you every hour of the day and night. I want to fill you with sons! I want us to be the greatest rulers Gwynedd has ever known, the beginning of an even more glorious line of Haldanes!"

She smiled a tiny, secret smile as he buried his face against her bosom again, gently stroking his sable hair for several seconds.

"Your wishes are coming true, then, my lord, for I think you have already filled me with sons—or with *a* son, at least."

As he pulled back to look down at her in astonishment, she lowered her eyes demurely.

"A son?" Conall breathed. "You're with child? Rothana, are you sure? How can you know so soon?"

She shrugged. "There are no objective signs yet, but Deryni women often—know. I have never been with child before, of course, but I believe that I have conceived. If so, your heir will be born next winter—a little Haldane prince."

"A—prince?" Conall whispered, awed. "Then, you know that it's a son as well?"

"Well, of course, my lord. One can—"

A commotion of some sort had been increasing in the castle yard for several minutes, and Conall held up a hand for silence as he strode to the window and pushed open one of the mullioned panes to look down. A large crowd of men, mostly on foot, many of them garbed in rough border tweeds and plaids, was surging through the gatehouse entrance and moving briskly toward the great hall steps. None of the men seemed belligerently armed, but Conall turned in alarm as booted feet pounded down the corridor outside and fists pounded against the solar door.

"Your Highness! Prince Conall!"

With sudden foreboding, Conall dashed to the door and wrenched it open.

"What is it?"

"The king, Your Highness! The king! He's come back!"

"My father's regained consciousness?" Conall gasped.

"No, King Kelson's come back!" the squire replied. "He's alive! And so is Lord Dhugal!"

Kelson stood holding the weeping Meraude in his arms as he watched Morgan, Duncan, and Dhugal bending over Nigel. Archbishops Bradene and Cardiel were in the room as well, but Ciard, Jass, and the escort of Saint Kyriell men stood guard outside to keep everyone else out. Bishop Arilan was nowhere to be found. Duke Ewan was gathering the court in the great hall, and spreading the word, but Kelson did not want to go down to them until he learned more about Nigel's condition.

"Oh, Kelson, he's dying," Meraude sobbed, shaking her head as Kelson continued to stroke her hair. "We thought you were dead, and then he had a seizure—"

A commotion outside the door announced the arrival of Conall, the only person the guards had orders to admit. Conall's face was white as whey as he slipped through the opening Jass allowed and came to fall to his knees at Kelson's feet. His hands were cold as ice as he took Kelson's hand to kiss it.

"Kelson—my Liege!—we thought you were dead! And then father took ill, and—"

"And you couldn't even wait a decent interval to wed my intended bride," Kelson said quietly, pulling his hand away and folding his arms across his chest as Meraude drew back a little. "Conall, even if you are proven innocent in every other point, I shall never forgive you for that."

"I only meant to secure the succession," Conall whispered, starting to get to his feet as his mother gasped at Kelson's implication. "Father was incapacitated, and I—"

"I have not given you permission to rise," Kelson said coldly, his mere glance causing Conall to sink back down.

"Kelson, that isn't fair," the prince protested. "I had no way of knowing you were still alive, and neither did Rothana. It's—incredible that you could have survived the waterfall. And then, when no bodies were found—"

"You still acted precipitously."

"Was it precipitous to attempt to secure the succession as soon as possible?" Conall retorted. "I was Regent of Gwynedd, for God's sake! No one had or has any idea how long my father might linger on. Why do you suppose the council has kept badgering *you* to marry, if getting an heir wasn't important?"

"Did they badger you?" Kelson snapped.

"No, not yet. But you and Rothana hadn't made any binding commitment, after all."

"Get up," Kelson said distractedly, for his attention had shifted suddenly to the men clustered at the head of Nigel's bed as Morgan drew back and beckoned him closer.

"As we feared, it was more than a simple seizure," Morgan said, as Kelson moved between the two archbishops at the foot of the bed, a wide-eyed and stunned Meraude hovering at his elbow. "There's a combination of actual physical trauma and some sort of psychic lock. We didn't see it before because we had no idea we should even look for it. It took a powerful Deryni to put it in place. Duncan and Dhugal are dealing with the actual physical damage, but we may need your help to resolve the other."

"A psychic lock," Meraude whispered, plucking at Kelson's sleeve. "Kelson, what is he saying?"

Kelson could not bear to look at Meraude, but he turned slowly to stare coldly at her eldest son.

"I fear you will have to ask your son about that, Aunt. Conall, do you know anything about it?"

"I? I don't even know what a psychic lock is. I mean, I sort of know now, but I didn't when he had his seizure," Conall explained. "Why are you looking at me that way?"

"Because I am Truth-Reading you, Conall Haldane, despite your efforts to cloud the issue," Kelson said, "and I don't like what I'm seeing. Did you do this to Nigel, your own father?"

Conall's shields slammed even tighter, before Kelson could get a clear reading, but the prince's mere belligerence could have been taken as an indication of guilt, even if it was not conclusive proof.

"How dare you ask me such a question?" Conall retorted.

"The King of Gwynedd dares to ask *any* question of his sworn vassal," Kelson snapped. "Or have you so soon forgotten the oath you swore me at your knighting?"

Before Conall could form an answer, Morgan reached out to beckon Kelson closer.

"He's coming around, my prince," Morgan said, watching as Duncan and Dhugal withdrew. "Breaking the lock wasn't as difficult as we feared, once we knew what to look for. The only problem may be a slight loss of memory."

But it soon became clear that whatever else had been impaired by Nigel's long incapacitation, his memory was not affected. In the course of dealing with the lock, Duncan had imprinted Nigel with the bare essentials of Kelson's rescue and return, so the royal duke was able to turn full attention to dealing with the cause of his previous condition as he opened his eyes and made them focus on Kelson.

"My king, you're alive," he whispered, his voice hoarse and scratchy with long disuse. "And my son, who wished me dead," he went on coldly, shifting his gaze to the terrified Conall, "would be better off dead himself, for having betrayed his blood and his sovereign. He killed Tiercel, Duncan," he went on. "I finally put the pieces together, after you had gone to fetch Alaric, and when I confronted him on it, he tried to kill me as well. I—suppose that being a Haldane myself is the only thing that saved me."

Conall tried to bolt at that, but the two archbishops and then Morgan were on him before he could reach the door, throwing him to the floor. Meraude screamed, and Dhugal and Duncan tried to keep Nigel from struggling to a sitting position.

Frantic, Conall attempted to bring his powers into play, but Morgan slapped the flat of a stiletto across his throat and searched for the right pressure points to knock him out as Cardiel and Bradene pinned his thrashing arms and legs, fighting the compulsion of Conall's mind.

"Conall, if you don't stop that, I swear I'll cut your throat!" Morgan barked. "Right now, nothing would give me greater pleasure."

"No, bind him!" Kelson commanded, as Morgan finally managed the right pressure points and the prince went limp. "He doesn't deserve that easy a death. But we'll have this settled once and for all, by the law. Duncan, I'll ask you and the archbishops to stay with my uncle. Dhugal, I want you to search Conall's rooms. Duncan told me that certain people wondered what ever became of Tiercel's drug satchel. I suspect you'll find it among Conall's things. I'm willing to wager that he was responsible for the *merasha* that went into your flask, so I'll give you the dubious honor of finding where he hid the rest."

"And where will you be?" Dhugal asked.

"In the Chapel Royal, convincing myself I should give this wretch a fair trial!" Kelson said, kicking the sole of one of Conall's boots. "And Morgan, get that Haldane tunic off him. He isn't fit to wear it. I'll have the Ring of Fire back as well, if you have to rip his finger off to get it."

Kelson left to the sound of Meraude weeping in Nigel's arms, but he could not bear to stay in the same room with Conall any longer, even with his cousin unconscious. He took Jass MacArdry with him and stationed that goodly knight outside the door of the chapel to see that he was not disturbed. There, after he had schooled his righteous anger to colder resignation—for there was little doubt of the outcome of the trial to come—he allowed himself to weep for what could never be righted, no matter what penalty Conall suffered for his crimes.

He was kneeling slumped over the altar rail, his face buried in one hand, when he heard the door open behind him. He turned his head, expecting it to be Dhugal, come to tell him it was time, but it was Rothana, muffled in a cloak of royal blue and with the hood pulled closer around her face. He rose awkwardly as she came toward him and the door closed, but he could read nothing behind her shields. She made him a profound curtsey, her head bowing nearly to the floor before she rose to meet his eyes. She had been crying, and she was no longer the fresh-faced, carefree innocent she had been before he left.

"I would throw myself and my husband on your mercy, my lord," she whispered, "but I know you can never forgive what we've done."

"And what have *you* done, that I could not forgive, Rothana?" Kelson asked, gently folding her hood back from her face. "Surely you had no part of Conall's treason."

But her hair was bound beneath the coif of a married woman, and Conall's gold and rubies weighted heavily on her left hand. Both of them knew that, even if losing faith was not an act of treason, things could never be as they had been.

"You are kind, Sire," Rothana whispered, "but I know my own guilt. I am no longer worthy of you."

"Rothana—"

"No, hear me, Sire. I gave up hope. And now I am Conall's wife, bound to him for life, no matter what his condition."

"His life," Kelson said sharply, "is almost certainly to be forfeit. Such is the fate of murderers and traitors. And when he is dead, I still would take his widow to wife, if she agreed."

"She could not agree, Sire," Rothana whispered, lowering her eyes. "The Church could not agree. We are consanguineous now, by virtue of my marrying your first cousin."

"A dispensation could be obtained."

"No dispensation could alter the fact that I am with child by him."

"With child!"

"I carry Conall's son, my love," Rothana said miserably, looking up at him with tears welling in her eyes once more. "That changes things."

"No! It only means that *our* children would have an elder half brother, also of Haldane blood," Kelson replied, without hesitation. "Rothana, I love you. Don't do this to us!"

"I wish I could do otherwise, in honor, Sire," she said. "But Prince Conall Haldane, my lawful, wedded lord, is the father of the child I bear, and his acts of murder and treason make me no longer fit to be your queen."

"No! His crimes do not touch you!"

"In law, perhaps not, Sire, but in fact, one has only to look at how my cousin Richenda has suffered for being the widow of a traitor to guess how much worse it would be for a queen—and for that queen's king. I could not do that to Gwynedd, my lord—and I could not let *you* do that to this land that you wed before you ever thought of wedding a queen. So do not take our former relationship into your reckoning, because I can never be yours now, no matter what you do."

Half an hour later, Kelson went down to the great hall, only Dhugal accompanying him through the cheering throngs. He deliberately had not changed into Haldane attire himself, letting the rough, slightly barbaric splendor of his mountain leathers and tweeds speak for the very uncivilized anger that still smoldered in his heart. He wore the Ring of Fire again, however, along with the Eye of Rom and his Saint Camber medal. In the crook of his arm, he carried the unsheathed Haldane sword like a royal scepter.

His steps faltered only once, just before he reached the dais, as he saw Rothana, in Meraude's company now, slipping in through a side door to huddle forlornly with her mother-in-law on a bench near the pallet where Nigel had been brought. The royal duke, attended by Duncan and Father Lael, was propped up on mounds of pillows, his eyes fever-bright as he struggled to rise at Kelson's approach, only to have Duncan command him to lie down again. Dhugal had Tiercel's water-stained drug satchel over his shoulder, with a look on his face that bespoke thoughts of murder, and Morgan waited just outside the rear doors with Conall, surrounded by the Saint Kyriell men and half a dozen fully armed knights. A further contingent of Haldane archers had been stationed in the upper galleries, arrows already nocked to bowstrings and ready to draw, certain proof against even a Deryni prisoner gaining very much advantage before he could be cut down.

The cheering continued as the king turned to face his assembled lords, and he stood a long time, caressing the hilt of the Haldane sword, as their shouts of acclamation echoed among the high beams of the hall. Bradene and Cardiel stood behind the throne to either side, and at Kelson's glance, as the shouting died down, the former brought forward the oldest and plainest of Kelson's official crowns: a band of hammered gold two fingers wide, chased with a design of Celtic interlace and set with small, round cabochon rubies in some of the interstices. It was also the most primitively designed and went well with the mountain leathers and tweeds he wore. The hall grew hushed as the king bent his head to receive it from the archbishop's hands with a murmured word of thanks and rippled in new but quieter comment as he took his seat.

"My lords, I thank you for your welcome," Kelson said, when silence at last lay like a tranquil pond before him. "It is good to be home and even better to know that your loyalty is unshaken. I wish I could say that all of my subjects had remained so loyal during my absence, but unfortunately, this is not the case in at least one appalling instance.

"Before proceeding to deal with this unpleasantness, however, it is my pleasure to bring you happier news—that my beloved Uncle Nigel, who has always served me and our family with such devotion, is back among us and recovering—if weaker than he would have us believe," he added, with a glance of mock disapproval in Nigel's direction. "But in a few weeks, his physicians and I have every reason to believe that he will be back to his full-time occupation of bullying my royal pages and squires into becoming fine warriors and young men of honor, as well as continuing as one of my most trusted and valuable advisers. I give you welcome and thanks, Uncle."

As the hall erupted in shouts of enthusiastic approval, Kelson glanced again at Nigel, who ducked his head awkwardly, blinking back proud tears as Meraude came to kneel at his side. Behind him, comforted by Duncan, the two younger Haldane cousins, Payne and Rory, stood ill-at-ease and frightened looking, trying not to be obvious as they searched the back of the hall for sign of their elder brother. And Rothana, huddling even smaller on her bench, would not raise her eyes. Kelson sighed as he turned his gaze away from that sad little family.

"Another thing I have to tell you concerns my faithful friend and confessor, Bishop Duncan McLain, the Duke of Cassan." He could feel Duncan tensing over his shoulder, but he did not turn his eyes back in that direction. "Many of you have been aware for some time now that Father Duncan is Deryni." He held up a hand to silence the murmurs of comment that threatened to disrupt the room again at this open and unequivocal admission of Duncan's Deryni status. "I am also aware that some of you have voiced concerns as to what this disclosure would mean to his status as a priest and bishop.

"I am happy to be able to tell you that I have just come from the synod now meeting in Valoret, and that the Ramos Statutes barring Deryni from the priesthood are in the process of being rescinded. Yesterday, as Archbishop Bradene will attest, the bishops voted unanimously to uphold Father Duncan's status as a priest and bishop in good standing, granting him pardon and absolution for any errors committed in the past because of this unjust former ruling. I am assured that this absolution will be extended to any other Deryni who may presently be in holy orders, thus mitigating the grave injustices perpetuated in the past against those who came to God's service in defiance of the laws of man and whose only sin was that they were born Deryni.

"All of which brings us to a major departure from our former official posture regarding Deryni. The law is being changed to remove merely being Deryni from any list of crimes. But part of the reason this has not always been so in the past is because the majority of people have not been aware of the true abilities and limits of Deryni—and it is a weakness of our race, human and Deryni, that we fear what we do not understand. Therefore, what I am about to bring before you will be conducted in all openness, so that all may know that being Deryni, or even being royal, is no bar to equal and just treatment under the law. Some of what may transpire will surprise, shock, or even frighten you—but I believe it is time that you knew the truth."

He raised his eyes to the back of the hall, where Morgan had moved into sight with Conall at his side.

"Alaric, Duke of Corwyn, bring in the prisoner."

A collective gasp rippled through the assembly as Morgan slowly walked Conall down the hall, his stiletto still held casually against the side of Conall's throat, the prince's hands bound before him, grey Haldane eyes blazing defiance and anger.

CHAPTER TWENTY-EIGHT

A king that sitteth in the throne of judgment
scattereth away all evil with his eyes.

—Proverbs 20:8

Nearly everything eventually came to light in the trial that followed, beginning with Conall's tearful, impassioned denial after Tiercel's drug satchel was produced.

"I didn't start out to betray you, Kelson," he sobbed, "but things—happened. It wasn't fair! Why should you have gotten everything, just because your father was older than mine? You got to be king, you got all the glory—and the power—and you were going to take the woman I wanted, too. I saw you with her in the garden, that last night before we left on the quest!"

"And so you decided to kill your rival?" Morgan said, as Rothana buried her face in her hands and wept silently, and Kelson went tight-jawed.

"No!" Conall replied. "I was jealous—I admit that—but I never actually would have done anything to Kelson. He was my king."

"Yet you put *merasha* in Dhugal's wine flask, knowing that Kelson might drink from it, too," Duncan said. "Surely you knew what it would do."

"I know nothing about *merasha*," Conall insisted, though none of the Deryni present had any doubt that he was lying. "I was—jealous of Dhugal, too, but I never would have tried to kill him."

"But you were quick to take advantage of the situation,

416

once you believed Kelson and Dhugal were dead," Archbishop Bradene said.

Defiantly Conall lifted his head.

"Fate seemed to have eliminated both my rivals, without my lifting a finger," he said haughtily. "Meanwhile, I had a responsibility to my royal line. *Everyone* believed that Kelson was dead—including Alaric and Duncan! And that meant that my father was king—and I was his heir. It was appropriate that I take a suitable bride at once and secure the succession, as my royal cousin had failed to do. Whatever else I may have done in error, I at least have fulfilled my dynastic duty, for my lady wife carries my child. Nor is there any crime in *that*."

And indeed, there was none; no man could say there was, though many might lament that it had occurred, after the fact. All eyes turned toward Rothana in shock, but she only kept her head bowed over her clasped hands, sitting forlornly on her bench near Nigel's pallet.

"And what of Tiercel's death?" Duncan asked. "Do you maintain that there was no crime in that, either?"

"It was an accident," Conall replied. "We argued. Both of us said things we shouldn't have. It degenerated into pushing, and he—went over backwards and hit his head. I didn't mean to kill him, but I was afraid I would be blamed."

"And you were feeling guilty, because you had been seeing Tiercel secretly," Morgan added coldly. "And the reason you were seeing him secretly is because you *were* engaged in a crime with him—for you were plotting to usurp the Haldane magic, which has always been reserved to the senior Haldane. You planned eventually to rival the king for the throne. That's why, when Duncan and I took measures to confirm you in the Haldane powers—after you had struck down your own father with your illicit power—both of us had the feeling that something was not quite right. We couldn't really confirm you in the power, because you had already usurped it for yourself, in defiance of the law."

"No! It wasn't that way at all!"

"Then, how was it, cousin?" Kelson demanded. "We know that Tiercel always maintained that more than one Haldane could hold the power at a time—and you two set out to prove it, didn't you? And now we know exactly why it was always forbidden before."

The interrogation went on for several hours. Partway through it, an overjoyed but fearful Jehana arrived, escorted by Father Ambros, but Duncan intercepted them and had Ambros take her to a seat in one of the upper galleries before she could interrupt, for Kelson did not need her distraction at a time like this. Kelson marked her arrival, but he did not allow it to shake his resolve. He sighed and slowly nodded when Conall at last wound down in his latest attempt at justification.

"It's pointless to continue this," the king said quietly. "Your very refusal to allow yourself to be Truth-Read condemns you, Conall. What would *you* do, if you were I? How would you resolve this sad, sad state of affairs?"

Conall, sitting dejectedly in a straight-backed chair, with Morgan and Jass MacArdry standing guard to right and left of him, lifted his bound hands in a weary, futile gesture.

"What else could I do but kill me, cousin?" he said bitterly. "You killed my chances long ago of rising to my true birthright. And no matter what I say, you will condemn me now."

Kelson shifted uneasily, knowing that it was so. But before he could open his mouth to say anything, Conall suddenly gave a desperate lurch to the left and looped his bound wrists over Jass's head, bearing him backwards onto the floor, with Jass's body shielding his. He had overturned his chair as he launched himself from it; but, before it could hit the floor, he kicked it deftly into Morgan's path so that Morgan tripped and fell with it. Simultaneously, he conjured a blazing aura of white light around himself and Jass that immediately made Morgan recoil.

"Call off the archers, or he's a dead man!" Conall shouted, wrenching his head wildly from side to side to try to watch them all as Jass subsided jerkily. "I don't want to kill him, but, if I'm going to die anyway, I've got nothing to lose. Morgan, get back! You know what I can do. And if one arrow touches me, I can kill Jass before it kills me. I mean it!"

Kelson had sprung to his feet as the struggle erupted, and Dhugal was halfway down the dais steps—as, indeed, half the court had started forward instinctively, while the archers took aim and the rest of the MacArdry men began to move—

but the king's stiff gesture halted all further notion of intervention, at least for the moment.

"Conall, don't be a fool!" Kelson said. "Don't add deliberate murder to your list of crimes. What did Jass ever do to you?"

Conall only smiled and whispered something in Jass's ear, his eyes bright with defiance. The young border knight had ceased his struggling, arms slack at his sides to further shield Conall, and his eyes were half-closed. The field of energy keeping Morgan at bay distorted Deryni perception of precisely what else Conall was doing, but not enough to disguise the fact that he had taken control of Jass's mind—for Jass's hands slowly raised to begin untying Conall's wrists.

"Why don't you go ahead and have them cut me down, Kelson?" Conall taunted, glancing up triumphantly at the hesitant archers as Jass worked at the knots. "Kill me, the way you cut down Sicard MacArdry last summer. But I don't think you'll risk Jass's life further, if you can bargain instead."

"I don't bargain with traitors, Conall," Kelson said coldly, raising a hand to stay the archers in the balconies above. "But, just to humor me, suppose you tell me what you want. Surely you don't think I'd let you walk out of here, after what you've done."

Conall, his wrists freed at last, slid his right hand back to twist it several times in Jass's border braid, keeping the young knight's head very close to his own while his other arm stayed close around the young man's neck.

"I want you to face me in a proper Duel Arcane," Conall said softly, a wild, crafty look lighting his eyes. "I want you to face me the way you faced Charissa at your coronation— except that this time, the outcome will be a little different, because I've got Tiercel de Claron's knowledge behind me to augment all the Haldane power we've both got."

A ripple of indignation and disapproval rose and fell in the crowded hall, especially among the Deryni, but Kelson only set his jaw, barely containing his anger.

"Do you really think that would solve anything? Even if you won, Conall, no one would accept you. If you killed me, you wouldn't walk out of this hall alive, no matter how many innocent people had to die to prevent it."

"Then I would make certain that they paid a high price

for my life," Conall retorted, "and I would die in battle—
not at the hands of an executioner."

"And are you so certain you have to die?"

Conall snorted. "Do you take me for an idiot? There's
no way you can let me live, knowing what I can do. If you
don't kill me, you'll have to keep your best Deryni busy
guarding me night and day for the rest of my life—because,
having tasted the full sense of what it means to be a Haldane,
I'll never rest now until the crown is mine."

And though he would have wished it almost any other
way, Kelson knew that this was true, for Conall permitted
him to read it. Nigel knew it, too, sitting propped against
Duncan's shoulder and shielded by him—though he knew it
not by any Haldane magic, but only honest human intuition
and knowledge of his son. His eyes were dark with righteous
anger as he struggled weakly in Duncan's arms to sit up with
more dignity.

"I am ashamed for the honor of my family, Sire," he said,
as Kelson glanced in his direction. "He is my son, and I love
him—but I do not like him. All apart from what he did to
his own father, he has tried to usurp the throne and kill my
king. For that I cannot forgive him. He is a traitor. He must
die."

Nor could Meraude honestly plead her son's case, though
she said nothing in words, only turning pointedly away from
Conall as Kelson glanced at her.

"My lady?" Kelson said softly, turning his attention reluctantly to Rothana.

She would not meet his eyes.

"Do not ask me to speak for or against my husband,
Sire," she whispered. "Nor should my future be a factor in
what you decide. I shall never marry again—never! So do
what you know you must. Do what you were born and have
been trained to do."

Sighing, Kelson turned back to Conall, whose face had
gone hopeful and then a little sad as Rothana spoke. But the
prince immediately resumed his expression of defiance as he
looked back at Kelson, his arm tightening across Jass's
throat.

"She's said it all, hasn't she?" he said. "Do what you
must. And I shall do what *I* must."

"Very well," Kelson said wearily. "I suppose you must have your Duel Arcane. Now release Jass."

"And how do I know you will not order the archers to shoot me before we can meet in combat?" Conall countered, as Jehana slowly stood, suddenly realizing what was about to happen. "Remember, I've used the archers before, cousin. I know what they can do."

Kelson snorted derisively, but his mere glance made Jehana sit down again.

"I shall give you my word."

"Truly?" Conall replied. "On your honor and on the Haldane sword?"

Kelson colored, but he knew Conall had read him correctly. Kelson Haldane could not break an oath thus sworn.

"I swear on my honor and by this Haldane sword that I shall give you honorable combat, according to the ancient tenets laid down for the Duel Arcane—with two qualifications. First, if at any time before or during the combat you violate the terms, all oaths go by the boards, and I shall be free to deal with you in any manner I see fit."

"A reasonable concession, since I do not intend to violate the terms," Conall agreed. "And the second qualification?"

"The second qualification is that the Duel Arcane shall not necessarily be to the death within the circle, but only until one of us has a clear victory over the other. Presumably that will be me."

"A somewhat arrogant presumption, don't you think, cousin?" Conall retorted. "Or are you afraid to die in the circle?"

Kelson only shook his head sadly. "I do not intend to die *anywhere* today, Conall. But I do intend that *you* shall not have an honorable death in battle, but shall face just execution in the manner befitting a traitor."

The answer clearly angered Conall, but he seemed to realize that no more concessions were likely to be forthcoming.

"Very well, then. The question is moot, in any case, since I do not intend to die, either. But I swear by *my* honor—for whatever you may think that is worth—that I likewise shall abide by the terms of Duel Arcane, with the two conditions you have set. Which settles *that*," he added, rolling the compliant Jass off him and getting to his feet.

The archers stirred uneasily, some of them starting to raise their bows again, but Kelson's gesture stayed them.

"Let no one interfere," he said, rising briskly to hand his sword to Dhugal.

His crown he gave into Nigel's keeping, in pointed recognition that Nigel was still the heir, even if Conall should manage to win. As Kelson came down from the dais, Morgan was helping the groggy Jass to a seat on the steps. The king paused to convey his concern, setting one hand on the young border knight's shoulder.

"Are you all right, Jass?"

"Aye, Sire. I didnae want tae let him use me like that, but I couldnae help myself."

"Not your fault," Kelson murmured. "Don't worry about it. Alaric, do I need to be concerned on Jass's account? Conall hasn't planted any unpleasant surprises, has he?"

Morgan shook his head, tight-lipped. "It was strictly a contact control. There are no residuals. But be careful, my prince. From his Haldane potentials, Conall could be as powerful as you are. And there's no way to predict what additional information and skills he may have gotten from Tiercel."

"Well, he still hasn't got Deryni blood," Kelson replied, glancing up at Jehana with a reassuring smile. "Maybe that will make the difference."

"That, or experience," Morgan agreed. "Fortunately, he's new at this game. That's a disadvantage, regardless of how good his teacher was. Good luck, my prince."

Kelson nodded as he straightened. Conall was standing alone in the center of the hall, arms crossed on his chest, a faint glint of anxious anticipation lighting his otherwise smug expression. Someone had removed the chair to the side. As their eyes met, Kelson came down from the dais. Instantly the assembled lords began backing off to clear a larger space in the center of the hall, for many had been present when Kelson and Charissa dueled and knew what kinds of energies shortly would be raised and exchanged.

"You're sure you want to do this?" Kelson asked quietly.

For just an instant, Conall looked uncertain. But then he nodded emphatically.

"You've given me no choice," he whispered. "I'm backed into a corner. No matter what I do, I'm going to die.

But if I take you with me, that's something, isn't it? I only wanted what was rightfully mine, Kelson, but you were the king, and you wouldn't give it to me."

Kelson snorted contemptuously. "When did you ever demonstrate that you deserved to be given anything beyond what your birth entitled you to, by courtesy? You could have followed in your father's footsteps, Conall. Would that have been such a terrible fate?"

"My father may be a great warrior, but he has no ambition," Conall replied. "He might have been content to be always in second place, but I can't be. It isn't in my nature."

"Is it in your nature to accept disgrace, then?" Kelson countered. "Because that's the only thing you can hope to gain by this display."

"*One* of us will gain disgrace, but it shan't be I!"

"This is pointless," Kelson murmured. "Cast the circle."

"Me?" Conall squeaked.

"Yes, you. You started all of this. You can start this final folly, too. Or don't you know how?"

The gibe had its desired effect. Drawing himself up in wounded pride, Conall backed off three stiff paces and, without further preliminary, raised his arms above his head and then to the sides, murmuring a setting spell under his breath. A semicircle of crimson fire sprang up on the floor behind and around him, sending watching courtiers scurrying farther back to flatten themselves along the south wall of the hall, those on Kelson's side also retreating into the window embrasures on the north side.

Kelson tested at the barrier Conall had raised, satisfying himself that it would not require a death to release it, once he completed his part of the spell, then swept his own arms up and outward in a graceful arc, holding as he uttered the words that would produce the counter. More crimson fire sprang up behind him, matching Conall's, enclosing them both now in a circle of red.

"Your turn again," Kelson said, lowering his arms.

The lightness of the king's tone, suggesting the triviality of whatever Conall might attempt, angered the wayward prince, but Conall only raised his arms to shoulder level again, his palms turned inward toward the center of the circle.

"If you're expecting some trite piece of poetry, don't,"

Conall said. "My teacher didn't believe in such things. I affirm that the circle shall contain all power that we shall raise within it, so that none outside may be harmed, and that it shall not be broken until one of us has achieved a clear victory over the other. Is that your understanding?"

"It is," Kelson agreed, also raising his arms again. And at Conall's nod, Kelson began to pour energy into the binding of the circle as Conall did likewise, only barely aware, in his concentration, that the fire of the two arcs they had cast was rising to define a dome above their heads. When they were done, it was as if they stood beneath a dome of pinkish, faintly opalescent glass.

Almost as soon as the dome was in place, Kelson shifted into an assault mode, not even bothering to glance outside as he stalked closer to the center of the circle, away from the barrier ring. Under the circumstances, he was not given to theatrics, so there was little outward sign of the energies he began to gather—for as challenged, he did not intend to forfeit the right of first strike simply because Conall was of his blood. The attack was launched almost before Conall realized that battle was joined.

Conall staggered a little, absorbing the force of that first assault, but his shields wavered not at all, and he responded with a series of traditional testing spells that Kelson had countered before. The king did so again, with ease, and launched the expected testing spells of his own—which Conall answered as readily as Kelson had answered Conall's.

What followed next became a more earnest battle of wit and power. For a time, Kelson decided merely to hold firm and let Conall spend his first exuberance on pointless assaults. Conall took up the challenge, fueling his attacks with increasingly vivid visual imagery—nightmare visions out of his own worst dreams at first, but then a relentless succession of images out of Kelson's past, people and events that had either threatened Kelson or brought him great hurt: the fanatical and slightly mad Archbishop Loris, who had so terrorized Duncan; the doomed Sicard MacArdry, Dhugal's traitor uncle, to whom Conall had alluded before, falling helplessly with a war arrow in his eye, shot down by Kelson himself within a ring of Haldane knights and archers, unable to escape; Sicard's elder son, Prince Ithel of Meara, choking out his life at the end of a rope by Kelson's order, unshriven and unrepentant; another Mearan prince, a priest and bishop named Judhael, bowing before the headsman; Prince Llewell of Meara, Ithel's younger brother, accusing Kelson of blame for Sidana's death, just before the executioner took his head—and finally, Sidana herself, drowning in her own blood in Kelson's arms, the gore defiling the sacred altar before which they had just recited marriage vows.

That last shook Kelson most of all—until Conall followed up with vivid, graphic images of his own wedding night with Rothana that reverberated in Kelson's memory with his own erotic dream about her, during his ordeal in the cavern.

But it also brought back the memory of that other visitation within the cavern shrine—of the shrine's patron, grey-clad and powerful, standing at the edge of his circle and asking admittance; and Kelson had given it to him. He called on Saint Camber's presence now, conjuring *his* image in as fine a detail as he could—the quicksilver eyes that a man could drown in, so very like Haldane eyes; the roundish, kindly-looking face surrounded by silver-gilt hair; the gentle but powerful hands reaching inexorably toward his head— toward Conall's head.

And suddenly, Conall saw the image, too, and stepped back, startled, raising his hands in an alarmed, warding-off gesture as the figure of the saint did not retreat but continued to advance. Kelson stood very still, only staring at it, hardly able to breathe, uncertain whether he was even controlling the image any longer—though how Camber could have entered the sealed circle was beyond his comprehension. The last time Camber had come to call, Kelson had had to open a door.

But this entity, whether Camber himself or merely an illusion of Kelson's mind, had not been deterred by the circle. As it advanced on Conall, the prince continued to retreat, until finally his black-clad shoulders were hard against the glassy curve of the barrier circle—and still the apparition continued to advance.

Conall's scream, as the ghostly hands gently clasped his head, was one of the purest terror and echoed shrilly within the misty confines of the dome. Nor did the apparition vanish when Conall at last had screamed out his final defiance and slid bonelessly to the floor, clutching his temples, either dead or unconscious. The figure knelt beside the motionless prince for several seconds, head bowed, then rose gracefully and turned toward Kelson.

Hail, Kelson of Gwynedd. Now shalt thou truly be a king for humans and for Deryni, the being spoke in Kelson's mind, echoing words that another such being—or perhaps the same one—had spoken to Kelson at his coronation.

Dumfounded, the king dropped to one knee and bowed his head, crossing himself reverently.

Are you who I think you are? he dared to ask.

The figure had moved much nearer while Kelson bowed his head, and Kelson gasped a little as the figure stopped an arm's length away.

And who do you think that I am? the being replied.

Kelson's throat was very dry, and it was all he could do to swallow, very glad he did not need to speak with words.

I believe you are Saint Camber of Culdi, whom I sought on my quest. You—came to my aid.

Did I? the being answered. *Or am I but a convenient image for that stronger and better part that is within you and, indeed, within all folk who seek the Light, and which can be called up when darkness threatens?*

Kelson blinked. It had to be Saint Camber. Only the irascible Deryni saint would be so evasive and yet speak so primal a truth.

It doesn't matter, he dared to say next. *I'm still going to restore the cult of Saint Camber. I promised that, back in the shrine at Saint Kyriell's, and I'm going to do it, too. I'll build you a shrine the likes of which no one in all the Eleven Kingdoms has ever seen!*

The saint's chuckle surely must have been audible, but Kelson's ears were still ringing with the silence.

Dear, dear young champion of Light, do you truly think that I need physical edifices to guard my memory? My memorial is in the heart of every man and woman down through the ages who has been willing to sacrifice everything in the service of Light and Truth.

I don't mean to contradict you, Lord, Kelson dared to reply, *but a memorial means more to many folk if there's a physical focus for it. You don't—mind, do you, if I build you shrines?*

The being's laughter rang like tiny silver bells in the hollow confines of the dome, and he shook his head.

Human frailty—and Deryni, he answered. *You may build your shrines, if it gives you and them comfort. But keep what I have stood for; that is far more important.*

Yes, Lord, Kelson replied meekly. *Ah, have you any recommendations on what I should do with Conall?*

The apparition's face grew pensive, even a little wistful.

You must do what you must do, Kelson Haldane. It is a king's duty to render both mercy and justice, according to the circumstances. Only you can decide.

But, can't you give me some hint? Kelson persisted.

You must listen to your inner voice—your higher self. With prayer and meditation, you will know what to do.

But when Kelson would have pressed him further, the figure only moved a little closer and stretched forth his hands over Kelson's head.

Go in peace now, my son, the voice said in his mind, as the hands descended to touch his hair lightly. *Life and prosperity to thee, King of Gwynedd.*

At the very touch, the figure was gone, vanished in less than a blink of an eye, and the dome of the circle was disintegrating into thousands of tinkling, musical shards that slid down the curve of the dissolving barrier ring to shatter and dissipate on the stone floor in a silent music. Not a soul moved for several seconds, only scores of eyes darting from Kelson to Conall and back again. But when Kelson finally sighed and stood up, weaving a little on his feet, the murmur of renewed life sighed through the hall like a cleansing breeze. Dhugal was thumping to his knees at Conall's side almost before Kelson could, pulling a blue glass vial from Tiercel's drug satchel.

"What's that?" Kelson murmured, thrusting his hand hard against the side of Conall's throat to feel for a pulsebeat as he glanced at the vial.

"*Merasha,* so we don't have to go through this again before you execute him."

Kelson grimaced, for his own two encounters with the drug had been all too vivid, but he knew it was the wisest course.

"You're that sure I'm going to execute him, are you?" he asked.

"You haven't any choice," Morgan said, crouching down beside him and lifting Conall's head as Dhugal pried loose the vial's cork. Arilan had appeared from somewhere and stood behind him with crossed arms. "Even if he were contrite, which I doubt very much he is, you can no more let him live than you could have let Judhael of Meara live. Romantic notions of redeeming the strayed prince from dishonor and death are all very well and good, but not entirely practical in the real world."

Dejectedly, Kelson bowed his head and sighed.

"I wonder if you realize how tired I am of buying life with the coin of others' deaths," he said in a very low voice.

Duncan, too, had come to overlook the unconscious Conall. At Kelson's words, he also crouched down to join the conference in progress, helping Morgan open Conall's mouth so that Dhugal could administer the drug.

"That's an old, old controversy that we're no more likely to resolve now than we have in the past, Kelson. It's an unfortunate but necessary part of being king. Incidentally, were you talking to someone, just before you broke the circle?"

Kelson blinked. "You didn't see him?"

"See who?" Dhugal asked, tossing the empty vial back into the satchel.

"Sa—never mind," Kelson murmured, as Conall stirred and moaned, and Morgan produced a cord to tie the prisoner's hands behind him. "Bring him. I'll tell you about it later."

EPILOGUE

*Thou hast granted me life and favor, and thy
visitation hath preserved my spirit.*

—Job 10:12

Several months later, on a seashore near Morgan's capital
of Coroth, the King of Gwynedd and his blood brother, now
Duke of Cassan and Earl of Kierney as well as Transha, rode
silently together just at the water's edge. It was high summer,
with a balmy breeze wafting in off the great southern sea,
and the day was sunny and mild. Both young men rode in
shirt sleeves and homespuns now, in comfortable contrast
to the silks and brocades of earlier in the morning. For the
king had come to Coroth with his court to celebrate the birth
of Morgan's first son and heir, and Duncan had baptized the
infant Kelric Alain Morgan.

"Little Kelric's a handsome bairn, isn't he?" Dhugal said
wistfully. "All those masses of pale hair. I wonder if his eyes
will be blue or grey."

Kelson shrugged distractedly, trying not to think of another noble infant, not yet born, who would almost certainly
be as dark as Morgan's son was fair, like both his parents;
and of the other child expected far sooner, and of far more
humble birth—both of whom would enter the world father-
less. He especially did not like to think about the children's
sire.

For Conall had died no better than he had lived, all but
weeping with terror as a stony-faced detachment of Haldane
lancers escorted him to the scaffold on a fine morning in
May. Nor had Conall's death been as quick as Kelson would

have wished. The poor executioner faltered during his first stroke, unnerved already at having to take the head of a royal prince of Gwynedd, and then was further distracted by Conall's violent flinch just before the blade struck. It had taken two more blows finally to end the matter—though at least Conall knew nothing after the first—and Kelson had been violently and wretchedly sick as soon as he was out of public view.

"Will you stop thinking so much?" Dhugal murmured, breaking into Kelson's grim reverie. "What is it this time? Rothana? Conall?"

Kelson sighed explosively, shaking his head. "It was Conall—and his son—and Rothana," he admitted. "*God*, Dhugal, why did he have to do it? He was my cousin. I would have been glad to give him so much, if only he'd been willing to earn it."

"Kelson, he *earned* exactly what he got," Dhugal retorted. "It's all very well to say that he was the victim of an odd chain of events, if that makes you feel better, but Conall *chose* to be attached to it. Regardless of what his true intentions may have been, when he put *merasha* into my flask—and we'll never know whether he was *really* getting cold feet and would have warned us not to drink—he got that *merasha* by killing a man and then fleeing his responsibility. He'd been seeing Tiercel for the express purpose of gaining the Haldane power, so he could someday challenge you—which he did. And he tried to kill his own father. There's no justification for any of that."

"No, you're right, there isn't," Kelson agreed. "But I can still regret the waste of what could have been a valuable and productive life, can't I?"

"Of course." Dhugal leaned forward irritably to smooth a strand of his horse's mane. "I just don't want to see you dwell on it to the point that it's somehow your fault that Conall went bad—because it isn't. I don't care if you *are* my king and my brother—I'll thrash you the next time you carry on like that."

Kelson nodded sheepishly. "And I'll deserve it," he agreed. "It's still hard. Now that Duncan's resigned his ducal duties to you, you'll soon have a far better idea just how hard. You're going to have some of the same kinds of headaches, you know. Ducal scale is only a little less grand than royal, especially if you're Deryni.''

"I'll keep that in mind," Dhugal replied drily. "Thank God, Father's left me a devoted cadre of deputies, at least. And most heirs don't have their predecessors to fall back on, as I will. I'm glad I didn't have to lose a father to gain a duchy.''

"You're not the only one," Kelson replied. "I put him up to the resignation, you know. It was the only way I could think of to keep him in Rhemuth. Someday, I have no doubt that he'll be archbishop; but in the meantime, he can stay at the capital indefinitely as auxiliary and stay my confessor and adviser. I've got to have *one* Deryni with me all the time that I can trust.''

"Well, I'll be there as much as I can; you know that.''

"Yes, I know.''

With feigned nonchalance, Kelson guided his horse around a tidal pool. He was gloveless on this fine summer day, and the horse's red leather reins were supple and smooth in his hands.

"Rothana looked well, don't you think?'' he said with forced cheerfulness. "I'm glad she decided to come and stay with Morgan and Richenda until after the baby is born.''

"Aye, she looked—radiant,'' Dhugal murmured. "Oh, Kelson, I wish—''

"I know,'' Kelson broke in, remembering the one conversation he and Rothana had had since he arrived at Coroth a few days before, refusing to recall the several others they had had while she was still in Rhemuth. "Actually, she's bearing up fairly well. No one seems to hold Conall's crimes against her. I think it's helped her to be here with Richenda— and Richenda's situation has improved as well. Now that she's provided Morgan with a proper male heir, his men seem finally to have accepted her.''

"As if either of the poor women had anything to say about their dead husbands' treason!'' Dhugal said with an indignant snort. "Sorry, I didn't mean to bring him up again.''

"It doesn't matter.'' Kelson sighed and stood in the stirrups, stretching. "God, my bum's asleep! I'm going to get down and walk awhile.''

"I'll join you,'' Dhugal said, also dismounting.

They walked in silence for several minutes, the horses

plodding easily behind them on slack reins, until finally Dhugal glanced at Kelson again.

"Listen, you don't have to talk about it if you won't want to, but has Rothana given you any indication what she plans to do after the baby's born?"

"Oh, yes. It isn't what I'd prefer, of course, but she'll be returning to the religious life," Kelson said quietly, fingering the ends of the red leather reins. "I suppose there *is* a bright side to that. She's been in communication with the Servants of Saint Camber, and they want her to come and help them revive the Order as it used to be, in Camber's time, with a women's Order to train for the old Deryni disciplines. She sounds very excited about it. And it's definitely something that we need."

"And the baby?" Dhugal asked.

Kelson grimaced. "He'll be brought up for the priesthood. Nigel's trying to be very fair about all of this, but he was most emphatic about the succession not passing through Conall, so Rory will be the next duke—not the eldest son's heir, so the boy will still carry the style and title of a Haldane prince, however. I insisted on that. None of this is *his* fault."

Dhugal nodded. "Maybe he'll be a prince of the Church someday. Wouldn't that gall Conall, if he knew?"

Sighing, Kelson shook his head. "I don't really care whether it would or not. He's paid his debt; let him rest in peace."

Neither of them spoke again for several minutes, only concentrating on walking in the damp sand, occasionally pausing to overturn a seashell or other piece of sea wrack with a booted toe. It was Dhugal who eventually broke the silence again, as they approached a rocky headland jutting out partway into the sea.

"Do you think it really was Saint Camber in the circle with you, when you fought Conall?" he asked.

"I dunno. It bothers me that none of the rest of you could see him, though. We really failed on our quest, too, even though we found the Servants. I so wanted to find some actual relic. Restoration on the shrine at Valoret is going splendidly, and the new side chapel at home will be finished by Christmas, but whoever was in the circle with me didn't seem to place a great deal of importance on physical places."

"Well, the priests at Transha always taught me that God

is in the heart, not in a structure built by human hands, so maybe it's the same for saints," Dhugal replied. "Oh, a focal point is fine, but these are all really things of the spirit."

"Yes, but Camber had a physical body at one time," Kelson said stubbornly. "And I'm not entirely convinced that he was bodily assumed into heaven, despite what the accounts say about the evidence for canonization. We know that some physical objects have kept psychic impressions, too—like Duncan's ring."

"Well, maybe you can get him to give it up for a relic," Dhugal quipped. "Not that it's likely, given its association with our newest saint, but—"

He broke off suddenly and stopped so quickly that Kelson ran into his outstretched arm. Ahead of them, sitting quietly on a rock just at the edge of the tide-run, was a man in a grey cowled robe, a wooden staff leaned across his shoulder.

"Do you see what I see?" Dhugal breathed, though Kelson was already staring at the obviously visible man, his face gone very white and still.

Without a word, Kelson took Dhugal's arm and started forward, dropping the horses' reins, their feet leaving deep, clear footprints in the wet sand. The man did not move or look up until they had come within a few yards of him, and his face was shadowed by his hood when he finally did raise his head. His feet, Kelson noticed, were bare.

"May I be of some assistance?" the man asked. His voice was low and pleasant, and his hands on the staff were smooth and uncallused.

"Who are you?" Kelson breathed. "Haven't we met before?"

The shoulders shrugged beneath the grey robe, an eloquent gesture that neither confirmed nor denied, but the movement brought the man's mouth into view.

"Many people ask that of me, my son," the pleasant voice replied, "but my name is not important."

"Someone very like you said the same thing to a friend of mine a few years ago, on a road not very far from here. Do you know Father Duncan McLain?"

Again the shrug. "I know many priests, my son."

"And do you know of Saint Camber?" Kelson dared to ask. "Can you tell us anything of him?"

"Ah, then, you seek the great Defender?" the man countered.

"We do," Kelson answered. "We went on a quest to find his relics this spring. We found some of his Servants, but we never found any sign of him."

"And what sign did you think to find?" came the next query.

"Well, some—tangible evidence that this has all been real, that the contacts we've had with him haven't just happened because we wanted so badly for them to be true." He paused a beat. "I don't know why I'm telling you all of this."

"Perhaps because an honest seeker always knows the teacher when he finds him," the man replied, shifting his staff to begin idly tracing designs with the tip. "Are you bold enough, young seekers, to trust a stranger-teacher who would help you with what you seek?"

The man was tracing a more intricate design now, in the wake of a wave that had come particularly high onto the sand, and Kelson felt himself beginning to slip into trance as his eyes caught and followed the pattern. It was not—quite—familiar, but he did not feel at all afraid. And Dhugal likewise was falling under the man's spell.

"Let go and follow what I would show you, young seekers," the man's voice urged, soothing, soft. "You will come to no harm."

It was against all logic, but Kelson sensed instinctively that he might trust the man. Withholding nothing, he let himself slip into deeper trance. After a few seconds, as the man's voice droned on, almost singsong now, in a language Kelson did not know, the wet sand seemed to take on a darker sheen, to deepen and then to clear. Suddenly Kelson seemed to be floating in another time and place.

He looked upon a great, vaulted chamber with a bier occupying the place of honor underneath the center of the dome. Upon that bier, covered by a network of scarlet silk cords, lay a body clad in robes very like those of the priestly elite at Saint Kyriell's, but of dark blue rather than grey. Like the nets Kelson and Dhugal had seen in the mountain burial chambers, this one was studded at its intersections with small *shiral* crystals, but all of these were polished very smooth and drilled to take the cord. The net seemed to delineate a shimmer of power shrouding the body, and the sense of peace surrounding it was almost palpable. A legend had been chiseled around the edge of the bier, and Kelson, in his vision, bent to read it.

Hic jacet Camber Kyriell MacRorie, Comes Culdi: carissimus pater, ministrator coronae Gwyneddi, Regum salvator, sacerdos et episcopos, defensor hominum. Natus est Anno Domini 846. Non mortuus est. Resurget.

He was still trying to make sense of it as a wave washed over the sigil and erased it, snapping him abruptly out of his trance. He swayed a little on his feet as he dragged himself back to normal consciousness, catching his balance on Dhugal's arm and stupidly watching the wave eddy around their boots.

But the grey-clad man was gone. Nor was there any sign of how he had contrived to disappear without leaving footprints. Both Kelson and Dhugal glanced around wildly, trying to imagine how he had managed it, but then Kelson suddenly fell to his knees in the receding wave and began grubbing in the sand.

"What're you doing?" Dhugal gasped.

"I saw something—there!" Kelson pounced on it before the wave could carry it out, and scrambled a little closer to the water to rinse it. What he held aloft triumphantly between thumb and forefinger was a small, well-polished *shiral* crystal, glinting wetly in the summer sun.

"Sweet *Jesu!*" Dhugal whispered, also dropping to his knees beside the king and pulling his hand down for a closer look. "If you tell me it's got a hole drilled through it, I think I'll faint."

"Prepare to get very wet, then, if you intend to do it right here," Kelson said, helping Dhugal up with his free hand and glancing around again, "because it does. Dhugal, you don't suppose this is from—you *did* see what I saw, I hope? The body on the bier, with a net of these over it?"

Dhugal nodded gravely. "A net of red silk cords, with *shiral* crystals knotted where they cross—just as in the tombs. Kelson, do you suppose they *know* where he's buried?"

"Their ancestors may have known," Kelson answered. "And I'd be willing to bet a lot that the fellow who was just here knows."

"You don't think that *he* was Saint Camber, then?" Dhugal ventured.

"No, but I'd be very surprised if he didn't turn out to be one of Camber's servants—in the broad sense, not a member of the group at Saint Kyriell's. In fact, it wouldn't surprise me if he's the same chap that your father saw near here, several years ago. The point is, we may finally have tangible proof that a tomb exists—or at least that it did exist—something physical that we can hold in our hands. And—"

He stopped talking as his eyes suddenly paused at the open throat of Dhugal's shirt, where the young border lord wore, along with his recovered Saint Camber medal, a small, honey-colored nugget of *shiral* on a leather thong—once the gift of his mother to his father, on their wedding night. Dhugal's face went very still as he realized what Kelson was looking at, and his hand was trembling as he closed it around the crystal.

"Kelson, you don't suppose that my *mother* knew about any of this?"

"I dunno," Kelson whispered. "But suddenly a few more pieces begin to fit together. Could there be more clues in Transha, do you think?"

It was a question that neither of them could answer just then, but it was one that would continue to be asked in the future, along with many others. Both young men were quiet as they rode back to Coroth a little later to tell the others, but Kelson was also more hopeful than he had been in months.

Perhaps joy might yet come out of sorrow. Perhaps the quest for Saint Camber was not ended after all, but was just beginning.

INDEX OF CHARACTERS

AGNES de Barra, Lady—a young lady at court.

ALARIC—see MORGAN.

ALEXANDER of Rhemuth, Archbishop—bishop who ordained Duncan.

ALROY, King—late King of Torenth, eldest son of Duke Lionel of Arjenol and Wencit's sister, the Princess Morag; killed in a fall from a horse while hunting, summer of 1123, shortly after his fourteenth birthday; succeeded by his younger brother Liam, now age ten. Many in Torenth believe the "accident" was engineered by Kelson to eliminate a rival who had come of age.

ARDRY MacArdry—eldest son and heir of Caulay; killed 1107, age twenty, in brawl with a McLain retainer.

ARILAN, Bishop Denis—Bishop of Dhassa, age forty-one; secretly Deryni and member of the Camberian Council.

ARMAND, Sir—a legendary hero of the Eleven Kingdoms, subject of many ballads.

ARNOLD, Brother—monk who guided Kelson and Dhugal to the ruins of Caerrorie.

BARRETT de Laney—elderly Deryni; blind co-adjutor of the Camberian Council.

BELDEN of Erne, Bishop—Bishop of Cashien, suspended for his part in the Mearan rebellion of 1123/24.

BENED—a *cyann* or chief of the hill people at Saint Kyriell's.

BENOIT d'Evering, Bishop—elected Auxiliary Bishop of Valoret at the Synod of Valoret in 1125.

BEVAN de Torigny, Bishop—one of the twelve itinerant bishops of Gwynedd; elected Bishop of Culdi at the Synod of Valoret in 1125.

BRADENE, Archbishop—scholarly former Bishop of Grecotha, now Archbishop of Valoret and Primate of Gwynedd.

BRAN Coris, Lord—traitor Earl of Marley and former husband of Richenda; killed by Kelson.

BRENDAN Coris, Lord—eight-year-old Earl of Marley, son of Bran and Richenda.

BRION Donal Cinhil Urien Haldane, King—Kelson's late father; slain at Candor Rhea by the magic of Charissa, 1120.

BRIONY Bronwyn de Morgan, Lady—daughter of Morgan and Richenda, born January 1123.

CAITRIN of Meara, Princess—the defeated Pretender of Meara, age sixty-two, now immured in a convent; mother of Ithel, Llewell, and Sidana.

CALDER of Sheele, Bishop—one of the twelve itinerant bishops of Gwynedd, with no fixed see; great-uncle of Dhugal; suspended for his part in the Mearan rebellion of 1123/24.

CAMBER (MacRorie) of Culdi, Saint—outlawed Deryni saint of two centuries previous; patron of magic.

CARDIEL, Archbishop Thomas—former Bishop of Dhassa, now Archbishop of Rhemuth, age forty-six.

CARTHANE, Earl of—Gwynedd earl whose daughter elicits much interest among the young men at Kelson's court.

CAULAY MacArdry (The Old MacArdry)—Chief of Clan MacArdry and Earl of Transha until his death in 1123; believed to be Dhugal's father until Duncan proved otherwise.

CIARD O Ruane—Dhugal's faithful old gillie.

CONALL Blaine Cluim Uthyr Haldane, Prince—eldest son of Prince Nigel, and Kelson's cousin, age eighteen.

CONLAN, Bishop—Bishop of Stavenham.

CREODA, Bishop—Bishop of Culdi after dissolution of his former See of Carbury, and a conniver in Loris' return to power; suspended for his part in the Mearan rebellion of 1123/24.

DERRY, Sean Lord—former aide to Morgan and now his lieutenant for Corwyn, age twenty-eight; also a member of
Kelson's privy council.

DHUGAL Ardry MacArdry, Lord—foster brother to Kelson,
age seventeen; Earl of Transha and Chief of Clan
MacArdry; son of Duncan McLain by Maryse MacArdry;
grandson of Caulay MacArdry.

DOLFIN—Kelson's new senior squire, age fifteen.

DUNCAN Howard McLain, Bishop—Deryni priest, cousin of
Morgan, age thirty-three; Duke of Cassan and Earl of
Kierney, following the deaths of his father and elder
brother; Auxiliary Bishop of Rhemuth under Archbishop
Cardiel; father of Dhugal MacArdry.

EIRIAN Elspeth Sidana Haldane, Princess—infant daughter of
Nigel and Meraude, born June, 1124.

ELROY, Father—Archbishop Bradene's chamberlain.

EWAN, Duke—Duke of Claibourne and hereditary Earl Mar-
shal of the Gwynedd Royal Council.

GELRIC, Brother—monk who guided Kelson and his party
toward the High Grelder Pass above Saint Bearand's
Abbey.

GILBERT Desmond, Bishop—one of the twelve itinerant bishops of Gwynedd, suspended for his part in the Mearan
rebellion of 1123/24.

GORONY, Monsignor Lawrence Edward—aide to Archbishop
Loris; executed by Kelson in 1124 for treason.

HAMILTON, Lord—seneschal of Morgan's castle at Coroth.

HELOISE, Mother—Abbess of Saint Brigid's Abbey.

HILLARY, Lord—commander of Morgan's castle garrison at
Coroth.

HUGH de Berry, Bishop—former secretary to Archbishop
Corrigan and longtime colleague of Duncan, now one of
the twelve itinerant bishops of Gwynedd; elected Bishop
of Ballymar by the Synod of Valoret in 1125.

ISTELYN, Bishop Henry—former itinerant bishop and assistant to Archbishop Bradene; briefly Bishop of Meara;
hanged, drawn, and quartered at order of Archbishop

Loris in 1123; sainthood is being discussed at the Synod of Valoret in 1125.

ITHEL, Prince—elder son and heir of the Pretender of Meara, executed by Kelson at age sixteen for treason.

IVO Hepburn—Kelson's new junior squire, age twelve.

JANNIVER, Princess—daughter of a Connaiti prince, formerly betrothed to the King of Llannedd.

JARED McLain, Duke—Duke of Cassan and father of Kevin and Duncan McLain; captured at Rengarth and executed by Wencit of Torenth at Llyndruth Meadows, 1121.

JASS MacArdry—a young MacArdry retainer knighted by Kelson in 1125.

JATHAM—former squire to Kelson, knighted by him in 1125.

JEHANA, Queen—Deryni mother of Kelson and widow of King Brion, age thirty-seven.

JENAS, Earl of—see ROGER.

JILYAN, Mother—a *ban-aba* or abbess among the hill folk of Saint Kyriell's.

JODOC d'Armaine, Father—a candidate being considered as an itinerant bishop.

JODRELL, Baron—one of Duncan's lieutenants in Kierney.

JOHN—Duncan's alias as a royal courier to Arilan at Valoret.

JORIAN de Courcy, Father—Deryni priest, close friend of Arilan, discovered to be Deryni and burned at the stake before Arilan's ordination.

JOWAN—Conall's squire.

JUDHAEL Michael Richard Jolyon MacDonald Quinnell, Prince of Meara—priest-nephew of Caitrin of Meara; illegally made Bishop of Ratharkin by Loris and executed for treason at age thirty-eight by Kelson.

KELRIC Alain Morgan, Master of Coroth—infant son of Alaric and Richenda, born spring 1125.

KELSON Cinhil Rhys Anthony Haldane, King—son of King Brion and Jehana, now eighteen; Deryni.

KEVIN, McLain—Duncan's deceased brother.

KILSHANE, Earl of—known as the "Bonnie Earl," subject of border ballads.

KYLAN—an archer at Saint Kyriell's.

KYRI, Lady—Deryni, around thirty, known as "Kyri of the Flame"; member of the Camberian Council.

LACHLAN de Quarles, Bishop—Bishop of Ballymar, in Cassan; suspended for his part in the Mearan rebellion of 1123/24.

LAEL, Father—Archbishop Cardiel's chaplain and battle-surgeon.

LAMBERT MacArdry—one of Dhugal's older retainers.

LARAN ap Pardyce, Lord—Deryni physician, sixteenth Baron Pardyce, about sixty; member of the Camberian Council.

LIAM, King—middle son of Duke Lionel and Princess Morag, age ten; King of Torenth since the death of his elder brother, summer of 1123; Deryni.

LLEWELL, Prince—younger son of the Pretender of Meara; executed at age fifteen for the murder of his sister Sidana.

LORIS, Bishop Edmund—fanatically anti-Deryni former Archbishop of Valoret and Primate of Gwynedd; stripped of his offices and sent into forced seclusion by his fellow bishops in 1121, but escaped in 1124; executed for his part in rebellion led by Caitrin of Meara.

MACARDRY—see ARDRY, CAULAY, DHUGAL, MARYSE, MICHAEL, SICARD.

MCLAIN—see DUNCAN, JARED, KEVIN.

MAHAEL, Duke—younger brother of the slain Lionel, and his ducal heir; regent, with Princess Morag, of the young King Liam.

MARYSE MacArdry—eldest daughter of Caulay MacArdry; died 1108, age seventeen; wife of Duncan and mother of Dhugal.

MATTHIAS MacArdry—one of Dhugal's retainers; thirtyish.

MERAUDE, Duchess—Nigel's wife, and mother of Conall, Rory, Payne, and Eirian; sister of Saer de Traherne.

MICHAEL, Brother—*coisrigte* or member of the priestly caste of the hill folk of Saint Kyriell's.

MICHAEL MacArdry—second son of Caulay; died in 1119, age twenty-nine, leaving Dhugal the heir.

MIR de Kierney, Bishop—one of the twelve itinerant bishops of Gwynedd, suspended for his part in the Mearan rebellion of 1123/24.

MORAG, Princess—Deryni sister of Wencit of Torenth and widow of Lionel; mother of the current king, Liam, and Prince Ronal.

MORGAN, Briony—see BRIONY Bronwyn de Morgan.

MORGAN, Alaric Anthony—Deryni Duke of Corwyn and King's Champion, age thirty-four; cousin of Duncan McLain and husband of Richenda.

MORGAN, Kelric—see KELRIC Alain Morgan.

NEVAN d'Estrelldas, Bishop—one of the twelve itinerant bishops of Gwynedd, captured in arms and suspended for his part in the Mearan rebellion of 1123/24.

NIGEL Cluim Gwydion Rhys Haldane, Prince—Duke of Carthmoor and Brion's younger brother, age thirty-eight; Kelson's uncle and Heir Presumptive.

NIVARD, Father John—one of several young secretly Deryni priests ordained by Arilan.

PAYNE, Prince—Nigel's youngest son, age ten; royal page.

RANDOLPH, Master—Morgan's physician at Coroth.

RASOUL ibn Tarik, Al—Moorish emissary of the Court of Torenth.

RATHOLD, Lord—Morgan's chamberlain and master of wardrobe at Coroth.

RAYMER de Valence, Bishop—one of the twelve itinerant bishops of Gwynedd, suspended for his part in the Mearan rebellion of 1123/24.

RHIDIAN—young Deryni woman, member of the Quorial of Saint Kyriell's.

RHODRI, Lord—Kelson's chamberlain at Rhemuth.

RICHENDA, Duchess—widow of Bran Coris, Earl of Marley, and mother of the current earl, their son Brendan; now wife of Morgan, mother of his daughter Briony, and carrying his son; Deryni; age twenty-six.

ROBERT of Tendall, Lord—Morgan's chancellor at Coroth.

ROGER, Earl of Jenas—one of Kelson's retainers.

RONAL, Prince—Deryni younger brother of the current King of Torenth, age seven.

RORY, Prince—middle son of Prince Nigel, age fifteen.

ROTHANA, Lady—novice nun at Saint Brigid's, age seventeen; Deryni; daughter of Emir Nur Hallaj and related to Richenda by marriage.

SAGART—dead *coisrigte* or member of the priestly caste at Saint Kyriell's.

SHANDON, Father—Duncan's young priest assistant.

SICARD MacArdry, Lord—younger brother of Caulay, Dhugal's great-uncle, and husband to Caitrin, the Pretender of Meara; killed on the field at Dorna by Kelson.

SIDANA, Princess—daughter of Caitrin and Sicard; briefly, wife of Kelson; killed on her wedding day, age fourteen, by her brother Llewell.

SIWARD, Bishop—Bishop of Cardosa.

SOFIANA—Deryni; sovereign Princess of Andelon, and Richenda's aunt; member of the Camberian Council.

SYLVIE—Rothana's Jacan maid.

TAGAS, Father—Morgan's chaplain at Coroth.

THOMAS, Earl of Carcashale—present holder of the lands of Caerrorie.

TIERCEL de Claron—Deryni, in his mid-twenties; youngest member of the Camberian Council; secretly instructing Conall.

TOLLIVER, Bishop Ralf—Bishop of Coroth, age fifty-two.

TRAHERNE, Saer de—Earl of Rhenndall and brother of Meraude, Nigel's duchess.

VANISSA—Conall's mistress, with child by him.

VIVIENNE, Lady—Deryni; elderly co-adjutor of the Camberian Council.

WARIN de Grey—self-appointed messiah who formerly believed himself divinely designated to destroy all Deryni; has healing power that does not seem to come from Deryni sources.

WENCIT of Torenth, King—Deryni sorcerer-King of Torenth and scion of the Festillic claim to the Gwynedd throne; slain by Kelson at Llyndruth Meadows in 1121.

WOLFRAM de Blanet, Bishop—Bishop of Grecotha.

INDEX OF PLACES

DESSE—a port town on the river south of Rhemuth.

DHASSA—free holy city and seat of Bishop Denis Arilan; known for its woodcraft and the shrines of its patron saints, Torin and Ethelburga, that guard its approaches south and north.

DOLBAN—formerly the mother house of the Servants of Saint Camber and site of a shrine to him.

DORNA—the plain where Duncan finally found Sicard's army.

EASTMARCH—former earldom of Ian Howell; ceded to the Crown on his death and subsequently given to Burchard de Varian to reward his loyalty in the Torenth War.

ELEVEN KINGDOMS—ancient name for the entire area including and surrounding Gwynedd.

FIANNA—wine-growing county across the Southern Sea.

FORCINN BUFFER STATES—group of independent principalities south of Torenth, including Nur Hallaj.

GRECOTHA—university city, former site of the Varnarite School; seat of Bishop Wolfram de Blanet.

GRELDER Pass, High—pass leading from Saint Bearand's Abbey, northeast of Caerrorie, down to the Iomaire plain.

GWYNEDD—central and largest of the Eleven Kingdoms, held by the Haldanes of Gwynedd since 645.

IOMAIRE, Plain of—former site of a shrine marking the place where Camber MacRorie fell in battle.

JENAS—a Gwynedd earldom.

KILSHANE—ancient coastal earldom bordering Transha.

KHELDISH RIDING—northeastern portion of the old Kingdom of Kheldour, famous for its weavers.

KIERNEY—earldom and secondary holding of the Dukes of Cassan, now held by Duncan McLain.

LAAS—ancient capital of Meara.

LLYNDRUTH MEADOWS—grasslands at the foot of the Cardosa Defile; site of the final confrontation between Kelson and Wencit of Torenth.

MARBURY—seat of Ifor, Bishop of Marbury, in Marley.

MARLEY—former earldom of Bran Coris, now held by his son Brendan, under the regency of Richenda and Morgan.

MEARA—formerly a sovereign principality, now a possession of the Crown of Gwynedd, west of Gwynedd.

PURPLE MARCH, The—meadowlands north of Rhemuth; one of the Lordships of the Crown of Gwynedd.

RAMOS—site of the infamous Council of 917, which ruled

stringent measures forbidding Deryni to enter the priesthood, hold office, own property, etc.

RATHARKIN—new capital of Meara after the union of Meara and Gwynedd in 1025, and seat of the Bishop of Meara.

RHEMUTH—capital city of Gwynedd, called "the beautiful," and seat of the Archbishop of Rhemuth, now Thomas Cardiel.

RHENNDALL—mountainous earldom in the southern portion of old Kheldour, famous for the blueness of its lakes; held by Saer de Traherne, brother of Duchess Meraude.

R'KASSI—desert kingdom south and east of the Hort of Orsal, famous for its blooded horses.

SAINT BEARAND'S ABBEY—abbey at the foot of the High Grelder Pass, near Caerrorie.

SAINT BRIGID'S ABBEY—Rothana's abbey in the Mearan border area, sacked by Prince Ithel in 1124.

SAINT GEORGE'S CATHEDRAL—seat of the Archbishop of Rhemuth, now Thomas Cardiel.

SAINT HILARY'S BASILICA—ancient royal basilica within the walls of Rhemuth Castle, of which Duncan is rector.

SAINT KYRIELL'S—lost village in the hills north and east of Caerrorie where some of the Servants of Saint Camber went into voluntary exile after the enforcement of the Statutes of Ramos.

TORENTH—major kingdom east of Gwynedd, now ruled by regents for the boy King Liam, nephew of the late King Wencit.

TRANSHA—seat of Dhugal MacArdry, Earl of Transha, in the border marches between Kierney and the Purple March.

VALORET—old capital of Gwynedd during the Interregnum, and seat of the Archbishop of Valoret (and Primate of Gwynedd), Bradene.

PARTIAL LINEAGE OF THE HALDANE KINGS

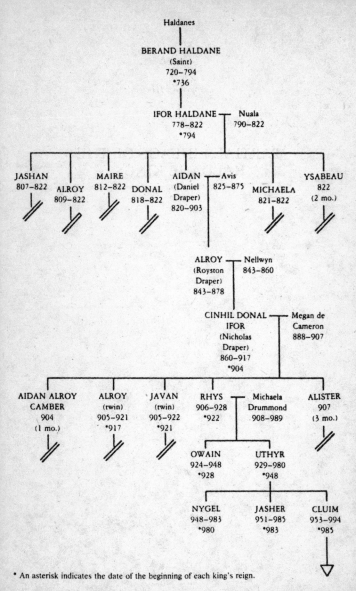

Haldanes

BERAND HALDANE
(Saint)
720–794
*736

IFOR HALDANE — Nuala
778–822   790–822
*794

JASHAN   **ALROY**   **MAIRE**   **DONAL**   **AIDAN** — Avis   **MICHAELA**   **YSABEAU**
807–822   809–822   812–822   818–822   (Daniel   825–875   821–822   822
                                            Draper)   (2 mo.)
                                            820–903

ALROY — Nellwyn
(Royston   843–860
Draper)
843–878

CINHIL DONAL — Megan de
IFOR   Cameron
(Nicholas   888–907
Draper)
860–917
*904

AIDAN ALROY   **ALROY**   **JAVAN**   **RHYS** — Michaela   **ALISTER**
CAMBER   (twin)   (twin)   906–928   Drummond   907
904   905–921   905–922   *922   908–989   (3 mo.)
(1 mo.)   *917   *921

OWAIN   **UTHYR**
924–948   929–980
*928   *948

NYGEL   **JASHER**   **CLUIM**
948–983   951–985   953–994
*980   *983   *985

* An asterisk indicates the date of the beginning of each king's reign.

448

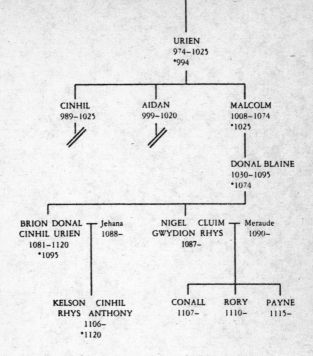

URIEN
974–1025
*994

CINHIL
989–1025

AIDAN
999–1020

MALCOLM
1008–1074
*1025

DONAL BLAINE
1030–1095
*1074

BRION DONAL
CINHIL URIEN
1081–1120
*1095

Jehana
1088–

NIGEL CLUIM
GWYDION RHYS
1087–

Meraude
1090–

KELSON CINHIL
RHYS ANTHONY
1106–
*1120

CONALL
1107–

RORY
1110–

PAYNE
1115–

ABOUT THE AUTHOR

Katherine Kurtz was born in Coral Gables, Florida, during a hurricane and has led a whirlwind existence ever since. She holds a Bachelor of Science degree in chemistry from the University of Miami, Florida, and a Master of Arts degree in English history from UCLA. She studied medicine before deciding that she would rather write, and is an Ericksonian-trained hypnotist. Her scholarly background also includes extensive research in religious history, magical systems, and other esoteric subjects.

Katherine Kurtz's literary works include the well-known Deryni, Camber, and Kelson Trilogies of fantasy fiction, an occult thriller set in WWII England, and a number of Deryni-related short stories. At least three more trilogies are planned in the Deryni universe, and several additional mainstream thrillers are also currently in development.

Ms. Kurtz lives in southern California with her husband and son, an orange cat called The Marmalade Bear, and a Bentley motorcar named Basil—British, of course. They hope soon to move to a castle in Ireland.

KATHERINE KURTZ *The first lady of legend, fantasy and romance!*

"A great new talent in the field of fantasy!"
—Bestsellers